THE BIG SQUEEZE

SELECTED BOOKS BY DAVE DeWITT

Fiction

The Mute Strategy

Avenging Victorio

Nonfiction

First Skin 500 Squirrels: Eyewitness Accounts
of Barbecue History

Precious Cargo: How Foods from the Americas
Changed the World

Da Vinci's Kitchen: A Secret History of Italian Cuisine

The Founding Foodies: How Washington, Jefferson,
and Franklin Revolutionized American Cuisine

The Complete Chile Pepper Book (with Paul W. Bosland)

The Field Guide to Chile Peppers (with Janie Lamson)

The Habanero Cookbook (with Nancy Gerlach)

THE BIG SQUEEZE

An ECIS Eco-Thriller

DAVE DeWITT

SUNBELT
EDITIONS

ALBUQUERQUE,
NEW MEXICO

This is a work of fiction. All of the characters, organizations, and events portrayed in this novel are either products of the author's imagination or are used fictitiously.

THE BIG SQUEEZE

Copyright © 2018 by Dave DeWitt

ISBN: 978-0-9832515-5-2
Covers and internal design by Lois Manno

Acknowledgments

*Thanks to Lois Manno and
the Mendel Media Group, LLC.*

BEFORE

The Everglades is the only ecosystem of its kind in the world. Often called a "River of Grass," it is neither. Neither river nor swamp, the Everglades is a flowing marsh that drops about two inches a mile as it moves south. Even if you stand in it, the flow is undetectable. And the "grass," specifically sawgrass that grows 12 feet high, is not a true grass but rather a sedge. More than a hundred years ago, before the building of 1,074 canals, 720 miles of levees, 18 major pumping stations and 250 diversion structures in an attempt to drain it, the wild Everglades was home to as many as a million and a half wading birds such as herons, egrets, ibises, and storks.

Then the habitat destruction, extinctions, and non-native species invasions began. The Florida red wolf was trapped and killed almost to extinction by humans to protect livestock and game. In 1980, it was declared extinct in the wild. Overhunting of monk seals for oil, and overfishing of their food sources, are the established reasons for the seals' extinction. The critically-endangered Florida panther is somehow hanging on with fewer than one hundred left in the wild.

Hunting and deforestation removed the Carolina parakeet from Florida and severely depleted the egret population of herons and egrets all because they had beautiful feathers that women loved in their fancy hats of the time. Habitat loss also doomed the ivory-billed woodpecker, and its numbers have dwindled to the point that we simply do not know if they exist any longer. Even if they do, almost no forests today can maintain an ivory-billed woodpecker population large enough to avoid extinction.

And then the invaders arrived, all caused by the hand of man. More than one-quarter of all the fish, reptiles, birds, and mammals alive in South Florida today are invasive species. The worst of the alien plant species are the Brazilian pepper trees, melaleuca, Australian pines, and Old World climbing ferns that grow just like kudzu. What they all have in common is that they take over the plant habitats for native wildlife by forming monospecific forests with dense canopies that birds, mammals, and reptiles don't like.

Invading mammals include the second largest infestation of feral hogs after Texas, black rats, and the largest rodents in the world, capybaras, which can weigh up to 150 pounds. Nonnative fish now swimming in the Everglades canals and Florida Bay include piranhas, Oscars, pacus, Mayan cichlids, tilapia, walking catfish, and the highly poisonous lion fish.

But invasive reptiles cause the most problems by eating the eggs, young, and adults of many important native species in the Everglades such as raccoons, opossums, bobcats, young deer, and many, many species of water birds. In descending order of danger and impact, they are Burmese pythons, Nile monitor lizards, yellow and green anacondas, African pythons, black and white tegus, and boa constrictors.

The estimated population of Burmese pythons in south Florida ranges from 30,000 to 300,000. In January, 2013, the Florida Fish and Wildlife Conservation Commission sponsored a "Python Challenge" that drew more than 1,600 hunters, the vast majority of them novices, into the Everglades in search of the invasive giant snakes that inhabit its marshlands. The result? The month-long event netted only 68 pythons. So the 2014 Python Challenge was cancelled, and the FFWCC announced they were forming teams of volunteer python hunters to help combat Post-Traumatic Stress Disorder in military veterans and local police officers.

1

Only the largest vertebrates are immune to attacks by the
hungry python of gigantic dimensions. Almost any not
too formidable creature weighing less than 125 pounds is a
potential victim, horns, armor, and spines notwithstanding.
–C. H. Pope, *The Giant Snakes*, 1961.

On a hammock, a small island in wetlands, Sam Dalton
braced himself against a solid melaleuca tree and strained
to hold the head of the writhing eight-foot Burmese python
caught in his modified snare pole with the custom catch-hoop.
Meanwhile, Chuck Gannon and Lloyd Vann were struggling
to place its midsection and tail into the snake bagger when a
second python, hidden in the thick brush beneath a palmetto, struck Vann's right foot. The thick leather of the Merrill
Wilderness Boot prevented the snake's teeth from reaching the
flesh of his ankle, but the python quickly coiled around Vann's
legs. Toppling into the murky water around the hammock, he
lost his grip on the first python.

Freed from one of its captors, the first python renewed
its efforts to escape, and Dalton could not hold on to it. He
dropped the snare pole and picked up his shotgun while Gan-

non scrambled out of the way. As the first python swam away with the catch-hoop around its neck, Dalton racked a shell into the shotgun's chamber and pulled the trigger. The loud explosion sent dozens of double-ought buckshot into the snake's head, killing it instantly and ruining the snare pole. The dogs were barking like crazy, but shut up at Dalton's hand command.

Dalton then jumped into the water and lifted up Vann's head and shoulders so he wouldn't drown as the snake's coils around his legs pulled him down. Gannon pulled his Mtech tactical knife out of its scabbard and proceeded to attack the python's neck to sever its spinal cord.

Three minutes later, the volunteers, the hoods of their camouflage Tyvek suits hanging down their backs, were laughing nervously at the sight of the python's severed head still holding a toothy grip on Vann's boot. Two of the volunteers snapped photos with their cell phones while Dalton replaced his Remington 870 tactical 12-gauge in the airboat's modified waterproof compartment that normally would have held bass rods.

"That was fun," Dalton said wryly, "and a good lesson for everyone."

Lloyd Vann, still shaking from the attack and the submersion, begged to differ. "Fun? You didn't get bit. I didn't sign on for this shit."

"Look, Lloyd," Gannon said, "how many python hunts you been on?"

"20-some."

"Until now, they've all gone according to plan, right?"

"Right."

"Then clearly," Gannon said slowly, "this is a case of reptile dysfunction."

Dalton couldn't help but laugh. The volunteers joined in, and even Vann smiled and nodded. "Okay, okay, I'm just a little rattled," he admitted, "and pythons aren't even poisonous."

"Back to the business at hand," Dalton said. "Numbers 153 and 154 for the month, but don't tell anyone. According to the Effin' Doubleyous, it's only 47 and all our snake baggers are ready to go for the official count, which will bring it up to 51."

His men grinned up at him, knowing that the stupid rules of Fish and Wildlife were not going to stop the Anti-Python K-9 Team from executing pythons instead of placing them in bags for veterinarians to euthanize and study. The turkey vultures were circling already, and Dalton wondered if the same ones were following the team. Probably. The goddamn snakes were eating up all the vultures' usual prey. A dead snake would be a treat for them. Birds were smart. They learned things. All traces of those pythons would be gone in a couple of days, absorbed into the Everglades.

"It's beer-30," Gannon said, prying the head off of Vann's boot with a long knife. Sharp python teeth snapped off as he moved the knife sideways. Dalton nodded, and one of the newbies opened the cooler and started passing around cans of Python Pilsner to the six men. He poured some bottled water into a metal bowl for the two Labs, Osceola and Abiaka, and everyone sat down in the shade of a Brazilian pepper tree— another fucking Everglades interloper, Dalton thought—and they toasted their achievement.

"To Sam," Vann said, holding up his beer. "We owe him big time."

"Hear, hear," came the chorus, and they drank. Not the best Florida craft beer, Dalton thought, but appropriate.

One of the newbies got to his feet and wandered off to take a leak.

"Find another place to piss, soldier!" yelled Dalton. "That's a Florida poisontree, like poison ivy on steroids. You don't have to touch it—some of that urushiol chemical is airborne."

"Well, how many have we killed since we started?" Vann asked.

"As of today, 1,261," Dalton replied. "Not too bad for nine months."

"A drop in the bucket," another newbie said. "They say there's 100,000 of 'em out here."

"Wait a goddamn minute," Dalton ordered. "What's your name again?"

"Ed McCoy, sir."

"What's our mission?"

"To get well, sir."

"Then the python count is irrelevant because killing pythons is our therapy, not our mission, right?"

"Yessir."

"Lloyd and Chuck know it's working, because...?"

"I'm sleeping better, only an occasional nightmare," Lloyd said.

Chuck stood up without using any support for his high-tech left leg. He was huge, former Special Forces until the land mine got him. "My panic attacks are gone, hopefully forever. I love these little pythons."

Everyone laughed. Laughing at PTSD was highly encouraged on the team.

"Let's go home," Dalton said. Osceola and Abiaka trotted to the airboats and sat, awaiting the command to board. The men picked up their gear and beer cans while the medic disemboweled the python to help out the vultures and get rid of the snake carcasses as quickly as possible. Dalton, Vann, Osceola, and a newbie got into the first boat, while Gannon, Abiaka, and the other two newbies boarded the second. They fired up the engines and took off for the 30-minute ride back to the landing. Within minutes, the first bald, black bird landed.

• • •

Dalton always disliked the initial workshop with the volunteers he called the newbies—and what the Effin' Doubleyous, the Florida Fish and Wildlife Conservation Commission— termed Python Apprehension Volunteers. Jeez, PAVs, like we need another acronym, Dalton thought. It was a waste of time because only five percent of the newbies stayed with the project for a year, even if they were paid a salary. It just might be the working conditions, he thought, so best to lay out all the negatives first. But then again, maybe they left because they didn't need the mission any more—they were cured of PTSD. Or at least thought they were.

There were 12 of them in the barely air-conditioned meeting room at the Oak Hammock Hall in the Long Key Natural Area and Nature Center in Davie, sitting in uncomfortable plastic seats and dressed like beach bums. Hey, it was south Florida in the winter. Tourist season.

"My name is Sam Dalton. I'm paid nearly minimum wage to run this anti-python operation, and I have to do it with mostly volunteers like yourselves who need some action in their lives. The problem is, there's a bunch of obstacles in our way, and I'm going to outline them for you right now. If you get up and walk out, no one will blame you. We've haven't shared names yet. Believe me, if you don't like this, leave now. It will save me from having to identify your body later."

The slouching men sat up straight at that. Dalton began his presentation. The first image showed the legs and khaki shorts of a Girl Scout hanging out of the severed head of a huge python.

"Her name was Melissa Stuart. She held the troop record for cookie sales. It was a picnic sponsored by the Homestead Methodist Central Church. Close to a slough known to have alligators. But the python was in the grass next to the soccer

17

field and when Melissa, the goalie for the Homestead Mana-tees, went near the water to retrieve a missed shot on goal, the python apparently bit her leg, got its coils around her, con-stricted her to death and proceeded to swallow her head-first. Her camp counselor grabbed a machete from the trunk of his car and killed the python."

Three guys, probably fathers with young daughters, got up and left. No one said a word.

"This deal is voluntary," Dalton reminded the rest. "You can leave at any time, no probs."

"Does this happen very often?" a black PAV in the front row asked. Beefed way up and with that get-it-done attitude. Former Army, Dalton thought, maybe Marines.

"She's the thirteenth killed by pythons in the US since 1980. This one's got the citizens freaked. I'm now promised real funds to solve this problem, but it's nearly impossible to do that."

"Because?" the black guy asked.

"The snakes are breeding too fast to stop 'em. One female we caught," he clicked ahead to the image of the egg sacs in a dissected 16-foot female, "had 85 eggs in her."

"Whoa," one of the newbies said.

Dalton clicked back through his slides. He explained how they used two airboats and two trained python track dogs. He called their names and Osceola and Abiaka hopped onto the small stage and sat next to him at the lectern. "Now I'm going to show you the dangers you'll face if you go with us and how we try to mitigate them."

He clicked to a shot of a red-faced volunteer leaning on a stick. "Exhaustion and dehydration are the biggest worries out there, so there are several ways we combat them. First, we test every volunteer for fitness—Mercy Hospital does this for us to support our project. Some of you won't make the cut, but no hard feelings. And we welcome your tax-free donation. In the 'Glades, we always bring adequate water, we wear Tyvek suits, always have Kevlar gloves on and everyone wears both cooling vests and Multi-Cool cooling towels around their necks. And we all have ventilated insect head nets over our safari hats. I should remind you that there are 45 different species of mosquitoes in the 'Glades that transmit diseases you've probably never even heard of, like Everglades Virus. We're not taking any chances. Let me tell you one more thing about them: entomologists report that the all-time record mosquito catch in one trap in one night was 365,696. Now there's some sun on our faces, diminished by the net and sunscreen, but no other part of the body is exposed to nature. Except when you have to take a leak. Then you're on your own. Oh, and I forgot about the scorpions. If they get inside your suit, we may have to airlift you out."

The usual nervous chuckles came from the audience. They were starting to get into his presentation. "Now let's take a look at some of the unpleasant plants and animals we will attempt to avoid."

Up came a three-part photo montage. Dalton used the laser pointer to indicate each species. "Poison ivy—everyone knows about this. Remember, the chemical urushiol gets on your suit and can spread, so we undress in outdoor stalls and keep our gloves on until the suits are placed in plastic bags for what the Effin' Doubleyous would call decontamination. And what we'd call dry cleaning. Now meet poison ivy's mutant and more dangerous cousin, the poisonwood tree—same chemical, but more of it."

Dalton noticed that the only woman in the audience was scratching her left arm, but there was no red rash. "And this is the one you really want to avoid. Manchineel, known in Spanish as manzanilla de la muerte. Little apple of death. It's the most poisonous tree on earth."

19

He paused and then laid it on thick. "Its sap can blind you and those apple-like fruits will, indeed, kill you. The tree has a notorious history. The Caribbean and Floridian Indian tribes poisoned their arrowheads with this tree sap. And the Calusas used them to wound Juan Ponce de León, who died from it. Not quite his fountain of youth."

Scattered chuckles. Dalton put up another montage. "We have two species of rattlesnakes in the 'Glades. The Eastern diamondback is the largest venomous snake in the US, reaching eight feet in length. If you hear a rattle, freeze. Your team leader will take care of it without harming it. Compare this huge guy to what looks like his baby, the dusky pigmy rattlesnake, which doesn't even reach two feet. Don't worry about him too much, but this one," Dalton pointed to a close-up of a viper's open white mouth and large fangs, "cottonmouth moccasin. Gets to five feet. They'll only strike in self-defense, but don't take a chance. We try to stay out of the water as much as we can— there are also red-bellied piranhas swimming around."

"Mr. Dalton?" the woman asked. Dark brown hair, medium length. Not much makeup. About 40, good looking.

"Yes?"

"Will those suits protect us from snakebites?"

"Good question. Probably, but no guarantee."

He moved on. "The pythons and boas in the 'Glades are invasive species, but the alligators and crocodiles are native. Alligator, fresh water. Crocodile, salt. But when you have a river like the Everglades flowing into the ocean, you get many degrees of brackishness, which either creature could live in. The alligator is more aggressive, despite what you might have heard from the Crocodile Hunter. There aren't any alligators in Australia, except in the zoos."

He showed them images of alligators eating pythons and pythons swallowing alligators. The military-looking guy said,

"Battles at the top of the food chain."

"Almost," Dalton replied. He showed them images of men in handcuffs standing in front of piles of neatly-packaged cocaine. "Here are the most dangerous animals we might encounter—smugglers of drugs and people. Always armed, always dangerous."

"What do we do if we run into the bad guys?" the woman asked.

"We leave the area quickly," Dalton said. "Since cell phone service is so spotty out here, we use satellite phones donated by Iridium. I can call police, the Coast Guard, DEA—all of the enforcement agencies. And I'll have a GPS location to give them."

Dalton passed out questionnaires. "If you want to discuss volunteering on some level, hang around. If not, or not right now, it would help us immensely if you could fill out this brief questionnaire. And for the last time, any donation you'd care to make helps pay for the gas to run the airboats. Thanks for coming—I really appreciate it."

And he did. He also appreciated the fact that two of the newbies stayed after the others had left. The big black guy and the woman.

The man extended his hand. "Kevin Cooper."

"Great to meet you. The Corps?"

"Yessir, master sergeant, retired. And you?"

"Special agent, NCIS, retired. And you?" he asked the woman.

She extended her hand and had a firm grip. "I was Army. Combat medic E-3. Jenny Rodriguez, retired."

"A trio of retirees. First names now. Have a seat." He arranged three chairs so they could all see each other easily. "First rule is you don't have to talk about it. No one will ever ask—all of us have our own ghosts."

"Good to know," Jenny said. "No trauma for me. I'm just bored to death." Everyone chuckled.

"Mine's the usual story," Kevin said. "I'm getting a better grip now, but it's taking longer than predicted."

"Took me three years and regular therapy," Dalton said, and they all went silent for a time.

"I've got an airboat," Kevin said out of the blue.

"Really?" Dalton asked. "Why?"

"I'm a fishing guide," he explained. "I have a flats boat, too. In fact, I'm the only African American fishing guide in the Keys."

"Sounds like an interesting story."

"It wasn't too bad since a lot of the guides already knew me. I grew up in Key Largo. I'll tell you all about it sometime."

"Why do you want to join us?"

"We've just got to do something about the fucking pythons—excuse my language—they are destroying the Everglades. I see it every day."

"Jenny," Dalton asked, "what's the deal with you?"

"That Girl Scout you showed, Melissa Stuart—she was my niece."

The silence in the room was palpable. "I'm so sorry, Jenny," Dalton began.

She waved him off. "No, that's okay. You did what you had to do. But she is one of the reasons I want to help you kill these fucking snakes."

"Makes sense," Dalton agreed.

"To answer your question, I'm a part-time emergency room paramedic. With my Army retirement I don't have to work full-time, and I don't want to be blood-spattered all the time. What kind of injuries has your team had so far?"

"A bruised knee and two cases of contact dermatitis."

"Not bad. Who's your medic now?"

"He's not really a medic. He's a dental hygienist named Lloyd Vann. He couldn't get the morning off or he'd be here."

"I'll sign on if you make me your new medic."

Dalton did not hesitate. "Lloyd will be relieved, actually. Of course you can be our medic."

"Good. I wanna go python hunting with him." She nodded at Kevin. "The sergeant and the medic—what a team."

"When's the next hunt?" Cooper asked.

"Saturday. Not sure exactly where yet, but we usually hunt on weekends. I have some paperwork for you two to fill out."

"Of course you do," Jenny said. "This is the new military, right?"

On the drive back to Homestead, Dalton reflected that he was a very happy camper. Expanding his team to three boats meant training another Lab, but that was no problem. He would assign Chuck Gannon to command Cooper's boat, and on the first hunt the newbies would only be observers, not hunters.

He figured that if he could just have ten boats operating throughout the 'Glades and Big Cypress, they would begin to get a handle on at least holding the python population stable— it was officially called "containment." What he really needed was what killed off all the aliens in War of the Worlds—a virus. One thing at a time, he scolded himself.

Dalton pulled into his carport at 4:13 p.m. He could hear the dogs going nuts in their runs as they recognized the sound of his F-150. It was more than an hour until their feeding. He knew they were a little hungry but mostly bored. He walked through the small house he called his "bungalow," and into the back yard. He freed the dogs from their runs and after greeting him, they ran around the fenced back yard like they had been caged for three weeks instead of five hours. The only reason they got along so well was that they were neutered litter mates.

He grabbed a Gnarly Barley ale from the refrigerator and checked his email. Just routine except for a note of thanks from his new medic Jenny and a picture of Kevin's large black airboat with the comment, "Let's go kill some big reptiles."

Dalton's cell phone rang and he checked the caller. Phil Everett, an Effin' Doubleyou, but also a close friend.

"Phil, where are you?"

"Everglades City. Better bring those dogs over here. We grabbed a 14-footer who couldn't move because he was trying to swallow probably the largest monitor lizard in the United States. We spotted two larger pythons, and we know where they live. Two different hammocks."

"What the fuck? Monitors that big?"

"Eight feet. It's a crocodile monitor 'cause it has big yellow spots on its back. It's definitely not a Komodo dragon."

Dalton mentally kicked himself for not telling the newbies about the monitors. Encounters with humans were rare, but they did happen. Phil had told him there were now eight species of monitors in the 'Glades and Big Cypress.

"You think we have a nest of 'em?" he asked Everett.

"Who knows? Come on over and we'll try to find out. The females don't need a mate, you know." Everett had a doctorate in reptilian zoology.

"I heard that. Partho-something."

"Parthenogenesis. Just what we need. The smartest reptiles in the world, and they're self-breeding. They only do that when they can't find a male python, for whatever reason. I've been fantasizing about training some invasive species to eat other invasive species. Gambian rats eating Latin American apple snails. Feral cats eating the Gambian rats. Feral swine eating the feral cats. And pythons eating the feral swine."

Dalton laughed. "Wouldn't that be great? Phil, we can come on Friday for a Saturday hunt. I've got three boats now and a new medic—a real medic. But still just two dogs."

"Want reservations at the Everglades City Motel?"

"Hell no. Find us a place to camp."

"The Chokoloskee Island Park and Marina, just a little south of Everglades City. They've got nice amenities and free Wi-Fi."

"We'll need room for nine tents. And can we launch from there?"

"Yes and yes. Done deal. See you day after tomorrow."

Dalton picked up his beer, walked into his office, and began planning. He had never hunted in the western 'Glades—hell, Everglades City was 80 miles from Homestead, and there was certainly enough hunting in the east to keep them busy. But this would be a good trip for the newbies with monitors in the mix and an Effin' Doubleyou as a guide. He made the assignments for the three boats and emailed all the information to his now eight-person crew. He had promoted Julie Loftus to interim captain of what had been Chuck Gannon's boat. Phil would ride with Dalton. He fed the dogs and then considered his own dinner—alone, as usual. He decided on a smoked pulled pork sandwich with some chips and pickles. There was another team killing animals in south Florida, and Dalton knew them well. Hog hunters. Florida had a large population of feral hogs, and his friend Dell killed the hogs then smoked their meat. Five bucks a pound for smoked pulled pork? Works for me, he thought.

Before he went into the kitchen to make it, Dalton plugged his phone into the stereo and selected the 70s mix. The random mix began with Todd Rundgren's "We Gotta Get You a Woman."

"Ain't that the truth!" He'd been living alone for three months now, ever since his live-in girlfriend, Laura Saylor, had said, "I can't live in this dump anymore," meaning Homestead, and not Dalton's "cute" bungalow, he had hoped. She meant both, she had said as she stormed out. She had been only his third lover since his wife had died. None had worked out. He wanted to believe that the pythons spooked them, but maybe it was just him, the formerly freaked-out PTSD vet. As he fixed his dinner, an odd thought came to him. Jenny, his new medic, didn't wear any rings at all. Interesting.

Rundgren's vocal was interrupted by the ringtone of Steel Pulse's "Drug Squad," so he picked up the phone and looked at the caller ID. Laura. I'll be damned, he thought.

"Hi there," he said pleasantly.

"Miss me?" There was a little catch in her voice.

"I do."

"I miss you terribly. Maybe I was wrong to leave. I was just so fed up living in Redneckville. Do you have somebody new yet?"

"Hell no. Do you?"

"Are you kidding? I've been too busy. I have a new job with odd hours…"

He took the hint. "Where are you working now?"

"Come up here and I'll tell you."

"What do you mean?"

"Let's start all over again. I'll give it a shot if you will."

"You mean…"

"Come up here. We'll go out to dinner. My treat. We'll celebrate my new job."

"You mean a date?"

"Yeah, a first date, so don't plan on getting any." She giggled.

Dalton mulled it over for all of two seconds. "What's your address?"

"Just meet me at the main gate of Fairchild Tropical."

"I'll be there within the hour," he promised.

• • •

Dalton explored his options as he locked the front door of his bungalow and went to the truck. The Florida Turnpike Extension was quicker, but if he took 821 to Old Cutler Road, it was a straight shot to the botanical gardens with the scenic Mangrove and Matheson Preserves between him and Biscayne Bay. He chose that route, wondering if Laura had gotten a job at Fairchild. She had worked for a time at Selby Botanical Gardens in Sarasota, so anything was possible. Basically, Laura was a self-styled "media gal," even had that title on her freelance business card. In her 40-some years, she'd been a radio morning show DJ, a lifestyles reporter for the Fox Miami affiliate, a freelance journalist for various south Florida magazines and newspapers, and had also worked in advertising and PR.

It was cooling off now, so he didn't even run the air conditioning. He liked the Florida winters—perfect temperatures, no hurricanes, and the occasional freezing air mass that dropped the mercury so low in the 'Glades that a lot of the pythons died. And that was a good thing. State Road 821 took him between Leisure City—what a fucking name for a town, he thought—and Homestead Air Reserve Base, just a third of what it had been before Hurricane Andrew.

It was getting dark. Dalton's mind wandered back to Laura. He'd thought he'd never see her again and then she calls him out of the blue, half-apologizing for her actions? Weird. But she was a little impulsive on occasion. They had met about three years ago when she interviewed him for an article on very unusual careers in south Florida for the Miami-Dade Weekly. She was about six years younger than he was, and he was attracted to her immediately because not only was she good-looking, she also had a sense of humor. He made her laugh several times during the interview, and he remembered his reply when she asked him how it felt to make a living killing animals. "I don't kill the pythons," he lied. "I just collect them for the Effin' Doubleyous. They euthanize them."

"The what?" she had asked.

"It means Fish and Wildlife, state or Feds. Don't quote me—I have to work with those people. Effin' Doubleyous is off the record." That's when she laughed and shook her head. "Great nickname. Your secret is safe with me."

"You like stone crabs?"

"Sure."

And 30 minutes later, they were cracking and eating the crabs at the Black Point Grill at the Dade County Marina. Three weeks later, Laura moved in with him.

There was still a little light in the western sky when Dalton pulled up to the entrance of Fairchild Tropical Botanic Garden. Laura was waving at him from the driver's seat of a new red BMW 3. She must have gotten a really good job, he thought.

"Follow me!" she yelled and peeled off. He dutifully followed in his beat-up F-150.

They ended up at Ortanique on the Mile, probably because Laura had given the owner, one of the top female chefs in Miami, a glowing profile in an article for American Way. Ten to one their meals would be comped. Laura got out of the BMW quickly, ran over to Dalton, and planted a juicy one on his lips. She was dressed in clinging black slacks, moderate heels, and a bright tropical shirt with jungle foliage and parrots. This time her blonde hair was in a pageboy cut, and he couldn't help himself.

"You look stunning."

She took his hand. "And you look rugged, Mr. Snake Hunter. Let's eat—I'm starved."

The hostess greeted Laura by name and led them to corner two-top, about as private as it could get in the popular restaurant. Quickly, a server took their drink orders—an Ortanique Mojito for Laura and the usual Python Pilsner for Dalton.

"This was a real surprise," he said, lifting his glass.

She touched his glass with hers. "Tell me about it. When I wondered who to tell about my new job first, I conjured up your face and realized how much I missed you. I've made a slight career change."

"Fairchild?"

She nodded and smiled. "Big time. I'm going to be the face of Fairchild—at least that's what the board of directors told me. Their on-camera spokeswoman, star of their Internet video ads, my face in the magazine and newspapers ads. I'll also be their 'Press Secretary' except I changed my title—"

"To 'Media Gal.'"

"Yep. It's so retro. Maybe I'll get to dress up like Katy Perry. And they're paying me 125 a year."

Dalton whistled. "Good for you."

"Have you two decided yet?" their server asked. Her name tag read "Judith, Cayman Islands."

"Let me order for us," Laura said. Curried crab cake and port-glazed short ribs for him, lobster bisque and the jerk chicken penne for her.

"Now, could I have done all this from Homestead?" Laura asked.

"Sure, it's only 37 minutes away."

"Not at rush hour. That means a two-hour a day commute six days a week. Would you do it?"

"No," he admitted.

"And neither would I. Done deal. Truce?"

"Truce," Dalton agreed. They bumped fists and grinned at each other.

"So what's going on with you?" she asked. "Are you still pushing that rock up a hill? Want to move in with me and be a kept man?"

Their meals were superb, and they shared tastes of each others' dishes like old times. Dalton realized he hadn't been so happy, well, since she left him. They were back in sync and making each other laugh out loud. As promised, Laura picked up the check for his meal—hers was comped.

They kissed at length in the parking deck and Dalton pulled back. "What's all this first date crap?"

"To hell with it. Would you like to follow me one more time?"

"Are you kidding?" He nodded at her vehicle. "So what's with the BMW?"

"Oh, some asshole rear-ended the Mazda. It's in the shop so the Beamer's a loaner."

"Nice loaner."

She batted her eyelashes. "I can be very persuasive."

"I know."

As he followed Laura back to her townhouse, he considered her invitation to move back into her life—on her terms. But what would he do? The python project wasn't over. People needed him, needed structure and discipline in their lives so the nightmares would fade along with the guilt they felt for surviving when their buddies had died. But he knew when the time was right he would stop the python hunts. After all, he had resigned from NCIS. He could do it again.

• • •

Ray Jacobs was the manager of the shipping department at World of Reptiles in downtown Homestead, but Bruno Zimmerman called him his "chief witness." It was Ray's responsibility to witness and report on every single incoming reptile shipment to document its origin—or, more importantly, to shield Zimmerman from any knowledge of its illegality. On the same day that Dalton interviewed the newbies, for example, he had set up the video camera as usual to record a meeting between Bruno and one of his main suppliers, Jed Stoddard.

Ray pointed the camera at the front page of the *Miami Herald* to document the date in case someone didn't believe the one on the recording. Then he focused on a sealed box with air holes on the side. Behind it stood Bruno and Jed. Bruno was tall and swarthy in a short-sleeved shirt and tie. Jed, a foot shorter and chubby, was wearing a Parrot Jungle t-shirt. Ray gave Bruno the cue.

"I'm Bruno Zimmerman, owner of World of Reptiles. With me today is Jed Stoddard." Stoddard sneezed from allergies and Bruno laughed. "Also known as Sneezy, one of my trusted suppliers. What did you bring me today, Jed?"

"Indian star tortoises," Jed replied, slitting open the top of the box and tilting it toward the camera. The perforated cardboard revealed 16 small compartments, each containing a black and yellow tortoise about four inches long.

"And what is the origin of these tortoises?"

"Myanmar, formerly called Burma." He reached into the box and pulled out an envelope. He opened it and gave some papers to Bruno. "Those are the captive-bred permits issued, stamped, and signed by the Myanmar Secretary of Game and Wildlife."

Bruno held up the documents, and Ray zoomed in on them. "These documents remain on file here at House of Reptiles. Thanks for these, Jed. Just take your invoice down to accounting, and they'll issue you a check." He stared at the camera. "And that's it for today."

As soon as the camera was off, Bruno and Jed shared a good laugh. Ray joined in with a chuckle as if to support them, but he was faking. If the box had contained cocaine, the three of them could have been arrested on the spot. If Jed had said the tortoises were smuggled in, the three of them could be in big trouble. Bruno was covering his ass perfectly. If he were later accused of buying smuggled reptiles, the video would prove he believed that they were not smuggled but captive-bred. He could only be convicted if the Feds could prove he knew that they were smuggled. That was assuming that they didn't find out that the permits were forged to begin with.

It was a loophole that Ray disliked with a passion. Fortunately for him, Bruno did not know how Ray felt about buying the smuggled reptiles. If he found out, Ray would be without a job. Or worse.

After Stoddard left, Zimmerman closed his office door and gestured for Ray to take a seat. "Ray, I'm amazed at the progress you've made in the short time you've worked for me. In fact, I'm going to name you Employee of the Year, and we're going to celebrate that award at a party I'm throwing at my place."

Surprised, Ray smiled. "Thanks, Bruno—that's quite an honor."

Zimmerman gave him his imitation of a smile. "It's more than an honor. You're getting a bonus. Have you checked your bank deposits lately?"

"No sir."

"Can you check it on your cell phone?"

"Sure."

"Then do so." Zimmerman waited patiently while Ray punched buttons on his cell phone.

"A $25,000 deposit went into it this morning."

Zimmerman nodded. "Yes. Your bonus—in a cash deposit. You'll get a 1099 form from me, so make sure you pay the IRS at tax time."

"You know my account number."

"Of course."

"Why didn't you just write me a check?"

"Ray. Then I wouldn't have anything to hold over you.

Even the IRS knows that if a person gets a bunch of cash, he doesn't deposit all of it."

There was a stalemate-like silence for a few seconds and then Ray blurted out, "But you made the deposit!"

"Did I? What's in your left front trouser pocket?"

Ray reached into the pocket and pulled out a slip of paper. He saw the logo for SunTrust Bank. Then he saw the date and the deposit amount of $25,000. Then he saw his available balance of $25,819.72. He was fucked. If Zimmerman ever accused him of embezzlement, how would he explain where the cash came from?

"Okay, Bruno, who do I have to kill?"

Zimmerman laughed. "No one, my friend. But there are a few other things I need done."

"Like what?"

"I want you to find out everything you can about this asshole Sam Dalton."

"The one killing the pythons?"

"They're not the only things he's killed."

"What do you mean?"

Zimmerman's stare skewered Ray. "My brother, for example."

• • •

Dalton woke up in her bed with the aroma of bacon heavy in the air. He got out of bed and called down the stairs. "Good morning! Do I have time for a quick shower?"

"Five minutes!"

Laura served his favorite breakfast: Bacon and avocado omelets with papaya slices and lime juice.

"I sure had fun last night," she said gently. "Thanks for coming up."

"Are you kidding? We're meant for each other. But circumstances only mean that we can't live together right now. It doesn't mean that we can't see each other or love each other."

She grinned. "So you won't be my kept man?"

"Not right now. I've got to work through the python season. I promised. Come spring, I'm going to re-evaluate the situation. I mean, my life goal is not to be a python hunter."

"I know, but what is the goal?"

"I'm not sure. Now I have more options than just living by myself in the bungalow in Redneckville."

Laura laughed. "Think we can get together, uh, maybe once a week? Up here?"

"You'll have to come down some time. You can't miss the Redlands Orchid Festival."

"Come on, Sam, that's in the fall. We'll be back living together by then."

"You optimist."

"A gal can dream, can't she?"

He finished his omelet, kissed Laura goodbye, and headed back to Homestead. On 821 he took the Old Dixie Highway exit and went to look at the scene of the "accident" that had taken the life of his wife and son nearly a decade before. He did this twice a year, feeling that he owed it to her memory. He drove east on Caribbean Boulevard wondering, as he always did, why Robin had taken this route. Especially at night. They had been at the mall getting Kenny fitted for a new soccer uniform. At ten years old, he was growing very quickly. He slowed down as he approached the 10340 block, where it crossed a canal. There was an approaching guard rail beside the road and a guard rail on the bridge, but between them was just a chain link fence to keep pedestrians out of the canal. The Homestead police investigator believed that Robin lost control of the Toyota Corolla, which crashed through the fence and hit an exposed pipeline over the canal. The vehicle flipped upside down into the canal. Robin and Kenny, trapped inside, had drowned.

He pulled off the road and got out of the truck. He walked onto the bridge and stared into the water, picturing their faces. Five minutes later, he was driving south on the Old Dixie Highway. Dalton had never bought into the investigator's theory. He had examined the Toyota and found scrape marks on the front and rear left door panels and a dent in the left rear bumper indicating that Robin had been forced off the road by a much larger vehicle, like a Nissan Armada or a Hummer. But the investigator, Florence Duval, told him that the fence had scratched the car and the dent was from a previous incident.

Dalton had gone over her head and appealed to the assistant chief of police, a nice guy named Garcia, who refused to open an investigation. "I know you were NCIS, so it's in your nature to investigate, but don't go there. I agree with Duval—this was a tragic accident." Dalton had racked his brain thinking about possible enemies from his days in NCIS, but he had drawn a blank.

He turned right after a couple of miles and entered the grounds of the Palms Woodlawn Cemetery, then parked the truck. He walked though the beautiful landscaping until he reached a slight rise that overlooked the pond. There were two graves, side by side, with modest markers. Robin W. Dalton and Kenneth C. Dalton.

"Again, Robin, I have followed your wishes." Their wedding vows had included a controversial promise: "If either of us passes before the other, the surviving partner, after proper mourning, will find another mate, and live a happy life, without guilt." It had been Robin's idea, but he had agreed with it. Still did. And the crazy thing was that he didn't feel guilty. Only sad.

Five minutes later, Dalton was back in the truck on his way to the bungalow, hoping his visit to the cemetery wouldn't trigger the usual recurring nightmare. Most of the men on his python team suffered from PTSD from dreadful combat experiences, but his was different. The bodies of his wife and son were recovered long before he arrived at the crash scene, but in sleep his mind created a slow-motion sequence. He would dive into the water with a powerful flashlight, swim down to the Toyota, and see that it was filled with water, the beam catching their bodies floating against the interior roof. They would turn in unison, eyes open and lips moving, silently mouthing "why?" over and over.

He had dreamt that sequence so many times that he had lost count. His own guilt was the trigger—he had done something that someone had avenged by killing his family. He was sure of that, but wasn't sure what he had done. He vowed that someday, somehow, he would find whoever was responsible, and kill him. Or her. It didn't matter which.

2

The Ever Glades are now suitable only for the haunt of
noxious vermin, or the resort of pestilent reptiles. The
statesman whose exertions shall cause the millions of acres
they contain, now worse than useless, to teem with the
products of agricultural industry…will merit a high place in
public favor.
—Buckingham Smith, 1846.

The Manatee Fish Meal Plant on Little Sukee Hammock,
eight miles northeast of Everglades City, had the revolting
smell of rotting fish that was all too similar to human excre-
ment. And that was exactly the reaction Big Ink wanted from
anyone who came within sniffing distance, which could be a
mile or two, depending on the wind. Big Ink, the owner along
with a few "investors," ran the plant efficiently, because, as he
put it, his equipment was "state of the fart." Gulf menhaden
and mullets were the fish of choice to make the meal and oil,
and he had long-time contracts with the fishermen who ran
the nets for him. In turn, he had agreements with many of
the members of the Central Florida Poultry Growers Association who had hungry chickens. Free range chickens? Ha! Little
cages were much more efficient. He sold the fish oil to several

paint manufacturers around the state, including his former employers, Tomat Technology.

Despite its aroma, the plant itself sparkled, a polished steel and concrete facility set on metal pilings, which, like bridge supports, had been hammered vertically nearly 150 feet down. The building's metal framework was triple-welded to the supports. "Hurricane-proof," Ink bragged to everyone. It had been tested only once and passed with, well, flying colors if you consider 91 mile-an-hour winds a hurricane. Many crackers would not. Since that hurricane had brushed Mexico first, Ink called it a "Category Juan." He denied it was a racial slur about Mexican laziness. "No more racist than the word 'niggardly,'" he said. Despite his appearance and his profession, Big Ink was a very intelligent man. He was fond of telling people that he had an M.S. in chemical engineering from Florida State and a Ph.D. in redneckology from Cracker University.

If a visitor to his plant had one of those 200-foot tape measures and could fight his way through the thick brush and the poisonwoods surrounding the building, he would find that it was 160 feet long. And if this same person walked inside and measured from the front door to the back wall, he would come up 30 feet short. That's because one of the Manatee Fish Meal Plant's subsidiaries was housed in the completely secure back section of the plant. It was a superlab called Methbusters, and it created 78 percent of the plant's total income. Big Ink thought it was amazing that something so smelly could launder money so cleanly.

On the same day that Sam Dalton was driving back from Coral Gables, Big Ink was giving a tour of his superlab to Gabriel Cypress, a member of the Miccosukee tribe. He hadn't wanted to—was suspicious of the whole damn thing—but Bone Mozell had insisted, and he was the money man.

"Hell, Ink," he had yelled over the phone, "This guy's got access to some disappeared tribal cash from their casino. He's goin' to spend 200,000 a month with us. I am personally guaranteeing him. His brother is on the Tribal Council. Give him the tour and feed him lunch—no alligator meat. Then, set up the deal."

Unfortunately for Bone, Big Ink and the Indian didn't hit it off. Maybe it started with the tattoo of an alligator eating a Seminole artistically needled on Ink's right calf. Ink thought that he should have worn long pants, but he didn't own any.

"That's funny," Gabriel Cypress said, pointing at Ink's leg. The Indian was wearing a traditional, colorful Miccosukee shirt with blue and red diamond patterns over a black background. It was the same shirt that the alligator wrestlers wore, but Ink held his tongue about that. Cypress' face was surprisingly light for an Indian, and clean shaven. He looked to be in his late 30s.

"No offense, Mr. Cypress. I had already passed out when the artist inked that."

"I couldn't care less about your tattoo. Let's get on with it."

They were in Big Ink's drab office at the back of the plant with worn furniture and photos on the wall. Big Ink holding up a sailfish. Big Ink supervising fish being transferred out of a boat's hold. Big Ink with a cute ten-year-old girl sitting on his knee. Big Ink eviscerating an alligator. Big Ink with the former governor on an airboat, cans of beer in their hands. Big Ink in a field of pot plants.

"Follow me," he said to Cypress. The sign on the door read "Plant Maintenance." They walked into what appeared to be a large closet with mops, brooms, and buckets. Ink played with the light switches: three on, two off, four on, four off and the back wall of the closet rolled up to reveal what looked like a food manufacturing operation. Gleaming steel tanks, glass tubes, a huge control panel.

"We have five stations," Ink explained, "Beverage—that's a joke on the reagents we use—Gaming, Weighing, Breaking Ice, and, of course the Main Lab."

Cypress looked incredibly bored, but he stopped before each station so that the QSee Surveillance Shadow pen in his shirt pocket recorded every detail, including Big Ink's narration.

"Obviously this is the main control panel. We got a FireIce fire suppression system. All venting is scrubbed. The partially scrubbed venting for the fish meal part of the plant covers for any of the Methbusters' fumes that might possibly escape before venting. Workers wear Responder Level A high-performance chemical suits—"

"Very impressive," Cypress said impatiently.

"This here's the oxide furnace and next to that is the hydrofluoric acid solution vat and the aluminum strip and sodium hydroxide mixing tank. That's your basic initial filtration system with the evaporation unit and the finishing tank. And there's the refrigerator where we keep the beer."

Cypress didn't seem to get the joke.

"At first we used pseudoephedrine but finding a million capsules of that shit was a pain in the butt so we switched to reductive amination using P2P—that's phenylacetone—and methylamine. The methylamine we get in drums from Mexico labeled 'diesel fuel.'"

"Okay, okay, I've seen the lab. Means nothing to me except it musta cost a fortune."

"Million five," Big Ink said proudly. "We made that back in the first six months. Say, I got some lunch for you in our cafeteria."

"Screw the lunch. Let's talk business."

Back in his office, Ink sat behind his desk in a specially-modified chair. "Okay, how much do you want?" He wondered if the Indian ever smiled.

"Ten pounds a month to start. First month I'll pay up front. After that, half and half."

"You know how we deliver?"

"Yeah. Bone said something about secure containers packed into fish meal totes."

"Exactly. So what are you gonna do with the fish meal?"

"Feed the pigeons, or doves, or whatever the fuck they are. Whatta you care?"

"Just curious. We're starting production again next week. Bring me the cash on Monday. You'll get your shipment the followin' Monday."

"Okay."

This asshole was not paying any attention at all, Big Ink thought. He decided to poke him—verbally, that is. "So what did you think of the lab, Tonto?"

The Indian was fast. Gotta hand it to him, Ink thought. The office lights flashed off the blade of the fish-gutting knife that Cypress was weaving in front of him.

"You got a lot of flab on you, Fat Ink. Wanna take a bet on how many times I'll have to stab you before you die?"

"Three," Ink said. "That's my bet."

They both broke out laughing. The Indian did indeed smile, Ink thought. "One would work for me," Cypress said, chuckling. "Through your right eye. Just kidding, of course." The knife went back into his boot.

Ink resisted the impulse to touch his right eyelid. "Deal?"

"Deal. I'll bring the cash on Monday. See you then, Kemo Sabe."

• • •

Big Ink grew up in Jacksonville in a seemingly normal middle class family. He wasn't called Big Ink then, of course, just Billy Draper. His father was an accountant and his mother taught middle school. He had a sister four years older than himself, so while he was in high school, she was down in Boca Raton at Florida Atlantic University. He looked it up and thought it was funny that she lived in Rat's Mouth, Florida, and he teased her about it. She thought her big little brother was insufferable. Their younger brother, Hal, dropped out of high school to become an automobile mechanic and eventually ended up in Georgetown, Texas.

Billy attended Englewood High School in Jacksonville, where he played offensive tackle for the Rams. When his teammates said he was very offensive, they were referencing his lack of hygiene rather than his football position. He was huge and very quick, although he rarely showered—and never in the team locker room. The standing joke was that everyone on the team was a Ram, but Billy was the only Ram who smelled like one. So for Christmas during his junior year, his friends—such as they were—all chipped in to buy him a case of Sure deodorant.

He was awarded a football scholarship to Florida State, and made the team. But a hit on his right knee from a teammate's helmet in practice ended his freshman year and his interest in the sport. But Billy didn't care—he had found a new fascination: chemistry. He had passed the subject in high school with an A-, but this was different. This was serious shit. That's because so many chemistry majors at state went on to the big time: nuclear science, petrochemicals, plastics, polymers, and drugs. Legal pharmaceuticals only, of course.

He had a knack for the subject. It just came naturally. He memorized the periodic table of elements in a single afternoon. Billy soon had a schematic of it tattooed on his lower back. He learned compounds, reactions, reagents, and how to make a very powerful explosive device for less than $20. You never know when you might need that kind of knowledge, he told himself.

Billy applied for a part-time job at Reynolds Paint and Toll Manufacturing, headquartered in Tallahassee with outlets in Tampa and Fort Lauderdale. He didn't even know what toll manufacturing was, but he made sure he learned a lot about it before he went for the interview. Jackson Reynolds, the owner of the company, later told him that he got the job because none of the other applicants knew that the company simply manufactured the base paints for retailers who would custom-mix them for customers.

It was Billy's job to help formulate paints that would resist Florida's heat and moisture. He was only a sophomore, but he worked for Reynolds through his senior year and one year in graduate school. The same month he got the job at Reynolds, he discovered a way to keep his weight below 330 pounds. First, reduce his intake of Landshark Lager from a six-pack a day to one bottle a day. Second, snort cocaine. But he quickly realized that even with a job, he couldn't afford it. After all, it was an import, and imports were always more expensive. That's why he drank Landshark instead of Andechser Doppelbock Dunkel for $35 a six pack. So why not a domestic weight-loss drug like black beauties, which he knew from chemistry were biphetamine capsules. They were easy to find at the Texaco Truck Stop in Monticello if you knew the right guy and said you were tired. If the right guy asked you how tired and you said you only got an hour's sleep last night, you were buying 60 capsules.

After he received his M.S. in chemical engineering, he had a meeting with Jackson Reynolds and asked for a full-time job and a significant raise. But Reynolds surprised him by saying that Billy, with all his paint and coatings knowledge, could find a much better job with a company like Tomat Technology in Miami. In fact, he knew the owner from the Florida chapter of the American Coatings Association. He told Billy that Tomat specialized in manufacturing polyamine epoxy coatings that provided corrosion protection for ships, oil platforms, pipelines, and piers. It was cutting-edge paint technology because those coatings could be applied underwater.

Reynolds' connection and Billy's résumé landed him an interview with Tomat's owners. He took their employment test—and got a perfect score. They offered him a job in the research and development department on one condition: that he lose weight and get in better shape. They didn't want him dropping dead of a heart attack. Billy agreed and began his search for a new speed connection.

Flash-forward a decade and where do you think Billy, still living in Miami and a lot more inked now, was scoring his speed? Mavericks Country Bar and Grill in Homestead, of course. Billy, now calling himself "Half Ink," had graduated from biphetamine to crystal methamphetamine—cowboy cocaine, as they called it at Mavericks. The key word for buying it there was "eight-ball," which meant that you were ordering about four grams of it from the guy in the parking lot wearing the shoulder holsters over his massive, naked chest. An eight-ball went for $200. Two of them would last Billy about a month. He didn't snort or inject it, he just smoked it in a glass pipe to keep his weight around 312 or so. He could afford it because he was formulating marine paint for $150,000 a year. Hell, his latest formulation, DRYCOTE 243TM had just been approved for use by the US Navy for underwater application on ship hulls. As a result of Billy's chemical engineering brilliance, Tomat Technology had gotten a huge contract from the Navy, and Tomat management had voted Billy a $10,000 bonus, which he calculated was more than two years of eight-balls.

Billy liked Mavericks a lot. The music, the people, the action, the sports betting, the meth. He wasn't born a redneck, he called himself an adopted redneck, but he was still part of the overall Florida family. All his friends were patrons, mavericks themselves, and they all knew what he did for a living. He figured his best friend was a chicken farm supply distributor named Bone Mozell, president of the prestigious CFFA, the Chicken Farmers of Florida Association. It was Bone who adopted Billy as an official redneck in a solemn ceremony in the bar with the Dixie Chicks on the jukebox singing "White Trash Wedding." Billy was wearing his favorite t-shirt that read, "I Beat Anorexia." It was a touching moment at Mavericks, and Billy bought a round for the house.

Bone, who looked to be about 47, had a mustache and goatee and dressed like a Vegas card dealer. He seemed to like chemistry and knew a bit about it. He had been teasing Billy about buying the eight-balls, saying, "Hell, make it yourself, you're the only real chemist around here."

And Billy would always reply, "I keep tellin' you I'm not a chemist, I'm a chemical engineer. Meth making is too dangerous and too much work. I'll just buy it."

But on June 2, 2008 (the date later became an anniversary), Bone said, "What if I told you about a way to make twice the money, be independent, and never have to buy meth again?"

"Here we go again," Billy said. "Okay, I'll bite. What's up?"

"Fish meal," Bone replied.

When Billy resigned from Tomat Technology three days after his bonus check cleared, the Tomat partners asked him what his future plans were.

"I'm going to open a rival company and run you guys out of business."

The two partners looked at each other in worried astonishment.

"Just kidding," said Billy. "But I am going to be an entrepreneur. I'm building a fishmeal plant."

The partners laughed and the older one said, "Come on, Billy. You've worked for us for a long time. Tell us the truth."

Billy unrolled some papers. "It is the truth. I brought the renderings and elevations for it so I could ask you guys to give me some advice."

After Billy left the Tomat building for the last time, the older partner said, "Was that the result of all the meth he does?"

"Gotta be," the other said.

"Good riddance. He resigned, so we don't have to pay unemployment. Or pay him royalties on DRYCOTE."

"Buy you a drink to celebrate?"

"Absolutely."

"I believe they stock that brand of vodka over at the Mermaid Tavern."

• • •

"What's my favorite tattoo on your body?" repeated Mary Sue Wheatley, who had just turned 17. She was Big Ink's "personal assistant" and he paid her $100 each time she came to the "Peee-Yewww Plant," as she called it, and pretended to be his girlfriend. She dazzled the plant workers—who really seemed to believe that Big Ink could have a teenage girlfriend. Or at least they were great pretenders.

"Well, I haven't seen the one on your butt, so I guess the python on your right leg is my favorite." They were sitting in the cafeteria having lunch. Mary Sue was dressed in an orange bikini top, short shorts, and flip flops, with no tattoos or piercings. She had changed in the ladies' room at the Marathon station—her mother would have never allowed her to leave the house dressed like that. She wore her hair parted in the middle with each side hanging straight down to her shoulders, light brown with blondish streaks. She was too young to be beautiful, but very pretty, with an oval face and green eyes. People said she looked like Jennifer Lawrence's little sister.

Big Ink raised his right leg and turned it back and forth. The tattoo artist had bunched the coils tightly together to suggest constriction and the python's head looked like it was locked onto Ink's kneecap. He had even put some drops of blood by the snake's teeth.

"Nice touch," Ink had told him.

The artist, who, in addition to being an albino, had no discernible body hair—not even eyebrows—but proudly displayed a thin, two-inch silver bone through his septum, shrugged. "Verisimilitude."

"It really does look like it's squeezing you," she giggled. Mary Sue was a junior at Lely High School in East Naples, home of the Trojans. She was, of course, on the cheerleading squad. The school mascot—a rampaging Trojan—was a huge joke, too late to change. One wag had tweeted: "No brand name mascots—call the team the Rubbers." Once a week Mary Sue drove a "company car"—a pink Smart Car Big Ink provided—over to the plant to keep the girlfriend fantasy alive.

The mythological Big Ink was the one into, well, teens of any age, and Ink often made statements that would be logically attributed to a child molester. But these were pronouncements made only to his close associates, the ones he needed. "They ain't little girls, they're little women," he would say. "There was even a book written about them. If they have tits and a bush, they're women. I'm not a pervert. I'm an aficionado."

But that was just Ink building his bad-boy image. In reality, the fish meal plant sponsored the Lely High School girls' soccer team and the football team's cheerleaders, so he always had cute young girls around him. His sponsorships were rewarded with advertising in the Trojans' sports programs. "Our Meal Feeds Your Meal-Ticket. Your chickens deserve the best food for their

health and your profit. So feed them all-natural and environ-
mentally-certified Chickens' Choice Finest Florida Fish Meal
every day, and watch them grow faster to the slaughter."

And Mary Sue's parents? He had told them in confidence
that he was gay. And anyway, Mary Sue's mom had a new high-
tech kitchen and her dad had a new red Harley. He was the surgeon who had removed Ink's appendix. "It was like operating
on a humpbacked whale," Dr. Wheatley had confided to his
associates. Big Ink was now a close family friend.

Big Ink stood up. "Thanks for stopping by, Mary Sue, honey, but I've got a meeting right now. He offered her his hand to
shake and passed her a $100 bill.

"Bye, dahling," she said to Ink, kissing him on the cheek
and playing her role to the hilt. She waved to everyone and flip-
flopped her way out of the cafeteria.

A little later, the three lunkers of the fish meal plant were
sitting around a table in Big Ink's office looking at an iMac
screen being operated by Derrick Fitzroy and Cutup Roberts,
chief chemist and production supervisor. Both men worked
equally for both divisions of the plant, meal and meth. In fact,
that was their mantra, their chant. The three of them studied
the production schedule on the screen.

"Since we're increasing our production by ten pounds,"
Cutup said, "I ordered the extra phenylacetone and methylamine. It should be here tomorrow." He was tall and lankly
with greasy, shoulder-length hair, a three-day scrubble of beard
and wore cargo shorts and a Nada Surf t-shirt.

"And the cash to pay for it is in the safe," Fitzroy added. He
looked like a golf instructor with styled blonde hair cut short.
He was clean-shaven and wore a green golf shirt with the insig-
nia of a manatee embroidered on it, white shorts with a sharp
crease, and highly polished boat shoes that had never touched
a deck. His glazed eyes betrayed his preppy appearance. "I went

to the safety deposit box yesterday. We're getting short on cash reserves."

"That will be taken care of soon," Ink said, thinking about the deal with Gabriel Cypress. "And after this cycle, we're throwin' the party to end all parties. So here's what I want. I need some pythons. We're going to do what the Romans used to do, except with reptiles and amphibians. They used to put lions, tigers, bears, bulls, and gladiators into the arena and the crowd bet on the outcome. Bring me two eight- to ten-foot pythons and a medium crocodile. We've already got the big alligator, Bill Hailey, and he's now a three-time champ."

"I can send Billy and Tomás to get the pythons," Cutup said. I know that World of Reptiles has a nine-foot crocodile hidden away from the Effin' Doubleyous, but it's gonna cost a few thousand."

"Just go catch one," Ink ordered.

Cutup disagreed. "Risky and very, very dangerous," he told Ink, and his head jerked to the left involuntarily in what Ink called an "anaphylactic twitch." "The Feds stake out Florida Bay and watch the crocs all the time. Many of them are tagged with GPS units."

Ink gave in. "Okay, okay, buy the goddamn croc. But I want you out there supervising the python hunt. If Billy and Tomás go out by themselves they'll be drunk and high and the pythons will collect them instead of vice-versa."

"Shit, Ink, I hate going out there—"

But Ink cut him off. "For the second round, I wanna put three or four starved pythons in the arena and then throw in a buncha cotton rats. We'll take bets on which snake eats the most. "I've got some snakes I've been savin' up for this. Haven't been fed in two months. I can't wait for this one."

"Yeah," said Fitzroy drily. "What a lot of fun that will be. Oh, I forgot to tell you—I tried to restore the scrubber after that last batch of meth we ran, but it wouldn't start up. We may have to replace it."

"I'll worry about that next week," Big Ink said, words that he would later regret.

3

It is almost impossible to name an animal or plant species anywhere on the planet that has not been traded—legally or illegally—for its meat, fur, skin, song, or ornamental value, as a pet, or as an ingredient in perfume or medicine. Every year, China, the US, Europe, and Japan purchase billions of dollars of wildlife from biologically rich parts of the world, such as Southeast Asia, emptying out parks and plundering wildlands, often newly accessible along logging roads.

–Bryan Christy, "The Kingpin," 2010.

Sam Dalton was dressed as a python ranger in dark green cargo pants and a light khaki bush shirt from Orvis. Why, you ask? Because he was playing the role of moderator for the CISMA Python Progress Meeting at Oak Hammock Hall in the Long Key Natural Area and Nature Center in Davie. How else was he going to dress? Coat and tie? Jumpsuit?

CISMA was another forced governmental acronym for the Cooperative Invasive Species Management Area, which was essentially all of the undeveloped public land south of Lake Okeechobee, including Everglades National Park, Big Cypress Preserve, and the Florida Wildlife Management Areas. The organization was composed of signatories—government agencies, totally—and cooperators. The signatories were the Florida Fish and Wildlife Conservation Commission, the Army Corps of Engineers, US Fish and Wildlife Service, National Park Service, Miami-Dade County, and the South Florida Water Management District. The usual suspects, Dalton thought.

The cooperators were a mixed bag of foundations, do-gooders, universities, Indian tribes, the Nature Conservancy, Florida Power and Light, and Dalton's own non-profit, PTSD: Positive Thinking Solves Distress, LLC. Fairchild Tropical Botanic Garden was also a cooperator, which explained why Laura Saylor was waving at him and pointing to her phone. He read her text. "Can only stay for half the meeting. Call me later." He texted back "ok" and looked out over the hall. Not only was it almost full, there was a lot of media in attendance including at least three television stations.

At precisely 10:00 a.m., Dalton took the microphone at the podium and called the meeting to order. "Welcome everyone. We have really good attendance today, which is great. This meeting focuses on pythons, but that doesn't mean CISMA isn't busily working on other invasive problems like monitor lizards, giant African land snails, piranhas, and Gambian pouched rats. They are just as important but because of public concern, this meeting addresses progress toward python control. Here's the agenda. We'll have the Python Patrol and Hotline updates from the Florida Fish and Wildlife Conservation Commission and the University of Florida. We have news from Everglades National Park and Auburn University on python research, data management, and what the next steps will be. We will present the planning for the Large Constrictor Workshop from the University of Florida. And I'll give my update on the success of the Python Apprehension Volunteers. This meeting will end promptly at noon, or before, I promise you that.

"But before we get to our side of the python debate, we have a guest speaker who has some opinions that many of you will disagree with. But because of the Florida Open Meetings

Act, she has just as much of a right to speak to this group as we do. So to begin, here's Diana Ventura, public relations manager for the Save Our Snakes Foundation."

To a smattering of applause, Diana Ventura stepped up to the podium. Her long black hair was secured at the back of her neck and hung halfway to her hips. Dressed in a powder-blue jacket and matching pencil skirt with an orange and dark blue blouse, she looked professional but nowhere near nerdy. Classy would be a better word.

"First, I'd like to thank the CISMA directors and moderator Sam Dalton for the opportunity to address you today. And don't worry—Save Our Snakes does not have any demonstrators with signs outside and we're not going to make a scene or try to shut down this meeting to get publicity. We don't operate that way—we do things logically. So I'm here today to suggest some alternatives to the way CISMA is handling the python situation in Everglades National Park and the surrounding preserves.

"I'm going to start with a simple suggestion and then give my reasons for making it. You should forget trying to eradicate pythons and focus on a far more serious ecological problem for the state of Florida: feral hogs. They cause far more damage to the land and the ecosystem, they breed even faster than pythons, and they're a hell of a lot easier to find."

Muted chuckles came from her audience, so she added, "And they're better eating and are not mercury-contaminated." Several people laughed. "You laugh, but Florida has the second-largest population of feral hogs after Texas. And Texas has a statewide program to accept freshly-killed hogs, process the meat under USDA supervision, and then sell the meat to supermarkets, butcher shops, and restaurant suppliers. Excess meat goes to homeless shelters. It's a self-sustaining program.

"Now, what are our reasons for not pursuing the attempted

destruction of pythons?" She held up her left hand and touched the fingers with her right forefinger. "You don't even know how many there are, with estimates from 5,000 to 500,000. No matter how many there are, they are here to stay and you can't destroy them all. Yes, they are an invasive species, but there has been no definitive study of the amount of damage they've done or might do. One preliminary study of dissected pythons found that their most common prey is cotton rats. No, not beautiful water birds or house pets, but the hated cotton rat. Finally, pythons are one of hundreds of invasive species, but Floridians have singled them out because they are snakes and 95 percent of American citizens—of any race, age, or gender—fear and despise snakes.

"What about crop-eating starlings? They're invasive, as are house sparrows. Other animals are self-invasive, like cattle egrets and Eurasian collared doves—both got here without human help. But nobody's out there killing them, right?

"And just how dangerous are these pythons anyway? Nature by definition is dangerous. So is domestication. Dogs kill approximately 25,000 people around the world annually—most of that by transmitting rabies like mosquitoes transmit malaria. Each year, horses kill 20 Americans, and cows kill another 20. Deer kill 200 people a year in car accidents. I could go on for an hour, but death by python usually only happens to careless hobbyists who should not have large snakes in the first place. We've had only one python-caused death in the wild in this country—a tragic one, yes, but still only one. Alligators are far more deadly, yet they're a protected species.

"And finally, groups helping veterans conquer PTSD, like Mr. Dalton's, might discover that feral hog hunts are far more interesting than python hunts. They are a better simulation of combat, and require guns instead of nooses and snares. And Labrador retrievers can be easily retrained to track hogs because they smell ten times worse than pythons. Now, any questions?"

"Ms. Ventura," asked a reporter she knew in the second row, "are you a herpetologist?"

"No, I'm not."

"Do you keep a pet snake?"

"No," Ventura replied, and gave the audience a sweet smile. "I find that cats are more lovable companions." More chuckles.

An obnoxious "Undercover Exposé" reporter from Miami's Channel 6 asked, "Is the Save Our Snakes Foundation controlled by World of Reptiles, the notorious importer and reputed reptile smuggling house?"

Ventura replied smoothly, without hesitation. "Certainly not. We are an independent organization supported by reptile enthusiasts like the Sunshine State Reptile Fanciers. It is true that House of Reptiles supports us and is one of our biggest donors. But they do not control us."

"How much do they contribute?"

"I'll tell you what, Ms. Peters, we're holding up the CISMA meeting. See me in the hall in a few minutes."

And then, to Dalton's astonishment, she winked at him, and he took it as a cue and stood up.

"Thank you for listening to me," Ventura said, and there was the usual low-volume polite applause given to a hostile speaker.

Dalton took over the mike. "Ms. Ventura makes some interesting points. I don't agree with most of them, but our group should be open to any and all comments and research about the python problem."

The remainder of the meeting took a little over an hour and 45 minutes. Dalton left the room and noted that Diana Ventura was sitting on an uncomfortable bench, working on her iPad and apparently waiting for him. She stood up and asked, "Walk with me to the parking garage?"

"Sure. What's up?" He really wanted an answer to that but got a question instead.

"What did you think of my presentation?"

"Well researched and well presented. Total BS, of course, but good."

"Thanks. I try. Just doing what I'm paid to do. I think we should have a meeting. There are some things you should know. I'll call you later."

"Let me give you my cell number."

"I have it."

"What's this all about, Ms. Ventura?"

"Diana, please. I will explain later. I just want you to know one thing."

"Okay," Dalton said, as curious as ever.

Diana took his arm and pulled him to her so her mouth was close to his left ear. "I hate the fucking snakes," she whispered. "Don't tell anyone."

• • •

Sam Dalton was born and grew up in Key Largo. His dad Stuart owned Dalton Marine Engineers and Mechanics, a large and very successful company, and his mom Melinda had a tourist retail shop—"make that a trap"—as she used to say. From his earliest memories, Sam was always on a boat. He grew up in the life of the Keys and particularly loved fishing and observing marine life. His first career goal was to be a fishing guide.

The fisherman Sam was a B- student at Coral Shores High School mostly because he was distracted by sports. Dalton was an ace pitcher on the baseball team, going to the state finals one year, and a striker on the soccer team. He lost his virginity his junior year, the same year he scored a school record 23 goals, to a woman we would now call a MILF. This woman, temporarily living aboard a yacht moored at the same marina as many of the Dalton Marine work boats, had asked Sam for a tour of their biggest salvage vessel, which actually had nice suites because management had to live aboard it on a job. How could he refuse? She was about 40 but sexy as hell in a white one piece bathing suit with some kind of gauzy shawl around it, and high-heeled flip-flops. Sam showed her the captain's suite and she—he thought her name was Shirley, or Sherry, or something—started taking off her suit.

"What are you waiting for?" she asked.

"For God to acknowledge my prayer of thanks." He thought he was very clever, but Shirley or whoever just said, "Get over here and I'll show you how fast I can disrobe a high school kid with a hard-on." Young Dalton's second career goal was that of becoming a gigolo.

After high school, Dalton enrolled at Florida Atlantic University in Boca Raton, where he devoted a lot more time to his studies than he did in high school. After four years, he had earned a B.S. in biology with a certificate in environmental sciences, and had found both a wife and a career. He met Robin in his senior year at the farewell party for a mutual friend, and a week later he attended a job fair. His father had wanted him to come to work at Dalton Marine full-time instead of the half-time position he'd had all through high school and college, but now that Dalton was receiving his degree, he wanted to keep his options open. Maybe some company needed a marine biologist but couldn't afford a Ph.D. It would pay half what his father would pay him, but it would be a hell of a lot more interesting.

At the job fair on campus in the student union building, Dalton noticed a sign for a booth that read, "NCIS. Not the FBI. We're better." Beside it was a sign that listed disciplines with open positions. Biosciences, computer experts, law enforcement, attorneys, and boat captains. Intrigued, he approached the booth and noted that it was casual.

"National Center for Information on Submarines?" he asked a recruiter in shorts and an NCIS t-shirt.

"Cute. We get that sort of thing all the time. Need a career?" he asked Dalton with a grin. "What's your field?"

"Biology with a certification in environmental science. What's NCIS?"

"Naval Criminal Investigation Service. But we are not navy—we're civilians. We investigate serious crimes by and against members of the US Navy and the Marine Corps. We are hiring qualified special agents. Are you interested in a career in law enforcement?"

"Well, my only other option at the moment is working for my dad's company, Dalton Marine. But I've been there, done that since I was 12."

"Your father owns Dalton Marine?"

"Sure."

"Could you come to our office for an interview on Monday?"

"What time and where?" Dalton asked.

"0900 and we're officed at Homestead Air Force Base. Give me some information about yourself and a visitor badge will be waiting. Here's a map."

Everything went smoothly at NCISRU Miami in Building 184. A security agent escorted Dalton to a small conference room with a table and four chairs. The only seat left was at the head of the table, so Dalton took it. The recruiter introduced the unit director and assistant director.

The director said, "I won't waste your time, Mr. Dalton. Have you thought about this over the weekend?'

"Yes, and I did some research. I'd like to apply."

"No need. We've already filled out your application and it's been approved. Next step is for you to read the job description and tell us if it's acceptable."

It was a one-page description of a position that offered Dalton the chance to use his biology skills in collecting samples and overseeing their forensic examination and use as evidence, his boating skills by piloting (at times) NCIS watercraft, and his physical and mental skills as an undercover operative digging for information related to suspected smuggling by navy airmen stationed at the Naval Air Station Key West. He would not only receive a reasonable salary from NCIS, he would be allowed to keep his half-time salary from Dalton Marine, because, and this was the kicker, Dalton Marine would provide the cover for him going anywhere from Fort Lauderdale to Key West any time he needed, for whatever reason, by company car or Dalton Marine boat.

"My father would have to approve this," Dalton said.

"He said you would say that," the director commented. "I spoke with him earlier—he's all for it. He said, and I quote, 'Put the fucking smugglers in the lockup, and while you're at it, get rid of all the jet skis in the Keys.'"

"That's good ole dad."

"We'd like you to start training the day after graduation."

"I'm not going to graduation—I paid the University the $100 fee to opt out. But I am getting married. Consider yourself invited to the ceremony. I'll start training right after the honeymoon."

"And how long will that be?"

"Just three days. It's an underwater shark-tagging trip."

The director's eyes widened and Dalton explained. "Just kidding. We're running away to Key West. Can't imagine what we'll be doing down there if I'm going to be in training for the next few months."

• • •

As she rode in the Mercedes with Helen Menuah, Diana's expression was neutral but her mind was grinning. Finally, after nearly three months, she was on her way to meet Bruno Zimmerman, owner of World of Reptiles. She had not pushed for the coming meeting or even mentioned it, for that matter. If it was inevitable, why queer the deal by suggesting it?

"Why is World located in Homestead?" she asked.

"Tradition," Helen relied. She was a woman of undetermined age—anywhere from 40 to 60—dressed in a lightweight grey summer suit and a white blouse. No jewelry, no fragrance, no makeup, no smile. "Homestead is not only the reptile capital of Florida, but probably the entire US."

"But what about Hurricane Andrew?"

Helen gave a little shrug. "Most of the dealers evacuated, and every facility was leveled. But nearly all of them had plenty of insurance, so they rebuilt and made every building not only much stronger, but very contemporary."

Diana could see what Helen meant as they pulled into the large parking lot of World of Reptiles. The building was like a scaled-down Cabela's—glass, exposed wood, and burnished metal. Above the entrance was a three-dimensional globe with a python girdling it. Its head seemed to look at everyone coming in the front door. It was creepy to her, but the customers, lovers of all things reptilian, undoubtedly thought it was really, really, cool.

As Helen led her back to Zimmerman's office, Diana believed spinal shivers would permanently debilitate her as she went past row after row of cages, aquaria with screened tops, signs for snake food ("Special Today: Large Rats—Buy Two, Get One Free!"), a life-sized diorama of an alligator and a python locked in a deadly embrace ("Those are fiberglass," Helen pointed out), all steeped in a dreaded odor that she could only describe as slimy. She knew snakes weren't but there were amphibians here too—"Chinese giant salamanders! Only two left!"

"Those are babies," Helen said, "they grow up to be six feet long."

There were abundant floral displays throughout the store, probably an attempt to soften the reptilian atmosphere of the place, but it didn't work for Diana. She was perspiring profusely by the time they arrived at the sign that read, "Herptile Offices," and walked through the door and into the mayhem of a packing and shipping facility.

"Hello, Ray," Helen said to a short guy with wild hair and a badge. Ray Jacobs, Shipping Manager.

"Hi, Helen," he said in passing.

Helen knocked, heard a prompt, "Come in, Helen," and they entered a large office with a bank of video monitors on the wall to their left and a large, ornate desk on their right. Bruno Zimmerman rose to greet them.

The phrase "lounge lizard" popped into her mind. He was a big guy but not fat. A bit of a roll around his waist, open-necked purple shirt showing chest hair and gold chains. Tight black curls on top of his head, no facial hair but a five o'clock shadow at 1:00 p.m. Some sort of too-tight designer jeans with metal doodads on them. He held out his hand, she shook it and he held her fingers just a little too long. Shivers again for Diana.

"I saw you on TV last night," he said. "You're good."

"Lotsa practice," she replied. The three of them now sat at a small table in front of the monitors.

"You were speaking with Sam Dalton after the meeting," Zimmerman said. "Do you know him?"

"Just met him that day," she replied, realizing that in the

future she shouldn't even speak with Dalton in a public situation like that. She wondered who had reported the encounter to Zimmerman.

"I'd like to find out more about that guy. Could you do some snooping for me?"

"Sure, if Helen okays it."

Helen almost smiled and nodded her head.

"Good. And thanks for defending SOS on camera."

"It's my job," she said, trying to be humble rather than just rattled and very uncomfortable. "What do you want to know about Dalton?"

"I just don't like people killing snakes. Sorta gives World of Reptiles a black eye. We sell Burmese pythons—US farm-raised, of course."

"No more imports allowed," Helen added.

Zimmerman gave her his serious stare. "Whatever you can find out about him that's not on the Internet would be helpful. The old coconut telegraph routine, know what I mean?"

Diana nodded her assent.

"Okay," Zimmerman said. "I have a new plan for SOS. Let's go over it."

• • •

Ray Jacobs waved to his boss as Zimmerman left for the day. Ray was always the first one in and the last one to leave. He wanted it that way. He needed to be Mr. Indispensable, the worker bee who just did his job well with no complaints. He was almost finished with his work for the day—just one more little thing.

With the key no one knew he had, he entered Zimmerman's office. Walking over to the bookcase, he reached behind Zimmerman's trophy for "Snakeman of the Year" from the American Society of Ichthyologists and Herpetologists, and retrieved the Jooney-Bug voice-activated flash drive voice recorder and replaced it with another one.

Jacobs locked the door behind him. Back in his cubicle, he plugged the flash drive into his iMac. He downloaded the MP3 of Zimmerman's meeting with the two women, listened to it for 33 minutes, and then opened his email and began typing up the circumstances behind the recording. He attached the MP3 to the email and sent it off to his superior at the Vero Beach office. Then he moved the MP3 to the trash and emptied it. He also deleted the sent message so that there was no evidence of the recording. He put the Jooney-Bug in his pocket.

Jacobs said goodnight to the security officer who would be on duty until 2:00 a.m., walked into the parking lot, put on his helmet, mounted his C600 Sport BMW, and headed home. As he drove, he considered his predicament, which was precarious at best. He was the de facto second in command, and although he could not make financial decisions or sign checks, he could make sure the customers were taken care of and the shipping of various reptiles ran smoothly. Ray knew that Zimmerman needed him, but Ray didn't care since he didn't really work for the man. His real boss was Harry Nichols, regional director of law enforcement for the US Fish and Wildlife Service, and his real name was not Ray Jacobs but Ray Lindsay.

There was no doubt that Ray was the perfect undercover reptile expert. He had been fascinated with reptiles as a kid, bragging to his friends that he had been bitten by snakes 40 times before he turned 13. He was the kid in the neighborhood who knew all about wildlife, specifically reptiles and birds. He knew many of the adults in Holmes Run Acres because he mowed their lawns, babysat their little kids, and went to school with their older kids. He always told the adults that snakes were good because they ate mice and rats. He was the one they called if they found a suspected poisonous snake, because he had them trained. Most of the time the "cottonmouth moccasins" were common water snakes and the "copperheads" were rat snakes. He'd catch them in the neighbors' yards, deftly transfer them to old pillow cases, and release them in the huge second-growth forest that Holmes Run ran through. He had virtually memorized his bible, How to Make a Miniature Zoo by Vinson Brown, and he had made a good one.

From the time he entered high school, he knew he was going to major in biology in college, and after he was accepted by the University of Kansas—"the Harvard of herpetology"—he worked hard and eventually received his masters degree in ecology and evolutionary biology with herpetology as his specialty. But when he looked for jobs, he soon discovered that unless he stayed in school for his doctorate, they were few and far between. He dreamed of getting paid for what he had always loved—field collection of snakes, especially endangered ones, but that was not going to happen. So he applied for an inspector's position at the US Fish and Wildlife Service and got it.

As a wildlife inspector, he was soon bored with opening people's suitcases in Atlanta, headquarters for Region 4 of Fish and Wildlife—he called it "being a bookkeeper on Noah's Ark." After working as an inspector for a year, he decided that being a special agent would be a lot more interesting. He passed the initial qualification tests and was sent to Glynco, Georgia, to attend FLETC. That would be the Federal Law Enforcement Training Center, where recruits for the Secret Service, the ATF, the IRS, and other law enforcement agencies were trained.

If he didn't pass FLETC, he couldn't become a special agent and he might not get his inspector's job back. First he went to Criminal Investigator School and after that Special Agent Basic School. He graduated third in his class and was assigned to the Environmental Crimes Section in Miami, a cooperative project of the US Fish and Wildlife Service and the Environmental

Protection Agency. Since 1992, the two agencies worked to-gether on cases instead of competing with each other. And Mi-ami was the center of animal smuggling in the United States.

Ray immediately felt frustrated. Under federal wildlife laws, possession of a smuggled animal was not good enough to prosecute—you had to prove that the person in possession knew it had been smuggled into the country. Also, the rules and regulations of CITES, the Convention on International Trade in Endangered Species of Wild Fauna and Flora, were not only confusing, they allowed the trade of "captive-bred" animals, so a few bribes to officials in the right countries could guarantee the proper paperwork for animals smuggled into Mi-ami International.

He was one of only four special agents in the Miami Divi-sion, and the only one undercover. Hell, there were just 217 F and W special agents in the entire country. To get that position he had joined Special Operations, the elite undercover squad, and that meant passing the in-service training at the National Conservation Training Center in Shepherdstown, West Virgin-ia. That was easy compared to the testing Bruno Zimmerman had given him after he applied for the job of shipping manager at World of Reptiles. Zimmerman had walked him through the showroom, stopping at seemingly random cages and asked Ray to identify what was in them.

"Shingleback lizard," he told Zimmerman, "*Tiliqua rugosa asper*, an armored skink from eastern Australia." Zimmerman had just nodded. At another cage he told Zimmerman that the little crocodilians in it were mugger crocodiles from India, not as rare as the gharials but endangered nonetheless. "*Crocodylus palustris*," he added.

The reptile that most amazed Ray was a white leucis-tic boa, a specially-bred near-albino boa with dark eyes that was called the Princess Diamond boa in the trade. A specimen like the one he was looking at was probably worth $20,000. "Captive-bred in the US, I assume," he told Zimmerman, who gave back just a little smile and another nod. In Zimmerman's office, the boss told Ray that he was the only applicant in the history of World of Reptiles to score 100 percent on the identification exam. He made Ray an offer that was immediately accepted. He was the new shipping manager at World of Reptiles. A few weeks later Zimmerman trusted him enough to add the unofficial position of chief witness to Ray's imaginary job description. Then Ray came up with the Monty Python Roundup Promotion, whereby if any citizen caught a feral python on land not belonging to the Feds or state, the catcher could bring it to World of Reptiles and exchange it for anything in the store worth $100 or less, including the 14-disc box of The Complete Monty Python's Flying Circus 16 Ton Megaset.

During the month-long promotion, eight pythons were turned in and the cost to the company was about a $1,000. Zimmerman calculated that with all the coverage by newspapers, TV stations, and social media, the promotion had resulted in publicity worth about $50,000. The store itself averaged 18 percent higher sales for the month. For that, Zimmerman had named Ray Employee of the Year and had deposited $25,000 in cash into his checking account. How the hell was he going to explain that to Harry Nichols, regional director of law enforcement for the US Fish and Wildlife Service?

4

When it strikes, as it does with a very wide gape to the jaws,
it fastens its teeth firmly in the prey, while the force of the
thrust often knocks the animal off balance. At the same time
the python rolls over, twisting itself round and round so that
its body encircles the animal it has caught.
—R. C. H. Sweeney, *Snakes of Nyasaland*, 1961.

Bruno Zimmerman had just turned 11 years old when he committed his first two murders. The bullies deserved it, of course. They were brothers, one 12 and the other 14, and their specialty was stealing students' lunch or lunch money. Bruno's mother, aware that her son checked all his snake traps for indigos after school, made him a hearty lunch, plus an afternoon snack like some cookies or a piece of her chocolate cake. That's what the Snyder brothers liked the best, the cake. And despite Bruno's best evasive tactics, Tim and Willie caught him every other day or so—and to avoid the black eye of the first encounter, when trapped, he opened his NASA lunchbox and they took everything in it. And laughed at him, calling him "Snakey Suzy."

Finally, Bruno got really pissed off about being a victim. He planned the murders carefully and on the chosen day, when the two boys accosted him, he called them assholes and ran for the piney woods next to the school. They were close behind and could outrun him, but he knew every trail in those woods and kept ahead of them, doubling back, going left, going right until they were lost. The bullies, that is. Bruno knew exactly where he was. After all, this was his snake-hunting territory.

He left his lunchbox full of Twinkies in the middle of the trail and vanished into the thick brush. He checked his watch then retrieved the axe he had stashed. After 40 minutes had passed, he carefully worked his way back to where he had left the lunch box. The brothers, sick as dogs and on their knees trying to vomit, were actually happy to see him.

"Bruno," the older one, begged. "You've got to help us. Something made us really sick and we can't even walk. Please help us."

"Sure, Tim," Bruno replied, smiling. "I wouldn't want you to suffer." Then he raised the axe and brought it down first on Tim's head and next on Willie's neck.

Then there was the problem of what to do with their bodies. But Bruno was a resourceful kid, and he had borrowed his uncle's garden cart. Fortunately, the school and the piney woods were very close to the North Canal in Homestead. Still, it took Bruno three hours to dismember the bodies, haul them to the canal, and dump them. Then he cleaned up, put on an old t-shirt and a spare pair of jeans, and caught hell from his mom for being late to dinner. And he was hungry. After all, he had missed lunch, especially those Twinkies he had filled with Cowley's Rat and Mouse Poison from the old bottle he had found in his uncle's shed. And, to top off his day, he had learned a new word: rodenticide. He liked the sound of it.

• • •

"He told me to snoop you out," Diana told Dalton. They were sitting together at Latte Da on 2nd Street in Homestead.

He had to drive to the Chokoloskee Island campground to get his team organized for the next day's hunt, so coffee at 7:00 was their only option.

"What's he want to know?"

"What's not on the Internet. He seemed pissed off that you're killing pythons—I know, I know, either the state or Feds do the actual killing and necropsies. But most people would call you a python-killer. Zimmerman does."

"Why are you telling me this when you're sorta workin' for the guy? Where's your loyalty, Diana?"

Diana hesitated, her eyes sweeping the room for familiar faces. There were only two other customers, and they weren't paying her or Dalton any attention at all. She was in her jogging outfit, with makeup on. Dalton wore cut-off jeans and a t-shirt that read, "Florida Piranha Fishing Guide Service—Eat Them Before They Eat You." The guide service was imaginary. The Florida piranhas were not.

Diana realized that she had been holding her breath. She exhaled slowly and looked at him. There was no use swearing him to secrecy or any of that crap. She needed his help and would either get it or not. Her dad always said, "If you don't make pitches, you don't make sales," so she just flat out told him what the hell was really going on.

"Look, Dalton, I'm going to level with you because I think we're on the same side here. I'm not trying to save any snakes," she began, and then it all came out in a rush. She was an investigative journalist and had convinced the editors of the two largest newspapers in the state—the *Miami Herald* and the *Tampa Tribune*—to jointly fund the undercover investigation of World of Reptiles and its reputed reptile-smuggling schemes that included some endangered species. And the newspapers had brought in two TV stations to help promote the stories, Channel 12 in Tampa and Channel 6 in Miami. At first all she had was circumstantial evidence and the word of one turncoat who despised Zimmerman. Then she lucked out with the job at Save Our Snakes and finally had a chance to get close to Zimmerman. But she needed more. Would he help her?

"I'm all for stopping reptile smugglers. How, exactly, can I help you?"

"Zimmerman must have excellent smuggling methods because he's never been caught. Help me figure out what they are. Maybe if we put some pressure on him he'll make a mistake."

He grinned at her and doubted that she knew he was former NCIS. "The first thing we have to do is figure out what you're going to tell him about me."

They spent another 15 minutes working up a plan to make Zimmerman really nervous about Dalton, and then he told her he had to go.

"He's going to try to fuck me," she said. "Maybe rape. I know his type."

"Play hard to get," Dalton suggested. "Somebody better might come along."

"You are a cruel man, Dalton," she told him. But she was smiling.

Damn, she's good-looking, he thought.

• • •

By 7:00, when the sun was down, the naked bulbs of the Chokoloskee Island Park and Marina campground cast a weird and weak light on the campers amidst the palmettos. Most of the python team had small tents, but Dalton preferred his Coachmen Viking because the pop-up also popped-down quickly, and self-locked. Dalton had hauled the pop-up while Phil Everett had trailered the air boat.

Dalton and Phil were drinking on campstools between the pop-up and the water. Their team members were laughing and clapping, which, to Dalton, indicated their excitement for the coming hunt.

"Wife and kids?" Dalton asked.

"Totally normal, not even a case of sunburn or poison ivy. Boring, almost. Sometimes boring is good—no crises. You?"

"Laura and I are dating."

Phil spit out a mouthful of Python Pilsner. "Dating? Turn off the time machine, Daddy-O."

"Her term. It's a private joke."

"Are you back living together?"

"Not at the bungalow because she hates it. Off and on at her place. Say, a question for you, Phil."

"Go."

"At the CISMA meeting, that Channel 6 reporter asked the SOS representative if they were funded by this guy Zimmerman from World of Reptiles. She called him a reptile smuggler. Your opinion?"

Phil brightened. "Slimeball—but smart. Everybody knows he's dirty but no one can prove it. And no one, from the Staties to Customs, to the FBI, to enforcement agents like me, can figure out his smuggling methods."

"He's askin' around about me."

"Oh yeah? How do you know that?"

"Diana Ventura, the SOS gal."

"You two buddies now?"

"Sorta. She is a real temptation."

"You were a goddamned monk for half a year and now you've got all the spermaids swimmin' right up to you. Okay, okay, Zimmerman's got Ventura spying on you supposedly, so I assume you're gonna chum him. See if he takes the bait?"

"Right, but I need to find the right bait. Can you share the department's files on Zimmerman with me?"

"I'll have to clear it with George, but shit, all the favors you did for him when you were NCIS? I don't think it will be a problem."

"Tell him I'll be an advisor on the investigation of Zimmerman, if there is one."

"There is. It's ongoing but not active at the moment because we have zilch—nothing new, no leads."

"Tell George we're going to chum one up."

"You mean?"

"It's known as extortion, but first we're going to track down his entire network of reptile sales."

And suddenly, without warning, Kevin was between them. They both jumped a little.

"Sorry to startle you," he said. "I guess I should've worn whiteface."

"Good one, Kevin," Phil said. "Join us. How 'bout a beer? "

"Love one, thanks."

They sat around shooting the shit about pythons and the one passion they all had in common: fishing.

"Instead of hunting pythons, take a day off and let's hunt redfish and bonefish. I'll take you into the Back Country. On me."

"No you won't," Dalton said. "We'll pay you fair and square."

"Whatever." Kevin grinned. "At least it will be prey we can eat. You two go way back, right?"

"You could say that," Phil told him. "Let me tell you about the NCIS clusterfuck."

That took Phil another beer and when he was finished with the story, Dalton said, "Your turn, Kevin."

"Let me tell you how I left the Army," Kevin began. "I was on a hostage rescue team. The Taliban had attacked the Red Cross office in Jalalabad, killed two guards, and were holding five of the staff hostage to trade for some of their people in our military prison. Our team's mission was to get them out any way we could. So we tried negotiating—on a sat phone. Our team leader spoke Pashto, so after two hours of back and forth, we reached an agreement. The staff members were all alive, but handcuffed together. The Taliban in prison would get reduced sentences. The ones in the Red Cross office would surrender to the Jalalabad police, who would escort them out of town and release them. Then we would move in for the release of the hostages."

"Uh oh," Dalton said.

"You see it?" Kevin asked.

"It was a trap."

"Yep. I watched the five Taliban soldiers leave the Red Cross and get into police jeeps. We moved in carefully, checking for trip wires, explosives, mines, everything. We checked all the offices in the building and then returned to the lobby where the hostages were having their handcuffs removed. And all of a sudden the floor exploded—not from a bomb but from automatic weapons fire from the basement. I took three in the leg and nearly fucking bled to death. Two of our team were killed, one Red Cross worker, and the ones who lived were shot up bad. There were six Taliban, and one stayed in the basement. He killed himself with a pistol when his automatic ammo was gone. I passed out, but the Red Cross workers kept me stable until the chopper could get three of us to the combat hospital in Bagram. Two surgeries there, then another in Japan. I retired, got about 95 percent use of my leg back, and now I'm a fishing guide with a wife and kids. Who dreams of exploding floors."

"Jeez," Phil said.

"And I still have all my Army skills," Kevin added with a big grin. "Pythons, beware."

• • •

Phil Everett's friendship with Dalton went back more than 20 years to when Dalton was NCIS and Phil was a lieutenant commander in the Coast Guard at Station Key West. They had worked together on the famous—or infamous—Operation Xterminator case, which to date was the largest drug bust in naval history, with 84 naval and marine personnel arrested along with 99 civilians. Nearly all the arrests took place at Camp Lejeune in North Carolina, but the only deaths had occurred off the coast of Key West, on Phil and Dalton's watch.

The massive manufacturing and smuggling operation had focused on ecstasy, cocaine, amphetamines, and Ketamine, which was nicknamed "Special K." The only imported drug was cocaine, and it came through Key West, which is why special agent Sam Dalton had been aboard the 27-foot Special Purpose Craft-Shallow Water (SPC-SW for short), piloted by Phil Everett with two petty officers armed with M4 carbines as backup. Phil was wearing a P229 semi-automatic pistol on his hip, while Dalton was similarly armed with a SIG Sauer P229R DAK.

NCIS Xterminator command believed that three enlisted men at Naval Air Station Key West, under the guise of fishing trips, were retrieving small, waterproof totes with GPS beacons containing bricks of cocaine. The men, in civilian clothes— namely shorts and t-shirts—and using a flats boat, would fish their way to the beacon location, retrieve the tote, and return to the dock, usually with some redfish or sea trout that they would give away to people on other boats docked at the Conch Harbor Marina. Carrying a federal search warrant, Dalton and Phil were attempting to intercept their boat and catch them with a tote. They had not expected resistance, but they got it anyway.

After the pilot of the flats boat spotted the Coast Guard craft, he attempted to escape by outrunning it. That tactic might have worked if the wind had been still, but the seas were running at nearly two feet, and no one would run a flats boat at 40 knots in that sea for fear of capsizing it. With its twin Honda 150 horsepower outboards and its 3.5-ton weight, the SPC easily overcame the flats boat, and that's when the shooting began.

Automatic weapons fire raked the cockpit and starboard side of the SPC and everyone aboard except Phil flopped to the deck below the protecting gunwales. Phil ducked as low as he could, cut the engines to half and turned to starboard to present a smaller profile to the shooters. The petty officers, without orders from Phil, opened fire with the carbines aimed at the lowest part of the flats boat, which had a draft of only a foot. That should have crippled and sunk the flats boat. Instead, a huge explosion and fire killed all three men and destroyed any evidence that might have been on board.

During the mandatory incident inquiry, the following facts didn't matter: That the suspects had fired first. That bricks of cocaine were found in their places of residence. That the petty officers had fired without direct orders. That neither Phil nor Dalton had discharged their weapons.

But the following facts did matter: That three young men, possibly innocent, were killed by the Coast Guard and NCIS. Horribly. That there was no evidence they had contraband aboard the flats boat. And that one of the men, Stuart Mc-Gregor, was the son of William McGregor, the state senator from Senate District 39, which included Key West. As far as the media and general public were concerned, the Coast Guard and NCIS had overreacted. And all sides agreed that Operation Xterminator needed a new name and acronym.

The US government settled with the families of the airmen killed, precluding any civil action against the two disgraced officers. Phil took early retirement from the Coast Guard and became a special agent for Florida Fish and Wildlife. Dalton received partial retirement from NCIS and, after burying his wife and son, went python-hunting. Now, they were partners again. "We better not fuck this one up," Dalton had texted Phil.

"Amen, bro," came the immediate response.

• • •

From 4.7 feet above sea level, Commander Dalton reviewed his anti-snake armada. He had three airboats now that Kevin Cooper had joined his team. And he had a new python dog in training, a young male named Kinhagee, after a Miccosukee chief. He would be part of the Boat One team, with Dalton, Phil, and a newbie named Carol Watson, on her second hunt. Boat Two would be commanded by Julie Loftus, with former medic Lloyd Vann, newbie Ed McCoy, and the most experienced dog, Osceola. Boat Three, Kevin Cooper's, would be commanded by Chuck Gannon and also included the new medic, Jenny Rodriguez, with newbie Kevin, and second dog Abiata.

They left as the sun came up, with Phil piloting Boat One. He had the GPS locations for the seven hammocks they were targeting first, and the boats would split up once they got close. All of the boats had GPS units that would guide them to whatever location was entered, but Dalton's boat was equipped with a Lowrance HDS-8 Gen2 Fishfinder/Chartplotter and a Davis Instruments 6250 Vantage Vue Wireless Weather Station. The combo enabled Dalton to find pythons underwater and also track weather changes that might occur while they were on the hunt—anything from ambient temperature to wind velocity to relative humidity to barometric pressure.

It was 59 degrees when they left the campground with an expected high of 81 under partly cloudy skies with no rain in the forecast. The armada headed up the Turner River and turned to port at the confluence of the Left Hand Turner River. In minutes they were in the black mangrove wilderness, but they weren't going to find any pythons there. They had to move further inland, where the mangroves thinned out into sawgrass and hammocks.

About half an hour later, Dalton reached the first hammock on his list. It was a little under an acre in size. He deployed Phil, Carol, and the new dog, Kinhagee, to track down some snakes. He decided to try the Lowrance while cruising around the hammock using a trolling motor. The water was deeper here than what he was used to in the eastern part of the park, sometimes as much as three feet deep. He removed his GoPro camera from its case and made sure it was charged. He opened the storage bin for fishing rods and pulled out his 29 by 34-inch Pro-Formance landing net with a four-foot handle. Maybe he could record another method of catching pythons— small ones, of course. There was no way he was going to catch a ten-foot python in a net less than three feet long. He readied his eight by 20-foot white nylon net snake bag just in case.

It took Dalton nearly an hour to find one. Finally he saw a four- or five-footer slide off a log and into the water. He maneuvered the air boat closer and turned off the trolling motor. He adjusted the Lowrance until he spotted the snake resting quietly on the bottom then used the GoPro to take a shot of the Lowrance monitor. He mounted the GoPro on the net handle and positioned himself for the scoop and grab. Fortunately, the little camera was waterproof to 40 meters. He felt the tip of the net reach the bottom and scooped the net quickly forward and then pulled up. The first third of the python was in the net, thrashing wildly with its tail section. Dalton realized it was a two-person job. Somebody needed to hold the snake bag open. Before the snake could escape the net, he transferred it to his left hand and used his right to pull the .22 pistol from his pocket. He fired and hit the snake three times with snakeshot before it flipped out of the net and escaped. Dalton doubted that the snake would survive, but he couldn't count it as a kill.

Phil, Carol, and the Lab returned, with Phil shaking his head. "We got skunked," he reported.

"Chuck to Dalton," came a voice on Dalton's HT. He pulled it out of his pocket.

Every volunteer carried a water-resistant Motorola Talk-About MB140R walkie talkie, or more properly, a handheld transceiver.

"Go, Chuck."

"We have a situation here, requesting assistance."

"What's the problem?"

"Three illegal python hunters in an airboat. With weapons. And they're drunk—or stoned—or both."

"What are your coordinates?"

Phil entered the location into the weather station GPS and nodded.

"On our way," Dalton told Chuck. He called Julie and gave her the same GPS location and told her to meet him. With weapons ready.

When Dalton and Phil arrived, the scene was a cracker stand-off. Chuck with his Sig Sauer P-220 against three Un-Subs, one with a sawed-off 16-gauge, another with a revolver, and the last one, improbably, pointing a spear gun. With spear. Dalton slowed the airboat, cut the engine, set the poles, pulled out a flare gun, and shouted as loudly as he could.

"This will light you right up and blow you to fucking hell. Drop your weapons!" Doofus number one made a threatening motion with the sawed-off, and then backed off when Julie Loftus slid her airboat to the other side of the UnSubs and pointed her flare gun at him.

Phil stood up next to Dalton with his badge facing the UnSubs, about 50 feet away. "Phillip Everett, special agent, Florida Fish and Wildlife. Drop your weapons and prepare to be boarded."

They were outmanned and outgunned and they knew it. The UnSubs dropped their weapons and sat down, wobbly, in the airboat seats. And then the fun began.

No, not a fight. Not a boarding with weapons drawn. Just some fun with the stoned suspects. Those assholes, Dalton noticed, were crashing. Coming down from what? Meth? Gotta be meth. They were starting to twitch. He'd have to drag them onto the hammock. He marshaled the crew and pulled his oleoresin capsicum pepper spray from his belt. One of them stood up and fell out of the air boat. Chuck and Kevin pulled him out of the shallow water and threw him face-down on the wet ground of the hammock. Kevin pulled the man's wrists behind his back and zip-tied them. The other two saw the inevitable and stumbled off the air boat to sit on the ground. They too were zip-tied. Phil searched them, removed everything from their pockets and bagged it all, including a baggie of crystal and a small pipe.

"Thought so," he said. "Let's make them more comfortable." They erected a shade screen and ran a line though their cuffed hands. Phil gave each one a good shot of cold bottled water and Dalton duct-taped their mouths shut.

Phil wasn't sure if they were in Big Cypress Preserve or Everglades National Park, so he took the sat phone out of its holster and called park headquarters for instructions. Dalton sent the other two boats back to the hunt with the newbie, Carol.

Phil and Dalton had these guys to themselves until cavalry arrived in whatever fashion.

"They're gonna call me back," Phil said. "They're not sure yet how to get these assholes out of here and into jail." Five minutes later his sat phone rang.

"Crap," Phil said when he disconnected. "This is gonna take a while."

"What's the problem? We can deliver the assholes to them."

"Well, Sam, there's lotsa problems. Look at the potential charges. Hunting without a license in a national park. Poaching. Possession of loaded weapons in a national park. Threatening a state agent. Drunk and disorderly, possession of methamphetamine with intent to distribute. Plus two pythons in the boat's hold. The park's got a couple of special agents who want to investigate the crimes in situ, as they say. It will take them at least two hours to get here."

"Good. That gives us time to do our own investigation. Let's go through their wallets, maybe a little interrogation after lunch."

They never made it to the interrogation phase, although they did learn that all three men worked for the Manatee Fish Meal Plant. They had business cards but their titles were so vague as to be useless: Assistant Manager, Supervisor, and Technician. All three had credit cards that looked legit, and they each carried at least $250 in cash.

"I don't get it," Phil said. "Three rich tweaker fish meal execs out on a boat catching pythons and getting fried?"

"Is the Bermuda Triangle still in operation?" Dalton asked.

The sat phone chirped loudly. "Everett," Phil said. He was silent for about three minutes as he listened to the instructions.

"Yes, sir," he said finally, disconnecting. "They thought it over," he said to Dalton. "And we're making a movie. Live. I'm the director. Better get the rest of the team back here. See if your iPhone has a signal."

With Dalton as the cameraman with the GoPro, and Phil as the on-camera narrator, the story of the weird arrest of three fish meal execs, as they were now jokingly calling them, was captured live and broadcast to park headquarters via the iPhone's my-fi signal. All Dalton had to do was follow Phil around and shoot what he was pointing at, mostly the perps and the evidence.

At the end of his delivery, Phil directed Dalton to pan all of the PAVs. "Here are all the python apprehension volunteers, witnesses attesting that my description of this incident is accurate, who will sign the appropriate paperwork at headquarters. Phillip Everett, out."

Each of the perps, a lot more sober now, was placed on one of the air boats and secured in the seated position with zip-ties. Slowly, they eased away from the hammock and made their way back to the mangrove channels. The return trip took 45 minutes.

Although Phil had not mentioned it, Dalton was not surprised by the destination of his armada, now under new command. Phil was guiding the air boats to the very white and very impressive US Coast Guard Cutter Mohawk, which was anchored between park headquarters and the Everglades Airport.

• • •

Dalton was five miles out of Everglades City when the smell hit him. Rotting fish, an aroma he knew well from preparing chum on fishing boats. It had to be that fish meal plant where the three crackers worked.

He called Phil. "Smell that?"

"Remind me not to puke."

"What county are we in?"

"Monroe."
"Drive faster."

• • •

Big Ink was apoplectic. "What the fuck're you telling me?" he screamed into the phone. "Where the hell are they? We start production in four days! Go find them!" He slammed the cell phone down on his desk, cracking it badly.

"You're shooting the messenger, Ink," Derrick Fitzroy told him. "What's going on?"

The big man sputtered, "Cutup, Toad, and Tomás went python huntin' and never came back. No one knows where the fuck they are. That was Billy askin' me if I knew where they went."

"I'll make some calls," Fitzroy said and left the office.

Big Ink sat in silence for a while, reviewing his options. He knew how to make the meth himself—hell, he had taught the method to Cutup—he just didn't like being in the lab doing it. But he would if he had to. Employees, he thought with disgust. What the hell good are they?

He pulled out his cell phone and called Bone Mozell.

• • •

When your typical conman of either persuasion—be it a short con or long form—met Bone Mozell for the first time, the initial reaction was always the same: there's another one in the room. Bone described it as "an instinctual pheromone operating telepathically among conmen that translates into, 'What line of con are you in?'" The typical exchange that followed was, "Oh, art scams. And you?" Most of the cons replied, "fake gems" or "smuggled teenage Asian girls." Bone's usual answer was a lot more prosaic. "Nuggets," he would say. "Of the chicken kind."

He was kidding, of course, because Bone was not an industrial poultry farmer. He was president of the Sunshine State Poultry Fanciers Association (SSPFA) and director of District 12 of the American Poultry Association (APA), which not only included Florida, but also Alabama, Georgia, and South Carolina. Thus, he was the overseer of the 14 APA-sanctioned poultry shows in the region, including the Alabama Chicken and Egg Festival, the Sunshine State Poultry Fanciers Association Classic, and the shows at two state fairs, Florida and South Carolina.

But indirectly, he was in chicken nugget production. He was a poultry supplier—meal, prefab chicken houses, wire, feeders, watering stations, egg cartons, and other equipment. Mozell Poultry Supply was his company, operating out of a large warehouse in Naples but with retail locations all over Florida. So besides the chicken fancy, as it was called, he also supplied the down and dirty world of commercial chicken production in Florida. This is why he was president of the Chicken Farmers of Florida Association—and known in Florida as "Chickenman."

Bruno Zimmerman had spotted Bone in the Gecko Gardens section of World of Reptiles years ago, holding a fat tailed gecko. He recognized him from TV. "So Chickenman likes lizards, huh?"

Bone rolled his eyes. It happened all the time since he had started running the commercials on small cable stations serving Florida's rural backwaters. Dressed up as a chicken on camera, he called himself "Bone the Chickenman" and transformed himself into a pitchman for his own Mozell Poultry Supply, with shots of the big warehouse just outside of Naples and retail centers in most of the Sunshine Hardware store locations.

"I like geckos, anyway. I have a leopard and a crested—they live in my pool enclosure."

"Living on roaches, flies, and chlorinated water, I'm sure." Zimmerman smiled and held out his hand. "Bruno Zimmerman."

Bone took it, gave it a firm shake, and smiled as well. "I've heard of you. Bone Mozell. I live in Naples."

"Reptiles and birds. We were bound to meet sometime."

That chance encounter was the beginning of a very special criminal enterprise, but it took them three months of waltzing around before they trusted each other enough to proceed with anything. They had lunch together. Zimmerman invited Bone to one of his parties at El Nido de la Víbora, his compound on Hibiscus Island in Biscayne Bay. They doubled-dated a pair of high-class escorts and swapped the two sisters back and forth. They went fishing in Florida Bay and caught reds and bonefish—by themselves because flat boats had no head and women lacked the proper plumbing for flats fishing. With paid dates, they watched the Miami Dolphins knock the Jets out of the playoffs. With volunteer dates, they did the Miami Beach bar shuffle a few times, where Bone was always asked to perform his Chickenman shtick at least once. It was male bonding at its finest, as Bone was fond of saying. And it was during their beach bar-hopping that they discovered another common interest: a passion for uppers.

"A touch of the toot," was Zimmerman's expression, while Bone spoke of certain things that became "crystal clear." They also had one other belief in common: nothing to excess, always stay in control. Never drunk. Never too high. Just feelin' alright, like the old Dave Mason song. That probably was what really bound them closely together, that sense of control.

One night they were drinking with some escorts, and when they went off to the ladies room together, Zimmerman said in a voice barely above a whisper, "I think we trust each other enough for me to ask you a private question."

"Sure, go ahead," Bone urged him, curious.

"Where do you get your crystal?"

"I make it," Bone said, watching Zimmerman's eyes widen in surprise. "And now you have to confess something to me. Tit for tat." It was his mother's expression and fun to use.

Zimmerman didn't hesitate. "I smuggle reptiles."

"Why does that not surprise me?" Bone asked.

"What's the one box no thief ever opens?"

"I give up," Bone said.

"The one marked 'Live Reptiles,'" Zimmerman replied, smiling. The girls were back from the john and ready to leave for the swingers' party. "We'll talk about this later."

No only did they talk, they took action. Bone told him about his meth and fish meal operation, to which Zimmerman commented, "Ingenious." Zimmerman then related some details about his reptile smuggling operation after they arrived in the states, but not the method of their introduction.

"I'm the only one who knows that. That way I can't be sandbagged. I hope you understand, Bone."

"Actually, I don't care how they come in. My operation is confined to Florida."

"For the moment, yes. But I have to tell you something really shocking."

"Note that my ears are tuned up," Bone said.

"There is a certain criminal element in the reptile business."

"No!" Bone feigned shock.

"Let's take your business national," Zimmerman suggested.

The trouble was Big Ink, Bone told him. Methmaking was difficult and time-consuming and his main meth man did not want to increase production. That fact did not please Zimmerman one bit. And there was something else as well: Zimmerman had met Ink and didn't like him. Called him a self-parody.

"I've heard he stages reptile battles. Pythons versus gators, that kinda shit."

"He does," Bone told him, and went into a description of some of Ink's more dramatic reptile events.

"That's barbaric," Zimmerman said without a trace of shame.

"It's just something that we have to put up with. We need Big Ink."

"I don't think so," Zimmerman countered, and laid out his plan.

• • •

Dalton was unhitching the pop-up in his side yard when Phil called.

"They're not talkin' except to demand an attorney," he said.

"How long can the Coast Guard stall 'em?" Dalton asked.

"Not long. They're being transferred in the morning from Coast Guard detention in Key West to the FDC in Miami. Arraignment is scheduled for Tuesday, so they'll need an attorney for that."

"What will the bail be?"

"We're taking bets on that now. I'm saying 100 thou each."

"Good." Dalton was very familiar with the Federal Detention Center in downtown Miami. When he was NCIS, many of the felons he arrested were housed there until their trials.

"I spoke with George. He's okay with you taking a look at our file on World of Reptiles, but you'll have to do it at our office. No photocopies allowed."

"First thing Monday morning? Your office at 8:00?"

"Sounds like a plan," Phil said. "Later."

He called Laura. "Hi, honey. I'm home."

"Get your ass up here," she said. "I'm making paella."

On the way to Coral Gables, he got a text from Diana.

"Looks like Z's going to file suit to stop your python-killing. We should talk."

He pulled the truck off the highway and stopped on the shoulder. "Call you Mon," he texted back.

Less than one minute later, his iPhone vibrated with another text.

"Stop killing pythons or we'll kill you."

5

Death by constriction is most likely the result of circulatory arrest followed by rapid tissue hypoxia of vital organ systems. Although suffocation occurs simultaneously with circulatory arrest, it is not the proximate cause of death.

–D. L. Hardy, "Constricting Snakes Do Not Kill Prey by Suffocation," 1993.

Dalton was in a great mood. He had dismissed the threatening text as some reptile-loving nut case. How the idiot had gotten his cell phone number was a mystery, but not worth pursuing. Meanwhile, he was in Laura's bed and her arms were around him. They had made love a few minutes before and everything was perfect. A happy Laura in her own townhouse was a hundred times better than a pissed-off Laura in Dalton's bungalow.

"We've got all day to be together," she murmured. "What should we do?"

"I think we should go out for brunch and then go to the reptile house at the Miami Zoo."

She hit him with her pillow and started laughing. "You almost got me."

The previous night, over a delicious paella dinner, he had

told her about the adventure with the stoned crackers. She had asked him why they were catching pythons, and he had no answer. It made no sense whatsoever. Workers at a fish meal plant out python-hunting?

"I liked the part about brunch, though," Laura hinted. They ended up at the Bagel Emporium on the South Dixie Highway where Laura ordered the lox and bagels and Dalton tried the corned beef hash topped with poached eggs and hot sauce.

Laura wanted Dalton to give a python presentation to a group of rich Fairchild donors and sponsors, and they discussed how it might work. She wanted a live python to be part of the presentation, but Dalton wasn't so sure.

"A big python is impressive but dangerous," he told her. "Smaller pythons are beautiful, as snakes go, and there might be some sympathetic people there who don't want them killed."

"Like that gal with Save Our Snakes," Laura said. "She was something else at that CISMA meeting. Intense. Have you met her?"

"Yes. Diana Ventura. I spoke with her after the meeting." He was reluctant to tell Laura about what Diana was really doing.

"And?"

"We agreed to disagree. Politely. I don't like her and don't trust her."

"She looks like the actress who starred in that TV show V. Remember that?"

"Yes, I do. I was in college. I had a huge crush on that actress. Jane Badler. The lizard gal. Remember the scene where she swallowed the live rat? That was, well, just amazing."

"It turned you on, right?" Laura was grinning at him.

"It sure did," he admitted.

"Well, if you treat me nice today, when we get back to my

place I'll swallow something a lot more appetizing than a rat."

"Promise?"

She winked at him and he wondered, was this for real? Could they make this second chance work? It sure was looking like it.

As they left the restaurant, on their way to the Cineplex for an afternoon movie, the coincidence hit him. The alien lizard lady, the one Jane Badler played, was named Diana. Goddess of the hunt.

• • •

The call Big Ink had been desperately waiting for finally came after nearly three days. It was 2:16 Sunday afternoon.

"Ink? How's it hangin'? This is Cutup. We sorta need your help."

"Where the fuck you guys been?"

"Shut up!" Cutup screamed back. "This is the only phone call they've allowed me. They've been interrogatin' us for two days straight and I ain't said nothin' except that I want a lawyer."

Ink moderated his demeanor, but it took a huge effort. "Where are you? What happened?"

"Federal Detention Center. We got busted for poaching pythons in the national park. Go figure, huh? The Feds are killing these snakes but they're protected because they're in the park. Does that make any sense to you?"

"We need to get you guys sprung," Ink told him, calmer now that he knew what was going on.

"Tuesday, 9:00 a.m. That's the arraignment. We'll know what the bail is after that."

"How bad is it?"

"Well, Ink, I can't talk much on this phone."

"I think I'll change your name to Fuckup. But I know who

to call," Ink told him. "You're going to owe me big time."

"Okay, just a few days. See you Tuesday."

"You won't see me. The attorney's name is Judith Banderas. Don't fuck with her. Tell her the absolute truth. Don't turn your back on her, either."

"She must be mean."

"You'll see soon enough. $500 an hour."

"Ouch."

"It's comin' out of your pay."

"Thanks, Ink, I guess."

Big Ink killed the call.

• • •

On Monday at 7:00 a.m., Diana met Dalton at Warren Municipal Park. "Go in the entrance off Palm Drive," he had told her on the phone, "take the first right and when you get to the roundabout, go around it and park on the left. I'll be waiting at one of the shelters with the picnic tables."

Dressed in a burnt orange blouse and tight gray slacks, Diana sat across from him on the bench of the picnic table and quickly told Dalton that Save Our Snakes was going to file suit against him and his non-profit for animal cruelty. World of Reptiles would help with another civil suit claiming that Dalton and his group were causing harm to its business by spreading rumors that they were reptile smugglers.

"Zimmerman knows he can't win either suit, so that's not the point," she said.

"He wants me on the run, off guard, paying attorneys. It's distraction tactics."

"And he gets all the publicity, through me," she added.

Dalton's eyes caught a brief reflection of light from across the park to his right and he noticed that the larger shelter at the crossroads just after the park entrance now had an occupant.

It had been empty when he arrived and checked out the entire park.

"Diana, listen carefully. Someone's watching us through binoculars. He wasn't here when I arrived, so either your phone or your car's being tracked. Don't look around and don't change your expression. When you leave here, go somewhere and buy a prepaid cell phone and text me the number. Now, lean over and kiss me on the mouth. I'm going to say some shit to you, so look disappointed. We're gonna have to be enemies for a while. When I call you on the throw-away phone, I'll explain everything. Do it."

She kissed him hard on the mouth, a little longer than necessary with quite a bit of tongue. His placed his hand on her chest above her breasts and pushed her away.

"Goddamn it, woman, leave me the fuck alone. I'm not interested in playing games with you." He stormed away from the shelter, got in his truck, and drove away, leaving her there. And thinking, that was a helluva lot of fun.

He called Diana's new cellphone number 45 minutes later. "Sorry about that. I was playing a role."

"I certainly hope so."

He ignored the cold edge in her voice. "Here's what's going on and what we're going to do about it."

After he disconnected from her, he called Laura. "I need a favor," he told her. "I'd like you to call some of your media pals and tell them you have a scoop for them."

She laughed. "No one's called it that since the days of the *Daily Planet*. Now it's 'inside information.' But I'll do it. What's going on?"

• • •

At 8:00 a.m. Dalton was in Phil's Miami office reading the World of Reptiles file. Phil had been good enough to print most of it out. Dalton set aside the printout from Customs and Border Protection that showed the date and location for every time Bruno Zimmerman's passport had been scanned in any country. Bruno had been a busy boy. Just in the past three years he had been in The Netherlands, Colombia, Kenya, Malaysia, and Germany. Buying reptiles? Buying off people?

"This file is huge," he said to Phil, who nodded in agreement.

"Trouble is," Phil noted, "it doesn't go anywhere. There's no big stamp on the cover saying, 'Case Closed.' In fact, there is no case. Not one complaint about Zimmerman or World that we can act on. And all taxes are paid, so we can't take the Al Capone route. Ernst & Young handles all the accounting and tax work, and they send us copies of everything routinely. Not in great detail, of course, but the summaries have convinced our department's accountants."

"How much does Bruno boy take out of his own business?" Dalton asked.

"About 150 a year. Not that much for a company grossing millions."

"Have you tried to rattle his cage, so to speak?"

"Like how?"

"Well, he must have some enemies. Most businessmen have a few—ex-wives, disgruntled former employees, that sort of thing."

Phil looked embarrassed. "No one like that has surfaced. Remember, I told you this case is still open but not active."

George Tompkins came into the office, pulled up a chair, and shook hands with Dalton.

"What would it take to make the case active?" Dalton asked.

"Someone like you as the co-lead investigator," George said. The office was suddenly very quiet, but Phil had a big grin on his face.

"Are you offering me a job? I didn't think you had a budget for this sort of thing."

"I do now, thanks to the governor. He saw you on camera explaining the python problem. He likes your style and he has a slush fund he can dip into."

"So, what's the deal?"

"Same salary as Phil, same special agent title. You two would head up a new reptile crimes task force."

"I hear that cage starting to rattle," Phil teased.

"Take the World file with you and study it," Dalton's new superior officer directed. "I'll assemble all the paperwork to get you hired."

He left the office and called Laura at Fairchild. "Is your offer still good?"

"Which one?"

"The one where I become your kept man and move in with you."

"Of course, darling. I meant it. I want us to get back together, but more on my terms."

"I'll move in, but I'm paying half of everything. None of this kept man BS."

"You'll pay half on your one-half NCIS retirement?"

"That, and my salary from the state of Florida. I've got a new job with a Miami office. Lots of stuff comin' down. I figure two weeks and I'll move in with you."

"Hallelujah! What job?"

"I'm a special agent for the Florida Fish and Wildlife Conservation Commission."

"You joined the Effin' Doubleyous? You? Groveling in the mud of bureaucracy again? They must be paying you a shitload."

Dalton chuckled after they rang off. Laura was so concerned about his financial condition. Nobody—except for his brother Rick—knew that in four months and 12 days, when he turned 50, he would be a multi-millionaire, thanks to his rather unusual father, Dalton Marine, and the trust that would mature and become his. His brother's trust would be available to him three and a half years later. Same crazy amount of money. Of course, when his father set up those trusts for $50,000 each 15 years ago, stock in Apple, Amazon, and Google had been real bargains. His father had always been an early adopter of technology.

• • •

Laura was sitting at her desk at Fairchild Tropical Botanic Garden thinking about Dalton and his new job. Things were looking better and better, not only for him but for the two of them as a couple. It had not been easy for them. He was mostly reclusive, while she, being a media person, was very social and tended to make friends quickly. She had to drag him to events and parties, and force him into conversations where she knew he felt uncomfortable. Tough shit, she thought, grinning.

She loved telling her friends the story of how they met because it was a cliché that she could spin in all sorts of ways—a blind date. At the time they met, she was going through her first and only attempt at being an entrepreneur, and it wasn't working. Laura had grown up in West Palm Beach, and had graduated in the top tenth of her class at A.W. Dreyfoos School of the Arts, where she was part of the exclusive Communication

Arts program, specializing in journalism and creative writing. That earned her a partial scholarship to the University of Miami School of Communication, department of Strategic Communications—which in reality was public relations—where she earned a B.S.C.

After college she worked doing PR for mostly media companies. She was assistant PR director for the Fox TV affiliate,

WSVN, then moved on a similar job at the Miami Herald, but that only lasted six months because she was lured away by Freeder, Dunne, and Lamont, one of the area's top PR agencies. As an account rep for that firm, she handled media placement for a number of top Miami companies, including the Marlins, Continental National Bank, Dadeland Mall, and Kendall Toyota. But the job was incredibly stressful, with 60 hours a week, odd hours, inconvenient meetings, and pressure from management to produce more and more billable hours.

After three years of corporate PR, she and her good friend at the agency, June Winter, decided to open their own "boutique"—she came to hate that word—firm, specializing in new high tech start-ups that truly needed their expertise. She and June worked quite well together for two years, making good livings for both of them. Then June got married, then pregnant, and left the firm to "spend more time with her family." Laura was left in the lurch, with no way to handle the workload.

Then Dalton called her. Mutual friends, namely Phil Everett and his wife, Janice, had been trying to set the two of them up for month. Janice told her that Dalton was good-looking, charming, and a widower. Phil told Dalton that Laura was smart as a whip, a real looker, and single. She was not about to call him for a date, so Phil badgered Dalton, who finally agreed to call her so that Phil would stop bugging him.

So he called, they went out, and romance bloomed. As her business slipped away, she began to cut expenses, and finally, when she asked him to move in with him at his bungalow in Homestead, she gritted her teeth and did it, moving her business there too, and saving apartment and office rent every month. But she hated it there, had moved out, closed her business, and joined Fairchild. Then it was her turn to call him, and maybe the second time really was the charm.

● ● ●

"I got something for you on Dalton," Diana told Zimmerman on her regular cell phone. "I finally got the asshole to meet me. In a goddamn picnic area. I came on to him, even kissed him, but the jerk doesn't like me because I work for you. So he was lording it over me, playing big shot. He said you were a quote, 'slimy reptile smuggler' and that I should quit my job before you took me down with you."

"That's very interesting," Bruno Zimmerman said in a neutral tone, as if he knew what she was going to say.

"So I have an idea. On Wednesday, Dalton has a big meeting of his python volunteers. Media will be there. I think you ought to serve him papers at that meeting, embarrass the shit out of him. I'll be there interrupting the presenter, who's some sort of do-gooder bigwig from Florida Fish and Wildlife. I'll make sure the media's there. SOS will get a lot of publicity.

"Let's do it. Good work, Diana." And the line went dead.

● ● ●

On his way to Davie for the meeting, Dalton called the Upper Keys office of the Florida Department of Environmental Health in Monroe County. He spoke with Inspector Raul Herrera, identified himself, and told him about the horrible fish smell along Highway 29 between Everglades City and the Tamiami Trail.

"Oh, we know all about that Manatee plant, have two complaints about it already."

"I'm going to make it three."

"Excellent. That will trigger an inspection. I'll do it myself."

● ● ●

"Our guest presenter today is Dr. Christina Reed," Dalton announced to the volunteers, guests, and media. "Dr. Reed is the resident expert on Florida pythons in the Fish and Wildlife

Conservation Commission. She and I wanted to know what the volunteers were curious about, what they didn't know about the python infestation. So I emailed all of them and asked them to submit questions. Dr. Reed has selected the most pertinent ones and will discuss those in her presentation. Please don't interrupt her—she will take further questions at the end of her presentation. And now, Dr. Christina Reed."

A smattering of applause filled Oak Hammock Hall in the Long Key Nature Center as Dr. Reed took the podium. She was small in stature, barely five feet tall, but she was lively and dynamic, about 45 years old, wearing jeans and a t-shirt that read, "Spongeorama, Tarpon Springs, Florida." Over that she wore a white lab coat, which had been Dalton's idea.

"Greetings everyone. Before I get to the volunteers' questions, I'd like to dispel one myth about the land we're dealing with here. You hear a lot of 'Save the Everglades' talk that what we have left is a very small remnant of what the Everglades once were. That is only true to a limited extent. What happens is that everyone compares the original size of the prehistoric Everglades drainage system to today's size of Everglades National Park. But they forget the 700,000 acres of Big Cypress Reserve and about the same size of the state wildlife management areas like Francis S. Taylor. When you add up all the acreage, it's about 3,000,000 acres or 4,500 square miles for the pythons to hide in. That's about the size of the state of Connecticut."

She let that sink in for a few seconds. "Now I'll answer the best questions from the volunteers, in no particular order. First, how did the pythons get into the Everglades in the first place? Well, the media has convinced everyone that the infestation started after Hurricane Andrew destroyed reptile breeding facilities in Homestead in 1992 and the snakes escaped. But this wasn't any ordinary hurricane. You have to realize that these buildings were hit by 175-mile-an-hour winds. They were obliterated. As bad as the worst tornado. It's doubtful that any of those snakes survived. Biological studies of python adaptation, expansion of range, and population growth have led us to the conclusion that a small group of pythons was released prior to 1985 around Flamingo at the southern end of the Main Park Road. I think there was a smuggling operation going on with drugs, reptiles, and whatever, and somehow those snakes got loose, started breeding, and given enough time and no predators to eat them besides the occasional alligator, here we are today."

"That's overly simplistic," Diana shouted from the third row. "What if they just got here naturally, floated here from South America on a mass of vegetation? It happens!"

"Please hold questions and comments until the end of my presentation," Reed said sternly. "Now, why did the python population expand so fast? Well, we believe that it was a perfect biological storm. A burgeoning breeding stock, plenty of food, and fast-growing snakes. The pythons encountered no predators except for alligators, a few scattered monitors that eat young snakes, and an occasional pack of feral hogs. We tend to think of snakes, especially large ones, as lethargic or inactive. In the summer, they are, hiding from the sun under brush or in the water. But during the winter, they're out sunning and traveling up to about a mile a day. The large females can lay up to 85 eggs at a time—"

"The python population is exaggerated," Diana yelled, standing up. "There is no need to hunt and kill animals now indigenous to Florida!"

Dalton grabbed the mike. "Ms. Ventura, you are out of order and are interrupting the proceedings. If you keep this up, security officers will remove you." Dalton noticed that the TV crews had already trained their cameras on Diana, which is what they both wanted.

"Bring 'em on," she shouted. "You cannot silence free speech! I'm here to save our snakes."

Dalton nodded to the county officers, who approached Diana while volunteers next to her scrambled to get out of the way. At first it looked like she would resist the officers, but she stood up and glared at Dalton and Reed. "You will regret this insult." Looking mad enough to eat a rat, Diana brushed past the officers, walked quickly up the aisle and out the door.

"And there you have a perfect example of irrationality in action," Dalton said. "Dr. Reed, please continue."

She was shaking her head as she took over the mike. "The next question is what's the weirdest thing that you've found in a python's stomach? That would be the partially digested body of a magnificent frigatebird. They only land to nest, and they don't usually nest in the Everglades, so this one's a real mystery.

"Next, how can a python kill and eat an alligator? By being bigger and stronger, and having the constriction edge, while alligators have the chomping edge. A 12-foot snake can take a five- or six-foot gator, but not a 12-foot gator. Sometimes the python wins, sometimes the gator, and sometimes they both lose.

"How smart are these giant snakes? Well, smarter than you think. They can find their way home—meaning where they were born—from 20 or more miles away. Several biologists have observed them—get this—looking both ways before they cross the street. And that street would be Alligator Alley. Snake lovers who keep them as pets swear that they know their keepers and are affectionate with them—like squeezing them a little." Laughter erupted in the meeting room.

"What about some sort of biological control? The ideal control would be a transmissible sterilization drug that works only on females. No sense giving such a drug to males because females would go into parthenogenic mode and give birth without receiving sperm.

"Can we ever get rid of them, really? Yes, but it would take about three days of lows in the 20s to kill off most of the pythons. We lost about half of the younger pythons during the 2010 winter freeze, but the population has already bounced back from that. So I really think that the pythons are here to stay and we can only try to keep their population from expanding."

Dalton's phone buzzed and he looked at the text from Phil. "Process server is here."

He texted back, "Tell him to wait."

"But if we can't control the spread of pythons and they run out of prey species, will they come after humans? First, they'll come after our pets. I'm not kidding. There is a documented incident in Dade County of a 14-foot python killing and attempting to eat an Alaskan malamute. A mass invasion of pythons after your children? No. More pet incidents like these? Yes."

Dr. Reed then opened the meeting up for questions before Dalton took the mike again.

"Thank you Dr. Reed, and thanks to everyone for attending the meeting. Since the media's already here, and as leader of the non-profit Positive Thinking Solves Distress, I'm declaring an impromptu press conference. It will only take about 15 minutes. You will find it very interesting, I promise."

• • •

"Your name, sir?" Dalton asked the little man with that deer-in-the-headlights look as the TV cameras and lights pointed at him.

"Frank W. Campbell."

"And why are you here, sir?"

"To serve court documents on you, assuming you are Samuel Dalton."

"I am. Do you know what these documents are?"

"No, sir. I'm just paid to serve them, not read them." Light laughter came from the media people. Nearly everyone else had left once the python talk was over.

"So serve me."

Campbell passed Dalton two envelopes. "Mr. Dalton, you are served."

As the process server left the room, Dalton tore the two envelopes open. "There are two separate actions in Dade County Circuit Court. First, Save Our Snakes is suing me personally and PTSD for, quote, 'Unlawfully killing native Florida animals, namely the Florida subspecies of Burmese pythons.' This will be immediately thrown out—they have the wrong court. Next, World of Reptiles, Inc. is suing me and PTSD for a $100,000 because the state and federal killings of pythons we captured is hurting their business of selling, again, what they fallaciously claim is a native Florida subspecies of Burmese pythons. They're going to have to re-file." Dalton dropped the papers on the stage. "Because I have resigned from PTSD before I was served, and I'm happy to announce that the new director, Chuck Gannon, has successfully conquered his PTSD. C'mon up, Chuck, and get sued."

Chuck laughed, there was some clapping, and he joined Dalton on stage, along with Phil Everett and George Tompkins. Dalton introduced him.

"I'm pleased to announce that the Florida Fish and Wildlife Conservation Commission has a new special agent we've hired to help with a taskforce implemented by the governor from his special law enforcement fund. "Former NCIS special agent Sam Dalton and F and W special agent Phil Everett will jointly head the new task force."

"And what's the name of this new taskforce?" Rhonda Peters from Channel 6 blurted out.

Tompkins smiled. "It's called "FRCSE, Florida Reptile Crimes Special Enforcement, pronounced 'firksee.' It will be the first complete investigation of the multi-billion-dollar Florida reptile industry ever conducted. Because agent Dalton has extensive experience in python eradication, he will also head a small team to figure out how to exterminate them all."

Peters jumped on that. "I'm sure mass snakecide is a noble goal, sir, but will this taskforce seriously investigate allegations of reptile smuggling?"

"Oh yes." Tomkins, nodded with a perfectly straight cop face. Then, as they had rehearsed it, the old finger point at the camera, he continued, "I'm warning you reptile smugglers: the FRCSE will uncover the truth about your insidious conspiracies. You won't be able to slither away from this one." It was the perfect videobyte.

As soon as he saw the video clip on Channel 6, Zimmerman picked up his cell phone.

6

After some time, the snake usually lets go its hold. It then passes its head all around the prey, playing over it with its forked tongue, and by some means other than that of sight, as the choice is made equally in the dark, selects the head of the carcass to begin the process of swallowing.
–P. C. Mitchell and R. I. Poccock, "On the Feeding of Reptiles in Captivity," 1907.

"**I**s 'clusterfuck' the right term for our present predicament?" Dalton asked at a back table at the Last Chance Bar & Package on the South Dixie Highway. Phil was on his right and Jenny Rodriguez, the new team medic, was on his left. They were all drinking Alligator's Asshole Ale.

"I'd like to know how catching pythons led to hunting reptile smugglers," Jenny said.

"Sam and I go back a long way," Phil explained. "We are law enforcement special agents—he came out of NCIS retirement as a special agent to take the position with me. We investigate, we follow leads. Reptile retailers are allowed to sell captive-bred Burmese pythons, the very ones we're trying to eradicate in the semi-wild. Does that make any sense?"

Dalton took over. "We think that World of Reptiles is part of—if not the leader of—the Florida reptile industry, which can afford lobbyists, advertising campaigns, lawsuits, and bribes. And very probably, they are runnin' a massive reptile smuggling operation."

"Do you have any proof of all this?' Jenny asked.

"Not yet. We have witnesses, we have sworn statements, and we have moles."

"Uh, say again?"

"We have agents planted in World of Reptiles as employees."

"Plural?" Dalton interrupted. "I thought we just had Diana."

"The Feds have another mole inside. I'm speaking of Fish and Wildlife."

"Crap! How many agencies are sloshing around in this investigation?"

Jenny held up her right hand as if she were back in third grade. "Uh, guys."

Phil beat Dalton back to reality. "Yes, Jenny?"

"Are you guys still on the python team?"

"In a fashion, yes, although we have more important things to hunt right now." Dalton shrugged his shoulders. He hoped he wasn't letting her down.

"Well, you're probably wondering why I asked you to meet me at this seedy bar."

"It crossed my mind," Phil said.

"You still want to kill pythons, right?"

"Of course," Dalton told her. "What's up?"

"This friend of mine, Ginger Delgado. She's a researcher at the Molecular Genetics Lab at USF. A python got Roxie, her cocker spaniel. That really pissed Ginger off, so after she chopped up the snake with her machete, she started researching pythons, and what really hurts them—besides alligators, of course."

That made them laugh. Phil called for another round of Triple As, as wimps called it.

"She found out that pythons and boas are very susceptible to a snake virus called inclusion body disease. Once they get it, they die. Sometimes it takes a while, but the infected ones don't survive. And they don't mate if they catch it."

Dalton and Phil looked at each other. "What's the vector?" Ph.D. Phil asked.

Jenny opened her purse and took a look at her notes. "A reptile mite called *Ophionyssus natricis*. IBD is highly contagious, too. So Jenny's trying to figure out a way to infect the pythons—she spends every night digging deeper into the Medline database. She asked me to get your opinion."

"Holy crap," Dalton said. "Can IBD infect other species of snakes?"

"Jenny said it can't, that it was species specific—only boas and pythons."

"There must be some law against infecting wild snakes with a virus," Phil mused. "Poisoning nature? Uh, threatening wildlife?"

"You're reaching, Phil."

"Yeah, I know."

"Jenny, don't tell anyone else. Just the four of us. Can you set up a meeting with Ginger?"

"Sure. When?"

"Just as soon as she can free herself from the online research pythons."

• • •

Big Ink held the management meeting in the private room at the Pelican Dive-In on Collier Avenue in Everglades City. He wanted a neutral site for the meeting—away from the plant— to help him keep his temper in check. He couldn't very well throw a fit at the restaurant like he did at the plant. Besides, it was All-You-Can-Eat Stone Crab Day at the Pelican, where Ink and the owner had a crab/crystal trade going—so they could all eat anything they wanted for sorta free. It was only four of them: Ink, Derrick, Toad, and Cutup. Tomás wasn't management.

Ink waddled over to the white board, grabbed a marker, and wrote "$30,000" on it. "That's what the bondsman charged me to post bail for you fucking idiots." He used an eraser to change the figure to "$32,000." "It was another two grand for the attorney." Under that, he wrote a list:

—Chemicals?

—Production?

—Bone?

—Cypress?

—Cash flow?"

"Our official agenda. Let's go through it."

"Well, the chemicals arrive tomorrow," Derrick said. "8:00 in the morning. All paid for."

"That's good," Ink said. He wanted to keep things as positive as possible. He looked at Cutup. "Ten pounds for our regulars. Ten pounds for Cypress—I'll get to him in a minute. From the amount of chemicals Derrick bought, could you squeeze out another pound or two?"

Cutup pulled out a calculator and began entering data. In less than a minute, he looked up at Ink and said, "21.39 pounds total yield."

"Better. Now, next on the list is Bone Mozell. I've not been able to reach the guy, and that's not good. Any ideas?"

Derrick was fiddling with a cigarette but he knew better than to light up. Ink, who had no trouble with the smoke from weed or crystal, hated tobacco smoke. "The last time I spoke with Bone, about a week ago, he said he was thinking about fishing the Dry Tortugas—that's pretty much out the range of the Key West cell towers. He sure likes to catch bonefish."

"That's how he got the nickname. I'll give him another few days. But what about the Miccosukee?"

Four taps on the door told Ink that lunch was ready. Toad, who not spoken once during the meeting, left the table and opened the door. Two servers who looked like college girls served up the boiled stone crab legs with sides of coleslaw, spicy ceviche, and Category 4 IPAs.

After the servers left, Big Ink resumed the meeting. "I guess it's kinda obvious that the Miccosukee never came by with the 200 thou he promised."

"Maybe he's out fishin' with Bone," Toad suggested.

"Could be," Ink admitted.

"We've got all the chemicals and we've got a schedule," Derrick told the group. "I say we make the entire batch. It doesn't take that long and there's no refund on the chemicals."

The men seemed to agree, nodding their heads as they used the large pelican-shaped mallets to crack the shells that were as hard as, well, stones.

"Okay, it's settled," Big Ink announced, "we make the entire batch and then sit on the extra ten pounds plus the 1.39 pounds of bonus crystal. When the tweakers start twitchin', we got 'em where we want 'em. Present company excluded, of course."

Unfortunately for the chemistry entrepreneurs eating lunch that day, things didn't go precisely the way Big Ink had planned.

• • •

Dalton was headed north from Homestead to Coral Gables with most of his clothes and a few personal possessions packed into the back of his truck. He had closed up the bungalow, leaving it intact and ready for either his return or that of a renter or new owner. He didn't know what was going to happen. And he recalled that he had been in this position before.

It was the uncertainty of his situation that reminded him of the confrontation with his father over the fate of Dalton Marine. He was married to Robin and about to leave for NCIS training when his father had called a family conference. It was such a rare occurrence that no one dared miss it, and Rick had even cancelled a performance in Panama City to fly back for the meeting at the house they had all shared for so long in Key Largo. It was just the four of them—mother, father, and two sons. No spouses or girlfriends allowed.

Dalton had dreaded the meeting for days—had the old approach-avoidance routine going. He and Rick had traded speculation over the phone. Their parents were getting a divorce. Their father had cancer, just a few months to live. Their mother was having an affair with a Muslim terrorist. Finally, laughing hysterically, they gave up the wild theories and just admitted that, as almost always, they would obey their father and be at the family meeting.

It wasn't as bad as they expected. Their father had finally accepted reality—that neither of his sons had any interest in taking over Dalton Marine. "I can't force either one of you to be a businessman, so I'm giving up. I have an offer from Heritage Yachts that is simply impossible to turn down. Your mother and I are going to sail around the world, spend most of our money and then find a place to retire. Maybe Hawaii. I'm going to establish trust funds for both of you based on stock, not cash. When you're 50, you'll get control of the trusts. Each of you had the chance to take over the business—no, no, let's not go there. That's over now. Let's just have a family dinner and talk about the future."

Three days later, Dalton was in Brunswick, Georgia at the

FLETC undergoing the SABTP. Translated from bureaucra-
tese, he was at the Federal Law Enforcement Training Center
enrolled in the 46-day Special Agent Basic Training Program.
He learned everything from how to process a crime scene
("Don't touch anything with your bare hands!"), to conducting
death investigations ("It's difficult for a suicide victim to shoot
himself in the head twice!"), to homeland security ("Not all
people wearing burqas are women!"), to unarmed self defense
("Kicking a man on his shin is just as effective as his balls!").
And there were brief courses on polygraph procedures, proper
surveillance techniques, the seven signs of procurement fraud,
debriefing of critical stress victims, maintaining rifle and pistol
accuracy, and advanced lock-picking ("When all else fails, use
a single-handed sledge hammer, not your shoulder, to open an
oak door.").

But the most important instruction he received was from
a clinical psychologist who told the beginner's class: "The suspect could be a Seaman Recruit in the Navy or a Marine Corps
General, but they are both human beings like us, which means
they are just as capable of committing crimes as we are. The
fact that they have rank is irrelevant. Special agents are civilians
who transcend military rank. A four-star general cannot give a
legal order to any civilian, much less an NCIS special agent."

Dalton vividly remembered when, in his first year of actual
duty, he had taken down a bad-ass drunk master gunnery sergeant who, caught in the act of pummeling his wife, had resisted arrest. He had tried shouting commands but Dalton simply
stomped on his right foot and then face-whipped him with the
expandable baton he always carried. The offender was convicted and given a dishonorable discharge from the marines. His
wife divorced him, too. His rank wasn't mentioned more than
twice during the trial. Dalton had received the less-than-cov-

eted Supervisor's Award for Meritorious Service. Let's not acronymize that one, Dalton thought as he pulled up to Laura's townhouse. Way too personal.

His cell phone vibrated with a text: "You stopped killing alligators as we ordered. The next step is to resign from the task force. If you don't, you'll be next, like your wife and kid. A family triple-header."

Dalton was stunned, torn between his memories and nightmares and his duty to investigate. He sat in the truck as if paralyzed. He was right—it was a murder. Was that good news? He forced himself to calm down. Think!

His phone buzzed. Laura texting, "I see you out there. Front door's open."

Laura. She could help him figure it out. He left the truck and hurried inside.

She knew instantly that he was upset. "You, sit," she ordered, pointing at the couch. Dalton sat.

She returned with two vodka martini rocks with olives, handed him one, and said, "Drink."

He took a gulp, shook his head and showed her the text on his screen.

"Oh my god," Laura said. "That's terrible. But at least you know for sure."

"I'm trying to figure out the next step."

"Track the cell phone?"

"Probably stolen and thrown away."

"Who's doing this?" she asked. "If we can figure that out, we can find out why."

"Oh, I know who's doing it. It's the next step I'm worried about."

She caught on. "And that perp would be Bruno Zimmerman."

"Yes," Dalton said, with a grim smile.

• • •

The truck unloading the Methbusters' chemicals had pulled into the rear dock of the plant by the same time Raul Herrera was pointing out to Big Ink the exact definition in Florida state law of "public health nuisance." It was funny to watch Raul try to be the aggressor against a man three times his weight.

"We're runnin' a load of menhaden and are too busy for a fuckin' inspection," Ink sputtered. "Can you come back later?"

"No," Raul said, his bald spot starting to turn red.

"So what if I throw your sorry ass out of here and fuck the goddamned inspection?"

"I will call my poker bud Little Billy over at Florida Power and Light and he will pull your plug in about five minutes. Some kinda outage or somethin'. Might be a week or two to fix it."

"Well, come on in," Ink said, forcing a smile. "It's about time we got inspected. Where y'all been, anyway?"

Inspector Raul was not amused.

• • •

They were halfway through dinner when Dalton's cell phone rang. Laura rolled her eyes and Dalton just shrugged.

"At least now I'm getting paid for this," he said as he took the call from Diana.

"What's up?" he asked.

"Zimmerman has disappeared."

"What exactly does that mean?"

"He didn't show up today at World of Reptiles."

"Well, maybe he didn't feel like coming to work."

She hesitated. "I don't like it."

"Nothing you can do about it. Just hang in there."

"The sooner I get this story written, the better."

"Don't push things," he advised. "As they say, chill."

"He's mad at me."

"How so?"

"You turned the serving of the papers upside down on us. Now you're an Effin' Doubleyou agent. Zimmerman hasn't said word one to me."

"Good. He's not going to blame you for my new job. He's coming after me, not you. That was the plan. Look, I'm in the middle of dinner…"

"Fuck you, Dalton." She hung up.

"Nervous Nellie?" Laura asked.

"Minor crisis of faith," he said, spearing a shrimp with his fork. "She'll get over it."

Later, when Laura was filling up the dishwasher, Dalton went out on the balcony, called Diana back and set up a time for them to meet. He didn't want Laura to hear the call. He had to reassure Diana—he didn't want her bailing out on him.

• • •

"We got a real fuckin' menagerie here," Bone Mozell said. He took a swig out of his can of Barracuda Bock, the setting sun making perfect dead-fish silhouettes of the day's catch. "We got us a Jew, a redskin, and a redneck." They were all dressed alike: cap, sunglasses, t-shirt, shorts, deck shoes.

"We Jews are not a race, Mozell," Bruno Zimmerman told him, "we're a culture."

"You think rednecks are a race?" Mozell asked.

"It would seem so," Gabriel Cypress answered. "He has an M.S. in gaming science from Southern Florida University On-line. A native swamp race."

"You callin' me a Swamp Ape?"

"You callin' me a fuckin' Miccosukee Squaw-Slave?"

That one got them howling. Well, hell, they were celebrating aboard Mozell's tacky yacht, Buoys in the Hood, which had all the charm of a Miami Port Authority tugboat. They had moored at the Conch Harbor Marina in Key West after a day of flats fishing near Sugarloaf Keys.

When they settled down, Mozell looked at them seriously. "So we're all in agreement—Big Ink goes away, then we take over the plant."

Zimmermann simply nodded his head but Cypress wanted more information. "Does 'go away' mean a cemetery or the sea bottom?"

Mozell shook his head. "There's no need for us to harm the guy."

Zimmerman grinned. "That's because addict that he is, he will do it to himself as we apply the pressure."

"So, nothing illegal, right?" Cypress was pushing a little but Mozell didn't seem to mind.

"I wouldn't go that far. We won't kill the guy. Maybe hurt him a little."

"Unless he fights back," Zimmerman added, "and then we'll flip some coins to determine who disembowels him."

Bone and Cypress were a little stunned, so Zimmerman continued, "Metaphorically speaking. We tweak too, but Ink's addicted. Don't underestimate your protégé, Bone. You made him the cracker that he is. A cornered rat is a dangerous rat."

"Not to a python like me, har har. Anyway, you can't trust an addict. A condition of our partnership was that he quit using that shit. He violated the terms of our agreement."

"So sue him. Addicts can't quit by themselves."

"You're rambling, Zim, so let's change the subject." Cypress rolled his eyes.

"We've talked about fishing, money, drinking, and Big Ink," Bone noted, "so there's only one thing left."

Zimmerman nodded. "Pussy."

"Where do we start the bar crawl tonight?" Cypress asked.

"The Green Parrot," Zimmerman said. "I like their slogan."

"Which is?" Mozell asked.

"A sunny place for shady people."

• • •

Dalton knew in his gut that Zimmerman was responsible for the death of Robin and Kenny. He finally took Phil's advice and turned over his iPhone to the Digital Evidence Department of the Crime Laboratory at the Florida Department of Law Enforcement, knowing full well that there was about a one in a million chance of finding any kind of a link to the reptile dealer. He was right: the texts came from two different stolen cell phones, one from a junior at Palmetto High School and the other from a UPS driver. The only person he told about the texts was Phil, who commented that he had a Remington 700 deer rifle with a Vortex PST scope, if Dalton wanted to borrow it.

Though sorely tempted, Dalton declined. He had to take care of this the right way—with his brain, not a rifle. To that end, he called Diana, who was understandably prickly. "Okay, Dalton, if you want to talk, take me some place nice, not a fucking park in Homestead with fake necking and some creep spying on us."

When they met at 3:30 at Blackbird Ordinary on 1st Avenue, Diana was considerably less prickly. It was her kind of place, a hipster hangout with good-looking people and pricey drinks. She walked in, spotted him sipping a Cigar City Jai Alai IPA, and came over to the table. He stood up to greet her and she gave him a brief hug and sat down.

"This place isn't ordinary at all," she said.

"An ordinary was a colonial tavern," he explained. "I read the blurb on the drink menu."

"Show off." Diana ordered a Scarlett Tanager—Fords gin

with fresh strawberries, ginger ale and herbs.

Dalton told her about the two texts and the death of his wife and son. Diana took a tissue out of her purse to blot her eyes before her makeup ran.

"Now I'm really scared," she confessed, "but I'm glad you told me. Better to know than not to know. Do you have some kind of a plan?"

"Well, the germ of one, anyway. Look, this is confidential, but you should know that Fish and Wildlife—the Feds, not us—has a mole embedded in World of Reptiles. If you could find out who that is, and what that person knows, it could be very helpful."

She thought for a while as she sipped her Tanager. "I'll work on that angle starting tomorrow. Say, there was one thing I did like about our adventure in the park, Dalton. Care to make a guess?"

He changed the subject, but not very well.

"Are you hungry? They have some jerk chicken wing snacks."

She moved her chair closer to his and crooked her finger at him so she could whisper into his ear, placing a hand on his thigh. "Damn right I'm hungry. I really liked kissing you at the park. Care for an encore?"

A blatant pass and he knew what he had to do. "Your timing is terrible, Diana. Let me tell you a little story." He did not remove her hand from his thigh—he just waited until she took it away.

Dalton launched into his best fake Texas accent. "This Texan goes into the ladies' undergarments department of Lord & Taylor in the Galeria in Houston—"

"What?"

He held up a hand. "Shhhh. The Texan's in the lingerie section when a young, good-looking clerk offers her assistance.

'Well, Cindy Dee is a little under the weather today so she sent me down here to buy her a new brahzeer. Here are her breast surgeon's bra specifications, but I don't know what brand.'"

"'Playtex?' asked the clerk."

"The Texan tipped his Stetson to her. 'Thanks for the offer, ma'am, but I'm a happily married man.'"

Diana laughed so hard that some of the Scarlett Tanager spurted from her mouth and landed on Dalton's shirt. "Sorry, Dalton. Want me to lick that off? Just kidding."

"You are quite a temptation, Diana. But as the Texan said, thanks for the offer, ma'am."

"I'll be damned," Diana said in amazement. "That's never happened to me before."

• • •

Big Ink was bothered by the video camera inspector Raul Herrera was wearing. "Can you turn that fucking thing off?" he asked. "It's staring at me."

"No," the inspector said. "I have to document everything."

"Well, did we pass the inspection?"

"No. Not even close." He reached in his briefcase and pulled out a metal clipboard and a multipart form.

"What are you writing?" asked Ink.

"I'm filling out an SDO."

"SDO?"

"Shut Down Order," Inspector Raul explained. "Note that I'm checking the red box that reads, 'Immediate.'"

"You can't do this to me!" Ink screamed. I'll be losing $10,000 a day!"

"One of your scrubbers has failed. Until you replace it, you can't operate the plant."

"But—"

Raul waved a finger and Ink shut the hell up. After all, he

was on camera. "Replace the scrubber, give me a call, and I'll schedule a re-inspection. If you pass that, I will issue an immediate PRRO order, and you can resume making fish meat."

"Uh, that's fish meal, inspector. What's a PRRO order?"

"Problem Resolved, Resume Operation."

"I thought so," he bluffed.

At the management meeting that followed the shut down, Cutup was optimistic. "Look, I'll get that scrubber back up and operating in a day. Then you call the inspector, tell him your genius of an engineer repaired it and we're ready for a re-inspection. We only lose a day and a half of production time."

"He could delay the re-inspection for weeks."

"Nah, I know the type. Herrera wants this cleared up, off his desk. You didn't try to bribe him, did you?"

"With him recording everything? You think I'm stupid or something?"

Toad moved quickly to cut off Cutup's expected reply. "Did you get ahold of Bone?"

"He's fishing in Key West. He texted me that he would be back to work in a day and a half."

"Did you tell him about our little problem?" Derrick asked.

"I forgot," Big Ink replied with a wink.

Cute, but what Ink didn't know was that his so-called partners were going to execute a hostile takeover in whatever way made the best sense to them.

7

After sixteen years at the port, McKissick had seen or heard of every sort of smuggler's trick: boxes with false bottoms, bags with hidden compartments, boots made from endangered species and re-covered in common leather. One man was caught with a boa constrictor around his belly; another had a pair of pygmy marmosets in his fanny pack; yet another tried to sneak in some live finches—he'd crammed the birds into pill bottles and strapped them to his legs.
—Birkhardt Bilger, "Swamp Things," 2009.

The four anti-python conspirators met in Dalton's bungalow for privacy. Shortly after Phil arrived, Jenny pulled up in the driveway with Ginger Delgado. Ginger was the epitome of what pornographers term a BBW—big, beautiful woman. Enough said. Jenny made the introductions while Dalton went to the refrigerator and rescued four Snapper Special Stouts, with the garish label featuring the open and dripping mouth and head of a snapping turtle. Sure beats Moose Drool for an image, Dalton thought.

He quickly disposed of the small talk and let Ginger update them. "I've made some progress. I can replicate the virus easily and infect the mites, which multiply well with unrestricted access to food. I placed infected mites on three young pythons that Phil provided. Within three days, the snakes started showing symptoms of IBD—mostly what's called stargazing, when the snake holds its head in the air and stares off into space. Two others have been vomiting, not eating, and mouthgaping. I estimate these snakes will be dead in a month."

"Can you make it any faster?" Dalton asked.

"Possibly, but it will take a while. I gathered that you were in a hurry."

"Well, I'd like to get it done before mid-spring, when the temps get hot and the snakes hide in the water. We need them on the hammocks."

"There's the problem," Jenny said. "How do we get the mites to the pythons on the hammocks? Any ideas?"

Dalton interrupted her. "First, let's have Ginger describe the process from the beginning, and then when she gets stuck, we'll start speculating."

"Well, we infect the host snakes with IBD, then we introduce the mites, and the mites feed on the snakes and keep reproducing until every mite the snake can support is infected. Then the snake dies—or we kill it—blood stops flowing, and the mites leave the snake to find another. That's when we vacuum them up. I can put the mites in very weak, water-dissolvable gelatin capsules. Any moisture would dissolve them and then the mites would find the snakes. The problem is transporting them to each hammock."

"There are thousands and thousands of hammocks," Phil noted.

"Well, we won't be working in the mangroves, so it makes sense to focus on the northeastern section of hammocks where the infestation is the greatest." Dalton looked around for any other suggestions.

"We ride the airboat up to a hammock, reach into our sack, grab a handful of capsules, and throw them on the hammock?"Jenny asked. "That's pretty damned low tech."

"I've got it," Phil said suddenly, and he had six eyeballs

focusing on him. "Drones. We'll use helicopter drones that can fly to each hammock and drop the capsules."

"That is one hell of a great idea," Dalton told him.

• • •

Diana's World of Reptiles investigation was stalled. Diana had to get something moving. Anything. Her editors were getting impatient. Even though she dreaded doing so, the store was the center of things so she decided to visit, see what was going on with Bruno Zimmerman. But as it turned out, he wasn't there.

"He took some time off," Ray Jacobs told her. Apparently, he was second in command. "But I can show you around, if you like."

His demeanor and clothes triggered the word "nerd" in her brain, but she could see that he was muscular underneath the too-large reptile t-shirt. She wondered if he needed the thick eyeglasses or whether they were just a prop. Lose the glasses and the stupid, bushy mustache and he wouldn't be all that bad, she thought.

"Sure, thanks. What's new around here?"

"We have a new shipment of Chinese water dragons and we built a special display for them," he said, guiding her through cages of hissing lizards that made her shudder. They arrived at what seemed to be a diorama of stuffed lizards, a fake rock wall with little caves and a pool below it. Startled, one of the lizards leaped into the pool and went straight to the bottom. She twitched.

She's trying, Ray thought, but she doesn't like this at all. "Aren't they beautiful?" he asked.

She nodded her head vigorously. "I love that shade of green."

Bullshit, he thought. She's faking it. "What's your favorite kind of snake?" Her appearance wasn't fake at all: black jeans, a yellow sleeveless top with a medusa emblem in the middle, and three-inch yellow heels.

Diana was asked this question often, so she had a standard reply. "The Honduran milksnake—I love that shade of orange. The emerald tree boa is also quite beautiful. What's yours?"

"The boomslang," Ray replied easily. "A beautiful green and deadly poisonous."

"Snakes like that make me very nervous."

But despite the fact that she didn't particularly like reptiles, she had to admit that the tour was interesting from a marketing point of view. Ray obviously knew how to sell the creatures. The displays were oriented toward children and emphasized what they could learn from pet reptiles. Turtles and tortoises were the main focus. Ray showed her the display of snapping turtles. The sign below read, "What Do Snapping Turtles Like to Snap Most?" and kids would try to guess by punching the buttons next to fish, hamburger, tadpoles, worms, and water bugs.

"Fish?" Diana guessed. Turtles bothered her the least of all reptiles.

"Nope, tadpoles," Ray laughed, watching her smile for the first time since she entered the store. "They're easier to catch."

"But hamburger's really slow."

"They'll eat it if they're super hungry," Ray explained, "but these little guys like to chase things down. Kids take bets on how long it takes them to catch the tadpoles—gets them ready for the casinos."

"Ah, education at work," Diana said.

Ray checked his watch. "Time for my lunch break. Wanna join me for a pizza at The Big Cheese? They have a seafood one with shrimp, mussels, and clams."

"What, no conch? Sure, I'm hungry. Who's driving?"

"I am, and you'll have to hold on real tight." He smiled.

"I'll bet you say that to all the girls."

"You win. I do."

He handed her a helmet and when he pulled out his keys to the C600, Diana noticed a bright blue flash drive hanging with them.

• • •

"The county shut us down because of a bad scrubber," Big Ink explained to a chicken farmer on the phone. "It's fixed now, but we're a week behind in production. Sorry 'bout that, Jimmy. I know, I know, your chickens are hungry. Goddamn it, ever heard of Purina Flock Raiser? I know it's more expensive. Tell you what, I'll make up the difference in cost, okay? Yes, and I'll add an ounce to your other order. Go with me on this, Jimmy—you won't regret it. Thanks, buddy. Say hello to Sally for me. Talk soon."

He was sitting in his office with Derrick, Cutup, and Toad, waiting for Inspector Raul, who had texted that he was on his way to the plant. "How many is that now?" Derrick asked.

"Six," Ink replied. "But I think I've got 'em under control, finally."

"What's the deal with the inspector?" Cutup asked. He was eager to get the meth plant up and running again.

"He's tuned up now."

"So you say," Derrick said sarcastically. The shut-down had everyone on edge, and the seven tons of menhaden arriving that afternoon would rot if they didn't get the processors up and running. At least the scrubber was repaired and Cutup had the print-outs of the tests to give to Inspector Raul.

"Heard from Bone lately?" Toad asked.

"He texted me. Said he's trying to get Cypress on track."

"What's the holdup?" Derrick wondered aloud.

"Somebody won big. Real big. The Swipe, Play, and Win promotion." Ink shook his head. The stupidity of gambling always amazed him. "A gal from Kendall won a million bucks. The casino tried to get her to take it in 20 payments, but she took a lump sum. Killed their cash flow—just temporary, Bone says."

"Smells like fish meal," Derrick noted, but Ink was distracted by the intercom. The receptionist told him that the county inspector was up front.

"Cutup, give me the reports. You and Toad go find something to do. Derrick, stay here. This should be fun."

The first thing Ink noticed about Inspector Raul was that he came without a camera this time. That was a good sign.

"Smells better around here," Raul said.

"Here are the scrubber test results from my chief engineer," Ink told him, handing him the print-outs.

"And here's your PRRO order so you can resume making fish meal."

"Thank you, sir." Might as well be nice to the fucker, Ink thought.

"And since the complaint is now resolved, the county can release the names of the complainants against you. Per the request of your attorneys, here are their names and addresses."

Inspector Raul stood up and handed an envelope to Ink, looking him in the eye. "Is our business here concluded?"

Ink also stood up, but they didn't shake hands. "It is." Inspector Raul left the office quickly and did not look back.

Derrick stared at Ink, who was chuckling. "What the fuck just happened? He was a pussycat. The county doesn't give out the names of complainants. You must've got something on him."

Ink grinned at him. "Inspector Raul Herrera is what used to be called a chicken hawk."

"And now?"

"Just a run-of-the-mill pervert. He likes boys between the ages of nine and 12. Indian boys in particular. You probably don't want to hear all the details."

"Maybe just one."

"He likes to tell his perv buddies how the Indian boys wrestle his alligator. With their mouths."

Derrick made the puking gesture with his index finger. "That's disgusting."

"Isn't it now?" Big Ink asked with feigned innocence. "Say, Derrick..."

"What?"

"You and Cutup and Toad..."

"Yeah?"

"Never underestimate me." Suddenly, Big Ink didn't sound like a cracker. He spoke like a businessman with an M.S. in chemical engineering from Florida State University. A crooked businessman, of course, but a very serious one. Derrick felt a little queasy.

Ink opened the envelope. "Well, well, guess who complained about us?"

"Dan Marino?"

"Nice try. Samuel T. Dalton."

"He's that python guy. One of bunch who arrested Cutup and Toad."

"We should do something about this fuckwad," Ink suggested. "He messed us up—twice."

"Like what, kill him?"

"Why not?"

"After we finish the production, I'll look into it."

"You do that," Big Ink ordered.

• • •

"What are you doing home?" Laura asked as she breezed into her townhouse. "I thought you'd still be at the office."

"Some office," Dalton snorted. "I'm sharing one with Phil. No windows and no desk for me yet. So your dining room is my temporary office."

"And what is that?"

It was a Wikimedia Commons image of the head and neck of a snake so black it was purple.

"That's an endangered Eastern indigo snake," he told her. "The largest native snake in the US, gets to nine feet long. Isn't it beautiful? For a snake, that is. This species gave Bruno Zimmerman his start in reptile poaching and smuggling." He held up a bound computer print-out. "The state and Feds' combined report on Zimmerman. I can't let you read it, but—"

"You can talk about it," she filled in for him.

"Yep. It's mostly hearsay, but interesting reading."

"Give me the abbreviated summary." Laura poured herself a glass of Chardonnay. "I know that's redundant, but snakes— you know how I feel."

"They're in first place for women's fears," he told her, opening up an EF-4, the hoppiest IPA produced by Plant City Brewery and named after the 220-mile-an-hour winds that hit Tampa in 1966. Its bitterness was refreshing.

"What are second and third?"

"Spiders and mothers-in-law."

"Har, har. So what's with snake boy?"

"His mother, father, and an uncle on his mother's side all owned Herpetological Research Laboratories in Homestead, a fancy name for a snake-breeding farm. When he was nine, his uncle, one Larry Curtis, taught him how to catch snakes by luring them to old carpet remnants in the abandoned orange orchards that surrounded the farm. Mice and other rodents would hide under the carpets and snakes would find them. The most valuable snakes were the indigos, which could bring $350 each when sold up north. They were a protected species—the first snake in the country to get that status, but no one paid any attention to the laws. Little Bruno averaged catching five indigos a day and his uncle was at least somewhat honest and paid him $20 apiece for them. Think about that, Laura—a ten-year-old making a hundred bucks a day in the late '80s."

"Did little Bruno go to school?" she asked Dalton.

"He graduated high school in the top half of his class. By that time, investigators estimated he had a nest egg of more than $100,000."

"College?"

Dalton nodded. "Yes, Hard Knocks University. In Jakarta. After his mom and dad died—I haven't tracked down how that happened, but it was in 1992—his uncle apprenticed him to Billy Wong, who was probably Asia's most notorious animal smuggler. He specialized in—you guessed it—rare snakes for the pet trade, including the albino Burmese pythons that were fetching thousands of dollars from US collectors. The plan was for Bruno, now a snake expert, to facilitate the export—read smuggling—of the snakes to the US."

"How many?"

"Thousands."

"You're kidding."

"CITES—you know what that is, right?"

"The group that monitors endangered species?"

"Yes. They reported that in 1998, 22,000 Burmese pythons entered the US—and they were mostly legal at that time. But of course, there were many other species that were transported illegally. To make a long story a little shorter, Zimmerman partnered with Wong to buy out Uncle Curtis, and over the years, Herpetological Research Labs evolved into World of Reptiles."

"Which you suspect is a major smuggling operation."

"Yes."

"But you have no proof."

"Exactly."

"And Little Bruno?"

"He lives here." Dalton hit a key and an aerial photo came up of a sprawling complex on the water, complete with a 20,000-square-foot house with seven bedrooms, two smaller guest houses, three swimming pools, a dock with a yacht attached, and a helipad. "It's on Hibiscus Island, off the Causeway between Miami and Miami Beach."

"Figures," Laura said. "So how are you going to catch this guy?"

"The Feds have a mole in World of Reptiles—an experienced undercover agent. I don't know who—yet."

"Do snakes eat moles?" Laura asked.

"I guess we're gonna find out pretty soon."

"Hungry?"

"I could eat in about an hour or so. Care to pull a Jimmy Buffet?"

"You mean 'Why don't we get drunk and...'"

"No, let's screw first—then get drunk."

She started unbuttoning her blouse. "Sure thing, special agent man."

8

A python's mouth is almost as dangerous as its coils. No
venomous fangs are present, but it contains over 50 long,
needle-sharp teeth, and makes a formidable weapon. In a large
python these teeth may be 10 mm long [nearly a half-inch].

A full strike is like a hammer blow, and the curved teeth
penetrate deeply, causing long, ragged wounds. A colleague
of mine required 57 stitches after being on the receiving end
of a defensive strike. –W. R. Branch, "Captive Breeding of
Pythons in South Africa," 1984.

It was the weirdest thing Diana had ever seen. She had been
called to an after-work meeting by Sean Lamposte, her editor
at the *Miami Herald*, not being at the newspaper's downtown
offices but rather at the Port of Miami Holiday Hotel near the
airport. She took the smelly elevator to the eighth floor and
knocked twice outside of room 816. Sean opened the door.
Her first thought was that she was trapped, but as it turned
out, it was a nice trap. A chair, small desk, queen bed with a
ragged bedspread with seahorses on it. Sean gestured to the
chair. Diana sat.

"Something to drink?" he asked her.

She looked around. "A glass of Bollinger Blanc De Noirs
Vieilles Vignes Françaises, please." Her pronunciation was perfect but her boss wasn't buying it.

"Eddie said you were a wise ass," he countered, referring

to his co-editor at the Tampa Tribune. "Okay, forget the Bud Light I bought specially for you. Eddie and I are pissed. This so-called reptile exposé is going nowhere."

"Grow up, Sean. It's starting to unravel. I'm inside. I'm linking up with Zimmerman's shipping manager, who's got to know something—"

"You fucking him?"

"That's the next step," she said in her faux-deadly serious voice.

"That's my girl, the backbreaker," he joked and Diana seriously considered removing her right leopard print Christian Louboutin spiked platform pump and smashing it into Sean's eye. But she didn't. This time.

"Why are we meeting, Sean?"

"Eddie and I have hired you some help. Meet the Chopper."

"He's invisible?" Diana asked sarcastically.

"I'm in here," came a disembodied voice from the bathroom. "You don't need to know my name or see my face. I'm what's known as a hacker, but I don't just hack, I chop."

"What the hell does that mean?"

Sean intervened. "Chopper is going to get into Zimmerman's computers and other devices."

Diana paused. "That is a really good idea, Chop. How can I help?"

"I need a key to get into the World of Reptiles computer system. Someone's login and password. Sometimes they're in what people think is a secure file on their computer. Some people write them down and hide them somewhere. Or use flash drives they carry around. Any of these files could be encrypted and most probably are, so that's where we come in."

"But I work for Save Our Snakes, not World of Reptiles."

"I know that. I'm convinced that SOS is part of the World

of Reptiles intranet, so if you could find Helen's login and pass-word, that would get us going."

"I can do better than that," she promised, thinking about the Pulitzer Prize.

"If you do," said the hollow voice bouncing off the cheap tiles in the bathroom, "after I've extracted all the data you need, I'll go into Chopper Mode."

"And that would be?"

"Imagine an office with a top pro paper shredder combined with a cross-chopper and you're feeding paper into it for 24 hours and it all spews out on the rug. Then I bring in a leaf blower and shoot half of it down the hall."

"Okay. And?"

"That's what all the data from World of Reptiles will look like on their hard drives and in their clouds. That is why they call me Chopper." Diana wondered if that was a fake Transyl-vanian accent.

"Let's go down to the bar for a drink, Chop."

"Not going to happen, Diana," Sean told her. "Now get to work. I need this story in two weeks or it's over."

"Yikes." But she was thinking, lead pipe cinch.

• • •

Whenever he needed someone killed, Bone Mozell called Mort. Bone didn't know if it was short for Mortimer or Mor-ton and he didn't care. As the man said, "Just call me Mort. That's French for dead."

The only trouble with Mort was that he wouldn't wheel and deal. No trading for drugs or women, no discounts for multiple murders, and always cash up front wired into his ac-count in the British Virgin Islands. This time, when Bone told Mort who he wanted killed and how he wanted it done, Mort seemed intrigued.

"I've never offed anyone using that technique before," he mused over his secure phone. "Risky, but very interesting. How's your bank balance, Bone?"

"I'm at my computer now, itchin' to push the send button."

"Push it. I'm taking the contract."

• • •

Big Ink needed a break. The fish meal and meth production was back on schedule. He was pretty sure his rather irate customers had settled down after they heard about the harassment Ink had suffered for them. So Ink's night out would be that break he needed so badly—and one that he had been looking forward to since Mavericks had announced it a month ago: the Bactrian Brewery Cameltoe Contest.

He and Toad joined three of the workers in the meal plant—who had showered twice after work. Toad had driven his Armada, one of the few vehicles with a shotgun seat big enough for Ink. As they pulled up, an electronic billboard flashed the four categories of cameltoes the customers would vote for: Spandex Tights, Bikini Bottoms, Short-Shorts, and Fancy Panties.

Ink and his crew walked into the crowded bar that seemed to be one half single men, one quarter women with male dates, and one quarter well-muscled dykes not even the drunkest cracker would mess with. Ink's table for five, set directly in front of the stage, had cost him a hundred bucks a head. There was a nicely designed program that listed the rules for the contest. Pretty faces did not count, nor did big boobs, nice legs, or pouty lips. That was because the customers couldn't see the whole woman until the voting was over. All they would see was a video shot of the cameltoe on the screen hanging over the stage.

Before the action began, Ink had time to memorize the Official Cameltoe Definition that was reprinted from the Bactrian Brewery website: "A vaginal wedgie caused by tight pants that work their way into the crevices of the pussy." He decided that he would try the Dromedary Doppelbock with the slogan "Two humps are better than one!" The rest of his crew, hooked on hops, tried the Ship of the Desert IPA.

Marginal Margie, one of managers of Mavericks, took the stage and went over the rules of the club and the contest, explained the Bactrian Brewery beer specials, and then announced, "And now your host for the first annual Bactrian Brewery Cameltoe Contest, heeeeere's Josephine, Call Me "Jo," Camel."

The crowd erupted in thunderous applause and started chanting "Cameltoe, Cameltoe!" Jo Camel, dressed in a tight white halter top with the image of a camel's face positioned so its eyes were precisely aligned with her erect nipples, used her fingers to frame her own wedgie that protruded from the red heart on the crotch of her seemingly painted-on pink satin short-shorts.

"Pussy power!" Jo screamed. "Let's go 'toes!"

So began the first annual Bactrian Brewery Cameltoe Contest, which the South Florida Convention and Visitor's Bureau website would later call "fine family fun," mistaking it for a petting zoo, which it sorta was.

In the humble opinion of Big Ink, the highlight of the entire contest was the winner of the Fancy Panties division. Her 'toe clobbered the competition with a 97.5, fully ten points above the closest competitor. Jo Camel described it as "puffy perfection" and introduced to the fascinated audience a woman called Moll Flanders who was a self-admitted 52-year-old bleached blonde with saggy tits but a perfect, shaved 'toe.

"Hell," Ink told Toad, "you gotta love a woman who says her favorite contact sport is double penetration."

But the Manatee Fish Meal crew's party time came to an

abrupt and unpleasant end when they returned to the Armada at 1:30 and found it was surrounded by eight drunken chicken farmers who wanted a refund from Big Ink for the meth money they had advanced him. Of course, the farmers were not inclined to discuss their request politely—as Ink found out when a bald guy in overalls lobbed an empty bottle of Ship of the Desert IPA at him.

Ink caught it easily and hollered, "Girly throw," hurling it back quite accurately. He caught the farmer directly in the mouth, shattering his teeth as well as the bottle. Then the melee was on. And although they were outnumbered, Ink's men weren't as drunk as the farmers—plus they had Big Ink, who was pissed. His only weapon was a Leatherman Skeletool, but it had a three-inch knife blade.

Two farmers engaged Ink, one jumping on his back while the other waved a broken beer bottle in his face. Ink's Leatherman blade stabbed the first man twice in his left thigh—just missing his femoral artery—before Ink bucked him off his back and into the arms of the bottle waver. They cracked heads and fell into the rough gravel of the parking lot. Someone fired a pistol and everyone momentarily froze, giving Toad some time to kick one of the farmers in the nuts, and then the rout was on with farmers staggering to their trucks while sirens screamed in the distance. Within a minute, Dade County sheriff's deputies had sealed off the parking lot and were arresting the farmers among the bodies of several unconscious men.

Big Ink knew one of the deputies and gave him a run-down of what had happened and the video from the parking lot cameras later confirmed his account. Two of the bodies on the gravel were almost-conscious farmers, but Ink felt his stomach lurch when the other—who was dressed like Toad—did not move at all.

Ink and the deputy hurried over to him. Ink was stunned

to see his employee lying on his right side with what appeared to be the handle of an ice pick protruding from his left ear.

• • •

"ATTACK OF THE CHICKEN FARMERS," screamed the headline on the front page of Section B of Dalton's *Miami Herald*. The accompanying photo showed the mostly inked, but very sad and upset face of a fat man. The caption revealed that the person in question was Big Ink—legal name—and that he owned the Manatee Fish Meal Plant. The same one that Dalton had turned in to the county as a health hazard. Hmmm. There was one death, a fish meal plant employee named Timothy Wheeler. Dalton remembered arresting him with the other python poachers. Toad. Stabbed in the brain. A chicken farmer from Immokalee named Walter Shipley was charged with the ice pick murder, which wasn't all that unusual in the state of Florida. Many felons just couldn't get real weapons. Dalton didn't know that the charges were dropped against Shipley three days later when a review of the parking lot footage showed that Shipley was nowhere near Wheeler, who was stabbed by a man wearing black clothing and a ski mask.

Dalton was sitting at his relatively new desk, which meant he was probably the twentieth state employee to use it. It faced Phil's desk, so their computer monitors partially blocked their conversations. But they could make it work. He felt the iPhone in his pocket vibrate with a text. From Phil. "Got a nice surprise for you. Don't leave."

He shrugged and finished the article. The president of the Central Florida Poultry Growers Association, one Martin Mozell, had blamed everything on Big Ink because he had raised prices. Mozell also claimed that the plant technicians had not removed lionfish from the catch, which polluted the meal with their toxic flesh. Dalton's inner marine biologist told him that

Mozell's claim was crap. Lionfish could not possibly be confused with menhaden, and every fisherman in Florida knew what a lionfish looked like. Shit, they were swimming in salt water tanks at the dentist's office!

"Dead chicks can drive a poultry farmer crazy," the president of the CFPGA was quoted as saying.

"Or eating too many McNuggets," Dalton thought out loud. Laura had read that they were 56 percent corn. His mind leaped to factoids like that when he was stuck—and stuck he was, with no momentum at all in the World of Reptiles case. And it wasn't even a case, because he had nothing—not a shred of evidence that Zimmerman was dirty. Diana Ventura was probably his only hope for a break and she was, well, a piece of work. A good actor, though. Save Our Snakes, my ass, he thought, remembering her over-the-top performance at the nature center in Davie.

"Solved anything yet?" Phil asked as he sat down. He passed Dalton a file folder.

"Wise ass. What's this?"

"The credentials of one Gabriel Cypress. They check out."

Dalton noted the photocopies of two IDs for the man: Drug Enforcement Administration and Miccosukee Tribal Member. "Undercover alligator wrestler?"

Phil grinned. "You got it. He wants to show us something."

"What?"

"Don't know. He's on his way over here. Maybe we should steal a chair for him."

Cypress was dressed like a tourist going to a golf tournament—white tennis shoes, long white trousers, a dark red golf shirt embroidered with the words "Miccosukee Raccoons," and to top it off, a red beret with white piping.

"What's your handicap?" Dalton asked after Phil introduced them.

"Bad knees, I guess. I don't know crap about golf. The casino is hosting a fuckin' tournament of some kind. Duty calls."

"What can we do for you, Mr. Cypress?"

Cypress pointed to the newspaper on Dalton's desk. "Your name surfaced in a complaint against the Manatee Fish Meal Plant. Owned by that jerk."

"Guilty as charged," Dalton admitted. "Three of their employees were poachin' pythons and gave us some grief."

"And one of them got himself killed."

"That would be Toad. Toad Wheeler."

"Right. Why did you file the complaint?"

Dalton glanced over at Phil, who gave him a slight nod. "I didn't like the smell."

"There was a reason for that odor. Wanna see it?"

"Sure."

Cypress handed over a flash drive.

"I got an inside tour of the plant from Big Ink. Better living through chemistry seems to be his motto."

The drive was loaded with time-stamped images of elaborate chemical apparatus. Dalton looked at Phil, whose mouth had dropped open.

"I didn't know making fish meal was this complicated," Dalton said slowly.

"It is when you're serving up a crystal methamphetamine dessert," Cypress told him.

Big Ink was in several of the shots. "How in the hell did you fool the guy?" asked Phil.

"I had a special pen in my pocket and he never noticed it. Dumb ass."

"Why us?"

"He means, why are you showing this to us?" Phil explained.

"You're investigating World of Reptiles, right?"

"How the hell do you know that?" Dalton asked.

"Fuckin' smoke signals," Cypress grinned. "I know everything. Let me tell you about my fishing trip—"

"Oh, get off it, Cypress," Dalton interrupted. He was getting tired of the guy.

"—With Bone Mozell and Bruno Zimmerman."

There was silence in the small office as the two F and W special agents stared at each other. "We're all ears, Gabe," Phil said finally.

"I know it's hard to believe when I'm dressed like this," Cypress told them, "but I think I conned a con. Maybe two of 'em. I need a drink. Is it noon anywhere?"

"Yes," Dalton said. "Bermuda."

"Close enough," Cypress said. "Let's go."

• • •

"Catch any fish?" Ink asked. He was dead tired and hadn't eaten anything since the fight at Mavericks, but Bone had insisted on meeting him right after his interrogation at four in the morning. It had taken the sheriff's officers three fucking hours to question and clear Big Ink and the rest of his crew. Fortunately, all the parking lot cameras were in good working order or it would've taken even longer. He had called Decker, woken him, and had Decker pick him up at the sheriff's office in his Expedition, which had a shotgun seat almost big enough to hold Ink comfortably.

Bone smiled. "As if you care."

"I do care. My guy gets killed while you're off on a boat playing fisherman."

"Quit whining, Ink. It was a fucking coincidence, that's all. Nothing to do with us or the late meth delivery. It was a personal thing between him and Shipley."

Ink looked at Bone skeptically. "Who's he? What was the beef?"

"Shipley works in my warehouse. He claimed that Toad had raped his daughter, age 14," Bone lied. "The sheriff's office is holding him without bail. They found the ski mask in the cab of his truck." Two more lies.

"Did he?"

"I meant to say 14, going on 41. The daughter, named Dawn, was hookin' for cigarette money. She looked 18, at least. Her mom left Shipley two years ago. Poor Toad never stood a chance. I think Shipley killed him because he thought Toad was going to take Dawn away from him, if you catch my drift."

Ink did catch it. "And which trailer park did the Shipley family live in?"

"Dixie's. On 8th Avenue. But Shipley's in the Naples lock-up. No bail. Dawn is living with her aunt and uncle in South Naples. What happened to Toad's body?"

"His brother had a funeral parlor pick it up," Ink explained. "The funeral's tomorrow."

"You going?"

"No, we're still working to catch up from the shut down."

Bone set a Tampa Bay Buccaneers gym bag on Ink's desk. "That casino deal's still on and Cypress just gave us a deposit."

Ink opened the bag and saw the stacks of hundreds. "How much?"

"50."

"Excellent."

Bone said, "Are we square?"

"If you promise to stay in touch better."

Bone thought Ink was buyin' it, suckin' in the bait. It was time to set the hook. "So promised. Now let's talk about the delivery route. We have to put the Miccosukee on it."

• • •

Diana was in her favorite position—on top of him, her hands on either side of his head, moving up and down on him

141

and adjusting her position and fantasizing that he was Bond, James Bond, in From Russia with Love and she was Tatiana. Ray had consumed much more alcohol that she had but he was holding his own, she had to give him that. Any man who could last longer than ten minutes when she was on top would get a plus mark in her little black book, if she had one. When she sensed he was ready she suddenly latched her mouth onto his and did the tongue thing as he grabbed her butt with both hands and released.

"Oh—my—god," he gasped as she rolled over and flopped beside him on the bed.

"Good, huh?" she asked with a little giggle.

"One of the best ever," he slurred. Five minutes, she guessed, and he would be sound asleep. Five scotches will do that to a man his size. Luckily, they had walked to the restaurant from his rather spartan apartment so they didn't have to worry about driving. And she'd had only had a single glass of wine and a little snort in the ladies room to keep her alert.

At five minutes Diana gave him a little poke in the arm. Nothing. She moved the sheet and noticed that the condom was still on him. She thoughtfully removed it and was rewarded with a soft snore. Ray was out.

Two minutes later she was dressed and pulling on her heels. His trousers were draped over the desk chair. She reached into his right pocket and pulled out his keys with a tissue, taking care not to rattle them. She removed the dark blue flash drive and replaced it with an identical one, then silently replaced the keys.

She left him a note on the counter in the bathroom. "That was so much fun! Now I have a new favorite reptile—your one-eyed trouser snake. Luv ya, Diana." She had always been a good liar. She glanced at her watch as she stepped into the hallway. Nine minutes from climax to exit. Not bad. Now for the dead drop.

That was Sean's stupid idea, of course. Instead of just meeting for coffee where she could pass it to him, he had to turn it into a fucking spy movie. As promised, his silver Altima was parked in his driveway. She pulled in behind it and killed the lights. She took an envelope out of her purse and sealed the flash drive inside. It took her less than a minute to slip the envelope through the half-inch gap in the Altima's left rear window, check to make sure the car doors were locked, and drive off.

Seduction: successful. Flash drive swap: a cinch. Dead drop: perfect. Time to relax, she thought. Diana pulled a joint out of her pack of Winstons and lit it up as she rolled her windows down.

• • •

"Hungry?" Derrick asked after Bone had left.

"Massively," Ink replied. They headed for the Waffle House.

Derrick ordered the country ham with two fried eggs and a bowl of cheese grits. Ink ordered the same—plus the pecan waffles and four grilled biscuits with sausage gravy. While stuffing himself, Ink explained the situation at Mavericks the best he could.

"Sounds like it's time for Plan B," Derrick offered.

But Ink wasn't through talking. "From these facts, give me your theory of what's going on." He held up his meaty left hand and touched his fingers with his right index finger. "One, on Bone's insistence we give a complete stranger a tour of our meth plant. Two, we make an extra ten pounds of product for the guy without even a deposit. Three, Bone disappears. Four, we get shut down. Five, our customers try to kill us and succeed with Toad. Then we get a $50,000 deposit from that Cypress jerk. It fuckin' stinks."

"Maybe Plan C."

"I'm thinkin' fail-safe."

"Holy shit," Derrick said.

"In fact, I've made up my mind. That is our only option."

"They'll really kill us this time."

"They'll try," Ink admitted, "but fail."

"Fail-safe." Derrick shook his head.

"You know what to do."

"Just the way we planned it."

"See you when it's all over," Ink told him. "You can drop me off at the marina."

"It's 5:30 in the morning," Derrick protested.

"I have a key. Let's get out of here." Ink just couldn't get the image of the ice pick handle out of his mind.

• • •

"Could you, uh, explain exactly what you mean by that conning a con comment?" Phil asked Gabriel Cypress. There were four of them in a booth at The Democratic Republic of Beer on northeast First Avenue. Kevin Cooper had joined them, and Dalton had told Cypress that he was a "special resource" of Fish and Wildlife. If sitting next to a stranger who was a large, fierce-looking black man intimidated Cypress, he didn't let it show. Phil and Dalton were having Harpoons and Cypress was drinking a Kudzu Porter, which actually had some of that weed in it. Kevin had a glass of water in front of him.

Cypress grimaced. "Most white guys don't really see an Indian, they see a stereotype. Tonto, or that crying fuck playing an Indian in that old clean water commercial."

"Are you speaking of Native Americans?" Dalton asked, messing with him.

"Fuck that, there's no such thing. All Americans came from somewhere else. There were no native Homo sapiens in the Western Hemisphere, period. Indians just got here first, that's all. You know, from Asia."

144

"Oh yeah, the Land Bridge—"

"Fuck that, too. We came in boats, followed the coasts, killing seals and eating oysters."

"If you say so. Now tell us about the con."

"The casino, that's all they can think about. Dumb Indians and all that money. Bone is an Ultimate Rewards Player, the highest level for a gamer at the Miccosukee. He was down like 30 grand one night and pretty drunk, but he didn't seem worried about the money. He let it slip that he'd be flush when the next shipment was delivered or something like that. I pretended to be just as drunk and started talking about the casino having so much cash that we were looking for some alternative investments. We waltzed around those ideas for a while, Bone paid his debt with a Black Amex card, and we agreed to meet for lunch. Away from the casino. That's when I gave him 50 grand in hundreds."

"Was he surprised?" Phil asked.

"You bet. I told him we wanted in on whatever he was doing. Said it was a down payment. Actually, it was DEA front money."

"And he bit?"

"Big time," Cypress said. "And he wanted me to meet his partner. Mr. Slimy, I called him. Bruno Zimmerman."

"Snakes aren't actually slimy," Phil interjected.

"I know that. But he is. I refused to meet with him."

"What?"

"Don't special agents take a course in confidence swindles?"

"Uh, more like advanced maritime safety," Phil said.

"Well, when you're runnin' a con, you gotta get them conning you. I just told Bone that I wasn't meeting anyone until I knew what the deal was. Then I asked him to give me the money back."

145

"You gotta pair, I'll tell you what." Phil glanced at Dalton, who gave him a thumbs-up.

"Bone then had to show off, so he asked me how much we wanted to invest if 50 K was the advance. I told him it depended on what racket they were running. We were stonewalled for a while and I could tell that Bone felt the deal slipping away. Then he asked me if I'd like a tour of a fish meal plant. 'Can't wait,' I told him, wondering what the fuck was going on."

"Where do we come in on this deal?" Dalton asked.

"I showed my photos of the plant to legal," Cypress told them, "and they shot me down. Can't use them to get a search warrant."

"Why the hell not?" Phil asked.

"Evidence illegally obtained and bordering on entrapment. It's the fruit of the poisonous tree—even if we caught them in the act of making meth, it could be thrown out because of a bad warrant."

"Jeez," Dalton said.

"But you guys arrested three fish meal plant employees for poaching on federal land," said Cypress, sounding more and more like a Fed and less and less like an Indian.

"Well, we were there but it was the Fed special agents from F and W who made the actual arrests."

"Whatever. Why were they poaching pythons?"

"They wouldn't say. The two perps, that is, one now dead."

"Don't you suspect that the owner is illegally harboring poached animals at that fish meal plant?"

Dalton suddenly understood where all this was going. "We do now. Right, Phil?"

"I know just the judge to help us with this sorta thing."

"Can I please tag along when you raid the place?" Cypress asked, back to playing his Indian role.

After Cypress left, Dalton looked over at Kevin. "We're going to need your airboat."

"What's up?"

"This is highly confidential, Kevin."

"Only four people know about this," Phil added. And then they proceeded to tell him about the pythons, IBD, and some infected mites that needed to be spread around on hammocks in the state lands in the 'Glades.

"Holy shit," Kevin said, shaking his head. "You can't use an F and W airboat?"

"No," Dalton said. "They have GPS trackers on board, and they can't be disabled."

"Of course you can use my boat. Want me to come along, fly a drone or something?"

"No need. We have the cover story all worked out."

9

African ball pythons were being sold in acrylic jewelry cases laid out on black felt—like diamond necklaces. Prices for genetically cultivated 'designer pythons' were skyrocketing. The $30 retail ball python was seeing its designed price climb to $15,000, then $45,000, then $85,000. One breeder ever paid $145,000 for a "completely white" ball python. And that was just one species. People were breeding designer lizards, albino turtles, and rare frogs.
—Bryan Christy, *The Lizard King*, 2008.

Bruno Zimmerman asked himself, as he often did, does it get any better than this? He was inspecting his estate on Hibiscus Island to make sure it was ready for the "World of Party Reptiles" event he was throwing to celebrate a record fiscal year for his company's sales. With 50 people in attendance, he didn't want any surprises.

He checked his floating dock, where a maximum of ten small boats could tie up, and saw no problems there. His tanks containing the larger specimens like Ernest, the alligator snapper, and Mildred, his largest alligator, had barriers around them, and security guards would prevent any drunks from swimming with his pets.

His horseshoe-shaped driveway could easily park 25 cars and he could use his neighbor's if he needed it. Security would handle all the parking anyway, and would carefully check IDs against a guest list to prevent crashers—like the media—from attending. The caterers had already set up serving stations under large red umbrellas and a band would use the built-in patio bandstand with a dance floor in front of it.

His encrypted Blackphone buzzed and the readout showed it was Lars checking in about the latest emerald tree boa morphs.

"Lars, do you have good news for me?"

"I do. They're not just emerald any more. Silver speckles on dark red, ruby chains on bright yellow, a blue paisley, and eight more beauties. I shipped them all this morning with the usual carrier. They'll get there before the Breeders' Expo."

"Excellent. What's the going retail price?"

"At least three grand each, maybe more if you auction them right."

"Okay, as soon as they arrive I'll wire the money, as usual."

He cut the connection and was giving the caterer last minute instructions about the drink service when a text arrived from Bone.

"Ink's 'on vacation.'"

"WTF?"

"That's the word from Derrick. Everything else normal. Shipment goes in a few days. They need to age it at least 21 days before shipping."

"10-20 on Ink?"

"No."

"Find him," Zimmerman ordered.

Crap. Just what he needed. Was Ink making a run for it? Well, even if he was, it wouldn't make much difference as long as the shipment went out on schedule and they could grab it. He and Bone had the whole heist planned out, but something unexpected could happen, like an alligator blocking the road. He grinned at the idea and banished all negative thoughts. Instead he focused on the party—and Diana, the enigma. She knew a lot about snakes but it was all "book larnin'," in cracker-speak. He had never seen her touch a reptile, and that gave her away. But it didn't bother him as long as she did her job, and she was a great spin doctor.

And he knew that she had hooked up with Ray—he couldn't keep his damned mouth shut and pretty soon his new accountant, Cathy Broussard, was telling her boss all about it, trying to suck up to him. He couldn't see Ray and Diana as a couple, but it sent him a message. She was making moves and it was his turn next. After the party—or maybe even during it.

• • •

Ginger Delgado called her disease-ridden mite-breeding operation Mitey Fine Productions. It consisted of three mite-infested ball pythons infected with a genetically-modified version of inclusion body disease that was much more infectious than the original strain. The snakes were living in her garage in Boca Raton in large, circular stock tanks. The snakes barely moved and anyone with a flashlight could see the dark red, eight-legged mites crawling in and out among the pythons' scales.

"Those snakes are on their last legs," she joked to Jenny.

The IBD plan, as they began to call it, was taking shape as the volunteers worked on their assigned projects. Dalton was in charge of planning the release of the mites and his first rule was no federal land, easy to remember: NFL. National parks, wildlife refuges, and preserves were out. State lands were in, and Dalton had selected three main deployment sites, as he called them: Collier-Seminole State Park, Francis S. Taylor Wildlife Management Area, and the Everglades Wildlife Management Area. His philosophy was to let nature do the work of spreading IBD from there to the federal lands.

Phil had perfected the drone drop technique and had bought and modified two Altura Zenith ATX4s. They were designed for aerial photography and could carry a payload of three pounds for 45 minutes on one battery charge. Each drone had four 16-inch props and they were controlled via tablet and GPS. Phil had rigged each drone to carry what looked like an SLR camera, which was really a mite dispersal device. He had also created the necessary paperwork for the Hammock Invasive Species Count, which was designed to monitor the spread of foreign plant species. Certain target species, like Brazilian pepper trees, melaleuca, Australian pines, and water hyacinths would be counted from the digital photos—Phil's cover story for the drones.

Ginger had calculated that Mitey Fine Productions would max out the mites in their protonymph and adult forms in less than two weeks. Phil and Dalton scheduled the dispersion expeditions. Only Ginger and Jenny were allowed to assist Phil, who would be the main drone pilot. It was need-to-know at a bare minimum.

• • •

A great party was all in the details, and Bruno Zimmerman was noted for great parties. The DJ, playing the Reptile Mix Bruno had programmed himself, was dressed in an alien lizard costume from The Amazing Spiderman, complete with fake muscles. The mix began with the blues legend Sonny Boy Williamson singing "Fattening Frogs for Snakes," segued into Bo Diddley's "Who Do You Love" with the great "cobra snake for a necktie" line, cut to "Snake Song" by Emmylou Harris, then "Snake Man" by the Doobies and then The Doors and their "Celebration of the Lizard."

A beer tent from the Hoppiest Corpus Brewery was in the center of the lawn, with girls dressed in fake snakeskin bikinis handing out their eight brews. Elegantly-dressed women were passing joints back and forth on the dock while guests filed through the snack service line for frog legs, rattlesnake pâté, and deep-fried alligator nuggets with habanero hot sauce.

About 45 minutes into the party, Zimmerman, dressed all in black except for his custom-made cobra snake tie, took over the microphone and presented the Employee of the Year award to Ray Jacobs—something all the employees expected—along with a fake bonus check for $5,000. He was given the traditional World of Reptiles loud hissing, followed by raucous applause.

Zimmerman's company party was nearly an hour and a half old before people noticed that the face of Save Our Snakes was not yet in attendance. Zimmerman texted Diana, then called her but there was no response. Ray, separately, tried to reach her too.

Zimmerman had asked her twice during the past week if she was going to be at his big party, and she had assured him that she couldn't wait for the event. And, Diana had added, she was especially looking forward to visiting the estate he called El Nido de la Víbora. She was bullshitting him of course, because he repulsed her. But Zimmerman assumed that every woman wanted him. He was a touchy-feely, invade-your-space kinda guy, the type she and her girlfriends had called cop-a-feeliacs in high school.

She knew that if she went to his party he would find a way to demand payback for her high salary and recent television fame with the story of the new elementary school on the Yamanomo Reservation in eastern Brazil built solely with the funds from reptile collectors. They loved the Indians' jungle-bred, designer red-flame miniature anacondas, which grew only to eight feet and 200 pounds. The collectors' going rate was a grand a foot for the snakes, which would, she figured, erect a school or two along the Amazon. She had made it all up, of course.

Zimmerman would try to seduce her or rape her if she showed up, Diana was certain of that. And Ray would be there, all over her as if they were an item, or something equally stupid, like she was his significant other. If she didn't show up, Zimmerman would probably fire her in a few weeks, after all the snake school publicity had died down.

Then two things happened that changed everything for Diana. She got a call from a head hunter letting her know that she was under consideration for the PR position at ARKAMERICA, the Association of Reptile Keepers of America, the main lobbying association for the US reptile industry. She told the woman that she would send over her CV before a Skype video interview. Then, the day before the party, she received a text from Sean: "Bingo! My office ASAP." That text wouldn't save her job at SOS, but it might well have saved her life in the long run. Her heart was pounding as she drove over to the Herald's office. It was only one little toot, she thought.

Diana took the elevator to the eighth floor. She knocked on Sean's door and he immediately invited her in. Of course, she'd been under video surveillance since she entered the front door.

Sean was at his desk, gesturing for her to come in. Sitting in a chair on the left side of the desk was a thin man, a paper bag over his head with holes cut in it for his eyes and mouth.

"Diana, meet Chopper, face to bag."

She started giggling and that soon turned to guffawing, and then Chopper pulled the bag off his head. "Surprise, you're now an administrator of the World of Reptiles intranet!"

Sean explained, "Chopper had to check you out before he could show you his face. You passed."

"Here's your login and password." Chopper, eager as a pup, passed her a slip of paper. "Theoretically, you'll have access to every part of the system, but if you have any probs, my contact info is below. Oh, and here's the decoded flash drive you gave me. It's basically copies of reports that Ray Jacobs was sending to his boss at US Fish and Wildlife."

"No shit," Diana said. "Why, that little, uh, snake in the grass. He'll be the star of my story."

"Sorry I had to look into your background," Chopper said. "I'll bet you were an awesome cheerleader in high school. Your split move on the school website is incredible."

"I have a DVD of all my best moves," she said, deadpan. "Clothing optional. $100 on Amazon. No rating. No panties sometimes. Look it up." She noticed that Sean was taking notes. Dumb fucks'll believe anything, she thought.

"Look, I'm disappearing now to write the story. This has been set up for months, and I used your money to do it. I'll find you if I need you, but don't bother me."

"Just send progress reports," Sean directed.

"And you find me a research assistant and an editor."

"I'll be your editor," he told her.

"Watch your back," she advised, and winked at him. "Do you realize how big this is going to break?"

"Why do you think we've invested more than $100,000 in this project?" Sean was a jerk but no dummy.

"I know why. Circulation. Sub rights. Book and video sales. Advertising. I'm going to deliver all that to you. And you'll give me a nice bonus when I win the Pulitzer Prize."

"When?"

"Delivery? Soon, very soon. Two, three weeks probably. I'm fast."

"So I've heard," Sean said.

• • •

"I owe you one big time," Dalton told Laura as he pulled

her Mazda CX-5 into the Ocean Center's garage on Earl Street in Daytona Beach.

"When you asked me to go to a show, I thought it would be more like seeing Jersey Boys at the Knight Concert Hall. Instead, you take me to a snake show."

"Just remember that big girls don't cry, Laura. I didn't want anyone suspicious that I was prowling around by myself as an agent for the Florida Fish and Wildlife Conservation Commission. And it's not any old snake show. This is the National Reptile Breeders' Expo, the largest reptile meeting in the world."

"Wow. What a treat," she said sarcastically.

"No venomous reptiles allowed in the show and no snakes or lizards heavier than 20 pounds."

"That's comforting."

"The reptile breeders want to distance themselves from the Burmese pythons and the Nile monitor lizards that are breeding like crazy over in Cape Coral." Phil had told him that the monitors were eating pet cats. They were such a nuisance that the city had a trapping program in place, with the largest one caught so far topping six feet and 45 pounds. And the city had started running radio public service announcements that urged people not to shoot the monitors, despite the liberal Florida attitude toward guns of all kinds, and reminded them that discharging firearms in the city was against the law.

Laura and Dalton strolled among the 150 exhibitors with Laura commenting on which reptiles bothered her and which did not. Turtles and tortoises were fine and some were "sorta cute." Frogs looked "slimy," toads were "just plain ugly," alligators—even babies—were "a walking nightmare" and all snakes were "very, very scary." She admitted that some of the designer snakes, the so-called morphs, had exotic colors and patterns, "but they still creep me out," she told him. And finally, one word of praise: the bearded dragon lizards were "striking" when they flared their flap of skin.

Dalton was more impressed with the reptile hardware: cages, specially designed aquariums and terrariums, rack systems, lighting and heating equipment, special gloves, and very detailed how-to books on the care and breeding of hundreds of species.

One of the more telling displays was of the one for ARKAMERICA. A sign in their booth reported that lobbying organization had completed the first comprehensive economic assessment of the industry and found its value to be $1,400,000,000 annually.

And Dalton knew that ARKAMERICA had challenged the US Fish and Wildlife Service's for recently listing the Burmese python, Indian python, Northern African python, Southern African python, and the Yellow anaconda as injurious under the Lacey Act. Dalton knew that money could buy any kind of loyalty for any cause. He had read the Lacey Act, which clearly stated that the Secretary of the Interior could declare those species dangerous to humans because they had killed people, and that they were dangerous to wildlife resources because they ate the wildlife, including the protected alligators. He wondered how much money World of Reptiles donated to ARKAMERICA.

It was obvious that World of Reptiles had the largest and best decorated booth at the expo. It was 30 feet on each side, decorated primarily with exotic plants and flowers, and each section featured a different aspect of the company's business: morph snakes; rare and unusual lizards; frogs, toads, and salamanders; turtles and terrapins; caimans and alligators, specialized cages and equipment; and World of Reptiles gear, with everything from t-shirts and caps to very elegant jewelry in every reptilian form imaginable. Laura turned down Dalton's offer to buy her a pair of hooded cobra earrings.

"Are you here to inspect us, agent Dalton?"

Taken aback, Dalton looked at the clerk's name tag. Ray Jacobs, World of Reptiles' Employee of the Year.

"I'm not inspecting anything, Ray," he replied. "That's not my job."

"Oh, that's right. You don't inspect snakes, you just kill them."

Dalton did not reply. He took his iPhone of his right pocket and quickly snapped two shots of Ray in front of the flower displays. "For my scrapbook, Ray. A very beautiful display. No wonder you made employee of the year. Congratulations."

He expected a look of hatred but instead detected a slight smile on the man's face. "Have a nice day, agent Dalton."

"What was that all about?" Laura asked as they moved toward the refreshment stand.

He showed her a shot on his iPhone. "I've never seen those flowers before. What are they?"

"King proteas, the national flower of South Africa. We have a display of them at Fairchild."

"And these?"

"I think they're called Tru-Blue Roses—they're GMOs."

"Are they common in the cut-flower business?"

"How would I know? Why?"

"Where did World of Reptiles get them?"

"You tell me," Laura said, shrugging her shoulders.

"I will when I find out."

• • •

For a journalist, the only thing worse than not having enough information was having too much of it—and that's precisely what Diana was facing. Between World of Reptiles' intranet material and all the reports on Ray's hijacked flash drive, there was such a massive amount of data that it was downright intimidating. The financials alone would take a team of accountants to decipher. She was in way over her head but at least she knew where to go for help.

"This is Dalton, Florida Fish and Wildlife. Leave a message and I'll call you back."

"I've got the information you need to take down World of Reptiles. Call me."

Dalton, who first was having dinner with Laura and then, later, making love to her, didn't get around to calling Diana for a couple of hours.

"What's up?" he asked casually when she answered.

"I've got access to World of Reptiles intranet, and Ray Jacobs is undercover for US Fish and Wildlife. I thought you'd like to know."

Dalton couldn't believe it—it was beyond left field, outer space maybe. He was speechless.

"Are you there?"

"Don't say anything more over the phone," he told her. It was 9:30. "How about a drink? You, me, and Phil."

"Oh goody, a threesome, F and W-style. Bring your laptop."

Diana was sipping on a Marlin Martini and Dalton was nursing a Hopalong Hemp Ale at Home Plate, one of the noisier sports bars in Dade County, when Phil joined them at about 10:15. Fist-bumps all around and then Diana got down to the nitty-gritty, explaining how she had received the login and password and how she had lifted Ray's flash drive.

Phil was doubtful. "We can't use this, any of it. This is the most poisonous fruit I've ever heard of. It would never hold up in court."

"I agree with you," Dalton said, "but why are you bringing up a trial? It will never come to that. To hell with the fan; after Diana's story runs, the shit is going to hit the wind farm. What we have to do is use this information to learn everything we can about Zimmerman's operations and how they can be sabotaged. I say we keep all this just among us. The three of us here in this bar and maybe a few consultants, but no one in Florida Fish and Wildlife."

"I don't know," Phil began. "If we tell them what we have, what will happen?"

"Your bosses will shut you down," Diana said, and Dalton nodded in agreement.

"All the law says is that evidence that is obtained by illegal means is not admissible in a court of law," Dalton explained. "It does not state that such evidence can't be used to really fuck someone up. Zimmerman must have an extremely efficient reptile smuggling system. If we can find out what it is, we can figure out how to use it without exposing ourselves. Diana can certainly help with that. Imagine a line in her story that goes, 'Officials close to the investigation have revealed that the reptiles are being smuggled into the US by remote-controlled personal water craft running at night,' or whatever the truth turns out to be."

"Okay, you win," Phil said. "I was thinking too much like a cop and not enough like a conman. Diana, you've had time to look at some of the information from Ray Jacobs' reports and Zimmerman's intranet. Give us a brief rundown."

Diana smiled. "The reports from Ray document the day-to-day activities of World of Reptiles and how Zimmerman covers his smuggling tracks with faked bred-in-captivity certifications from Myanmar and Malaysia. I found the PDFs of them, complete with the right signatures, on Zimmerman's hard drive. His intranet is nothing more than his method of spying on his employees, so the real treasure here is that hard drive. It has all the contact information for the reptile suppliers he uses, plus what seems to be two different accounting files for World of Reptiles. I downloaded all files on his hard drive and put them on this." She reached into her purse and produced a black hard drive that was about twice the size of a cell phone. "This is for you guys. I have another one at home."

Dalton ordered another round for the table. "Let's divide up the duties for the first round. Diana?"

"I'm going to skim all of Zimmerman's sent and received emails for at least the past year, plus look at his personal bank accounts."

"Okay. Phil?"

"I'll take a look at those accounting files. Becky did some bookkeeping for a while—hated it, but learned a lot. Maybe something will jump out."

"Okay. I'm going to check out Zimmerman's suppliers. They can't all be legit. I'll also go over all of Ray's reports. You never know what he might have uncovered."

Diana held up a hand. "Whoa, boys. Let's get the rules straight. We meet regularly and share all information. What you do with it is your business and what I do with it is mine."

"You mean we don't get to read your story before it runs."

"You got that right, Dalton."

He grinned at her. "Next meeting in three days—same time, same station. Cheers!"

• • •

"Florida F and W and the DEA, in action together," Dalton said as he turned off the Tamiami Trail on his way to the fish meal plant. Phil had begged off participating in the search, saying he was deep into the two financial records of World of Reptiles and didn't want any distractions.

"With backup, thank God," Cypress noted.

Dalton parked in a space marked "Visitor" and the Jeep Cherokee with the other DEA agents pulled in beside them. Cypress rolled down his window and said, "We'll call you if we need you. Or come on in if you hear gunshots."

Dalton and Cypress entered the factory, showed their IDs to the plus-sized receptionist, and asked to speak to Big Ink.

"Mr. Ink is on vacation. I think he's on a cruise somewhere."

"In what hemisphere?" Dalton asked.

"You'll have to speak to Mr. Fitzroy about that. I'll get him for you."

Fitzroy was wearing his usual golf shirt and shorts. "Can I help you gentlemen?"

Dalton knew something was fucked when, after they showed their IDs and the warrant, Fitzroy said, "Well, if you have a warrant, search away. Can I get you some coffee?"

"No thanks," Dalton said. No one was this cooperative, he thought.

"What are you looking for?" Derrick asked. "Maybe I can help." He sounded like a clerk at Walmart.

"Carnivorous contraband," said Cypress, pointing to the specific wording on the search warrant.

"Ain't got none a that shit," Derrick replied in a perfect cracker accent, and Cypress laughed.

"Should we even bother?" Dalton asked, certain that they wouldn't find squat.

"Quick run through," Cypress said. "I know right where to go."

But he didn't. Instead of the meth lab Cypress had toured with Big Ink, they found only vats that a crew was cleaning—and the sickening odor of fish guts.

"Sorry about the smell," Derrick said. "You get used to it after a while. Our scrubber's working normally, Mr. Dalton. Your complaint actually helped us."

"How did you know I made a complaint?"

"That county inspector—Raul?—gave us a copy of it. Mr.

Ink realized his error and had the scrubber back working the next day."

"Oh yeah? That's interesting."

Back in his truck, Dalton looked at Gabriel. "Do you know the definition of the word 'sandbagged?' Because that's what just happened to us. I'll bet the meth plant is just busted up lab equipment at the landfill."

Dalton was wrong. The lab had been carefully disassembled, packed in padded boxes, and was halfway to Georgetown, Texas aboard a UPS truck. Big Ink had sold it to his brother Hal. They needed meth bad down in central Texas, where they called it "cowboy candy." Ink had agreed to supply Derrick and Cutup as Hal's consultants for ten percent of the net, half in product, half by wire transfer. He figured to work the ingredient suppliers in the other direction for a ten percent commission, all by wire transfer to his account at the Royal National Bank of the Caymans.

10

A python about six meters in length was shot in about
1921 at Monze in Zambia after it had swallowed six goats.
Admittedly, two were lambs and the goats appeared to be of
the rather stocky and small variety. However, a snake of such
size, appetite, and determination could probably have also
handled a human being.
—W. D. Haacke, "A Possible Further Incident of a Human as
Prey of the African Rock Python," 1981.

The news of the killing in southwest Florida not only
stunned area residents, it quickly topped state news and
soon went national. It was particularly poignant because the
killing was recorded by a professional videographer who was
perched in a tree stand in Charlotte Harbor Preserve State
Park, photographing wood storks. When the incident began,
he switched his Nikon D7000 to HD video, and recorded the
entire, horrific scene. As soon as he realized the value of what
he had, he sold non-exclusive rights to Fox 4 Now in Fort My-
ers. The station persuaded a professor of herpetology at the
University of Florida to narrate a one-minute segment of the
longer clip, which was posted on You Tube. It wasn't every day
that an endangered Florida panther was killed and eaten by a
pack of Nile monitor lizards.

"Watch this sequence carefully," the professor intoned,

"and you'll see why the panther lost the battle. He was holding his own until that large monitor grabbed its tail and did not let go." The footage was in slo-mo, and when the monitor lizard, which weighed about 30 pounds, bit the tail, it completely ruined the panther's balance and ability to turn quickly, giving the other lizards the openings they needed to swarm over the cat. Soon, a pack of monitor lizards was dismembering and swallowing the panther, bite by bloody bite. Reptile porn. The monitors killed in the attack were eaten by still more monitors. The footage ended with more than eighty monitor lizards at the kill site.

In a follow-up interview, the professor explained in detail how the attack was possible. "The Nile monitors have taken over Cape Coral. Literally. There are untold thousands of them and although they mostly eat the eggs of alligators, when they're hungry, they'll eat anything—including your dogs and cats. Now, about the panther killing. Call me a nitpicker, but this is not true pack hunting. This was not a roving pack of these lizards looking for food, like a pack of wolves—they were not a social unit to begin with. This is more like a mobbing. Like when a group of, say, kingbirds join up to run off a Cooper's hawk. Remember, first, the panther attacked a monitor. Its screams alerted other monitors in the area and they came running—at 15 miles an hour—and when they reached the panther, instinct took over and they worked together."

The interview, though not as bloody as the footage, had its own fascination, especially when the bleached blonde reporter asked the professor if people were in any danger from the monitors. He stopped being professorial.

"What the hell do you think? We've just seen a few 20- and 30-pound lizards kill and devour a 145-pound panther. Put yourself in the panther's place: could you have done any better, unarmed?"

"Holy crap," Dalton said to Phil. They had watched the footage online. "The newspapers will blame this on Florida Fish and Wildlife and demand that we start a monitor holocaust. Then the reptile-lovers will go berserk and get even more attention."

"Well, they just lost one of their superstars," Phil said, looking up from his iPhone. "Diana has resigned from Save Our Snakes."

• • •

"I'll be goddamned," Bruno Zimmerman said to no one. He sat in his elegant office, staring at an email addressed to Helen Menuah and copied to him and Ray Jacobs.

Dear Helen: Sorry to have to do this to you, but it looks like some better offers are coming my way. I'm one interview away from signing with ARKAMERICA as vice president for media relations. So, effective immediately, I'm resigning my position with Save Our Snakes, Inc. It has been nice working with you and good luck in the future. Sincerely, Diana G. Ventura

Zimmerman picked up his iPhone and texted, "my office" to Jacobs.

A text came in from Helen. "We should meet very soon."

Jacobs knocked and entered. Zimmerman gestured toward an alcove that held a glass-topped cocktail table and two patio chairs. Beneath the glass, in a LED-lighted terrarium, a pair of elegant and deadly emerald boomslangs were feeding on chameleons.

They sat and watched the hungry boomslangs for few seconds. "Did you know she was going to resign?"

Jacobs, naturally a little nervous, did not avoid his stare. "No."

"Well, she must have given you some sort of hint, considering that you were fucking her."

"Just once. I haven't spoken to her since then and she's not returning texts or calls."

"Same with me," Zimmerman relented. "And I never got a chance to fuck her. Any ideas for a replacement?"

"Yeah. You know the South Florida Herp Society? The gal who runs it, Sara Tucker, is also an actress in TV commercials, so she's good on camera. She's no looker like Diana, but she actually loves snakes, unlike Diana."

"Bring her in for an interview," Zimmerman said, shaking his head. "That Diana is a piece of work."

"As fake as they come about reptiles, but great in the sack," Jacobs said mildly, needling his boss. "Very enthusiastic. Called me Bruno when she came."

Zimmerman laughed at that. "Good one, Ray. Wait a second." He picked up his iPhone, selected a contact, and put his finger on the screen.

"Bruno, what's up?" Bill Snedeker said on the speaker. He was president and CEO of ARKAMERICA.

"Why are you stealing away my favorite employee?"

"What do you mean?"

"Diana Ventura just resigned and wrote she was signing with you."

"We use a headhunter service for human resources. I know that she's been approached and that they have her CV, but that's as far as it's gone. She'd be good for us, Bruno."

"Bill, you're a lousy snake. But I'll still make my usual donation." He hung up and turned back to Jacobs.

"I could queer the deal for her, but why bother? If she doesn't like it here, to hell with her."

"She's history," Ray said. "Let's move on. We have one final meeting with Bone before we take that shipment."

"Agreed. Let's go." Zimmerman was pleased. Jacobs was now totally corrupted.

• • •

Phil hauled Kevin's airboat to the boat ramp at the Broward County Rest Area just off Alligator Alley, or I-75. With him in the cab were Jenny Rodriguez, navigator, and Ginger Delgado, mite control specialist. They were all dressed alike: jeans with Florida Fish and Wildlife work shirts and caps. The Drone Squad, as Phil called it, looked very official.

They had caught pythons in this area before, so Jenny had the GPS coordinates for the hammocks that had produced the most snakes. They would focus on those hammocks as the logical places to start seeding the IBD virus in the Francis S. Taylor Wildlife Management Area. It was a perfect day for dropping capsules loaded with virus-infected reptile mites—overcast with a high for the day predicted to be in the mid-70s. The forecast also called for rain that night, which Phil hoped would dissolve the gelatin capsules and free the mites.

He carefully backed the truck and borrowed airboat down the boat ramp. Phil left the truck in the parking area while Jenny moved the boat to the dock. He boarded, carrying the Remington 870 12-gauge—you can never be too careful. They set off into northern 'Glades at sunrise, 7:05.

Just 16 minutes later they reached the coordinates N26.09, W80.37, and Phil threw out the small anchor. He placed the Altura Zenith ATX4 in the bow of the airboat and Ginger handed him the mite capsule dispersal unit, which held 30 mite-filled capsules. He fitted it onto the drone and picked up the iPad, which would be his flight controller. He started the four rotors, lifted the drone off the deck of the airboat and flew it to the closest hammock, one Jenny had indicated was FST43.

"We shot an 11-foot female there two months ago," she said.

"Well, maybe we'll get some of her babies," Phil joked as he released three capsules. "Okay, now we are officially criminals."

What they were doing was a Level Three Violation of state wildlife law. Phil had read the statute so many times he had it memorized. Section 379.231: It is unlawful to import for sale or use, or to release within this state, any species of the animal kingdom not native to Florida unless authorized by the Fish and Wildlife Conservation Commission. For punishment purposes, Florida laws transferred wildlife violations into general crimes, so a Level Three Violation became a Misdemeanor of the First Degree. They could get a year in prison and a $1,000 fine. The problem was not the mites, for an attorney could argue that the mites were indeed native to Florida, mostly in captive snakes. But the yet-unnamed IBD-carrying arenavirus was a non-native species. Phil had read up on the arenavirus and was a little worried when he discovered how closely it was related to the Ebola virus.

As he made the drops, getting into the rhythm of the repeated mechanical actions, Phil realized just how much he loved this huge marsh with its slightly briny smells, the heavy moisture in the air and the sounds ranging from the squawks of gulls to the explosive sound of a flock of mallards taking flight off the water. A flock of snowy egrets passed over the boat and he couldn't help but smile.

No matter how it turns out, I am doing the right thing, he thought, trying to convince himself as the capsules floated down to the hammocks. I am doing my part to help save the Everglades. And it wasn't the fine or the possible jail term that bothered him the most, it was the thought of losing his job—and what it would mean to his family. He wondered about his retirement and how that would factor into his possible arrest and termination from Fish and Wildlife. Stop it, he told himself. Don't think negative thoughts. Think about how killing all the pythons would save the 'Glades. He and Dalton would be fuckin' heroes when the word got out. Public sentiment would be on their side, and they'd probably get a parade down Biscayne Boulevard. Everyone would love them, he thought. Except for the snake owners, that is.

The three criminals paused in their efforts to watch a large bull alligator swim by with a dead six foot Burmese python in its jaws. They gave him a polite round of applause.

Breakfast in the 'Glades, Phil thought.

• • •

While Phil Everett was trying to infect the pythons, Dalton was reading Ray Jacobs' reports on World of Reptiles. He was amazed that an undercover agent could actually rise to the position of unofficial second-in-command in such a short time, and was especially impressed that Jacobs seemed to love his job and his undercover position equally. After all, he was World of Reptiles' employee of the year.

After he read the reports from the flash drive, Dalton watched the videos Jacobs had created, courtesy of George Tompkins, who had made a deal with the head of the Southeast region of the US Fish and Wildlife Service. Dalton took notes on suspicions and evidence and came up with a chart that boiled down what Jacobs had discovered, chronologically.

1. Suspicion: Zimmerman is siphoning cash from the business. Evidence: Examination of deposit slips versus cash register receipts show that the cash received by the store was not deposited at Community Bank of Florida. Possible Crime: Tax fraud.

2. Suspicion: Snakes claimed to be captive-bred were actually wild-caught in Myanmar and Malaysia. Evidence: Zimmerman produces those photo-shopped certificates on his own computer and printer, and Jacobs had witnessed it. Possible Crime: Reptile smuggling.

3. Suspicion: Zimmerman was somehow smuggling rare and endangered reptiles into the country and selling them to private collectors for cash. Evidence: Jacobs had overheard Zimmerman discussing US arrival times for prohibited species, like the Cuban green anole, the Javan filesnake, and the spectacled caiman. Possible Crime: Reptile smuggling.

4. Suspicion: Zimmerman was using reptiles as a cover for shipping drugs. Evidence: Jacobs was shipping manager, so he had access to all shipping records, not only through World of Reptiles, but also through the shipping companies. After cultivating a friendship with a FedEx sales rep, he learned that Zimmerman had a private shipping account that was billed to him separately. Also, Zimmerman would on occasion remove a regular reptile shipment from Jacobs' queue, saying he wanted to write a personal note of thanks. Jacobs would never see it again. He did have the names and addresses of all the recipients whose boxes Zimmerman had snatched. Possible Crime: Interstate transportation of illegal substances.

The mention of drugs triggered Dalton's memory of the aftermath of Operation Xterminator. And that of course led to thinking about his wife and son. He shook them out of his head and watched the last video that Jacobs had shot, apparently with a video pen in his shirt pocket. He and Zimmerman were at a party. Dalton could hear a band playing and several conversations. The camera was focused on Zimmerman, who was in front of a swimming pool asking Jacobs about an incident at the store earlier in the day.

Jacobs: "The customer got pissed off because I wouldn't sell him a yellow anaconda."

Zimmerman: "You told him about the ban?"

Jacobs: "I sure did. I said we couldn't risk a felony violation of the Lacey Act. That's a five-year prison term and a $250,000 fine. He started yelling at me, so I asked him for his card and said you'd call him."

Zimmerman: "Maybe he's grandfathered in."

Jacobs: "Meaning?"

Zimmerman: "Maybe he had one before the ban. You're allowed to keep it but can't take it out of state."

Jacobs: "Well, he did say something about a replacement."

Zimmerman: "I'll call him."

Jacobs: "Where would you find a yellow anaconda?"

Zimmerman: "Paraguay." He winked before the screen went black.

Zimmerman looked familiar to Dalton. He had never met the man, but maybe he had spotted him somewhere, read an article about him, or seen a news clip about pythons that quoted him. He couldn't find Zimmerman's complete bio online, just mentions here and there that he owned World of Reptiles. The World of Reptiles website had a rather useless description of him: "Owner Bruno Zimmerman is a Florida native and a noted reptile expert." BFD.

Dalton checked the Florida Department of Law Enforcement database for wants and warrants for Zimmerman and found nothing. He did the same thing with the Florida Department of Corrections. Zip. NCIC. Nada. He chuckled, thinking, a real law-abiding citizen.

Well, maybe not, but he was a registered voter in Dade County with 1968 listed as his date of birth. Thank you, Florida Division of Elections. He called the Bureau of Vital Statistics at Florida Health, asked for a supervisor and spoke with a woman named Carol Rice. After telling her he was a special agent for Fish and Wildlife, he asked for a temporary login and password to search the EDRS, which was the Electronic Death Registration System. He figured that if Zimmerman was 46, perhaps one or both of his parents had died. He searched for a combination of "Zimmerman" as surname and birth dates between 1948 and 1952. There were twelve names, all with death dates.

He scanned through Florida obituaries. Bingo! The *Miami Herald* had run an obituary of Gilda S. Zimmerman of Boca Raton. Automobile accident, 1992. "Zimmerman is survived by her sons, Frank Miles and Bruno Zimmerman."

The name Frank Miles jumped out at him He was one of the Navy men who had died during Operation Xterminator. What a coincidence, he thought, and began searching for more information on Frank Miles. He began with his own files on Operation Xterminator, which he had copied before being drummed out of NCIS.

• • •

"I heard a rumor," Ink said on his encrypted Blackphone.

"Oh yeah?" Derrick asked. "What?"

"That someone was going to jack our shipment."

"That's not good."

"Maybe it is."

"Meaning?"

"Make it a very special shipment. Don't add the ethoxy-quin to it."

"I think I see where this is going."

"Is that old truck still runnin', the one we can put the open trailer on?"

"Yes. We fixed it."

"Use that truck. And just the driver—no helper on this run."

"Okay. Where should I stash the M?"

"At Hideaway." Ink had chosen the storage company because of its highly appropriate name.

"The one on Pine Ridge?"

"Yeah. We'll pick it up when things settle down."

"Everyone's been asking about your 20 and what the hell's goin' on. What shall I tell 'em?"

"Tell 'em I'm in tattoo rehab."

"That'll get a laugh out of 'em."

"But it's true. I'm a patient at TRIA, here in Fort Lauderdale."

"What's TRIA?" Derrick asked.

"Tattoo Removal Institute of America, of course."

"What the fuck? Why?"

"I think the Big Guy's sending me a message. Toad dying like that. Telling to change my ways or else."

"What do you want me to do?"

"Hide. Zimmerman and Bone will be coming after us soon."

• • •

Diana, Phil, and Dalton's second meeting was held in the living room of Laura's condo while she was at work at Fairchild Tropical Botanic Garden. Laura told Dalton they could use the condo if he promised to give her the scoop on what was coming down. He did give her an update, in a much-edited version. Need-to-know played a large role in his editing of the tale, but there was no holding back among the three of them at the meeting.

"Zimmerman's skimming off all the cash sales from the store," Dalton said, giving them the rundown on the bank deposits.

"Becky and I agree," Phil offered. "He's running two sets of books, one for the IRS and state of Florida and one for internal use."

Diana looked like she was on her way to a boat party—white short shorts, a tight, black "Free Pussy Riot" t-shirt with

175

a circle of multi-colored lip prints on it, and pink deck shoes. Dalton thought she looked stunning, but then she ruined her entire sexy presentation by opening her mouth.

"Dinky shit," Diana said, "the minor leagues. We need something big."

"I read all of Jacobs' reports and watched the videos he shot. Here's my report." He gave Diana and Phil a single page print-out.

"Jacobs is making out okay, guys, double-dipping the way he is. Playing both ends for the middle, which is Ray himself. Two salaries. Cash bonuses. Must be nice."

"He does seem to be having fun," Phil remarked.

"Smuggling snakes and shipping drugs," Diana mused, "and just circumstantial evidence. If you guys could just get a search warrant for some of those packages Zimmerman sends personally…"

"No probable cause, no search warrant," Dalton reminded her.

"Damn."

"What about the snake smuggling? Does Jacobs know more than he's reporting?"

"Ask him," Dalton suggested. "Isn't he your buddy?"

Diana grinned. "A one-time fuck buddy, that's for sure. He's been calling and texting me. I was ignoring him, but maybe I'll give him a call."

"Diana," Phil said suddenly, "do you have anything for us?"

She switched back to reporter mode. "Several things. First, there's a very large folder on Zimmerman's hard drive that I can't open. Must be doubly encrypted."

"I gotta guy who can help," Phil told her. "What's the name of the folder?"

"Documentation."

"Okay, what else?"

Dalton interrupted. "I'm not sure how this information works into this whole mess, but take a look at these two photos. The full facial images came up on the screen of his iPad. "On the left is Bruno Zimmerman, who we know and love. Care to guess who the guy on the right is—I mean, was?"

"They look like brothers," Diana said.

"Actually, half-brothers. That's Frank Miles, Zimmerman's older half-brother, now deceased."

"And I'll bet you're going to tell us how he died. Eaten by a python, maybe?" Diana was grinning again.

"He burned to death. On our watch. Operation Xterminator, that drug deal we busted in Key West when I was NCIS."

"Shit," Phil said, "you don't think..."

"I have no direct evidence that Zimmerman was responsible for the death of my wife and son."

"Just a suspicion, like me," Phil said.

Diana's eyes were wide and her mouth had dropped open. "You think Zimmerman killed your family to avenge his brother?"

"I don't know. I guess it's possible. Anything else to report?"

Diana hesitated, still trying to grasp the implications of what Dalton had told them. "I think I found out how the original pythons got loose in the Everglades. Zimmerman was joking about it in emails to one of his suppliers in Malaysia. It did involve Hurricane Andrew, just not the way everyone thought. It won't help our investigation, but it's wonderful background for my story."

"So tell us," Dalton suggested.

She teased them with a cute little smile. "All in good time. You'll have to buy a copy of the *Miami Herald* and read all about it."

Bitch, Dalton thought, but he didn't say it.

"Where's the cash?" she asked. "All the skim? Is it stashed or has he put it to work?"

"Is that rhetorical?"

"I guess. Just throwin' out ideas. But I did notice something odd about his accounts payable."

"What's that?" Phil asked. "We examined those pretty closely."

"Zimmerman seems to love flowers. He buys an awful lot of them for the store displays, and they're quite expensive."

"I've got his financials right here," Phil said. "What's the vendor?"

"Tropical Ornamentals."

"Let's see. Last year they were paid $118,000 and change. That's a lot of flowers."

"Take a look at this," Dalton said, pulling up an image on his iPad. "This was the World of Reptiles display at the reptile breeders' show. See those flowers there? They're king proteas, the national flower of South Africa. And these are blue roses—real blue. Maybe you should find a floral expert and find out where they came from, and how they got to Zimmerman."

Diana looked at Dalton and gave him a nice smile. He stirred a bit. Then she opened her mouth again. "I'm on it like flies on dog shit."

11

But one day a big, strong, water monitor grabbed the python by the neck. The teeth of those lizards are strong but blunt, so although it had apparently been trying for some time to tear the skin of the python, it had not succeeded in doing so. The python, however, wearied at length of the lizard's attentions, and throwing three coils round its body, crushed it to death and forthwith swallowed it.
—F. W. FitzSimons, *Pythons and Their Ways*, 1930.

In 2011, all of the Florida Department of Transportation motor carrier compliance officers were merged into the Florida Highway Patrol and became troopers. That's why their blue-and-white patrol cars were now serviced by Sanibel Auto Care, which had the maintenance contract for the southwestern part of the state. Sanibel was owned by Jess Doster, Bone Mozell's brother-in-law by way of his sister Sammi. This was precisely how Mozell was able to "borrow" one of those patrol cars for a couple of hours after Doster's mechanics had replaced its alternator.

Using forged credentials, Bone was also able to purchase two authentic highway patrol khaki uniforms and two black campaign hats online from National Uniform Supply. The gun belts and attached gear were an easy purchase from CopSupply.com, and Mozell already had the two Glock 37 semi-automatic

.45 caliber pistols in his weapons collection. The gear outfitted two of his warehouse workers, Grace Duran and Wayne Foster, who would receive $500 bonuses to hijack a load of fish meal that technically and officially belonged to Mozell in the first place, because he was the majority owner of the Manatee Fish Meal Plant.

"Raise your right hands," Mozell directed his officers before they left the warehouse. He laughed when they complied. "Just kidding. You know what to do."

For a pair of amateurs, Duran and Foster completed a very professional, almost military-efficient hijacking of Ink's old truck. Since Mozell knew the timetable and route, the two fake cops parked just off the highway and waited until Cutup Roberts, who was driving the load of fish meal, turned east onto the Tamiami Trail. Duran activated the lights and siren. Cutup, warned that something like this might happen, obediently pulled the truck onto the shoulder of the highway.

"Please step out of the truck, sir," Foster said. Cutup did so and Foster handcuffed his wrists behind his back. He directed Cutup to follow Officer Duran, who placed him in the back seat of the patrol car. Cutup didn't bother protesting. Foster climbed into the truck, pulled a U-turn, and headed toward Naples on Route 41. Duran followed for a while, then on the outskirts of Naples turned off toward Sanibel Auto Care. She only had one stop to make along the way. Foster headed to the Mozell Poultry Supply warehouse and pulled the smelly truck inside.

• • •

Nearly 40 miles north of the fish meal truck, Dalton was in a heated discussion with the Reverend Hixon Stemmons, pastor of the Deep South Baptist Church in Cape Coral. With the reverend were twelve teenagers, all armed with pellet guns of various shapes, sizes, and powers and wearing t-shirts which read, "Deep South B.C. Monitor Hunt Club."

"Are we breaking any state game laws, agent Dalton?" the reverend shouted.

"No, but—"

"Then please let us get on with the hunt. We have a quota, you know—20 monitors per hunt."

"You are discharging firearms within the city limits of Cape Coral, which is illegal," Dalton bluffed.

"I know the law and you're wrong. Pellet guns are not firearms, they are defined as gas-operated guns of two calibers, .177 and .22. Kids over 16 can shoot them as long as they are not endangering anyone or causing damage."

"Are all those kids at least 16 years old?"

"They are," Stemmons said defiantly, "and I'm supervising them—even though I don't have to by law."

"What are you doing with the lizard carcasses?"

"We freeze them and donate them to the Naples Zoo. They feed them to the sea lions."

"But what does the hunt have to do with the Baptist faith?"

"We are helping the Lord. 'Surely He will save you from the fowler's snare and from the deadly pestilence.' The pestilence is the population of Nile monitor lizards, and it is our duty to help the Lord in removing them. Besides, it's a good youth group experience. Keeps them off the infernal Internet and all its temptations."

"A killing club for Christ?"

"Exactly."

"Reverend, you are one sick puppy," Dalton told him and stormed off.

• • •

Bone Mozell found Cutup behind the abandoned gas station on Country Road. He was gagged and tied at his wrists to an old air pump. A tall concrete block wall completely obscured them. Without any hesitation, Mozell pulled his silenced Beretta 92FS 9mm pistol out of his pocket and shot Cutup in his right temple. He didn't want Cutup telling the detectives that he was hijacked by two troopers in a blue-and-white marked 8776. Especially when they figured out that the 8776 was in his brother-in-law's shop. He hauled Cutup's body to his car and lifted it into the truck. Then he drove off.

The first stop was his own 23-acre farm. He unlocked the gate, moved the Sentra beyond it, and relocked it. He drove past the house to the barn, where he retrieved two 45-pound barbell weights which he wired to each of Cutup's feet. The body could wait until his fishing trip the next day with Billy, his warehouse manager. They would move it to his Bayliner 215 in a large duffel bag, and sink it 20 miles away in the Gulf.

• • •

By the time Mozell got back to the warehouse it was 4:30. The news was not good. He called Zimmerman on his cell.

"We opened all the bags. There was nothing in 'em except stinkin' fish meal."

"That is highly disappointing," Zimmerman said.

"And now we're gonna have to pack up all that meal and move it to a different truck. Police will be looking for Ink's truck. I don't want to pay overtime to do it tonight."

"It'll wait for a few hours. Where are you taking it?"

"Gainesville. I gotta guy who'll buy it all."

"We'll have some unhappy M customers." Zimmerman's voice was cold.

"After Ink is out of the picture, and we get the lab, we'll make it up to them. Blame everything on the big guy."

"Has anyone seen him?"

"No."

"Heard from him?"

"No."

"Where the fuck is he?"

"Hopefully, swimmin' with the fishes in concrete boots."

"Somehow," Zimmerman said, frowning, "I don't think so. And that was a mixed metaphor."

"And what is that?"

"Look it up," Zimmerman suggested, and hung up, irritated and frustrated. First Ink fucks up and now Bone has lost the meth, he thought. That guy's gotta go.

• • •

Because it was late winter in Florida, the air conditioners had been turned off. The temperature in the warehouse had reached about 90 degrees. When Mozell cut open the polyethylene-lined burlap bags, the fish meal from the Manatee plant was exposed to oxygen. The bacteria in the meal caused the proteins in it to decompose quickly, yielding heat, because Ink's workers had left out the antioxidant, ethoxyquin. The unsaturated fats in the meal began to smolder. The burlap flamed up and ignited the lower sections of hundreds of boxes of cardboard egg cartons. Soon, the temperature in the warehouse reached 165 degrees, triggering the overhead sprinklers.

But Bone's warehouse workers had stacked metal chicken coops too close to the ceiling, which diffused the sprays into a fine mist that could not extinguish the flames. The fire was raging out of control even before the first engines arrived. The building was a total loss estimated at $1,800,000. Two firemen were killed in action when three stacks of chicken coops collapsed.

Derrick had filed a police report on the hijacking. As soon as the police matched the license on the truck in the warehouse to the one he gave, they charged Mozell with grand theft in the second degree, which called for up to 15 years in prison and a $10,000 fine. But that was nothing compared to the charges for aggravated manslaughter for the deaths of the firemen—another 30 years total. Bone was, in effect, facing life in prison. The police could charge him all they wanted to, but they couldn't arrest Bone—because he had, like Big Ink, completely disappeared. They didn't know where he'd gone, and they couldn't know that he had a body of a redneck in his trunk.

• • •

"Let's go for a little ride," Zimmerman said.

"Where to?" Jacobs asked.

"A little north of Everglades City."

"What's down there?"

"A fish meal plant that I've invested in. I tried to call but got a recorded message that says the plant is closed. That's it, that's all. I want to take a look at it, see what's going on."

Jacobs knew well that his boss didn't like any kind of a loose end. "Let's go," he said.

Zimmerman drove them, of course, in his BMW 760. They talked about business and the coming baseball season. World of Reptiles had an MVP Suite at Marlins Park at the Lexus Legends level on third base line that could—and did—host 16 people for the entire season. Zimmerman was constantly planning which bigwigs he would invite to the home games.

Traffic was light but Zimmerman kept to the speed limit, joking that he wouldn't want to run over any pythons on the road. The distance from Homestead to the plant was only 80 miles, but the trip took just over an hour and a half. And they soon discovered they had wasted their time.

The front gate was locked and two guards were stationed in front of it, sitting in a modular guard shack. Zimmerman pulled up in front of it and one of the guards stepped out. He was dressed in First Spear body armor and wearing a Safariland drop-leg holster with what looked like a Glock 9mm semi-automatic in it. His name tag read, "First Response Group, Sgt. F. Ryan."

"Can I help you, sir?" the sergeant—if he was one—asked.

"Any of the owners around?"

"No sir, the place is locked up tight. You might give them a call." He pointed to a sign for Marsh Realty that read, "Available—19,000 sq. ft. Manufacturing Plant. Contact Susan Maldonado, Broker. 239-557-9045."

"I'll do that. Thank you." Jacobs made a note of the number on his iPhone, while Zimmerman headed north. "Are you going to call her?"

"Maybe," Zimmerman replied. The meth's still in the plant, he thought. Why else would there be armed guards be out front? At least it's safe there.

It was 7:00 in the evening when they got back to Homestead. Zimmerman dropped Jacobs off at his motorcycle and drove away. Jacobs stopped at Chefs on the Run, picked up a mango chutney turkey burger, and took it back to his apartment, where he washed it down with an Anhinga Amber.

He wrote his weekly report and emailed it to his boss at US F and W, but when he went to save it to the flash drive on his key ring, the drive was blank. Absolutely nothing on it. Oh shit, he thought, Diana.

• • •

Diana was obsessing over cut flowers in general and one variety in particular—blue roses. This was because of the photo Dalton had shot at the Reptile Breeders' Expo—in addition to the king proteas, the arrangement included blue roses. For centuries, blue roses had symbolized unrequited love or the quest for the impossible. Her online searches brought up numerous attempts to develop a blue rose after traditional breeding methods had failed. A while back, Suntory, a Japanese company, had teamed up with Florigene to insert a delphinidin-producing gene from a pansy into a Cardinal de Richelieu rose. They named the result Applause, but it was more of a lavender-colored rose. Still, it had sold for ten times the price of a normal rose.

But the roses in the photo were cobalt blue. A mutated soybean gene was the key to the Tru-Blu Rose®. They grew in Colombia and Ecuador. And that variety was owned by Tropical Ornamentals, Inc. of Fort Lauderdale, the flower distributor Dalton and Phil had found in the World of Reptiles financials. Diana searched for the nearest retail location of Tropical Ornamentals in south Florida then headed to South Beach.

She stepped into the overwhelming aroma of exotic flowers and the clerk rose from his desk to greet her. He had dark blue hair and was wearing a badge that said, "Hi, I'm Freddie Venus. Ask me about the Tru-Blu Rose®."

"Freddie Venus?"

"Yes, love. 'Freddie Mercury' was already taken. Besides, Venus is hotter than Mercury, and I want to be the hottest there is."

"But Mercury is closer to the sun." He was tall, thin, and quite good looking, but it was obvious that he played for the other team.

"And with no atmosphere. Venus has cloud cover. You know, I've got to say that you are the most beautiful tranny I've ever seen. Pre- or post-op, love?"

No one had ever asked her a question like that. "Thank you. Or how dare you, Freddie, as the case may be. I've had female plumbing since I was born."

"But straights never shop here."

"I'm not here to shop, Freddie." She pulled out her ID

from the *Miami Herald*. "I'm doing a story about how Miami is the hub of the floral industry in the US, focusing on the new flowers that are all the rage—like the blue roses and the king proteas."

Freddie Venus wiggled a little and clapped his hands. "I love it! The new Lois Lane in person. Are you going to mention us in your story?"

Oh God, she thought, what would Dalton do in this situation? Ignore it and go on, she figured. "Of course you'll be mentioned. But first, Freddie, tell me about your shop."

Freddie revealed that he and his partner Luther had used the money they had made producing gay rock and roll cruises to Saint Barts to buy the exclusive Tropical Ornamentals franchise for south Florida. They were planning to open more retail locations, but retail was soooo much work that they might just sell everything and retire. Diana decided to head this digression off at the pass.

"Who are your biggest customers?"

"Well, we work closely with Fairchild Botanical. Whenever they have a big flower event, we're their official exotic flower supplier. We exhibit at all their shows. We work with Laura Saylor. Do you know her?"

Dalton's squeeze, Diana thought. "I've heard of her. Do you supply flowers to other shows? I saw a display up at that reptile show up in Daytona Beach."

"Oh yes, we supplied those flowers to that scary man from World of Reptiles, Bruno Zimmerman. Luther says he'd like to swallow him up, but I think the man's creepy. I mean, he touches reptiles all day long. But his money's good."

"I guess the owners up in Fort Lauderdale like flowers."

"Oh, they're not the owners, they're just the home office."

"Who are the owners?"

"Something called the Frank Miles Trust. At least that's who we send the bills to."

She wrote the name down on her pad. "This is going to make a really interesting story. How often does World of Reptiles order flowers?"

"Once a month, like clockwork," Freddie answered. "They like to decorate their store with them. Exotic flowers and creepy reptiles. Go figure!"

"My readers will love that. Do you deliver the flowers to them?"

"Oh no, they pick them up. It's on a regular schedule."

"So, every month on a certain day, they come here—"

"No, not to the shop," Freddie said. "They pick them up at MIA after they've cleared customs."

"Are there flowers for your shop on the same flight?"

"Of course. It's just easier for them to pick up their part of the shipment. Otherwise we'd have to hold their flowers here, in the cooler, and we don't really have the room."

"What flight do they come in on?" She had a quick thought that she was being way too obvious, but Freddie was oblivious.

"It varies, but usually Centurion Air Cargo. The next one's due in Thursday." He checked the calendar on his smart phone. "Flight 302, arriving at 5:42 a.m."

Diana wrote that down, too, thanked Freddie Venus and left the shop. He certainly was talkative, she thought. And so helpful.

• • •

"This is the one we were looking for," Phil said. He touched the drop interface on the iPad and the drone released the last of the capsules. It had taken them ten straight days of work, and Jenny estimated that they had released around 2,000 capsules on 250 hammocks in three strategic sections of state wetlands.

No one had interfered with their project. In fact, except when they were around a public boat ramp, they had not seen another boat of any kind out in the grassy wilderness.

"I sure hope we haven't wasted ten days," Ginger said as the drone landed on the bow. One its rotors slowed to a stop, she retrieved it, set it on the deck, and threw a plastic tarp over it.

"Well, with all the work you did raising the mites, you have more time invested in this effort than Phil and me put together," Jenny said, pulling on the line so the airboat moved closer to the anchor.

Phil popped open three cans of Lizard Lager and passed them around. "Well, my vacation time is shot, so I'm hoping that the infection is setting in and spreading."

Jenny began singing the chorus of the old Dusty Springfield song "Wishing and Hoping" and they all laughed.

"This ends our criminal enterprise for now, fellow conspirators," Phil announced, starting the airboat engine and turning the craft south. "Cheers!"

• • •

The chemist formerly known as Big Ink had never felt more alone in his life. He hadn't been able to reach Derrick since Bone Mozell's warehouse burned down. More than a week. He had no one else he could trust, and now Bone, his former buddy and financer, was maybe a tad pissed off about his warehouse. He wondered if Bone took Derrick out. Ink now called himself William C. Draper. Bill to his friends. But Derrick had set up everything for the fish meal plant sale, Bill thought. He had spoken to the broker herself. He had also spoken to the manager of Hideaway Storage who said that their code was entered into the computer on the same day as the hijacking. Bill could only assume that it was Derrick dropping off the meth into storage.

Which reminded him that his personal stash was running very low. He couldn't just drive down to the storage area on his yacht. Maybe it was for the better. He didn't really need the meth that much anymore. He had lost 63 pounds since he began tattoo rehab. Not eating very much will do that to a body. Without the temptation of the deep-fried barbecue and bean sandwiches from Mavericks, he had developed a fondness for fruit and fat-free yogurt. He had also started walking a few miles in the morning and swimming in the afternoons after the tattoo removal laser sessions and his Tae Kwan Do lessons.

The laser therapist had refused Bill's request for country music during the sessions and had dialed up an alt-rock station instead. Bill discovered that he actually liked Kings of Leon and Foo Fighters. They distracted him from what felt like ten rubber bands snapping on his skin at the same time. But the treatments were working and all of his head, facial, and neck tats were faded to only seven percent of what they had been. The spiders on his knuckles were almost gone too. After that, he wanted Tinker Bell off his ass.

Bill spent some of his time reading the want-ads, looking for any sort of chemical industry job that didn't involve marine paint or narcotics manufacturing. And, one amazing thing had happened—he had gone out on a date. With a woman who seemed to like him. He had spoken with Jamie in the waiting room of TRIA a couple of times and thought she was cute. She was having a tramp stamp of Joan Jett and Blondie kissing removed from her lower back and she was bored too. When she asked him to go have a drink with her, he eagerly accepted. They ended up at the Wreck Bar, where they laughed at the mermaids swimming up to the portholes above the bar. Jamie had ordered a Sex on the Beach and Bill was drinking iced tea, telling her he was slowly eliminating his bad habits. He had never felt that way before.

"Don't drop all of them," Jamie suggested. She had a streaked pageboy haircut, bright red lips, and she was about his age. She was starting to stir some romantic notions in him.

She drove Bill back to the marina and his yacht, where they made plans for dinner in two days, and Jamie kissed him on the cheek. At least I'm not alone anymore, he thought. Back aboard the Queen Anne's Revenge II, he found his stash of meth and dumped it overboard. Before he dropped off to sleep, he recalled the handle of the icepick sticking out of Toad's ear and he shivered. A fuckin' shitload of guilt on me, he thought.

• • •

It was one of those quirky things you find while searching the Internet that gave her the idea. Diana was trying to find out exactly what path the flowers took from the South American plantations to Miami International when she ran across the story. In 1988, Avianca Airlines had been fined more that $13,000,000 after 14 loads of cocaine—more than two tons of it—was found hidden among cut flower shipments. So there was some historical evidence to support Dalton's theory of reptiles smuggled among the blossoms.

Using her cachet as a reporter for the *Miami Herald*, Diana requested a tour of the Cargo Clearance Center that consolidated all the federal agencies at the airport—Customs, FDA, Fish and Wildlife—and Plant Protection and Quarantine, where the flowers were supposedly inspected for insects and the like. She called the four offices and over the next few days managed to speak to the public information officer about a tour of their facility for "Bloomin' Miami," her article about the burgeoning cut flower business. She wanted to reveal the challenges facing each shipment of flowers. Everyone smiled and nodded but their tape was redder than Dolly Parton's lips.

She turned to Sean for help. Apparently, the publisher not only liked the flower story as a cover for the smuggling story, he wanted to publish "Bloomin' Miami," too. He called his drinking buddy, US Representative Stanley Matson (as Sean told her later), who made a personal visit to all those offices, And as Sean texted her two days later, the wheels were greased. Soon her phone rang and she was speaking to a male senior public information officer who wanted to simplify things and get the tour handled in one afternoon. Tomorrow at 1:00.

"Perfect," Diana told him sweetly. "See you then."

"I'll email you the terms and conditions of your visit," he said.

"You know my email?"

"Ms. Ventura, we know that your Aunt Cindy lives on Maple Street in Duluth."

And that put a little shiver down her spine—despite the fact she didn't have an Aunt Cindy. Then she got it. A Fed joke. The guy was flirting with her. Perfect, until she read the terms and conditions. He would be her guide through the facility. No conversations or interviews with the workers. No photography or recording of any kind in the secure facilities. Individual agencies would provide photos. The smiling faces of happy employees looking sharp in their uniforms, Diana thought. But what choice did she have? She added her digital signature to the PDF and returned it to Mr. Senior Public Information Officer.

• • •

Laura was on her way to play the role of chambermaid at one of her least favorite places in the world, Dalton's decrepit Homestead bungalow. All because Diana had called and asked for a big favor. To quote her, "The shit's gonna hit the fan big time, Laura, and I need a place to disappear to for a little while. Since you and Dalton are living together in Miami, what about his old place in Homestead?"

She had tried to talk her out of it, but Diana could be, well, insistent. "How do you know all this?" Laura had asked her.

"Dalton told me. I thought you two had broken up. I sorta made a pass at him. Sorry, girl. But he wasn't even tempted. Then he had me thrown out of a meeting. I was kinda embarrassed to ask him, so that's why I'm asking you."

At least that was some good news for Laura, but she had to admit that it was difficult to believe that any man could resist Diana. Laura only knew her in passing, seeing her at media receptions, air kisses, that sort of thing. But Diana was also in the media, and there were very few secrets in their business. She had heard the phrase "Diana the hunter" used several times in reference to her sexual exploits.

"So what shit is going to hit which fan?" she asked Diana.

"Just three words, Laura. World. Of. Reptiles."

"I heard you quit that job."

"It wasn't a real job. I was working on a story. Still am, but almost done. I really need this favor, Laura."

"The last time I saw the bungalow, it was trashed. Dalton doesn't do much house cleaning. That's one of the reasons I moved out."

"Don't worry about it—I know how to operate a vacuum cleaner."

Laura couldn't let Diana see the place in a mess, so that's why she was pulling into the driveway of the bungalow. The first thing she noticed was the For Sale sign in the front yard. The second thing she noticed was that the house was immaculate, or at least as clean as it could possibly be. Then she noticed a brochure for Ready Maid Services on the coffee table. It was just like Dalton and his military manner—always find the right personnel to do the job. He had even moved the dogs and their kennels to Chuck Gannon's place. She smiled as she closed the door, locked it, and went back to the Mazda. She texted Diana that she could come by her townhouse for the keys, gave her the address, and added, "We'll have a glass of wine and visit a bit."

• • •

The senior information officer assigned to handle her tour was named Bradley Richards and he was a big guy, 6-2, maybe 190 pounds, broad shoulders, dressed in a conservative blue suit with an ordinary tie. Salt and pepper hair, cut short, his face a little craggy, tanned, like he fished a lot. Richards was a take-charge guy and Diana liked that because she was the same way. They were sitting facing each other in a meeting room at the Cargo Clearance Center. The guard had not patted her down, but he had examined her purse before he let her drive through the gates to visitor parking, where Richards stood waiting for her with his card in hand.

"I'm going to give you a very quick tour of this facility and the Plant Protection and Quarantine Inspection Station, because what you're really interested in is flowers, and we have a completely separate, dedicated facility for that, with its own customs station and APHIS inspection. That would be—"

"I know the acronym," she told him.

"Then let's get going." Richards was obviously in a hurry, wanting her out of his hair as quickly as possible. He was definitely not flirting with her.

Both of the facilities were modern glass, metal, and concrete three-story buildings that looked nothing like warehouses. He showed her the flow of goods in and out of the facilities but did not introduce her to a single person. Then, driving a modified golf cart, it was on to the Flower Clearance Center, which looked exactly like warehouses, 80 of them, to be exact. The facility processed about 90 percent of all imported flowers that entered the United States, according to Richards. 20,000 tons of flowers a year, worth nearly $1,000,000,000.

"That's seven flights a day, six days a week, carrying nothing but flowers."

"I'm impressed," Diana said, and she meant it.

"Every flower shipment is x-rayed," Richards told her. "The machines are all over there. A typical shipment goes through in five minutes."

"How many x-ray analysts are watching the screens?"

"We don't release that kind of information. Enough, believe me."

She didn't believe him. From her vantage point, it looked like four analysts were watching 100 screens. How could anyone do that for 15 minutes much less eight hours? So she asked him.

"It's not possible to physically inspect the entire shipment, so we look at a percentage of each shipment," Richards explained. "That percentage depends on risk analysis we have done over the past few years. Generally speaking, it's about ten percent."

Bullshit, thought Diana. She had done her research and knew that the percentage was two, not ten.

"The inspections are conducted by Customs and Border Protection, with APHIS standing by in case the Customs inspectors run into something they can't immediately identify." Diana was sure that Zimmerman must have someone inside this facility coordinating the inspection when the shipment arrived from Bogota. Someone who could watch the monitors at just the right time and personally select the two percent for inspection.

"Okay, I've seen enough. Let's go back to the conference room. I have just a few questions for you. I've only been bothering you for 30 minutes."

"You are no bother, Ms. Ventura, believe me."

Second time he's used that pat phrase, she thought as they drove back to the CCC and reassembled in the meeting room.

"Mr. Richards, thank you for a very enlightening tour. Now, why don't you show me some identification? Something more than a phony business card. I'd like to know who I'm really dealing with. FBI, right?"

"Was it that obvious?" he asked, pulling his ID out of his right pocket.

"Yes. My father was a chief of police and I grew up around FBI agents. But that's okay—maybe even great. Have I stepped in some of your shit or something?"

"It's more curiosity than anything else, as you're a very visible person in the media. First, we know you were undercover at World of Reptiles—your publisher was forthright with that. But then you want to take a look at our inspection procedures, and if those two facts somehow connect, then you know more than we do. And we want that information, please."

"Pretty please. Let's get a few things straight, Brad. First, I want immunity—in writing and signed by a federal judge for any and all nonviolent crimes we may have committed in the compilation of this information. That's for myself, several of my friends, and two newspapers."

"This is the new FBI, Diana. We can do that. 24 hours, back here?"

"You got it. Look, some advice. When you do the inspection, remove the entire team on the floor and replace it with your own hand-picked team. And I want to be there exclusively for the Herald and Channel 6. And I want Dalton and Everett around, too. Email me an agreement while you're working on that judge."

Richards' mouth dropped open a little and Diana thought that was cute. He knows who's in charge of this case, she thought.

12

In 1993, 15-year-old Derek Romero was crushed to death by his older brother's 11-and-a-half-foot Burmese python. In 1982, an eight-foot python escaped from its enclosure and killed a 21-month-old boy in his crib. In 1980, a seven-month-old baby girl was killed by her father's eight-foot reticulated python. And in 2001, eight-year-old Amber Mountain was asphyxiated by a ten-foot pet Burmese python that had escaped its enclosure. The snake was one of five owned by her family at the time.
—Larry Perez, *Snake in the Grass*, 2012.

The night before the shipment was scheduled to arrive, Diana called Dalton.

"Ready for a little fun?" she asked him.

"Get off it, Diana. We've been through that before."

"I not talking about the beast with two backs, Dalton" she said, "but rather if I'm a heroine or a fool."

"What on earth are you talking about?"

"I think I've cracked the smuggling case; that is, how Zimmerman is smuggling reptiles."

There was dead silence on the line. "Are you still there, Dalton?"

"Just give me a brief rundown."

She quickly recited the entire story, starting with his hunch about the flowers.

"So while you're solving the mystery of the smuggled

snakes, the state assigns me to Cape Coral to dissuade minors from shooting monitors with pellet guns. Go figure."

"We won't know if it's solved until they open some boxes of blue roses tomorrow. Just like I said, a heroine or a fool. Wanna watch? I cleared you and Phil with the FBI."

"What does the FBI have to with it?"

"Tell you tomorrow. Meet me at the CCC at MIA at 5:30 in the morning. I may need a shoulder to cry on."

"Okay. See you in the morning."

"Bye."

When he told Phil what was going on, his friend replied, "Aw, shit. How in the hell did she do that in just a few days?"

"Despite what we think about her, she's one hell of an investigator."

"If the flowers are filled with snakes," Phil said.

"Are you taking bets?"

"Even money there are no snakes."

"Two to one there are snakes," offered Dalton. "$20."

"You're on."

• • •

"There are 2,000 boxes on that plane coming in," Brad Richards told her. They were having coffee at the little commissary at the Flower Clearance Center.

"Why are you here with me?" Diana asked. "Shouldn't you be...uh, doing something?"

He laughed. "I told my superiors everything and they called Customs and Border Protection. It's their job to inspect, not mine. I did pass along your suggestion about changing the inspection team, and they liked the idea. It's a done deal. So now we wait."

"Is the plane on time?"

"It is."

"I'm getting nervous," she admitted.

"I can imagine. You don't want people laughing at you. Think of all the Snakes on a Plane jokes you'll be hearing."

"Oh shut up," she said, smiling, and gave him a little shoulder punch.

"You look great," he said unexpectedly. She had chosen a black, V-neck top and a string of pearls because she would be taping a report live for Channel 6, regardless of the outcome of the inspection. She was prepared to eat crow and admit she was wrong if necessary. The TV crew would show up soon.

"Thank you, sir."

"You could be an anchor, you know."

"I've had several offers and turned them all down."

"Why? Isn't the money good?"

"The money's great, but the job is boring. Reading to the great unwashed what other people have written. No thank you. I am a writer, first and foremost."

They noticed a security guard escorting Dalton and Phil their way and waved them over to their table. As they sat down, Richards answered his cell. "Thanks. The Eagle has landed. Let's do it."

Diana later recalled that the entire incident came down like a good dream—very surreal, like she had scripted it in her mind. They had replaced the inspection crews on the floor and it took less than ten minutes for one of the new workers to shout, "Stop the line!" A still-frame on one of the monitors revealed that something was blocking the x-rays of several boxes. All of those boxes were pulled and inspected. Bingo! She thought. The live broadcast would begin in less than ten minutes.

"Where's the director?" she asked the cameraman.

"She called in sick."

"Bitch. Well, then I'll direct it. Have we got live video back to the studio?"

"Yep."

"Good. Carl, right? Better get me wired up. Don't touch my breasts. I need to talk to the studio director. You get a slow pan of the facility and a still shot of that monitor there. Quit blushing, Carl—I was just kidding."

Carl was shaking his head and trying not to laugh, but he got the mike pinned to the top of her blouse and she ran the wire inside the blouse down to her waist at her back, where Carl plugged it into the transmitter he had hooked on the belt of her slacks.

The live shot started with the pan of the facility and Diana's voiceover. "I'm live from the huge Flower Clearance Center here at Miami International, where we've just had a real incident of snakes on a plane. 20 of them, in fact."

Cut to Diana standing with a man in a suit and tie. "With me this morning is Inspector Arturo Sandoval of Customs and Border Protection. What happened here today, Inspector?"

Tight shot on the man's head and shoulders. "Well, Diana, based on a tip from a knowledgeable person—and that would be you—we isolated a certain shipment of roses coming in from Bogota, Colombia. Under x-ray, 20 of the flower boxes showed sections of opaqueness on the monitors." Cut to a static shot of a monitor showing an x-ray of a box. "Meaning they were partially covered with lead foil. We isolated those boxes and opened them carefully, like this."

He opened a box and revealed bunches of roses then removed the roses to find a section of cardboard, which he took out. He pointed to the foil on the side of the box and then to the three objects that the roses were hiding. "You can see the foil here, and that's what tipped us off. At the bottom of the box were three things: a two-foot yellow anaconda, a hand warmer, and a kilo of cocaine. Presumably, the hand warmer was used to keep the snakes warmer than the roses, which are chilled to 34 degrees for shipping."

Tilt up to the two of them standing. "Who was the shipment going to?"

"That is under investigation right now—we have to use a barcode reader—but when we know, you'll know."

Pan and zoom to Diana, full face. "Thank you Inspector Sandoval. Channel 6 will have an update on News at Noon, and be sure to read my story on this reptile and drug smuggling ring on the front page of this Sunday's *Miami Herald*. This is Diana Ventura, reporting live from the Flower Clearance Center at Miami International for the Channel 6 News Team on the Scene."

She recorded another close for Channel 12 in Tampa and then moved in the direction of the commissary to rejoin Dalton, Phil, and Richards. They gave her a round of applause as she approached their table. She stopped, gave them a slight bow, sat down, and said, "You know, adrenaline is the best upper there is. I'm totally wired."

"I love the way you started the report with the Snakes on a Plane reference," Richards said.

"Thanks for putting it in my mind. When will we know who the consignee is?"

"Ten to one it's a floral distributor," Dalton interrupted, and Richards nodded in agreement. "That puts one more level of confusion into the mix."

"Go on," urged Diana.

"If the consignee is a distributor, they may want to protect their customers, further delaying their identification. Or, the company making the original order for the flowers could be doing it cash-in-advance under a false name."

"Whoever the consignee is, it most certainly will not be under the name of World of Reptiles," Richards added.

"You guys are spoilsports," Diana said, "and you're not thinking in the right direction. Why don't you put some pressure on the reptile dealers who ordered the anacondas?"

"How would we know who they are?" Phil asked.

"They were on World of Reptiles intranet, under 'Special Orders.' It was coded, but I know all the codes. Eight people ordered the 20 anacondas. I'll email you their contact information. Anyone up for an early three-martini lunch?"

"I'd be honored to take you to lunch," Richards said, "but it's not even 8:00 in the morning."

"Oh, I'm sure we can find something interesting to do until then. Memorize some files or something." She had a fetching smirk on her face.

In the nude, Dalton thought.

But Richards looked at his watch again and said, in a semi-official voice, "I've got some things to take care of. Meet me at noon at La Boca, okay?"

"Yessir, you bet." Diana winked at him.

Diana the Hunter, on the prowl, Dalton thought.

• • •

"Holy fuck," Ray Jacobs said aloud after watching Diana's report from the airport. Staring at the monitor in his office in the shipping department of World of Reptiles, he had figured out exactly what had sabotaged his year and a half of undercover work for the Fish and Wildlife Service: his own stupidity.

Diana had been undercover at Save Our Snakes while he was doing the same thing at World of Reptiles. She stole his flash drive, replaced it with a blank, somehow broke the encryption, took over his entire case, and was probably going to expose him. All for one lousy fuck. Actually not so lousy, he thought. In retrospect, it was pretty damned spectacular. But still not worth it.

He reviewed his options. He could run and then call his boss, Harry Nichols, and tell him everything that came down, including the cash deposited into his checking account. But he was fairly certain that Zimmerman had video of the two of them discussing all kinds of illegal things, murder included. He felt a surge of panic. Where should he go? Calm down, he told himself. Time for lunch.

As normal, he entered the time he would return on the employee board. "See you after lunch," he said to the receptionist, got on his BMW cycle, and drove to the only branch of SunTrust Bank on 8th Street, where he withdrew all but $100 from his account. He bought a small sub sandwich and hit the road to Atlanta, Georgia, 662 miles due north. Nine fornicating hours, including piss stops. Gotta love adrenaline and caffeine, he thought when he checked into the appropriately-named Sleep Inn near the airport on Sullivan Road with a government credit card that could not be traced. On the way up there, he had pondered, among other things, finding a new career and finding a better place to hide out. He wondered if Zimmerman's elaborate World of Reptiles' scams were over. He thought about Diana, and what she might be up to. And finally, he wondered, was it possible for him to totally disappear?

"I'm in deep shit," he texted Harry Nichols at F and W, "and my life is in danger. I'll be out of touch for a while." That was the last communication anyone ever received from Ray Lindsay, aka Ray Jacobs.

• • •

Talk about gone to ground, Mozell thought. It doesn't get much grounder than this. And that ground was underground. Namely, his family's bomb shelter on the abandoned chicken farm just outside of Dundee, Florida. His grandfather, Sterling Mozell, built the original bomb shelter in the mid-1950s.

Bone's father, Jasper Mozell, expanded it into a small apartment with a kitchenette. Bone had further upgraded it, adding all of his favorite high tech trappings, like a surveillance system for the farm, a secure Internet connection, and satellite TV service. The best part about the bomb shelter was that no one knew of its existence. The next best thing about it was that it was almost impossible to locate without ground-penetrating radar. Its entrance was a concealed trap door in the basement of the original farm house, now a ramshackle shadow of its former elegance. A family trust still owned the property, but since Bone was the last remaining family member, the farm was essentially his. He had watched it disintegrate as the old chicken cages turned from rust to dust.

But the old farm had come in handy, especially the old chicken shit dump of partially composted feces from decades past. The dump brought back Bone's less-than-happy memories of carrying millions of buckets from the barns to the large hollow surrounded with extremely healthy post oaks. It was the perfect place to bury Cutup's body.

Mozell had altered his appearance as much as he could and now sported a shaved head, a mustache and beard, horn-rimmed glasses, and a Stetson Stallion Bullock black straw hat. Instead of a pickup, his vehicle of choice was now a beat-up blue 1999 Chevy Cavalier registered to his late brother, Lyle Mozell, with current registration and tags thanks to Bone's foresight.

As he sipped on a bourbon and branch one night in late February while listening to his Merle Haggard drinking mix that included "The Bottle Let Me Down," "Misery and Gin," and "I Don't Want to Sober Up Tonight," Bone considered his fate and his future. First, the bad news. Zimmerman had been trying to reach him, and his texts and emails were more threatening each time. Mozell himself was going stir-crazy and was very horny. There were open arrest warrants out and the police were looking for him. But other than those minor inconveniences, life was good.

Bone believed in the philosophy of positive thinking, so he mentally listed the good news. He had ordered the execution of Big Ink, and that was easily done with one phone call to Mort.

"I think he's on his yacht somewhere," Mozell had told Mort. "It's called Queen Anne's Revenge II."

"I'll find him. I've got one other job first. Wire the money."

Mozell had plenty of money in a Bank of Caymans account, which was further good news, as was the new passport from a contact of Mort's. Its only drawback was the pussy name on it, Durwood Wilkins. But it would get him into Canada untraced.

• • •

"Yes, that's what I said, Mort. Big Ink. It's his legal name." Zimmerman was, of course, using his Blackphone.

"But I already have a contract to off that guy."

"What?"

"Bone Mozell hired me."

"What if I take over Mozell's contract and you hit him, too?"

"Can't do that, Bruno. I took his money, so he's a customer. I don't off my customers—unless, of course, they don't pay me. And Bone has."

"What the fuck, a hit man with ethics?"

"Just sound business practices. Look at it this way, Bruno: you get your wish and you don't have to pay for it."

After a slight pause, Zimmerman said, "Good point."

"So gimme a call if you think of anyone else you want terminated. I've gotta get back to work."

"There will be more, I promise you that."

"Good to hear. I got some markers comin' due."

Zimmerman was tempted to give Mort Diana Ventura's name, or even the faggot Freddie Venus, who likely told her about the shipment, but he couldn't just go around killing people who were closely linked to World of Reptiles. That might look a tad suspicious, unless Mort could arrange an accident like he had for Dalton's wife and kid. And what kind of an accident would be perfect for a cunt like Diana? A heart attack during a Zumba class? One of her spike heels breaks off and she falls in front of a bus? Something electric falls into her bath?

His musings about Diana's accidental demise were interrupted by the ringtone of his Blackphone, "Crazy Train," by Ozzy. It was Anson Zhou, calling from Johor Bahru in Malaysia.

After some informal chit-chat, Zhou got serious. "Do we have enough insulation, Bruno?"

"Absolutely. Everything stops at Floriculture Specialties. No connection to us at all."

"Tell me about the leak that caused the shipment seizure."

"We were infiltrated by two experts," Zimmerman told him, "one at SOS, Diana Ventura, and the other was at the store, Ray Jacobs. My fucking employee of the year. Ventura tracked down Freddie Venus, who told her when the shipment was coming in. I think Jacobs is a US Fish and Wildlife agent. He knows as much about reptiles as I do, maybe more."

"And where are these two people right now?"

"Ventura is right here in Miami, apparently working on a story for the Herald that's going to be published Sunday. She's on Channel 6 as well."

"Can you make her disappear?"

"I don't advise doing that. She's already closely linked to me because of SOS. And she's probably already turned in the story, so what good would it do to off her?"

"What about Jacobs?"

"He didn't come back to the store after lunch a few days ago. Right now—" He paused to check the GPS monitor. "He's still at the Sleep Inn near the airport in Atlanta. Or at least his motorcycle is."

"Here's what I want you to do," Zhou began, bringing a smile to Zimmerman's face.

Five minutes later he had Mort on the phone again. "I thought of someone.And I'll double your fee it you take care of my project before Mozell's. It has to be finished by Sunday."

• • •

Tracking down the ultimate recipient of the anacondas turned out to be impossible, and Diana was frustrated. She wanted a direct link to World of Reptiles, but she wasn't going to get it though the bust at the Flower Clearance Center. Richards had told her that the initial consignee, was, indeed a flower distributor, Super-Fresh Floral Distributors. Part of the Tru-Blu® shipment was going to Tropical Ornamentals in South Beach, and the other part was going to be held for pickup by an outfit called Floriculture Specialties.

"I gave the owner of Super-Fresh what I call a hard interview," Richards told her, "but I couldn't shake him from his story. It had happened three times previously, he said. A shipment would arrive, was cleared through Customs and transferred to Super-Fresh's chilled warehouse. Then a phone call would come in from Floriculture Specialties asking if the prepaid shipment was ready for pick-up. A truck with the Floriculture Specialties logo on the door would arrive, pick up the shipment, and drive away. There the trail ended.

"I think Floriculture Specialties is a truck with a logo. Period."

"With 20-20 hindsight, I can see that we fucked up. We should have removed all the snakes and most of the cocaine and let the shipment go through for pick-up. Then we could have followed the truck to its destination."

"Well, we couldn't really do that once Customs was in the mix. They have procedures to follow. It would have taken high-level coordination with the FBI for Customs to allow any contraband into the country, and we couldn't have that until we knew what was in those rose boxes. See?"

Diana nodded. "A Catch-22."

"Want to have a little fun?"

"Night on the town? Dinner and dancing?"

"Not quite," he told her.

Richards' idea of a little fun was to place Diana in an observation room at the FBI offices on 2nd Avenue in Miami Beach where she could observe live video of his interrogation of one Ralph Hickson, a snake enthusiast who had ordered one of the yellow anacondas from World of Reptiles. Using the evidence of the seizure at the Flower Clearance Center, Richards had persuaded a federal judge to issue a search warrant for the World of Reptiles intranet and Zimmerman's hard drive, which had allowed his interrogation of Hickson. With his attorney present, of course.

Watching on the monitor, Diana did not hear the name of the attorney, but the woman was very aggressive, trying to control the procedure at the beginning by saying that anyone could have put Hickson on the list without his knowledge.

Richards turned to her. "Shut the fuck up."

"What?"

"You heard me."

"But—"

Then her own client looked at her and said, "You heard the agent, now shut up. I want to hear what he has to say." Hickson was middle-aged with thinning hair, a body people would describe as chunky, and a very round face. He did not seem to be nervous or frightened one bit.

"I arrest you for conspiracy to smuggle snakes and cocaine into this country. Beside your attorney's fees, you will have to come up with ten percent of the bail money, in cash and up front for the bondsman. Or you will stay behind bars until the trial."

"Or?" Hickson asked.

"What do you mean?"

"Cut to the chase, offer me a deal."

Richards knew that although Hickson didn't have a record, he had been through this before.

"Or," Richards said, "you tell us everything we need to nail Zimmerman, agree to testify against him, and we give you immunity from prosecution."

Hickson stuck out his hand. "Deal." Richards shook it. "I never liked that Zimmerman asshole anyway."

It was that easy. Diana grinned. She had her direct link to World of Reptiles. An eyewitness. Perfect.

• • •

"World of Reptiles' Owner Linked to Anaconda-Cocaine Plot," screamed the stacked front-page headline in the Sunday *Miami Herald*. Dalton stared at the newspaper on the kitchen table with some trepidation. He poured a cup of coffee and sat down. "By Diana Ventura, Special to the Herald," he read, "The Python Report, Part 1 of 3." Then, the disclaimer and editor's note, that an "allegiance" of two newspapers and two televisions stations had sent Diana undercover as the face of Save Our Snakes to get her inside the Zimmerman kingdom. Working with the FBI and federal and state wildlife agencies, Diana had broken the case wide open. The editors wrote that they had contacted Bruno Zimmerman and offered him first read of the story, but he never responded.

Diana's lead sentence was a grabber. "The seizure of the recent shipment of snakes and cocaine being smuggled together at Miami International Airport recalls a similar incident from more than twenty years ago that may explain why there are thousands of feral pythons roaming south Florida today."

She flashed back to late August, 1992, with a story she had pieced together from Zimmerman's emails, eyewitness accounts, and police reports. A shipment of 200 young Burmese pythons packed into cardboard boxes with air holes was part of a cocaine shipment coming into south Florida from Colombia on a large yacht. The shipment was to be delivered to Lorenzo Zimmerman, a convicted marijuana smuggler who had just been released from prison. The yacht was headed for a rendezvous with Zimmerman at the Loggerhead Marina in Lantana, but it was driven off course by strong winds from approaching Hurricane Andrew. The yacht was forced to seek shelter at the Flamingo Marina at the Everglades National Park's Visitor Center, which had been evacuated.

Lorenzo Zimmerman, along with his wife and an accomplice, foolishly decided to pick up the shipment despite the coming hurricane. Zimmerman drove the pythons and cocaine north up the Main Park Road unril the full force of Hurricane Andrew's 170-mile-an-hour winds flipped his vehicle. The wreck killed all three passengers and threw the boxes of snakes all over the road. Park rangers found the wreck two days later, and one of them noted that the intense rain had softened the boxes and whatever was inside had escaped into the Everglades. Most of the cocaine was recovered and seized by the DEA.

Lorenzo, of course, was Bruno's father, and Diana neatly brought the story back to the present with some teaser quotes about what was coming in forthcoming articles. Dalton looked up from the paper and saw Laura pouring a cup of coffee.

"Well, what do you think?" she asked.

"Diana did a great job. I would imagine Zimmerman's furious. This could push him out of business. Eyewitnesses to the conspiracy could bring him down. And she actually figured out how the pythons got here in the first place."

"Any word from Richards?"

"Well, technically, he is an advisor. So he'll have to persuade the Customs brass to take the smuggling plot to the grand jury. Zimmerman better find a good lawyer."

"I'll have to read it." Laura was dressed in white shorts and a clinging, green sleeveless top. "We've both got the day off for a change," she said. "Any ideas for fun?"

"Do you like the Key Largo area?"

"For what purpose?"

"Living. Let's take a run down there. I want to show you some things where I grew up."

"What kind of things?"

"Well, houses for one."

"Why would we go house hunting in such an expensive area?"

"Because of my birthday."

"Weirding out about the big five-o?"

"On the contrary, I'm looking forward to it." He grinned at her. "I'm coming into a little inheritance from my father. I'll tell you all about it on the drive down."

Laura came up to him, hugged him, and kissed him hard on the lips. Then she pulled back and looked at him. "How little?"

"Millions, but how many of them depends on the stock market."

"Why the hell didn't you tell me before?"

"If I had, would you have left me?"

"Hell no. It was never about you, it was that stupid bungalow."

"We'll take the profit from the sale of it and buy a boat."

"Maybe a rowboat." She smiled at him.

"You might be surprised. Let's go house hunting."

• • •

The next morning at 7:30 a.m., when Justin O'Brien, the RAC—Resident Agent in Charge—of the Miami office of the U. S. Fish and Wildlife Service, went down the steps to his lap pool for his morning 30-minute swim, he couldn't help but notice a clothed man floating in the middle of it. O'Brien was nude, but carrying a towel and his cell phone. "Police or FBI?" he asked himself. On a hunch, he called Brad Richards.

"Got a floater in my lap pool. Could be Ray Lindsay."

"Give me a half-hour," Richards said. "Better call Nichols."

Bad news, Nichols thought when O'Brien told him about the body. Nichols had been the director running Lindsay at World of Reptiles, and the undercover agent had gone missing days ago, much to the aggravation of the top brass in the region. Nichols was feeling the heat, and if the body in the pool was Lindsay's, he knew exactly what he had to do.

"Text me when you know," he told O'Brien.

But it would have been a very long and difficult text, for what happened next was just a bit gruesome. So O'Brien choked back his nausea and called Nichols.

"It's Lindsay, all right," O'Brien, now in bathing suit and robe, said to him. "Only with some of his parts, uh, altered."

"Like how?"

"Well, the word 'Mort' was carved into his forehead. That means dead in French. The symbolism in the butchering leads us to theorize that Lindsay was suspected of being a spy."

"Ya think?" yelled Nichols. "O'Brien, you're a friggin' idiot." He disconnected and then told his assistant to file the retirement papers he had filled out the same day he had given Lindsay his assignment to infiltrate World of Reptiles.

• • •

Bruno Zimmerman had to calm down, think clearly and take positive action, but his rage had overwhelmed him. He wanted to strike out, exact more revenge on his tormenters. With Ray Jacobs dead he could focus on Diana, the fucking cunt. How was it possible that she had fooled him? He knew that part of it was his own ego and arrogance, but it was also her natural acting talent and her sexual appeal that seemed to inflame all men. How dare she bring his father into this?

No matter the risk, he had to stop her, shut her up for good. He had tried reaching out for Mort, but so far there was no response. "I'm on the job, leave a message," was the recording on his voice mail. Texts and emails went unanswered, which was unlike the guy. He had left messages telling him that Diana Ventura needed the Ray Jacobs treatment, but Zimmerman hadn't heard anything back. No word about Big Ink. Nothing from Bone either. Zimmerman was isolated, totally on his own. "Where's a goddamned hit man when you need him?" he asked himself.

And then there was the convening of the fucking federal grand jury that Richards had engineered because some stupid, chicken-shit customers of his had cut deals for immunity. Zimmerman briefly considered having them all killed, but that was stupid. Mort would demand overtime. He poured another glass of Appleton Estate 30-year-old rum, lit up both a Monte Cristo Number 4 and a spliff of Super Lemon Haze, and thought.

There were people out there who not only owed him plenty of money and favors, but also were scared to death of him. One in particular was a venomous snake aficionado with a gambling addiction named Jules Dangelo. Jules owed him about

$17,000 and it was time for a payback. Zimmerman dialed his number and it was answered on the first ring.

"Bruno, what's up?"

"You know that little debt that we talked about?"

"I'm taking care of it, I promise."

"Not to worry, Julie. You still got those Ems?"

"I do."

"Here's what I want you to do with them. If you do it, the debt is cancelled."

Jules listened to what Bruno wanted, then said, "Consider it done."

"Good man," Zimmerman said, severing the connection.

He tried calling Mort one more time to tell him that he was having someone else take care of Diana Ventura, but Mort couldn't answer his cell phone because he had bitten off a little more than he could chew.

13

In May, 1897, a python nine feet in length was found in the King's Palace. I was told it had swallowed a pet cat and then had become too fat to get away through the hole through which it had entered. On opening the snake I found a full-grown Siamese cat with a bell hung round its neck.
—S. S. Flower, "Notes on a Second Collection of Reptiles Made in the Malay Peninsula and Siam," 1899.

Mort had been watching the two of them for a day and a half. He was pretty sure the man was Big Ink, but he didn't really match Bone's description of him. The guy was big, sure, but not really fat and he didn't have any facial or hand tattoos. So he had taken a photo of him through the telephoto lens, transferred it to his laptop and compared the facial photo with the one Bone had sent to him. Same guy, no doubt about it. But who was the broad? Bone hadn't said anything about a woman.

He thought about what weapon to use. He did not have a silenced pistol because his specialty—with a couple of notable exceptions—was to make his killings look like accidents. What he preferred in this case was to knock the guy out and have him fall into the water of the marina and drown. But he was never alone—the woman was always with him. Kill them both? Not an option because he wasn't getting paid to off them both. He had standards, and one of them was no free homicides, god-damn it!

His best bet was the 15-inch Fusion Tactical Tomahawk. It wasn't designed for combat use, but if it could split a log, it could chop a human head in half. Mort remembered the day it had done just that, as he had photographed it afterward and showed his art to the client who had requested the technique. "This is no way to get ahead in the world," he had said. She had given him a one-grand bonus, and after thanking her, he said to the tough-looking bottle blonde of 50 who had hired him, "Excuse me ma'am, but if you don't mind, what did he do to you that was so bad it got him killed?"

"Oh, he started smoking again, and I'm on a health kick." Mort vowed to never ask that question again.

The choice of weapon solved, Mort looked for the right place to commit the murder, and the choices weren't good at all. The marina was brightly lit, and the streets nearby were jammed with boaters, tourists, vagrants, college kids, and se-curity cameras. He gave serious consideration to cancelling the hit and refunding Bone's money, but he had promised Emma Sue he would replace the pool enclosure that had collapsed when six large pythons used it as a sunning station. It was very difficult getting them out of the pool. He needed the money. And a drink. So he'd kill the guy tomorrow. What difference did it make?

• • •

Bill—the former Big Ink—and Jamie were celebrating their two-week anniversary of couplehood, as Jamie called it. They were dining at The Wreck at the Sheraton Fort Lauder-dale again, in honor of their first date, and Bill thought it had been the most wonderful two weeks of his life. He wondered, am I really becoming a normal person? They were living together on the yacht, to save Jamie money, and sleeping in the same bed. For the first time in a month he was having a beer to celebrate, a Bass Buster Brown Ale.

Jamie drove them back to the marina and parked the Honda in the lot. But when they got out, things got so confusing that Bill later had to write it out slowly to make in gel in his mind.

Jamie punched the code into the gate lock on the dock and pushed it open for me because I was carrying the leftover boxes. I saw a guy to my right, hunched over, sitting on the dock fishing, which was not allowed. I paused to say something to him. Jamie shut the gate with a loud clang, and as if that was the bell to start the fight, the man, wearing a ski mask, came at me waving some sort of long hatchet with a rope tied to it. I threw the leftovers at him but he just swatted them away. He got close and took a swing, but he had telegraphed it and my football instincts took over. After the hatchet went by, I tackled him and drove him back into the fish gutting sink, which caught him in the middle of his back and he yelled in pain and slumped to the dock. I grabbed the hatchet out of his hand and moved back, only to see him pulling a pistol out of his jacket pocket. My new instincts took over. As he was getting up, I gave him a right side kick to his neck and he slumped over without a word.

Mort, as they say in France, was mort. "Oh my god," Jamie screamed, "You killed him!"

"Tae Kwon Do," Bill said, amazed. "Check him out."

Jamie bent down and reached for his neck to feel for a pulse that wasn't there and then jumped up and started hyperventilating.

Bill hugged her. "It's okay, honey, it's over."

Jamie shook her head from side to side, broke free from Bill and pulled her cell phone out of her back pocket.

"What are you doing?" he asked quickly.

"Calling 911."

"No! Jamie, listen to me."

Jamie hesitated and Bill said in a low voice, "No one saw this. We can't have the police here. This guy was sent to kill me. I've endangered your life. Now we need a new plan."

"An assassin? What the hell's going on?"

"Help me get this body off the dock and I'll tell you."

He grabbed the guy under his arms and Jamie grabbed his ankles. "Wow, he just passed out and fell down," Jamie said loudly in case anyone was watching them carry the body. "He was doing shots straight out of the bottle!"

"Let's get him back to the yacht so he can sober up," Bill chimed in, playing his role.

Inside, Bill held the body upright while Jamie spread out some 30-gallon yard and leaf bags on the carpet of the small cabin. "In case of post-mortem seepage from the eyeballs or anus," she told him nervously. Bill eased the corpse onto the bags and Jamie covered it with a white sheet with blue anchors.

"What are we going to do with the body?"

"Gulf Stream," Bill replied. "I have two spare boat anchors aboard."

A half-hour later Jamie had calmed down enough to discuss the next steps.

"Ever been to Nassau?" he asked her.

"Nope."

"We'll stay at the Atlantis Resort. But first, let's do what I should have done months ago—sweep the boat."

"I'll get the broom."

"Not that kind of sweep, Jamie. I know a TSCM guy I can call. That's Technical Surveillance Counter Measures. If anyone can find bugs and GPS locators, he can. We used him at the fish meal plant."

"For what? Bill, I think it's time you told me everything."

"I'll tell you later. Before the sweep, why don't we leave at first light and feed the body to the Gulf Stream. It's only 12 or 15 miles out there."

"I'll make a picnic brunch," Jamie said, occasionally glancing at the large lump lying in the cabin.

• • •

What later became a story even bigger than World of Reptiles started as a small story in the New Times Broward-Palm Beach by a naturalist named Carole Wilson, who wrote the semi-weekly environmental issues column for the paper, "'Glades Diary." It was originally called "'Glades Monitor," but then those damned lizards showed up and the editor changed the name. Wilson's story concerned a highly usual event: Nine dead pythons were found against the north levee that Alligator Alley was built on, near the Broward County Rest Area. State workers were taking the snakes' bodies—one 12 feet long—to the Florida State Wildlife Laboratory in Tampa for necropsies and specialized pathologic analysis.

"It's too early to say anything definite, but dead pythons are always good news in south Florida," Wilson concluded.

Maybe this is the beginning, Phil thought. He called his contact at the laboratory in Tampa.

"Hey Phil, what's up?" Dr. Nestor Lowery asked. He was the assistant director of the lab and he and Phil went back 15 years.

"Those dead pythons?"

"We tested them. They died of a virus that causes inclusion body disease. It is highly transmissible. Strikes only boas and pythons. Very odd to find it in South Florida. Caged pythons get it because of the mites, wild ones don't because those particular mites don't occur naturally in the 'Glades."

"What's your theory?"

"I think a diseased captive snake or two escaped and infected some wild pythons. How about you?"

"You're the doctor, Nes, and I like your theory. Let's stick with it."

"Well, I already gave the reporter that theory. Wilson?"

"Yeah, that's her name. I read her column but don't know her," Phil said. "Thanks, Nes."

"You bet."

Phil was highly relieved. The seed was planted that would cover up the activities of the Drone Squad. He couldn't wait to tell Dalton.

• • •

The call came late in the afternoon from the SAC—Special Agent in Charge, Miami. Her name was Martha Fowler and she had good news for Brad Richards.

"We got a double whammy warrant thanks to the grand jury," she told him, "arrest and search. Two searches, actually, home and store. Since you helped uncover this mess, you get the job of serving all the warrants."

"Gee, thanks. When will the paperwork be ready?"

"It's here. Come pick it up, assemble your team, and go."

"Got it, Martha." This is getting interesting, he thought as he drove to the Miami Beach office.

An hour later he pulled up in front of the gate to Zimmerman's complex on Hibiscus Island. He had two other agents with him but neither one was a locksmith. The gate was sealed up tight, and it took another 45 minutes to get a locksmith from Keyed Up Locksmith Services to the island. Opening the gate took six minutes, and Zimmermann's front door five more, and they were in. Complete silence greeted them as they entered. They split up to search the mansion and grounds.

As Richards later told Martha Fowler, they searched for an hour and a half and found nothing. Not only was no one around, they could not find an office for Zimmerman or much evidence that he lived in the place. It was like a model home in a development, or a mansion up for sale. There was nothing personal. Refrigerator and cupboards were bare. There was furniture all right, and art on the walls, but no magazines on coffee tables, nothing in the trash cans. Sanitized, thought Richards, cleaned and polished.

So they started interviewing the immediate neighbors, two of whom had witnessed Zimmerman leaving. The previous night, a medium-sized yacht had pulled up to Zimmerman's dock—an unusual occurrence that had grabbed their attention. The flood lights were on at the complex and the neighbors swore that Zimmerman had walked out the back door and boarded the yacht. No, they had not seen the name of the yacht. The yacht left, the lights went out, and that was it. Another suspect on the run.

• • •

"Zimmerman Indicted; World of Reptiles Closes, Forfeiture Likely," read the headline for the next installment of "The Python Report." Bone had picked up a copy of the Sunday Herald at the Pic 'n' Pay in Winter Haven during his weekly venture out of the bomb shelter for food and supplies. His plan was just to lie low (har, har) and wait it out until everything, as they say, blew over, which was an apt expression in Florida. He tried to look as nondescript as possible and so far no one had given him a second glance, much less recognized him. Of course, he couldn't stay underground forever. In a month or so, he would start driving north until he reached Detroit. Then he would take the Detroit-Windsor Tunnel, enter the country using his Canadian passport, and disappear forever.

He unloaded the beer and groceries near the bomb shelter entrance, drove the Cavalier to an old barn about a mile away, and walked back to his underground apartment. He popped a Jai Alai IPA from Cigar City Brewing and read the article in the Herald. He was amazed at how fast Zimmerman's world was collapsing. He knew what the guy was capable of and was surprised that no one had been killed—yet. Witnesses had seen Zimmerman leaving the compound in a yacht, but Bone was skeptical. It was probably some sort of feint. Bone didn't have to worry about Zimmerman coming after him—the man had enough to worry about. Like the forfeiture of his greatest money-generating operation. Bone knew all about that—the state of Florida now owned his ruined warehouse and the land it was on.

He put the paper down and dialed Mort's number. Voicemail, for the tenth time. What the hell was going on? What should he do now? Watch porn? Read the rest of the paper? Bone was stir-crazy, fucking bored out of his mind.

• • •

Dalton liked the fact that Diana was forthright in detailing her undercover role at Save Our Snakes, which had shut its doors for good after Zimmerman's indictment. "Let's tell it like it was, a huge public relations con designed to sell snakes," she had written. "I was playing the role of media spokesperson so I could spy on World of Reptiles and obtain information. In fact, I despise snakes and am scared to death of them."

Diana then explained how forfeiture worked. Criminal forfeiture was the loss of rights to property used in the commission of a crime, but only after the criminal defendant was convicted. In the case of World of Reptiles, the federal government was using civil forfeiture, and that does not require the defendant to be proven guilty, just to be obviously associated with the crime.

"The fact that witnesses were on the World of Reptiles books as purchasers of illegally imported snakes, complete with down payments, will be presented in federal court before a judge as prima facie evidence that World of Reptiles was part of the conspiracy and therefore can be seized," she had written, and she was right. Dalton knew that civil forfeiture was often abused because law enforcement agencies were allowed to keep 90 percent of the profits of all assets sold during seizures, thus helping enormously with their budgets. But Diana didn't get into that aspect. She was just delighted that soon, Customs and Border Enforcement would be the new owner of World of Reptiles.

Dalton was giving Diana an imaginary high five for her clever article when he noticed an email from his principal researcher, Toni Murphy. Attached was the background report on Martin "Bone" Mozell. Under "Properties Owned," Dalton noticed that Bone had inherited his parents' seventeen-acre chicken farm in Dundee 20 years ago. It was abandoned, but all the property taxes were up to date, and Toni had discovered that the electricity was still on and the account was current.

Odd, thought Dalton. Why? A couple of lights? Security system? He wrote a quick email to Toni. "Please check with FP and L about current electrical usage on that abandoned chicken farm in Dundee."

Then he left the office. He had a meeting with Phil about the python deaths and how to play them. First, everyone involved had to re-zip their lips.

• • •

Mortimer "Mort" Cooley, naked as the day he was born but not as alive, was getting wired by Bill and Jamie. "Not the neck," advised Jamie, "because it's broken, the head will be the first thing to pop off and the wires may come loose."

Bill couldn't really see what difference that would make with the body a half mile down and anchored. But now somewhat wise to the ways of women, he just nodded and focused on Mort's ankles. He wrapped them securely with 12-gauge steel galvanized wire and then ran the wire up to the back of his shoulders. After wrapping the shoulders, Jamie helped Bill lift the body over the starboard gunwale, head over the side. Bill then wired the two spare anchors to the bound ankles and placed them on Mort's back.

He hummed "Taps" while Jamie did the honors and pushed the body off the gunwale and into the Gulf Stream. It disappeared immediately. Bill piloted the boat into calmer water and Jamie set the table for brunch.

"This is some kind of quality time we're spending together," he said with a chuckle.

"Can I ask you a personal question?" She looked serious as she put the shrimp quiche in the microwave.

"Sure, anything."

"Are you some kind of criminal?"

"Former criminal," he corrected her, knowing right then that he had to tell her everything.

• • •

"So you were completely wrong about that the insulation I asked you about," Anson Zhou said, calling from his penthouse condo on the seventieth floor of the Astaka Serviced Apartment Tower A in the City Centre of Johor Bahru.

"I was indeed," Zimmerman admitted.

"My people and I are very unhappy with you," Zhou said ominously. "Where are you now?"

"Hiding in plain sight. Look, we were running a criminal enterprise that went south. It happens."

"So we should just forget everything? Ignore our investment in you? Forgive you for your own stupidity?"

"You made a shitpot full of money with me."

"We dispute that, Mr. Zimmerman," Zhou insisted. "I have the accounting right here. You still owe us RM 420,475. That's $219,000. Not all that much, now, is it? You can wire that to us today, correct?"

"And what are you going to do if I don't? Take out a contract on me?"

"Oh, we've already done that, Mr. Zimmerman. However, we will cancel it if the transfer arrives."

"With all due respect, Mr. Zhou, fuck you." Zimmerman disconnected and blocked all incoming calls to his Blackphone.

14

The whole of his wife's arm had been drawn into the monster's
throat and the upper part of her body was slowly but
surely following. Not daring to attack the monster at once
for fear of causing his wife's death, the husband, with
great presence of mind, seized two bags within reach, and
commenced stuffing them into the corner of the snake's jaw,
by means of which he succeeded in forcing them wide open
and releasing his wife's arm.

—C. Gould, *Mythical Monsters, Fact or Fiction?* 1884

The reason that Diana frantically called Dalton at 3:00 in
the morning was the fact that there were three large snakes
slowly slithering around the carpet in her bedroom. She was
perched and shaking in the center of the bed with a quart of
water in a plastic bottle between her thighs and a Smith and
Wesson J-Frame snub nose .38 in her right hand, which was
also shaking. And she had to pee like a racehorse.

"I've got snakes in my bedroom, Dalton," she half-gasped
and whispered. "I had to learn a lot about snakes to get that
stupid job, and I know for a fact that these are African black
mambas. Vicious, Dalton. You gotta help me. You know, who
you gonna call? Mambabusters?"

Dalton turned military. "In order to help you, Diana, I
need to know where you are." He kept his voice low, and beside
him, Laura slept on, oblivious.

"I'm at your house, of course," she snapped. "The shitty little bungalow in Homestead."

"What the fuck?" Hit me with a snake stick, he thought.

"Laura said I could use it! She gave me the keys! Didn't she tell you?"

"No—"

"Hey, Dalton, there's mambas all around me. I. Need. Help."

"I'll call my crew—40 minutes at the most. Don't move even if they crawl on top of you."

"Easy for you to say," she started, but the line was dead.

• • •

"Prominent Local Exterminator Reported Missing" was the small headline in the local news section in the Del Ray Beach tabloid, The Pineapple. Missing was the legendary "Roach Ranger," Mortimer Cooley, "Mort" to his friends. His wife, Emma Sue, told police that her husband had driven to Fort Lauderdale because of some giant roach infestation at a marina. That was three days ago, and she hadn't heard from him since.

"I'm worried sick," she told The Pineapple. "I made pot roast, his favorite, but he never came back to eat it. I'm offering a $100 reward for information."

The reporter from The Pineapple had asked Mrs. Cooley, "which was giant, the roaches or the infestation?"

"I don't know. That's one of the great mysteries of his disappearance."

But since no one called the new widow to reveal that the body of her beloved Mort was resting on the seafloor 6.23 miles due east of Fort Lauderdale and was currently being savaged by crustaceans, the appropriately-valued reward was never collected.

• • •

Dalton called Phil and Lloyd Vann and gave them their assignments. Phil was the medic this time instead of Lloyd because he was a Certified Venomous Snakebite First Responder—called simply a Snakebite Medic because, face it, CVSFR was not a memorable acronym. Lloyd would be the spotter, armed with a powerful 1,000-lumen MF Pro Tango T6 LED tactical flashlight. And Dalton would be the killer with his 17-round Glock 19 loaded with 9mm Luger CCI snakeshot shells. It was like having a mini-shotgun in his holster.

They all met at the bungalow, dressed in their python-catching gear without the hoods. Dalton unlocked the front door and swung it open. Floyd's flashlight immediately spotted a mamba on the living room rug moving quickly away from the light. Dalton didn't hesitate and fired four quick rounds. The snake stopped moving.

"One down," Dalton said.

"Clear," Lloyd yelled after he had checked under all the furniture. They moved on.

When they got to the main bedroom, Diana had company in the bed, a coiled six-foot black mamba that hadn't detected the shots in the living room, and Dalton knew why. Since snakes had no eardrums, they felt vibrations from the ground through their jawbones, and the snake on the bed had been insulated. It was a good thing for Diana, who had not been able to hold her urine, and the smell of it was sharp in the bedroom. It had not fazed the mamba.

"Stick your fingers in your ears," he ordered. She started to say something and he yelled, "Do it, goddamn it!" She did. He moved closer to the snake, pointed the Glock at the mamba and pulled the trigger, turning its head into mamba mush. Diana screamed.

229

"Two down," Dalton called out.

When she recovered, Diana said, "Dalton, you're going to need a new mattress."

"Goddamn it!" Lloyd screamed from the bathroom, "I'm hit—I mean, bit."

Dalton found Lloyd pushing the bathroom door against the wall as hard as he could. "The son-of-a-bitch was behind the door. I thought he was in the tub."

"Stand back, Lloyd." The mamba pushed the door open, and Dalton blasted it with three quick shots.

"Three down and we stand down," yelled Dalton, and Phil rushed over to Lloyd, made him sit on the toilet seat, and removed his right boot and sock. Taking no chances, Dalton took Lloyd's flashlight, used his phone to call 911, and carefully examined the rest of the bungalow. It was blissfully mamba-free.

He went back to the bathroom where Phil had just finished the intramuscular injection of South African polyvalent antivenom, the third in the series that began with subcutaneous near the bite just below Lloyd's right knee and intravenous through the brachial artery in his right arm.

"We're in luck," Phil said. "The envenomation is either mild or moderate. Lloyd, open your mouth. No gum bleeding—yet" Phil knew that the black mamba's venom was classified as rapidly fatal. Lloyd would have died within 30 minutes if untreated. Fortunately, Phil had applied the antivenom within two minutes of the strike. Probably a new record, if anyone was keeping track.

"How do you feel?" Phil asked.

"Nah berry goo," he replied.

"The ambulance should be here any second," Dalton said.

Two minutes later, an ambulance pulled into the driveway, siren blaring at first, then silent. Lloyd was quickly loaded into it, and Phil was by his side, injecting yet another vial of antivenom as it pulled away, lights flashing and siren blaring again.

Dalton poured Diana a stiff scotch on the rocks, plus one for himself. "I feel bad that Lloyd got bitten."

"I'll find that asshole Zimmerman," he promised.

"And?"

"I think Lloyd's going to recover," Dalton told her, changing the subject. "Phil gave him a lot of units of antivenom and his signs were better when the ambulance got here."

"You're looking at the bright side, so I will too. At least I was sleeping in your bed. Hey, it's a start."

All Dalton could do was laugh at that one. "Well, soon you'll be sleeping on our sofa."

"Woo hoo," Diana said.

On his way back to Miami with Diana and her luggage, Dalton called Kevin Cooper down in Key Largo.

"If you're calling me this early," Kevin said after the third ring, "you must need some help."

"I do. I've got a damsel in distress."

"Who?"

"Diana Ventura."

"Oh, then you've got a hottie in distress."

"Tell me about it. Here's the situation. I just had to kill three black mambas that I think Zimmerman put it my house, where Diana was trying to lay low. Maybe she has a tracker on her car or something, but Laura was letting her use the bungalow. Anyway, I've got to get her off the radar. Don't you have a guest cottage? Nobody can track her down there."

"That could work. Is she going to drive down?"

"Could you drive up here and pick her up? I think that would be safer."

"Okay, I can do that."

"I owe you one, Kevin."

• • •

Bill had learned a lot more about Jamie over their two-plus-week romance than she knew about him. She was a jock from the get go. Field hockey, basketball, and swimming in high school, where she was a B student. She had a degree from the University of North Florida in medical laboratory science and was an EMT supervisor for the City of Jacksonville Emergency Preparedness Division. Never married, Jamie had once been engaged but had backed out because, she said, her fiancé was "a bit swishy at times."

On their 20-hour run to Nassau, she "ordered" him to tell her everything about himself, so he started with his education.

"You have a what degree?"

"Master of Science in chemical engineering from Florida State."

"That amazes me. When I first met you I thought you were a cracker."

"Honorary redneck," he corrected her. "But that was in my previous life. I've given up all that shit. I mailed my certificate back to Mavericks."

After he finished explaining his criminal career to Jamie, he thought he was done with his personal history, but oh no. Jamie had questions.

"Are there any warrants out for you?"

"I don't think so."

"Why not?"

"All the proof they have are photos of chemical equipment, which is not illegal."

"Do you have any meth?"

"Not on me or on the boat, no."

"Stashed?"

He hesitated just a second. Derrick was supposed to have put it in Hideaway Storage. "I don't know. I just sorta gave up keeping track of the illegal stuff."

"Well, what are you going to do in the future?"

"I guess I need a new career."

"Duh. What about money?

"What do you mean?"

"You know, cash. Are you broke?"

"No, I'm not broke. Why are asking me all these questions?"

She paused. "Because I care about you, Bill. We're a couple now, remember? I'm a little worried, seeing as I'm an accomplice in killing a guy and feeding him to the fishes."

"Okay, listen to me. There were no witnesses. It was self-defense even if there were. If we're ever questioned, the guy was a mugger. I hit him and he ran off. I checked the entire dock area, and believe it or not, no CCTV. I have nearly $1,000,000 in cash stashed in various places, this yacht is paid for and so is my house. I could retire, Jamie. So please, stop worrying."

"I'm okay, Bill, really. Thanks for explaining everything." She had brightened considerably and kissed him on the mouth. He kissed her back then held her at arms' length.

"Now, would you like to try the other bunk for a change?"

• • •

"Lloyd's fine, making a full recovery," Phil told Dalton on the phone. "The doctors are releasing him tomorrow. He resigned from our python team, which we probably won't need anymore, anyway."

"Please explain."

"All kinds of snakes are dying, Sam," Phil said, "Not just pythons. This will be a media frenzy. Let's get the four of us together. It's CYA time."

"Agreed," Dalton said, cover-your-ass time indeed. He called Kevin and Diana and discussed Kevin's "rescue" of her later that day. Diana was staying at Laura's condo, working on the third part of "The Python Report," and apparently the two of them were getting along, which Dalton thought was a bit strange.

The four conspirators met at the Impact Zone, a surfer brewpub and grill on 2nd Street in Miami Beach that was decorated with every surf cliché imaginable, including surfboard tables, most of the big wave posters ever published, and Endless Summer playing on the big screen behind the bar. Real surfers had issued an official SoBe boycott of the place, but it hadn't worked. Japanese tourists jammed the Zone.

The owner was a friend of Phil's who let him use a private room if the group was four or more and ordered drinks and lunch, which they did. Dalton had a Junkyard Dog, a grilled bratwurst topped with cheese, mustard, chopped raw onions, and sautéed jalapeños. The entire menu was filled with mostly obscure surfing terms. A Mushburger, in addition to being a wave of poor quality, was a Sloppy Joe made with Wagyu beef for $19. A Pipeline was a rice paper-wrapped chopped shrimp and stone crab burrito with a spicy lemon sauce, and so on. They split a pitcher of Hang Eleven Stout, which the menu advised, "Is when a male surfer rides his board in the nude." Gnarly, dude, Dalton thought.

"Are we in some sort of trouble?" Jenny asked. Nervous anyway, she was having difficulty handling her Wipeout, a sandwich that looked like it was designed to fall apart when bitten into.

"Not yet," Phil answered. "And not if we keep our mouths shut. Here's what going on. Yes, the pythons are dying—thousands of them. But so are other snakes, mostly water snakes, moccasins, king snakes, that sort of thing. But some threatened species too, like Eastern indigo snakes and the Florida pine snakes."

"Does anyone know how or why the other snake species got infected?" Dalton asked.

Everyone looked at Ginger Delgado. She blushed and stared at her untouched plate. "I'm very sorry and very sad," she said finally. "We have not yet figured out why this happened, but we suspect a mutation. Thank God it's just limited to snakes—no other reptiles have been infected."

"We have to weather the shitstorm that's brewing in the media," Dalton said. "No matter how guilty we might feel about harming cuddly little creatures like the Eastern diamondback rattlesnake, the pythons will be all gone. The other snakes can be re-introduced. Phil, what's the bottom line here?"

"I've probably studied this more than anyone in south Florida," Phil said, "and here's my prediction. Our supposedly species-specific eradication project is going to kill every single snake south of Lake Okeechobee. Then the virus will slowly burn out because as the mites travel north, the snake density lessens. I've spoken with George about this and he's convinced that we should be proactive with the media and start planning the re-introduction of the native Florida snake species. We're calling it 'repopulation,' a nice, positive term. We'll solicit reptile support groups to ask for donations of certain species for the repopulation of snakes in south Florida. As a matter of fact, Carole Wilson, the environmental reporter for New Times, is now covering the snake situation for the Herald, and she's re-starting Save Our Snakes."

"And what does Bruno Zimmerman have to say about that?" Dalton asked.

"Well, no one's heard from him. Richards and his men searched the compound on Hibiscus Island and found literally nothing. Zimmerman's vanished, and besides, Save Our Snakes is an independent, 501 C-3 corp with its own board, now led by Wilson. They amended their mission statement away from pet ownership to repopulation, which will be the new buzz-word."

"Okay, gang," Dalton said, "I'm going to say it one more time. If what we did ever gets out, we are all ruined and may do time. Dispose of anything you have that's related to the python project—notes, emails, photos, voicemails, anything. If you are asked how the virus got started, it's infected pet snakes that escaped into the wild. Do not speculate further or vary from that line. Always be positive—pythons gone, repopulation planned. Okay, let's do it."

He held his fist out. So did the other three. Then they had a four-fist bump and the meeting was over.

Dalton was on his way back to a condo inhabited by two beautiful women when Richards called him.

"Brass has pulled the plug on the Zimmerman case," he said.

"Why?"

"It wasn't really our case to begin with—it should have been Customs and Border Protection's problem, but it broke so fast that I had to run it and was stuck with it. But now the US government owns both World of Reptiles and Zimmerman's compound, and except for capturing the perp, the case is essentially closed. I'm turning copies of all my files and reports over to you and Customs. We have, as they say, bigger fish to make ceviche out of."

"Okay. Good working with you and good luck," Dalton said. "Is World of Reptiles still closed?"

"It's reopening tomorrow. Customs figures it's easier to sell a business that's open so they found a guy to run it."

"Anything new on where Zimmerman might be?

"No, but off the record, I checked some files around the office. We can't prove it yet, but both Bone Mozell and Bruno Zimmerman are stone killers."

"From what I've heard, I'd have to agree."

"Watch your back."

"Thanks," Dalton said, thinking, *if you only knew what I'm going to do to those two assholes, Brad, you'd arrest me right now.*

15

IBD is a serious, fatal viral infection of boid snakes. First identified in the mid-1970s, it is thought to be a retrovirus. Because the transport of captive snakes in the pet trade and between different zoological institutions frequently occurs, and snakes can harbor and shed the virus before manifesting overt clinical signs, we can expect this virus to spread worldwide eventually. The incidence of IBD in wild snakes is unknown at this time. The disease can rapidly progress to nervous system signs, such as disorientation, corkscrewing of the head and neck, holding the head in abnormal and unnatural positions, rolling onto the back or stargazing. Stomatitis, pneumonia, undifferentiated cutaneous sarcomas, leukemia and lymphoproliferative disorders have all been seen.
—Margaret A. Wissman, DVM, DABVP,
Reptiles Magazine, 2014.

Diana looked up from the pink tube of lipstick in her hand and said, "Dalton, you're going to make Laura jealous if you keep buying me gifts."

Laura laughed. "Take the top off and see if you like the color." Unlike Diana, she knew what the tube was for.

Diana did so and looked up quizzically.

"Pepper spray," Dalton explained, "specifically, oleoresin capsicum, 1,000,000 Scoville Heat Units. That one goes in your purse. Five one-second shots, six foot distance. And this one," he held up a small purple cylinder with a metal ring on one end, "is your new keychain."

"It's so cute," Diana gushed, holding it up. "You shouldn't have, Dalton. All my girlfriends will be so jealous."

The doorbell rang and Laura went over to let Cooper in. The two of them had met during her and Dalton's house hunting excursion down to Key Largo, so she gave him a chaste hug. Then she led him into the living room and introduced him to Diana.

"This is Kevin Cooper, Diana, a Back Country fishing guide who's very, very married."

"Oh, just like Dalton," she cracked, an innocent smile on her face. "Did you say 'black country?'"

Kevin rolled his eyes. He'd heard it a hundred times. "For a damsel, you don't look very distressed," he said, shaking her hand.

"That's because some very nice people are helping me, and now I guess that includes you." Laura and Dalton glanced at each other, waiting for a punch line that never arrived. Diana was totally serious. "Thank you all so much."

"Let's get a move on," Kevin suggested. "We have an hour's drive, at least." Hugs all around and Kevin picked up the heaviest piece of luggage. Diana got the smaller, wheeled suitcase and followed him out the door with a wave of her right hand.

"That Diana is something else," Laura pronounced.

"She is indeed," Dalton agreed.

"She told me that in her entire life you're the only man to ever turn her down. You told her some Playtex joke."

Dalton laughed. "Do you believe her?"

"That you turned her down, yes. Only man ever to do that, no."

"I'm sure she's scared away a bunch of men, including me."

"It's just a game she plays. Her career is more important to her than men, anyway. She probably has 'Pulitzer Prize' tattooed above her private parts."

"I must've missed that," Dalton cracked and Laura threw a sofa pillow at him.

"I kinda like her," she said.

"Me too, but I like you better," Dalton replied, taking her in his arms.

• • •

Zhou's men, four of them, came for him on a cloudy night with no moon or stars just after 2:00 a.m. They pulled a Solstice Sportster 310 inflatable up to his dock, which had alerted the motion-sensors and sent a beeping signal into Zimmerman's small bedroom in The Pod, as he called it. Instantly, he was awake, out of bed and moving quickly toward the monitors. First, he doubled the intensity of lights on the back patios. He could see the men looking at each other in confusion and then one of them waving for the others to follow as he rushed the house.

Zimmerman pushed the master button and all the steel hurricane shutters began to roll down over the windows and doors. The men, armed with what looked like assault rifles, arrived at the now-steel back patio doors and actually touched them as if they were not real. Zimmerman chuckled as he watched their confused faces. Without acetylene tanks and cutting torches, the men had no way to get into the house.

He dialed Miami-Dade Marine Patrol and gave the dispatcher details on what was happening and the GPS coordinates of his house. "And I almost forgot. They have automatic assault rifles. I don't know what kind. And they're wearing ski masks. I think they're terrorists."

241

Zimmerman turned off all the lights outside to further confuse the men and he wondered what they had thought of his artwork on the outside of the metal hurricane patio doors. His favorite graffiti artist had painted a huge, clenched, cartoony fist with the middle finger extended to greet a hurricane—or four frustrated bad guys who were definitely not United States citizens.

"Three Dead, One Critical in Smugglers' Firefight with Marine Patrol," ran the headline in the *Miami Herald* a day and a half later.

• • •

Dalton and Phil met the two Customs agents at the front gate of Zimmerman's compound, but all those agents did was hand over their keys and ask Phil, as the senior F and W agent, to sign a receipt for them.

One of the agents said, "And don't worry about Zimmerman's reptiles biting you. They have new homes at Zoo Miami. That huge alligator snapper is quite a draw."

Dalton figured that the case was closed for Customs. But not for them. Zimmerman was still on the loose. As a result of the invasion of the compound and the subsequent deaths, as it turned out, of all the suspects—four members of the purported Malaysian-American Mafia—Phil and Dalton had decided to take over the case. That was easy—no one else wanted it.

The caller who reported the intruders had to be Zimmerman, Dalton figured, and that meant he was probably holed up somewhere in the massive main house. They split up and checked the two guest houses first, but both had been so thoroughly cleaned that Dalton doubted that they would find a single fingerprint.

It was Phil who had the bright idea of turning off all the electricity to the compound. They found the large junction box mounted on a concrete pad on the right side of the main house. It was secured by a padlock too large even for a bolt cutter.

Dalton called George, explained the situation to him and asked if he had an inside contact at Florida Power and Light. Of course he did. About 35 minutes later, an FPL truck pulled into the compound. After checking out the locked junction box, one of the workers opened a tool chest and pulled out a Steelmax S9 portable metal-cutting saw. Two minutes later, the box was open.

"Now?" the worker asked, and when Dalton nodded, he pulled the main power lever down. Dalton watched the front porch lights flicker for a second, shut off, and then came back on.

"Generator," the worker said. "The house has a gasoline-powered backup system."

"Let's find it," Phil suggested.

They heard it before they saw it—in the large pool house next to the water filter, pump, and pool heater. Another large tank presumably held the gasoline for the generator, and the room felt cramped to Dalton.

"Poorly designed," the electrical worker said. "You should never have a gas tank indoors."

"It probably would look unsightly next to all of Zimmerman's modern art sculptures," Phil joked.

"Why does this building look larger from the outside?" Dalton wondered.

"Because of all this stuff crammed in here?" Phil asked.

"Anyone have a tape measure?"

"We have a 100-footer in the truck," the worker replied, and left to fetch it.

As it turned out, the outside of the building was 15 feet longer and wider than its inside dimensions, so they carefully search of the closet labeled "Tools and Maintenance," pulling out skimmers, lifesavers, children's floats, and finally, eight-foot tall rolls of outdoor artificial turf. And there it was—a small keypad.

"Well, if he's in there he probably can't get out with the power off," Phil said.

"Keypads have batteries, Phil. I'll call for backup—and a locksmith," Dalton told him.

• • •

Carole Wilson covered the joint press conference of the US and Florida Fish and Wildlife services for the Herald and was impressed that the bigwigs didn't sugar-coat the news. Cindy Maldonado, southeast regional director for the US Fish and Wildlife Service nailed it.

"The good news is that all the invasive pythons in south Florida will die. The bad news is that most of the other snakes will die, too. Our veterinary disease specialists are calling this a Viral Snake Pandemic, or VSP for short. We do not know the cause of this VSP, but I have a lineup of experts on this subject who will bring you up to date on what we know right now. After that, Q and A limited to 30 minutes."

Carole recorded everything on her iPad. One by one, the experts gave their summaries and opinions, but nothing they said altered the bottom line of a massive snake die-off. Phil Everett emphasized the mystery of the infection, how it would burn itself out, and that after that happened, the repopulation would begin. "Approximately 95 percent of all snake species lost in south Florida can be reintroduced from existing populations in other states," he told the overflow crowd at the Miami Convention Center.

As they always did during the question and answer period, the media asked questions already answered and questions they knew perfectly well couldn't be answered. So Carole soon realized that her story would not be about the press conference but rather the responses to it. She was on the phone as soon as she returned to her home office.

In her article, which ran two days later, Carole placed the initial blame on Congress for failing to pass more restrictive laws on reptile importations into the US. She noted that around 6,000 pythons were imported into Miami from 2003 to 2005, and that the total US importation of pythons since 2005 was 140,000, which stopped only when the importation of Burmese pythons was banned in 2012.

But the highlights of her story were the quotes. The media representative for the Herpetological Society of America told her: "What we are seeing in the Everglades is serpenticide at its worst. This was a deliberate act by reptile haters and nobody seems to care." In fact, the reptile hobbyists were worried sick, and pet stores had all run out of miticides.

On the other hand, many people, including politicians, were delighted with what had happened. The conservative US Representative from Florida's 12th Congressional District, Gus Spanos, told Carole: "If it takes killing all the snakes in the known universe to be rid of the pythons down here, so be it."

But even Carole had to shake her head while entering the comment from Reverend Hixon Stemmons, pastor of the Deep South Baptist Church in Cape Coral: "I remind you of Genesis 3:14, 'God said to the serpent, "Because you have done this, cursed are you more than all cattle, and more than every beast of the field; on your belly you will go, and dust you will eat all the days of your life."' This is the Serpent Apocalypse in south Florida."

She resisted the urge to change "dust" to "swamp water," knowing it would never make it past the copy editor.

• • •

When it rang, Phil was surprised to see "Diana Ventura" on the screen of his cell phone. "Hey there, Diana," he said.

"You're not going to believe this." She sounded upset, rattled.

"Try me."

"You remember that encrypted folder on Zimmerman's hard drive?"

"Vaguely."

"Chopper finally cracked it. He discovered it wasn't encrypted using prime numbers, but rather using the latest video game encryption. That's why it took over a month—he's had a software program working on it the entire time. The folder contains videos—"

"So?"

"Of murders."

"Of murders by Zimmerman?"

"Yes, he's in some of them. We now know what happened to his missing bookkeeper."

"What?"

"She was dismembered and fed to his reptiles like that huge snapping turtle."

"I'm seriously considering vomiting," he told her.

"Better not watch it, then. And there's one video clip you should know about. It's only 20 seconds long, but it shows a car being run off the road and into a canal."

"Jesus," Phil muttered. "Dalton's wife and son, you think?"

"I think it could be, yes, but I didn't dare call him."

"Can you send it to me?"

"I'll attach it to an email. Doing it now."

"I'll call you right back."

Phil watched it with a huge lump in his stomach before calling her back. "It's a red Toyota Corolla, the right color, make, and model."

"Are you going to show it to him?" Diana asked.

"I guess I have to."

"Let me know what he says. And somebody's got to stop Zimmerman."

"We're at the compound right now and we may have him trapped."

"If you catch him, call me. It would be the perfect ending for my python report running Sunday."

"What did you think of Carole's article?" Phil asked her, sure that Diana would bitch her out.

"She did a good job," Diana said with enthusiasm. "What a great bunch of quotes. She found some real loonies."

"Dalton's waving at me. Gotta go."

"Call me!"

• • •

The power was back on at the compound, the locksmith had unlocked the door, and Dalton and Phil plus three backup agents were ready. All of them were wearing Chief Millennium CBRN gas masks because the second Dalton opened the door, two of the backup agents fired tear gas canisters into the room behind it. Dalton slammed the door shut and they waited. Nothing happened. Two minutes went by, then five. No sound at all.

After 15 minutes, when most of the CS gas had cleared, they went in with pistols drawn, not knowing what to expect. They found an L-shaped series of rooms, nicely furnished, but empty. Zimmerman was not there, but what was left of his life was very much there. His books, his videos, his papers, three file cabinets, another computer, a landline phone. Leads? Evidence? Dalton wondered.

"Jeez, it's going to take days to go through all this stuff," Phil said.

"Well, it's better than no leads at all," Dalton told him. "Maybe Zimmerman has another hidey hole somewhere." His iPhone dinged and he checked his text messages. "Well, isn't this interesting. Florida Power and Light came through for us, Phil. They read the meter at the old chicken farm in Dundee, and guess what? Usage surged the day after the fire in Mozell's warehouse, and it's still going strong."

"Shall we cruise on up there and have a look?"

"Call George first and have him get some people over here to sort through all this stuff. Then we can go for a ride."

"Let's have lunch before we go. I have to show you something."

Dalton took it much better than Phil expected. He simply nodded after watching the video twice. "I knew it," he said, "from the text Zimmerman sent me. And here's the proof."

"Diana was reluctant to tell you about it. I'm supposed to call her."

"I'll do it," Dalton said, and reached her on the phone at Kevin's guesthouse in Key Largo. "How's the vacation going?" he asked her.

Diana literally snorted through the phone. "I was expecting Phil to call. Are you okay?"

"Only in a cold-blooded, avenging sort of way. Are you putting all this in your story?"

"Of course."

"Good. I have a quote for you—I want to goad Zimmerman, poke him, get him to take some action."

"He might just try to kill you."

"That is precisely what I want him to do. Ready?"

"Go, Dalton, I'm on my laptop."

He spoke slowly to make sure she got it right.

"Oh my god," Diana said. "If that doesn't motivate the bastard, nothing will."

"You'll use it?"

"Damn right. It's perfect."

• • •

Phil was driving them up to Dundee in his personal Nissan Sentra so as not to attract attention in an F and W truck. Dalton had been very quiet on the drive and didn't speak until they had reached Port Saint Lucie.

"Are you happy with the scenario where we catch these two assholes and turn them over to the Department of Law Enforcement?" he asked Phil.

"What do you mean?"

"What if we exacted our own punishment on them?"

"That would be breaking the laws we're sworn to enforce," Phil scolded.

"So? What if no one ever knew?"

"Well, let me think on that a bit. This is pure revenge, right?"

"Yes."

"We'd have to do everything by ourselves. No one else could know."

"We need one more person to pull this off. Two can't do it. I was thinking Kevin."

Phil nodded. "Might work. You got a plan?"

"It's starting to come together."

"Where are we going in Dundee?" asked Phil. "The old chicken farm?"

"The library," replied Dalton. "Conveniently located in the Town Hall building."

16

PRETORIA, South Africa [UPI]—A South African army recruiting campaign is under way—not for soldiers but for pythons. A statement released Wednesday by defense headquarters appealed for citizens to donate pet pythons to the army because South Africa is losing its war against an infestation of rock rabbits on the Botswana-Zimbabwe border. The army asked anyone owning a "problem python" to contact headquarters in Pretoria and hand it over—out of patriotism. (August 15, 1980)

It had been hell getting to the Palm Cay Marina down the east coast from Nassau. He thought he had a reservation at the Atlantis Marina, right there at the resort. So he set his Humminbird 898 GPS unit to N25.075, W77.32 and cruised in moderate seas for a little over 20 hours. When they were five miles out, Bill was totally exhausted from being up all night, so he thought he heard it wrong when the harbormaster told him his reservation did not go through because he had forgotten to specify the length of his boat.

"How long is your craft?" the harbormaster had asked.

"It's 42 feet," he had replied and got a chuckle from the harbormaster.

"I'm sorry, sir, but your craft is not long enough. It's a minimum of 80 feet to dock here. We're a mega-yacht marina." Bill felt like a second-class yacht owner.

The harbormaster had suggested the Palm Cay Marina, so Bill had reset the Humminbird to N25.01, W77.16 and finally found a place to dock.

"We can take a cab to Atlantis, or just sleep on the boat."

"That sounds like the name of a rock group," Jamie had said.

"What, Asleep on the Boat?"

"No, silly, Cab to Atlantis."

What Bill didn't realize was that when he registered with the harbormaster, his boat permit sticker was scanned into a database to compare it to wants, warrants, and inquiries. And that's why a programmed email alerted special agent Bradley Richards of the FBI in Miami.

• • •

Sometimes, you just get lucky. It was one of those days for Dalton. Mildred Pierce, of the line, "I know, I know, James M. Cain, but my mom never read him," was not your stereotypical librarian—if, in fact, there was such a thing. She looked like a runner-up in the Miss Florida Sunshine competition, despite her modest blouse and slacks. Dalton noticed that she was not showing off any rings on her fingers and that her blonde hair had no roots showing. About 40, he thought. Classy. Probably smarter than I am.

He and Phil had showed her their IDs, and she had said with a grin, "What do the Effin' Doubleyous need from the Dundee Library?"

"Information," Dalton smiled back at her. "Who knows the most about Dundee and Polk County?"

"That would be me." Ms. Pierce was not modest at all but had a slightly less outrageous personality than, say, Diana Ventura. "I'm a published historian."

"We're interested in that abandoned chicken farm out on Ridgewood."

"Oh, the old Mozell place? They're kinda famous around here."

"For the chicken farm?"

"No, for the Cold War. Old Sterling Mozell built the first bomb shelter in Florida in 1947. Right here in little old Dundee. After that, everybody wanted one."

Dalton and Phil stared at each other.

"Do you happen to have a file about that?"

"Only a vertical file. I haven't had the funding to digitize everything yet."

"Could we see it?"

"Sure, for a small donation to the Digitize Now! Fund."

"We could get a warrant," Phil warned.

Mildred smiled. "Sure. Go to the county courthouse and see Judge Waylon Pierce."

Dalton laughed. "And he would be your…"

"Grandfather," she finished.

"Is 20 bucks enough?" Phil asked her, and two minutes later they were photocopying the entire file, but focusing on the yellowed clipping from the *Winter Haven News Chief*, which included a cutaway diagram of the shelter.

By then it was noon, so Dalton asked Millie, as she like to be called, "What's the best lunch place in Dundee?"

"Aporkalypse Now. They have the best barbecue in the county. Smoked mullet to die for."

"Join us for lunch?"

"I thought you'd never ask."

And during that memorable, smoky lunch, Millie Pierce told them the story about how the former town manager had persuaded the TV star Paul Hogan—Crocodile Dundee—to be the grand master of the parade at the first Dundee Crocodile Festival. He had simply tracked down the star's US promoter of his upcoming tour, and told him, "Croc's gotta come—we changed the name of our fucking town to honor him, just like Hot Springs did, changing to Truth or Consequences down in New Mexico."

"He was lying his ass off, "she said, but Croc Dundee showed up. "It was a big success, and we produce the Dundee Crocodile Festival every year on the weekend closest to his birthday. Since he croaked, the crowds have been huge."

"Uh, Millie, there are no crocodiles within 100 miles of here," Phil advised her.

"I know that. We borrow all the crocs, snakes, and lizards from World of Reptiles. They're a big sponsor."

Both of them remained silent on that subject. "Who was the town really named after?"

"Not who, but what. The first inhabitant of our town, a Mr. Mungo Menzie from Dundee, Scotland, decreed in 1910 that his tiny settlement here should be called Dundee, after his former home."

"And what was the real given name of Crocodile?"

"What is this, *Jeopardy*? His name was Mick, but that was a fictional character played by the late Paul Hogan, as mentioned."

Dalton shook his head. "You are one helluva smart woman."

"And single, too."

"The right croc will come around sometime," he told her.

"Nice pun," she said, eyeing him.

And Dalton fought off the urge to follow up on that one. Jeez, he thought. They drove Millie back to the town hall and reluctantly dropped her off.

"Let's get back to business," Phil said as he drove out of the town hall parking lot.

"Bone's holed up."

"Or down, in this case." His phone interrupted them. The caller ID read, simply, "FBI."

"What's up, Brad?"

"The honorary redneck formerly known as Big Ink and who's now reverted to his given name, William Draper, has his yacht docked at the Palm Cay Marina on New Providence Island in the Bahamas. Could you and/or Phil fly down there and convince him to return to Miami?"

"And being out of the United States, with no authority to arrest him, how do we accomplish that?"

"Tell him we have an offer no sane person could ever refuse. It beats the hell out of life in prison."

"But Brad, this Ink or Draper guy is not a part of my caseload —"

"Let me explain," the agent insisted. "It's all about the meth—and World of Reptiles and the health of Florida wildlife."

"Bullshit. I can't do your work for you without a direct order from George Tompkins."

"I spoke with him—he's good to go."

"Tell him what I just said. Tell him to call me and give me that order."

• • •

Dalton was amazed that the *Miami Herald* actually published the final portion of "The Python Story," considering the fact that it was essentially a diatribe against the still-at-large Bruno Zimmerman. Subtitled "The Reptilian Murderer," the article tracked the crime-line, as Diana called it, of "the deranged reptile king and serial killer," beginning with his brother's death and Zimmerman's revenge against Dalton, and ending with the story of the mamba attack against her. In between, she covered the videos found on Zimmerman's hard drive in which he dismembered his former bookkeeper, the horrendous death of Ray Jacobs, and Zimmerman's subsequent indictment for multiple murders and smuggling, by first a Miami grand jury, and then a federal one.

The final sentence in the story was designed to "poke" Zimmerman, as Dalton put it, and spur him into action. "Sam Dalton, special agent for reptile crimes for the Florida Fish and Wildlife Conservation Commission," she wrote, "issued a statement on Friday: 'Convicted murderers sentenced to the death penalty under Florida law may request that the method of death be the electric chair. I certainly hope, Mr. Zimmerman, that you exercise that option, because I want to witness the flames shooting out of your skull like the last time Old Sparky was fired up, in 1999.'"

To celebrate the publication of the final installment of Diana's python series, Dalton and Laura drove down that Sunday to Key Largo to join Kevin Cooper, his wife Judy, Diana, and several of their neighbors for a barbecue. Dalton was in a great mood—they had probably located Bone Mozell, three state and two federal agencies were hunting Zimmerman, and Dalton was leaving the next day for Nassau to attempt to persuade Big Ink to come back to Florida. He had a feeling that the case was on the verge of being wrapped up, despite the fact that Zimmerman was still on the loose.

As Laura drove them down US 1 in her Mazda, Dalton decided it was time to ask her about Diana.

"Got a question for you, darling."

"What's that?"

"How come you didn't tell me that Diana was staying at the bungalow?"

Laura hesitated, and Dalton could see her cheeks starting to redden. "I guess I didn't want to bother you with it. You were so busy with the new job, and all. I thought she'd be gone in a week or so. Instead, she was dancing the mamba."

Dalton chuckled. "No big deal. Everything's okay now."

The Coopers lived in a two-story concrete house, the bottom floor consisting of the garage and utility rooms, the living quarters on the second floor in case of a storm surge. A large screened-in porch ran the entire length of the house, facing the dock and deep-water boat basin. That was where Kevin was staging the barbecue. The guest house adjoined the main house on the right side with its own separate entrance.

Laura joined Judy and Diana in the kitchen and after greetings offered to help with the side dishes, but they were already prepared. Judy poured glasses of Chardonnay. As she passed a glass to Laura, she said, "I met Kevin at Naval Base Subic Bay. I was his surgeon. We kept in touch and got together when we left military service. We get a lot of questions about how an Asian American got hooked up with an African American."

"How do you handle that?" Diana asked, ever the reporter.

"I ask them what they think our two kids are called. The nosy ones always make stupid guesses, like Asian-African Americans. So I get a little snooty with them and say, 'Well, both of them were born in Florida, so does that make them Floridian Americans?'"

Dalton laughed and took a Dorado Golden Ale from the Fishy Brewery out of the fridge and joined Kevin, who was on the porch turning the ribs over in his Yoder 640 pellet smoker.

"That aroma will drive the neighbors crazy," Dalton predicted.

"Well, some of them are coming over later," Kevin said as they shook hands. He was dressed in cargo shorts and a t-shirt with an octopus image and the line, "Eight Arms to Hold You." "How goes the battle?"

"It's going. And I have a plan for the end-game."

"Remember, I told you…"

"I accept. Phil and I can't finish this thing by ourselves."

"Let's discuss privately when you get back from Nassau."

"How do you know where I'm going?"

"I may be retired, but people still tell me things," Kevin answered.

"Say Kevin, you said you were going to tell me how you broke into the fishing guide circle in the Keys."

"Actually, it was quite interesting. Everyone knew I could fish. But could I guide? My first charter was Lloyd Evans."

"Really? I've heard of him."

"Oldest guide still working in the Keys. He told me straight up that it had nothing to do with race, just fishing, which was a helluva lot more important. I took him out and we had a great time. Caught our limits of reds and bones. From then on, he recommended me. I'm doing fine and no one cares. The fishin' times in Florida, they are a changin'."

Diana joined them. "I can smell the testosterone. What are you two plotting?"

"You're smelling the smoked ribs," Dalton said. "We're plotting an excursion into Florida Bay. For permits."

"You need permits and fishing licenses?"

"Permit is the name of a fish," Kevin told her.

"That's a stupid name for a fish. Have you seen this?" she asked. She showed him a clipping from the local news section of Saturday's Herald, written by Carole Wilson. "Snake Expert Disputes Cause of Python Infection."

Diana said, "The gist of Carole's story is that this herpetologist from the Florida Museum of Natural History plotted the top locations for all the dead snakes by date and concluded that it was impossible for the IBD infection to spread so rapidly in nature. It's his theory that a person or persons unknown deliberately introduced the infection in multiple locations on state land in south Florida."

Abruptly, Dalton's mood switched to worry mode, but he

didn't let it show. "A theory is still just a theory, Diana. Why are you showing this to me?"

"Because it's the subject of my next series for the Herald," she said pointedly. "I'd like to get a comment from you or Phil about this guy's theory."

"My comment is no comment for right now," Dalton told her. "I need to have more details about the guy's rationale."

"I can get that for you since I'm interviewing him tomorrow. Call me in the afternoon."

"Sorry, I'll be busy in the Bahamas tomorrow."

"A little vacation, huh?"

"Call it a fishing expedition."

"Well," she smiled, "I hope you catch a big fish."

"Me too."

• • •

Standing on the dock with the Queen Anne's Revenge II in front of him, Dalton yelled, "Permission to come aboard, sir?"

"Who is it?" came a woman's voice.

"Sam Dalton, Florida Fish and Wildlife. I need to speak with Big Ink."

"No one on board with that name."

Dalton checked his notes. "Okay then, how about William Draper?"

"Oh, Billy, you mean. He made a run to the store but he'll be right back, so come on aboard."

She offered him a Stingray Stout, which he accepted, and they sat down at the tiny galley table.

"I'm Jamie. Billy and I are a couple," she said. She was nicely dressed in a t-shirt and shorts and it looked to Dalton like she had the faint hints of tattoo removal.

"I met Billy at tattoo rehab in Fort Lauderdale."

Tattoo rehab, the latest health craze, Dalton thought.

They talked for a few minutes about how amazing the Atlantis resort was, particularly all the glass sculptures, then a booming voice came from above.

"Hi, honey, I'm home," Bill joked. He came down the steps and into the galley.

Dalton was flabbergasted. He had seen numerous photos and now Big Ink was no longer all that big. He wasn't fat at all. And he had no ink, at least not on his head, neck, face, or hands. The rest of him was covered in workout gear. Big Ink was now a fitness freak named Bill Draper.

Dalton stood up, took out his ID and showed it to Bill. "Sam Dalton, Florida Fish and Wildlife."

"Oh shit, are you arresting me?"

Dalton shook his head. "I have no authority to arrest you in the Bahamas. And besides, there's not even a warrant out for you—yet."

"How did you find me?"

"The marina here reports all boat numbers to a law enforcement information service."

"Why are you here, Mr. Dalton?"

"You're in big trouble, Bill, and I'm here to discuss your options. First, you show know that I'm under orders to discuss this with you, and even negotiate. Personally, I don't care about you or your problems."

Bill took a deep breath. "How big is this trouble?"

"You sold the meth lab equipment to your brother. That DEA guy, Gabriel Cypress, checked on all packages leaving the Manatee Fish Meal Plant, and the recipient of that equipment—your brother Hal—showed up on a suspect list for meth trafficking. As far as the DEA and the FBI are concerned, you are guilty of being part of an interstate conspiracy to manufacture and distribute methamphetamines. It's a federal offense, and then state charges would be added on. You are literally facing the rest of your life in federal prison."

Jamie gave a little yelp and Bill put his arm around her shoulders. Dalton held up his hand. "But wait, there's more. Why do you think no warrant has been issued?"

"The authorities want something from me?"

"Exactly. World of Reptiles has been taken over by Customs and Border Protection. Were you aware of that?"

"No, sir."

"They're trying to sell it, but they've had no luck finding buyers."

"What does that have to do with me?"

"Tell me, Bill, how much do you know about keeping reptiles?"

"A shitload."

"Can you scrape together $500,000?"

Jamie looked at Bill with complete fascination.

"Yes," he said finally.

"Here's how it would work. You have to give up any meth you made at the plant. Where is it now?"

Bill was now a little more animated, and Dalton believed he was going for the idea.

"Derrick has it. I told him to store it at the Hideaway Storage Center in South Naples."

"Okay, good. DEA will confiscate that, but no charges will be brought against you if you buy World of Reptiles from Customs. This will be huge news, because at the press conference you will announce that the goal of the new company will be the restoration of the native snake population of south Florida. Have you heard what happened?"

"Yes, I read that the pythons got sick and then the rest of the snakes did too."

"A snake virus is now burning itself out. We wait six

months to be sure then repopulation can begin. So, what do you think?"

"Do I really have a choice in the matter?"

Dalton shook his head. "I don't think so. Look, In—uh, Bill, you know you only have yourself to blame for all this. You're getting a second chance."

Bill hung his head. "Will any of this interfere with Jamie's and my plans?"

"What do you mean?"

"Well, Jamie and I are going to get married at Monkey Jungle in Miami. If I agree to all this, will you come to our wedding?"

Dalton started laughing, Bill and Jamie did too, and soon they were guffawing so hard they all had tears in their eyes.

"Yes," Dalton said finally, "I'll come to your wedding, and no, your getting married will not interfere with anything we're doing."

He said goodbye to Jamie and climbed out of the galley and onto the deck, Bill right behind him. Bill gestured with his head toward the dock and they walked together away from the boat.

"Where's Cutup?" Bill asked in a low voice.

"Missing in action. Murdered by Mozell, most likely."

"Where is that prick?"

"We know where he is and we'll be arresting him very soon."

"Good. And Zimmerman?"

"No idea. He's disappeared completely."

"When I buy World of Reptiles, will he come after me?"

"I can arrange protection for you and Jamie." Dalton was warming up to the former Big Ink.

"So can I," Bill said.

"Tell me something, Bill. Why did you change your life so radically?"

"Two things. I really liked Toad and I thought, fuck, Ink, you're doing things that get people killed. What is the purpose of all that? Second, I met Jamie and fell in love for the first time in my life."

"Good for you," Dalton said and they shook hands on it. "See you in Miami. Soon?"

"Leaving tomorrow," Bill promised.

17

ROMPIN, Malaysia. In one of the most uncommon reptile attacks, an adult monitor lizard bit an eight-month-old girl and tried to drag her away in Tioman Island. The lizard had sunk its teeth into the girl's head and tried to take her out of the staff quarters of a holiday resort into nearby bushes early Monday. The infant was saved when her loud cries attracted the attention of her mother, Nor Raudah Abdullah, 38, who rushed to her aid. She was shocked to see the monitor lizard with its sharp claws trying to drag her daughter away. She hit the lizard, forcing it to release its grip before chasing it away. The girl was bleeding and nearby villagers sent her to the health clinic in Kampung Tekek.
—Simon Khoo, *The Star Online*, September 23, 2014.

"**N**ew windows," Kevin said as he wrote it on his list. "Probably use glass-clad polycarbonate."

"What will that cost me?" Dalton asked. Already, Kevin wanted bullet-proof floodlights, a backup electric generator, tanks for potable water, and an unbelievably complicated system of sensors, alarms, and triggers for various devices, mostly video.

"This is a small house, so only ten grand or so."

"I don't have that kind of money available," Dalton protested.

"You'll have to refinance this bungalow."

"This is a nightmare."

"It's better than the three of us being dead," Kevin said. "And I could help you with the money for a nice percentage of the rent we collect when it's finished."

"Rent? How much could that possibly be? A bungalow in Homestead? A grand a month? That would barely cover the refinanced mortgage payments."

"It's not a mere bungalow in Homestead, Dalton," Kevin said loudly, feigning outrage. "It's a super-protected, high-tech, impregnable safe house in Homestead designed specifically for police and military use. Smaller is safer, that's our motto."

Dalton had to laugh. "And now you're an entrepreneur, Kevin."

Kevin was grinning. "You and Phil and I can pull off this remodel in ten days, with me managing it."

"I'll call Phil and we'll start raising the money."

"I'm in for a third of the investment and a third of the profit, if Phil goes along."

"He will," Dalton promised.

"One last thing," Kevin said. "I'm going to have our bungalow painted. What color would you prefer?"

• • •

The day after the work on the bungalow was completed, Dalton, Phil, and Kevin were at the site of Sterling Mozell's bomb shelter, now home for a very wanted family member. Dalton was holding a photocopy of the shelter cross section that had run in the *Winter Haven News Chief.* He knew that when Bone's granddad Sterling built his bomb shelter in 1947, he took no chances. There was a possibility of getting trapped inside the damned thing. Suppose a tornado hit and plopped a tree on top of the entrance? The shelter needed an escape hatch, a tunnel to freedom, so to speak, that led from the bottom of the shelter through the hill it was set in, and out the side of it.

Dalton said, "It should be somewhere about halfway up that hill. Let's split up and see if we can find the tunnel exit."

"What exactly are we looking for?" Kevin asked.

"All the article said was a small wooden door, but it's probably rotted away since the shelter was built."

"I'll bet it's like a small cave entrance with brush grown over it," Phil suggested. "Let's split up."

It took them three hours to find it, and Bone's Achilles heel was his love of fried hamburgers. Kevin was the one who smelled it, and the hamburger aroma grew stronger as he climbed the slope and finally spotted the large timbers of the shaft covered with vines that he recognized as poison ivy. Good thing they weren't going into the tunnel, he thought, because the plan was for Bone to come out that way. The escape tunnel was part of the bomb shelter's ventilation system, Kevin figured.

He spoke into his walkie-talkie, "I found it. Get over here." When they did, Dalton showed them the perfect spot where he would hide for the ambush.

"Okay, you guys know what to do." Kevin and Phil left and went back to the entrance of the shelter in the basement of the farm, a square hatch made out of anodized aluminum and locked from the inside. Kevin had wandered around the ruined buildings that once held thousands of chickens, and found what he was looking for: a three-foot-long section of steel pipe. He positioned himself by the hatch and waited for the go-ahead.

Phil found the electrical box and clipped the lock with his bolt cutter. He then pulled the lever down to shut off all power to the farm.

"Power's off," he yelled, and Kevin started banging the hell out of the hatch and making an enormous racket.

Bone, who had just finished his second hamburger, was watching interracial porn and was stunned when everything went dark, and nearly panicked when the banging on the hatch replaced the one on his big-screen TV. But he forced himself to remain calm, remembered where the flashlight was, picked up his AK-47, and made his way to the tunnel entrance.

Dalton wasn't even thinking about Bone. For him, that part of the case was a done deal. He and Kevin—who now seemed to be much more than a Marine staff sergeant—had been working on a plan to trap Zimmerman. It involved Dalton moving back into his bungalow, mostly for the protection of Laura, who had reluctantly agreed to the plan. Kevin knew someone who could sweep all of their vehicles, and so far only two trackers had been discovered—TrackPort GPS units attached to Diana's Lexus, which had been removed, and underneath Dalton's truck, which had been left in place. His yard and his bungalow were now covered with security and surveillance systems, and Dalton had stored enough food and drinks for three people for two weeks. They figured if Zimmerman didn't come by then, he wasn't coming at all.

Dalton heard a noise in the tunnel. Bone came out of the tunnel through the poison ivy, holding an automatic rifle in his right hand and a flashlight in his left, and ran in the direction of the car they had located. He rushed past Dalton, who came up from his crouch behind a bush, raised his rife, and shot Bone Mozell in the back.

• • •

"Rule number one," Zimmerman said to the two Chechen-American assassins and pit viper enthusiasts he had hired, "is that you can't kill Dalton. Wound him if you have to, but I'm the only one who gets to off the prick. Got it?"

"Da," they said in unison, as if mocking him.

Zimmerman shook his head. Just can't find good help these days, he thought, but the two Chechens had come highly recommended. After all, it wasn't that difficult. Three against one, storm the little house, shoot Dalton between the eyes, and leave. Easy. It was the last thing on his to-do list before he could leave Florida and start his new life in Zagreb, Croatia. It was all set up, a bargain for just 300 K. New identity, new passport, new Croatian work permit and visa. It was all set.

Bruno Zimmerman was a positive thinker, and that philosophy had gotten him through his recent hard times. He chided himself for his arrogance, his feelings of omnipotence, and the errors he had made, but all that shit was now in the past. It was time to move on. Yes, the Dalton bastard and the Ventura bitch had blindsided him and fucked him over, and Dalton was going to pay for that. Too bad the mambas hadn't killed the bitch, but scaring her that much was probably enough. He had no time for more revenge against her, especially since she had disappeared and none of his connections could find her. Dalton would have to do.

He had used Google Earth to find an aerial photo of Dalton's house and property to show the Chechens how he wanted the assault to work. One at the front door, one at the glass patio door in the back, he thought. What lousy security you have, Dalton!

All of them would be wearing body armor, of course. He would use his Orion 25mm flare launcher to start the fires and create as much confusion as he could. Maybe not between the eyes, he thought, I could be so much more creative than that. Between-the-eyes would be over too soon and no pain at all for the prick, and he should suffer big-time. Maybe I should blow out his knees first with my 9mm and then use my SOG SE14-CP Spec-Elite folding tactical knife to cut off his dick and balls. I don't like the idea of touching a man there, but I could wear latex gloves, he mused.

His mind briefly drifted away from Dalton's severed package to the new life ahead of him. He had set it up six years ago after realizing that if things blew up and went to hell for World of Reptiles, he would need a refuge. He had visited Zagreb during a European vacation and really liked the place because it fit his escape needs. First, the country had no extradition treaty with the US. Next, half of the population spoke English. And third, there were numerous business opportunities, both legal and not so legal, and he intended to do a little of each. While in Zagreb, he had kept a list of things that were hard to find there, like American cigarettes, specialty foods, books, and children's toys. So, with a Croatian partner he found through the EU Reptile Forum, he had funded the opening of Američki Trgovina, or The American Shop, on Frankopanska Street in the heart of the downtown shopping district. Amazingly, it had been profitable from the start, and he would make it even more so when he settled down in an apartment in Gornji Grad, or Upper Town, one of the better sections of Zagreb.

Zimmerman snapped back to reality. The raid was planned. The weapons were in place. They would hit the little house two nights from now. He looked at his checklist, and all the details had been checked off. The one thing he didn't realize was his miscalculation about the Chechens. They were expert assassins but had no training in surveillance at all, and it bored them to attempt it.

• • •

Jenny refused to cooperate. He had the unconscious body of Bone Mozell on a bed in the spare room of his bungalow, his hands, feet, and mouth all bound with duct tape. Now he needed the paramedic to keep Mozell unconscious until they could capture or kill Zimmerman.

"I won't do it," she said. "What do you have planned for him? Are you asking me to be your accomplice in murdering him? There are warrants out for him—just turn him in to the state troopers."

"Jenny, I really need your help with this," he began, trying to sweet-talk her. Kevin was with him in the room and began frantically shaking his head and pointing to himself. Finally, he drew his finger across his throat. Shut up and get rid of her was his message to Dalton

"But I understand your position. We'll talk soon. Bye."

"I know how to keep him under," Kevin said. "I just need some pentobarbital."

"So you're a medic now?"

"Everyone on my old team was. The Army takes no chances with training. We have to learn how to cope with any emergency."

"How long will he be out?" Dalton asked.

"Hard to tell," he replied, "too many variables. Weight factors in, along with exact dosage in the dart, physical health of Mozell, that sort of thing. Ketamine is essentially a short-acting anesthetic, so that's why I need the pento. When he starts waking up I'll have to give him some to keep him under. I'll rig a drip for short-term PN, and then I can just inject the pento into it."

"Translate, please," Dalton requested.

"PN is parenteral nutrition, feeding people through their veins when they're unconscious or their gastrointestinal tract has a severe problem. I don't want to keep him that way for more than three or four days, but we may have to."

Phil came into the room holding his ATN PS15 night vision binoculars and chuckling. "We're under surveillance—sorta."

"Oh?"

"There's a vacant house for sale up the street, and there's a car in the driveway with a clear view of the front of this house. There's a guy asleep in the driver's seat."

"Should we grab him, get him out of the way?" Dalton asked.

"Nah, that would just tip off Zimmerman. At least we know it's happening soon. But not tonight or the guy wouldn't be sitting there."

"I'll make a list of what I need," Kevin said. "Get all of it for me while I do some scouting around. If he starts to wake up, dart him again."

• • •

The American Eagle Super ATR 72 made the flight from Miami to Gainesville in an hour and 14 minutes with Diana seated in C4 and no one next to her in C3. She was one of the first passengers off the prop plane at 3:30, found her way to Dollar Car Rental and picked up a blue Kia Rio, which she considered a huge step down from her Lexus ES—but it got her to Bartram-Carr Hall at the University of Florida in 15 minutes. She parked in the small visitor lot and entered Carr Hall, where Dr. Jeffrey "Call me Jeff" Gordon had his office. She had looked him up—he was field curator for herpetology at the Florida Museum of Natural History, which is part of the University of Florida.

"It's a little complicated," he had told her on the phone when she called for an appointment. "Let's just say I work for the state of Florida."

He was in his office on the computer when she knocked on his open door. He waved her in and pointed to the chair next to him. He was dressed casually in a tropical shirt with macaws on it and khaki shorts. They made small talk for a few minutes and then she got down to business.

"Dr. Gordon, tell me about your theory that the pythons were deliberately infected."

"Please call me Jeff. I never said it was a theory. It's my hypothesis only."

She gave him a blank look. "Isn't that the same thing?"

"Absolutely not. A hypothesis must precede a theory and is based on a very specific observation. A theory comes from verified, proven hypotheses. So I'm suggesting that the pythons may have been infected deliberately, but that hypothesis has not been proven because we have no real, physical evidence."

"How do you prove a hypothesis?" she asked.

"The same way a detective solves a case—either by inductive reasoning or deductive reasoning. Everyone thinks that detectives finding clues that lead to a suspect is deduction, but that's not correct, because it's inductive reasoning. True deduction is what I'm trying to do: first an hypothesis, then I try to find the evidence to prove it—if I can. I think the hot spots I've found indicate deliberate IBD infection."

"But isn't IBD found mostly in pets? How much do you know about IBD in nature rather than in captive pythons?"

"Excellent question." He apprised her. "You know a bit about snakes. Are you a reptile hobbyist?"

"Heavens, no," she said with a grin. "You don't have to like these creatures to write about them. Are you?"

"No, I study and appreciate snakes, but I'm more interested in frogs and turtles. Anyway, I plotted the IBD hotspots and here's what I found." A Google map was on his screen. Diana saw what looked like clusters of small dots in several widely separated areas.

"Large numbers of dead snakes of many species here, here, here, and here," he said. "It's not a slowly spreading pattern emanating from a single place, but from many places, all on state land. They are the hotspots. There are no hotspots like this on federal land like Everglades National Park. Dead snakes everywhere, of course, but no concentrations."

"What does that tell you?" she asked him.

"That someone infected the snakes at these hotspots. Impossible to prove, of course, unless someone confesses. It's just my hypothesis," he repeated, now sounding even more like a professor.

He checked his watch. "Just about quitting time—we work 8:00 to 4:00, usually. Are you flying back to Miami or staying the night?"

"I'm staying at the Paramount Plaza," she told him. "Room with a lake view."

"Why don't we continue this discussion over a couple of drinks, and then I'll take you to dinner?"

Diana looked at him. Nice looking guy maybe five years older than she was, a trifle overweight, mustache and goatee. Normally she would be curious or tempted. But for some reason, romance was not on her mind.

"Thanks for the kind offer, Dr. Gordon, but I have a previous engagement," she lied. "Could you please print out a copy of that map for me? I'll give you credit if we use it."

"Sure," he said, hitting a few keys.

"Thanks. I have one last question for you."

If she had offended him with her refusal, it didn't show. "Go ahead, Ms. Ventura." Tit for tat, keep it formal—she liked that.

"What kind of a virus are we dealing with here?"

"Ah, the $1,000,000 question. Researchers at the Steinhart Aquarium in San Francisco analyzed the genetic material of IBD-infected snakes from south Florida and found genetic material from a previously unknown virus. Everyone thought IBD was an arenavirus, but the new snake virus contains a gene closely related to one found in the Ebola virus, which belongs to a different class known as filoviruses."

"Are you telling me that we're dealing with a kind of python Ebola?"

He laughed. "Well, scientists wouldn't put it like that, of course."

"How would you put it?"

"I think this new snake virus was created by a recent hybridization of an arenavirus and a filovirus and that's why it's so virulent."

Diana was ecstatic, with the partial headline "Mutant Python Ebola" running through her brain. But Dr. Jeffrey Gordon was not finished.

"It's a myth, of course, that all of the snakes in south Florida are dead."

"What do you mean?"

"There's nothing automatic about a virus. Some animals—just like some people—recover, survive, and keep on breeding. Most of the common snakes, like the garters, water snakes, cottonmouths, will naturally repopulate their native locations after the virus burns out. It's the endangered and threatened snakes that we herpetologists worry about. Like the Atlantic salt marsh snake and the rim rock crowned snake, to name two of them."

Diana knew that her readers wouldn't give a shit about obscure snakes like that. They wanted more dirt about pythons—particularly if someone deliberately infected them.

"So who infected the pythons at these hot spots?"

"You have to consider who would have the greatest motive for wanting the pythons to go away forever."

"Big Sugar? Arch conservatives? Bible bangers?"

Dr. Gordon just shook his head.

"Who, then?" she pressed.

"The Florida Fish and Wildlife Conservation Commission."

"I'll look into that," she promised. His guess was the same as hers. "Thanks for the interview, Jeff."

"Please call me Dr. Gordon," he replied, and Diana couldn't help but laugh.

"Okay, okay, you win. Where are we going for dinner?"

"The Butcher Block."

"A butcher shop?"

"And brewpub," Dr. Gordon said with a grin.

"Can you run me by the hotel so I can change into something more comfortable? Five minutes, max." She would feel ridiculous wearing a spring suit to a campus hangout.

"Sure. I'll just wait out front." While she was changing, Diana realized with a start that her last date, well over a month ago, had been with Ray Jacobs, now deceased. A shiver ran down her spine. She emerged from the hotel and entered Jeff's Hyundai Sonata in designer jeans and a Death Cab for Cutie t-shirt.

"Much better," Jeff said.

It was a butcher shop—in the front part of the building, anyway. The back was a typical sports bar/brew pub combo with big screen TVs, modified butcher's blocks for tables, and restroom signs for Rams and Ewes. The servers were dressed like medieval wenches, with cleavers in holsters on their hips. The greeter, a large guy in a butcher's white outfit, led them to a two-top, and handed them menus as they sat down, and a wench who looked about thirteen came by to take their drink orders. Undoubtedly a student, Diana thought.

The beers didn't look particularly appetizing to Diana so she ordered a glass of Virginia Viognier. Jeff decided to have a Bloodwiser, saying to Diana that he preferred it to the other two main brews at the Butcher Block, Slitz and LiverLager.

"This place is either ingenious or incredibly tacky—I can't

make up my mind which," Diana said.

"It's the most profitable restaurant in Gainesville."

"Then it's ingenious all right," Diana said. "What do you recommend for dinner?"

"It sounds weird, but the GumboBurger is pretty good."

"What about the Florida Fajitas?"

"They're great if you like alligator."

Diana ordered the GumboBurger and Jeff requested the special of the day, Lamb to the Slaughter—a sub with thinly sliced Greek leg of lamb, sautéed onions, feta cheese, chopped pickled pepperoncini, and a spicy yogurt sauce.

"I've been thinking about your hypothesis, Dr. Jeff, and I have a couple of potential suspects I'd like to bounce off of you."

"I showed you my hypothesis, you show me yours."

"Good one." She told him about Sam Dalton and Phil Everett, and how Dalton had previously run a squad of volunteer PTSD-fighting veterans that captured pythons for state execution.

"They're true swamp-lovers," she said, "and I think they're the ones who infected the snakes, but I have no evidence or way to get it."

"Doesn't the conservation commission require a log for each airboat?" Jeff asked.

She looked at him. This guy is pretty damned smart, she thought. "I have no earthly idea. But I can find out."

"If you find the logs, they may have GPS location notes in them. If those points and their dates coincide with my hotspots, you may have some circumstantial evidence, at least. How's your GumboBurger?"

"Better than I expected." She looked around The Butcher Block, taking it all in. Shaking her head, she smiled at the absurdity of it all. "You sure know how to treat a girl right," she said. "Come on down to Miami and I'll return the favor."

"I'll take you up on that," he promised.

18

Monitor lizards—commonly kept as pets—and iguanas produce venom, according to surprising new research that is rewriting the story of lizard and snake evolution.
Until now, nasty swellings and excessive bleeding as a result of a lizard bite were blamed on infection from the bacteria in the creatures' mouths. Venom had been considered the preserve of advanced snakes and just two species of lizard—the Gila monster and the Mexican beaded lizard. And scientists had thought these lizards evolved venom production independent of snakes. —Emma Young, *New Scientist,* November 16, 2005

Gabriel Cypress and his DEA team had been working on busting Bill Draper's brother Hal and his new best friend, Derrick Fitzroy. Cypress had subpoenaed the UPS shipping records from the Manatee Fish Meal Plant and discovered where Big Ink had shipped the meth lab to in Georgetown, Texas. It was 450 Doe Run, the last "farmhouse" on that particular street that dead-ended into typical Hill Country scrub, with live oak trees, dense brush, and a creek. It was perfect feral hog country, and that was their cover. The rancher who owned the land next door had hired them to kill the large pack of hogs that were tearing up his land.

He had met Hal Draper by calling him first, and then dropping by to warn him to stay out of the brush because they were hunting and had given him a business card that read, "Texas Hog Rangers: Total Eradication Is the Only Answer."

The house that Cypress had under surveillance was not a true farmhouse, but rather a city-slicker farmhouse and barn that screamed show horses, although there were none around. The nearest house was a half-mile away and with the Hill Country spring breezes, whatever odors that escaped from the meth lab in the barn would be difficult to detect. Cypress was waiting until they actually started cooking to pull the raid. It was a lot more dramatic that way, and much more newsworthy than busting a lab that "could possibly" be used to make the stuff.

He had been in contact with Dalton, so he knew what the deal was with the asshole formerly known as Big Ink, now Bill Draper. He was supposed to bust the lab, seize the meth, and scare the shit out of Hal Draper and Derrick—but not arrest them because of the deal Customs and Border Protection had struck with Bill Draper. There was only one problem with that scenario, according to Cypress: he didn't take orders from Customs or any state agent. Screw 'em. He was busting these fuckers and he wanted the case closed.

Cypress had called Draper yesterday and had him come out to the front gate to view three dead hogs in the back of his pickup.

"These are the last of 'em," he told Draper. "We got sixteen of 'em, so we're pullin' out now. Gotta big job over in Round Rock, another pack of 'em ruinin' the Teravista Golf Club, diggin' up the greens, eatin' the grass, wallowin' in the water hazards."

Gabriel was betting that Draper and Fitzroy were nervous about the hunters and wouldn't start making the stuff until they left the area. Then they would crank up the operation, so to speak.

So, when he saw the gray smoke come out of a small chimney on the side of the barn, as if it were from a pellet stove, he signaled his men to start the raid. A pellet stove when it was 84 degrees outside? No way.

The raid was a snap. No resistance, no one hurt, and two meth-makers enjoying the hospitality of the Williamson County Jail on 4th Street in Georgetown. Then, for Gabriel Cypress, the shit hit the fan. With his reputation as a somewhat loose cannon, no one who knew him at DEA would doubt that he had deliberately ignored a voicemail from his superior demanding that he postpone the raid on Hal Draper's barn.

• • •

The pressure was starting to get to Dalton. For five days now they had been hunkered down in the bungalow, waiting for the attack that never came. It was driving the three of them nuts, but Dalton more so. Laura had called, frantic with worry, and left a message. George had called because Diana Ventura was demanding access to the commission's air boat logs for the past four months through the Florida Freedom of Information Act. Bill Draper had called, outraged that his brother was in jail, demanding a meeting and threatening to pull out of the World of Reptiles deal.

Dalton tried to put all negative thoughts out of his mind and called Laura back.

"Don't worry, I'm still ticking," he told her.

"Thank God. I'm so worried about you. And Phil."

"We're fine, but bored out of our minds. We need some action around here. I had a big day buying a new mattress. That snake gut smell was starting to get to us."

"How much longer?" she asked.

"Not sure. Probably a couple of days." Then he told her about their precautions, the super-protected bungalow and the rotating outside backup team—when those volunteers could make it. He laid it on thick that anyone attacking would be outnumbered two-to-one. He told her he loved her but had to go put out some fires, figuratively speaking.

Next he called George, who was furious with Cypress.

"I called his supervisor," he told Dalton. "Cypress is suspended, had to turn in his ID and pistol. Gary, the supervisor, told me that Cypress refused suspension and had resigned to 'do Indian stuff.'"

"Good riddance. When can you get those guys out of jail?"

"Working on it. Customs had to send another guy down there to take them to the Federal Building in Austin to officially release them."

"Fed red tape," Dalton noted.

"Redder than red," George told him. "And one other thing—Diana Ventura and those airboat logs. Phil said go ahead and give them to her. Is there any reason to deny her request, drag it out?"

"No," Dalton lied. "We're not hiding anything."

"Okay, she'll get them then. Maybe that will shut her up."

"Don't count on it," Dalton advised.

Dalton then called Bill Draper and gave him an update, but Bill was not a happy camper, complaining that his brother was still in jail and the terms of the deal had been broken, and on and on. A first class whiner. Dalton had had enough.

"Fuck you, Ink. You and your brother are goddamned criminals and should be in prison. You caught a lucky break and things will work out eventually. Now shut up and leave me alone. Don't want to do the deal? Okay, I'll have the state issue a warrant for your immediate arrest, as will the DEA and the FBI. Oh, and your yacht has been temporarily confiscated and your passport has been temporarily suspended. You're back in the USA to stay." Then he hung up.

• • •

"Now I've really pissed him off," Bill told Jamie. "He called me 'Ink' and said he would have me arrested."

"You were too hard on him," Jamie said, wide-eyed.

"My temper is a lot better, but still not normal yet. I'm sorry, honey, I was worried about Hal in jail in Texas."

"Text Mr. Dalton and apologize, right now."

"Okay. I'm writing, 'Mr. Dalton, I'm sorry I lost my temper and bugged you. It won't happen again. We're on for the WOR deal.'"

"Perfect," Jamie said.

Later, while eating dinner in the hotel restaurant, Bill, worried again, told her, "Tomorrow I'm going to try to see Dalton. I want to apologize in person."

"Oh, Bill, I don't think that's such a good idea."

"I think I have to. I know where he lives in Homestead."

"Please, give it a day. If your brother gets out tomorrow, everything will be okay. Just one more day," she pleaded.

"Okay honey, I'll do that."

He needs me, Jamie thought. A lot. And I wonder if Dalton's still coming to our wedding.

• • •

Diana was rarely shocked by anything in the mindbogglingly complex world of journalism, but the response from George Tompkins of the Effin' Doubleyous flabbergasted her. It was a text that read, not even one day after she filed the Florida FOI request, "Diana, would you like to pick up the logs or should we mail them?" That was the good news.

The bad news was that the logs contained no information on or connection with the snake death hotspots. She scanned the logs and sent them to Jeff Gordon.

"The logs are legitimate," he told her. "I had a friend of mine check them out and they are authentic."

"Fuck," Diana said.

"Good idea, but impractical right now," he offered, and she had to chuckle. She liked his sense of humor.

"Hey, Dr. Jeffie," she teased, "I have a plan for how to deal with the log issue in my article."

"And that would be?"

"Tell the truth."

"A new low for journalism."

"Sure, but then the Effin' Doubleyous will like me."

"I know this must be going somewhere."

"You and I will then double-team Dalton."

"What do I have to do?"

"Forget the fucking pythons, they're dead. But those Nile monitors are even scarier. Ask the python hunter how he would get rid of the lizard packs that have taken over Cape Coral."

"I can do that. What's in it for me?"

"Me."

"Done deal."

"Get your ass down here, you cutie." Diana was officially horny, and, by a strange coincidence, so was Dr. Jeff.

• • •

Zimmerman, on the other hand, was anxious, nervous, impatient, and furious all at the same time. The cause of his discomfort was the fact that he was forced to postpone Dalton's death. One of his hired Chechens, Moysar Basayev, was incapacitated from the malaria he had contracted while working as a military advisor and assassin during the last civil war in Sierra Leone.

Moysar's condition had started with chills, followed by fever, and then copious sweating accompanied a severe headache, exhaustion, and shooting pains in his muscles. Then came the nausea, vomiting, and diarrhea. Hell, for all Zimmerman knew, it could have been the flu. The delay was in its fifth day, and Zimmerman was bored. So in preparation for the attack on Dalton, he went to the former veterinarian for World of Reptiles and had her implant a GPS-enabled radio frequency identification chip in his right shoulder. Should he be captured, his rescuers would be able to track him down.

Then he had to find some suitable rescuers—no easy task for a murderer on the run like he was. But money talks, and ten grand down, with a promise of double that after he was rescued, had produced some friends of his late half-brother—fellow smugglers of course, but of automatic weapons rather than reptiles. He would check in with them via text once a day, and if he missed two days in a row, they were instructed to track him down. Fat chance that would ever happen, he thought, but still…

The implantation accomplished, the next thing on his to-do list was to get laid, and that was easily accomplished with a simple call to his favorite escort service in Miami, South Beach Babes, one of 96 such services in the area. For regulars like Zimmerman, the management provided a Two-Fer Service: two babes for two hours for 2,000, tip included. Live porn—nothing like it, he thought. That was when he received a text from Moysar that read. "I am better mostly. Tumorow we can kill."

Indeed we can, thought Zimmerman as he watched the two escorts ditch the dildo and change into their thongs and cheerleader outfits emblazoned with "Horlick High." Especially since my other Chechen found three more desperate countrymen eager to assist in the assassination. Life is good—and about to get much better.

• • •

Less than a day after Dalton had told him off, Bill received a brief text from his brother that read, "We're out. Call me when you get a chance."

Bill did a couple of fist raises, a little dance around the hotel room, and then he called Hal, who answered on the first ring.

"Thanks, Bro. No charges against us, but they took the meth and the lab equipment. Coulda been a lot worse."

"Fucking Cypress," Bill said. "You weren't supposed to be arrested at all."

"No big deal. We had beer and pizza behind bars. We had to pay, of course, but they were pretty nice to us."

"And the Feds got all the meth?"

"Are you still usin'?"

"No, but answer my question."

"They got every fuckin' gram, man." he said, which was a brotherly code for, "We've still got a bunch stashed in another location."

"Good. You better be looking for a real job."

"I'll text if I get work," Hal promised.

Jamie was ecstatic about the news because now Bill would calm down considerably and she could quit worrying about him.

Bill's phone rang and it was George Tompkins. Bill knew who he was but had never spoken with him.

"I guess you know that Customs released your brother and his co—uh, his friend."

"Yes sir."

"Are you ready to proceed with the purchase of World of Reptiles?"

"Yes sir."

"We've got a preliminary meeting set next Tuesday at 10:00 a.m. at World of Reptiles to work out the details of your purchase. Can you make it?"

"Yes sir."

"You'll need to bring proof of solvency."

"Like what?"

"Like a bank statement showing a balance of at least $500,000."

"Uh, my solvency is not in the bank. Do you take cash?"

Jeez, thought George, what Diana could do with this information. The Feds allowing William Draper to buy a confiscated reptile smuggler's business with methamphetamine trafficking money.

"There's no sense in carrying that amount of money around. I believe you. We'll assign some agents to assist you with the cash delivery at closing. You can inspect everything at the meeting. Volunteers from the South Florida Herpetology Society have been taking care of the reptiles during the transition. Where are you staying? I want to messenger over all the financial documents related to World of Reptiles—you should know what you're getting into."

"Good," Bill said. "Can I bring Jamie to the meeting?"

"Who's that?"

"My fiancé."

"Sure. And Mr. Draper?"

"Yes sir?"

"Congratulations to you and Jamie on your new business."

"Thank you, sir."

• • •

Jeff was waiting curbside at MIA with a small black carryon when Diana pulled up in her Lexus.

"Where's your snake net?" she asked as he climbed in.

"Retired forever. But I've been thinking a lot about big lizards."

"Nile monitors?"

287

"Yes. And Velociraptors."

"Fill me in."

"Famous dinosaur in Jurassic Park, the movie. The extinct Nile monitor, I'm calling it."

"What are you saying? This sounds sorta creepy."

"Don't you want that to titillate your faithful readers?"

"Get with it, Jeff!"

"Think of a title like, 'The Dinosaur of the 'Glades,' or 'The Modern Velociraptor in South Florida.'"

"Holy crap! You're onto something here. Are you hungry?"

"Starving."

"Then we're having an early dinner, but no damned brew pub. On me, as I promised."

Diana took him to The Stoned Crab at the huge outdoor shopping mall, The Falls. It was the sister restaurant to the one at the Ibis Bay resort in Key West. Her drink of choice was the usual glass of Viognier. He ordered a vodka tonic. The restaurant décor was artificially sea-funky, with nets and blue glass floats hanging from the walls, a mural of a harbor with fishing and shrimp boats behind the bar, and old photos of movie stars everywhere—many of them showing off their dead marlins and sailfish.

For dinner, Diana ordered the lobster-stuffed ravioli with shrimp and sherry cream sauce, while Jeff decided to try the steamed mussels in Thai coconut red curry sauce. They held up their glasses.

"Here's to big lizards," she toasted.

"That's so incredibly romantic," Jeff grinned.

"So, tell me about the Velociraptors."

"They called them Velociraptors in the movie, although they were modeled after Deinonychus, a larger and fiercer-looking dinosaur. But Velociraptors and Nile monitors have a lot in common." Jeff opened the file folder he had carried from the car and removed a single sheet of paper it. "Take a look at this comparison table. I thought this would be a good angle for your story."

Dr. Jeff, the scientist at work, she thought, staring at the table:

Attributes	Velociraptor	Nile Monitor
Length	7 feet	5-8 feet
Max. Weight	~33 pounds	20-44 pounds
Food	Reptiles	Mammals, reptiles, birds
Max. Land Speed	40 mph (on 2 feet)	30 mph (on 4 feet)
Stands on hind feet?	Yes	Occasionally
Strong tail?	Yes	Yes
Pack hunter?	Unknown but maybe	Sometimes

"This is great—I'm getting some ideas already. We'll work on this tomorrow. Tell me about yourself, Dr. Jeff." They traded biographical stories, had some very nice food, and felt comfortable with each other. Diana paid for the meal with her gold Amex and he thanked her.

"I've never understood why men think they have to pay for everything on a date," she said as they walked to her car.

"An ingrained tradition that men can't shake," he suggested. "Can you take me to Miami Beach? I've got a reservation at the Pelican Hotel. Room 314, the 'Me Tarzan, You Vain' Room."

"To hell with the hotel. Cancel the reservation. You're staying with me. Only one bed though, sorry."

"I'll tough it out somehow."

And then she planted a big one on his lips and he could feel the tip of her tongue run along his teeth and gums. Oh boy, he thought.

Later, after they had made love, Diana turned on the late news and they watched the report from Channel 4 about a pack of monitors that had attacked some campers at the Pepper Ranch Preserve in Collier County, near Immokalee. One person was dead, an eight-year-old boy, but the campers had driven off the pack with shots from their .22 target pistols and recovered his body.

19

The most dangerous trait the monitor lizard possesses may
be its aggressive and extremely ferocious personality. The
monitor lizard is much like the pit bull dog, in that it will
attack relentlessly. However, unlike the pit bull and other
short-tempered breeds of dogs, the monitor lizard cannot
be tamed. To go along with its venomous razor-sharp bite,
the monitor lizard has other weapons at its disposal. The tail
can account for more than half of the body's total length, and
the lizard is naturally disposed to use this formidable weapon
with whip-like action. When confronted or even mildly
agitated, the monitor will whip around with its muscular tail
in an attempt to incapacitate its prey or any perceived enemy.
—"All About Monitor Lizards," EarthsFriends.com,
December 20, 2017

On the night of the fifth day, at a few minutes before
midnight, a perimeter alarm went off. Phil, who was on
watch, hit the switch that alerted everyone sleeping and within
20 seconds the three of them were at their assigned positions
and the backyard lights lit up—to reveal a bewildered raccoon
looking for table scraps near a secured trash bin.

At 1:05 in the morning of the seventh day, the perimeter
of the backyard was violated again. This time the lights showed

a huge horned owl on the patio with its prey, a cotton rat. The owl flew off into the darkness with the rat still wiggling in a futile attempt to escape from the talons that gripped it.

At 2:21 in the morning of the eighth day, five Chechens and Zimmerman stormed the bungalow from four sides. The attack began with the Chechens' flare guns firing projectiles at three sides of the bungalow, including the front. The projectiles were supposed to explode and catch the bungalow on fire with burning potassium perchlorate, but they bounced harmlessly off the windows. When they hit the recently painted house siding, the perchlorate burned out, but the paint did not ignite.

"See why we painted the house?" Kevin said over the radio. "Fire-retardant paint."

Next came the attackers, wearing balaclavas and all black clothing, and carrying—what else—old Kalashnikovs. Kevin was on watch in back and Dalton, guarding the front of the house, heard him say on the radio, "They're wearing body armor—shoot for the legs." But he didn't follow his own instructions because when the backyard lights came on, the Chechens were still wearing night vision goggles. One of them didn't see the trip wire in the booby-trapped backyard, and fell flat on his face. Kevin had time to train the laser beam on his head and punch the bullet through his right eye socket.

A spray of bullets punched through the front door and one ricocheted, striking Dalton's vest over his lower right ribcage. It didn't draw blood, but it hurt like hell. The front light had been shot out, but Dalton had night vision goggles too, and peeked through a corner of the shattered window to see a black-clothed figure on top of the front wall, about to jump down. Dalton fired a burst from his Heckler-Koch G36 at the man's legs, and he fell back over the wall and out of sight.

Another Chechen, probably the one who shot through the front door, didn't even make it to the porch because he stepped on an M-14 that Kevin had activated at midnight after he locked the tall front gate. The blast tore off the Chechen's right leg and he bled out in less than two minutes.

Zimmerman was fucking terrified. He had expected—foolishly, he realized—that Dalton would be alone and that he would get to administer the coup de grâce once the Chechens captured him. But instead, Zimmerman was crouched behind Dalton's storage shed in the backyard and hadn't fired a single shot. There were explosions, suppressed automatic weapons firing, and he could hear sirens in the distance. Paralyzed with fear, he had no idea what to do.

Kevin had noticed someone on the left side of the storage shed but could see that the bandit was not firing his weapon. He hurried out the back door and around the right side of the shed. Before he got there, all gunfire stopped and he heard Dalton shout, "All clear! The rest of the fuckers ran away!"

But Dalton was wrong.

"Drop the rifle, asshole!" Kevin yelled from behind the man crouched in front of him. The man started to turn. Kevin struck him on the temple with the barrel of his Heckler-Koch, the man toppled over, and his unfired Kalashnikov slid over the gravel.

"Back here!" Kevin shouted. "I've got a live one! At least I think he's still alive."

Walking gingerly because of his severe bruise, Dalton found Kevin by the downed man, rolling his body over and feeling for a pulse. There was one. He pulled the balaclava over the guy's head, and stared at the unconscious Bruno Zimmerman. They both started laughing.

"What a pathetic jerk-off you are, Zimmerman," Dalton said, shaking his head.

Then there was a loud crack and Kevin fell on his side and

Dalton dove behind some metal trash barrels—not that they would stop a bullet.

"Sniper," Dalton said. "Kevin?"

Deep breaths came from Kevin, so he was still alive, and finally he managed to say, "Body armor saved me but I was really punched in the gut. Turn out the lights."

Dalton pulled the remote out of his pocket and everything went black. The sirens were closing in now. "Where is that fucker?" he asked. Their eyes slowly adjusted to the ambient light of the city.

"Rooftop, I think." Kevin pointed up the alley. "There, I saw movement. You move Zimmerman into the house. I'll be back in a few."

Dalton was hurting so badly he knew he couldn't move a kitten. "Phil, do you copy?"

"Loud and clear. I chased one down the street but couldn't catch him."

"Back alley. I need you move a body. I can't lift anything—got hit in the ribcage."

"No problem," Phil said, and in less than a minute he reached Dalton, grabbed Zimmerman's boots, and dragged him up to the house, the man's head bouncing on the three wooden steps up to the back porch.

The Homestead police arrived first, and Dalton was glad Kevin had alerted them a week ago about what was going on. Lieutenant John Montoya called out, identified himself, and Dalton answered, then opened the front gate, holding out his F and W ID out for Montoya to see.

"I see two DBs here," Montoya said. "Any more lying around?"

"There's another in the backyard."

"Jesus, you guys weren't kidding about an attack. Where's Cooper?"

"Chasing a sniper."

"I'd better call this in. Central, Montoya here at Dalton's bungalow. The Effin' Doubleyous are okay, but we've got three bad guys dead—"

A shot rang out from a block away. "Make that four," Dalton said. "I hope."

Kevin arrived back at the bungalow at the same time Brad Richards and his FBI team showed up. Dalton had just enough time to text Laura, "It's over. We won."

They won all right, but it was quite a ways from being over. After all, Dalton had two captives in suspended animation in his spare bedroom.

• • •

In her entire journalistic career, Diana had never worked with a coauthor, but since her story was reptilian in nature, it was extremely handy to have a live-in herpetologist assisting her with her new series on the monitors, which she was now calling "Forget the Snakes and Fear the Lizards." Like the python series, this one would also be a three-parter, and she had bounced the idea off of Sean Lamposte, who gave her enthusiastic approval.

The first article, "Dinos in the 'Glades," relied heavily on Jeff's comparison of the monitors to velociraptors, complete with the table of similarities which Sean said he would run alongside an artist's renderings of the two species, whose heads would look much the same. Jeff had given her an authoritative lead quote that went, "Much like the late Burmese pythons, the Nile monitors are perfectly adapted to the Everglades and now share the title of top predator with the American alligator."

The next article, "Davey Sinclair: Lizard Victim," would cover the attack by the pack of monitors at Pepper Ranch Preserve and the sad story of the death of little Davey Sinclair. She would touch on the monitors that killed the endangered Flori-da panther. And, with the help of Dr. Jeff, she would advise the public on how to avoid a similar fate.

But where she would really shine would be in the final installment, "$10 a Tail," where she—with the official help and support of Dr. Jeffrey Gordon, herpetologist first-class—would call for a bounty on the monitors. She figured that the rednecks, crackers, and gun nuts, not to mention motorcycle gangs and teenage hoodlums, would enthusiastically support the idea of killing lizards for fun and profit. And she could take a jab at Dalton by suggesting that the Reverend Hixon Stemmons, of the Deep South Baptist Church in Cape Coral, had been right all along to encourage his bored teenagers to start using their pellet guns. With a bounty of $10 a tail, think of all the money the church could raise! And as Jeff had mentioned, she emphasized the fact that monitors were a lot easier to find than those sneaky pythons.

When she mentioned this idea to Sean, he took the liz-ard ball and ran it into the end zone. The Herald, the Tampa Tribune, and Channel 6 Miami would be the media sponsors of the LEP, or Lizard Eradication Project, and he told Diana that he had pitched the sponsorship idea to Florida Power and Light, the City of Cape Coral, and the Florida Fish and Wildlife Conservation Commission—with all of them likely to come on board for $50,000 each. LEP had so much money coming in they could hire a PRES, a professional reptile eradi-cation specialist, to manage the slaughter.

Meanwhile, she and Jeff were rutting like rams and ewes at least three times a day—well, for the first two days, anyway. Diana was riding high, on top of the world, as happy as a clam, or any other cliché of that sort. Then Sean called again, and this time he told her that she was a finalist in the Pulitzer Prize for local investigative specialized reporting for her python series.

While Phil was taking care of the "patients," as they called them, Dalton and Kevin had arranged to meet at the Resurrection Beer Bar, where there were no microbrews in sight. In fact, a large sign hanging above the bar read, "IF YOU WANT A MICROBREW, GO TO HELL."

The bar had on tap all the old, resurrected beers and their cheesy slogans, including Pabst Blue Ribbon ("This one has the touch."), Olympia ("It's the water."), Schaefer ("The one beer to have when you're having more than one."), Schlitz ("The beer that made Milwaukee famous."), Ballantine ("When you see the three-ring-sign, ask the man for Ballantine."), Falstaff ("The choicest product of the brewer's art."), Rheingold ("If you've got the time, we've got the beer."), and Colt 45 ("It works every time."), plus sixteen even more obscure brews in cans, like Courage and Blatz.

There were no servers, so customers ordered at the bar, just like in an authentic English pub like The Drunken Duck in West Palm Beach.

"PBR," Kevin said to the barman. Dalton, with some trepidation, ordered a Schaefer, although knew he didn't have the time for more than one. He paid and they took a table far away from the big screen that was playing a loop of grainy old TV beer spots.

"Now, what do we do, summarily execute them?"

"I think that's too gentle for them," Dalton replied, "not enough suffering."

Kevin nodded. "I get that. We could turn them in—that would be some suffering."

"But they wouldn't necessarily die if we did that. Zimmerman would probably get the death penalty because some of his murders were videotaped. But Mozell—who knows?" He took a sip of his beer, thought, yuck, and walked back to the bar for a glass of water.

Back at the table, he looked at Kevin. "What about that sniper?" They hadn't had a chance to talk since all the excitement because they were separated so each could give a statement to the police at the nearest substation.

"I found the house, but I couldn't cover both the back and front doors, so I staked out the car."

"How did you know it was the right one?"

"It was the same one they'd been using to surveil us. I memorized the tag last week. Idiots. Anyway, I was across the street, behind a pickup. When the Chechen got to the car, he started fumbling for his keys, and I shot him in the back of the head."

"Of course you did. I noticed how you took charge during the raid, and Phil and I sorta naturally followed your lead."

Kevin just nodded.

"Where did you get the M-14s? They were retired in the seventies. I looked it up on Wikipedia."

Kevin looked off into space. "I'd rather not say." His dark face was frowning and he was uncomfortable.

"You are—were—more than just a Marine sergeant. It showed even before the raid. You knew exactly what to do, no guesswork at all. Were you some kind of Marine special forces?"

"Why are you asking?"

"Because Phil and I quit Fish and Wildlife yesterday. We had a meeting with our supervisor, George Tomkins, and told him about our new business. We want you to join us."

"What kind of business?"

"It's called ECIS—Environmental Crimes Investigative Service."

Kevin relaxed a little. "Well, I have to admit that I really liked the recent action."

"Hopefully future investigations won't be quite so dangerous."

"Is telling you about my past a requirement for being a partner?"

"No."

"Good. In that case, I'll tell you. I was Force Recon Marines."

"Like Navy SEALS?"

Kevin smiled a rare smile. "We had quite a competition going on with those guys. Too bad they got picked for taking down bin Laden. But I'm glad that somebody got him. Anyway, I have to say all my PTSD symptoms are gone, I feel alive again, and that was a helluva lot of fun."

"Fun?"

"Okay, exciting, stimulating, interesting. Whatever. How are you going to fund this new business? Where will you find the customers? How much money can we make?"

They spent about 15 minutes discussing Dalton's coming inheritance, how they would set up the business and run it, but they couldn't avoid the inevitable forever. Dalton told him his plan for Mozell and Zimmerman.

"That plan is sound," Kevin said. "And fair to the perps." So the only loose end is Jenny. Do we tell her?"

"She doesn't need to know and doesn't want to know. She's no longer part of our team, anyway."

"When do we do it?"

"The sooner the better. First thing tomorrow."

"I'll join you and Phil in ECIS. I can fish in my spare time."

They shook hands and looked at their still-full beer glasses.

"The Resurrection Beer Bar is going to fail," Kevin said.

"Agreed."

• • •

Bill and Jamie were house-hunting in Homestead, and it wasn't going well. Bill had reasoned that if they were buying World of Reptiles, they should live nearby, but neither of them liked nearby. They simply didn't like Homestead. They had looked at 12 houses and none of them had clicked. Neither of them could figure out what was wrong with the area. There were the requisite palm trees, outlet malls, fishing shops, car dealerships, and citrus markets. So what was wrong?

Bill pulled into the empty parking lot at World of Reptiles. "Someday, darling, all of this will be ours. Like next week."

Jamie looked at him askance. "Billy," she said slowly, "I have a confession to make."

"You're seeing another guy with fading tattoos behind my back."

"No, silly. My confession is that I hate snakes. I don't think I could work in a store like that. I'd feely antsy."

"Antsy," Bill repeated.

"Yeah, like things were crawling all over me."

"Jamie, no one said you had to work here."

"But I thought, I mean, we're a team and I want to help with the family business."

"I'm sure that a trauma nurse like you can find work if you want to."

"Maybe we could live in Coral Gables or Boca and commute."

And then it hit Bill that he wasn't looking at the situation in the right way. World of Reptiles was not a career, it was an investment. He hadn't even looked at the financials that George Tompkins had sent over. He was paying half a million for a business that was worth—what? The most important thing Bill had learned from running a fish meal plant was that business connections were essential to success. And one of the most interesting connections he had made over the years was a business broker named Wilma Noggins, who had tried over and over again to get Bill interested in diversification. She had plenty to sell, this being south Florida.

Bill called her and she answered on the first ring, "Noggins Brokerage, your business is my business."

"Hi, Ms. Noggins, this is Bill Draper. You used to know me as Big Ink."

"Well, where the hell have you been? I heard the fish meal plant closed. What's going on, Inky?"

"It's a long story. I'm buying a business called World of Reptiles and I need some advice. I'll pay you, of course."

"Where are you right now?"

"In the parking lot of World of Reptiles in Homestead."

"Get your ass over here."

"Yes, ma'am."

Jamie was taken aback a little when she met Wilma Noggins, not expecting an 83-year-old woman with bright red hair, in a business suit and high heels.

"Look," she said to Bill after a brief hug, handing him a hardcover book, "I finally got it published."

Bill looked at the cover of the book, which had a photo of Wilma when she must have been 40—and a real looker. "Back in the day," she confided to Jamie, "they used to call me Wilma Knockers. That was before I had the breast reduction surgery." Her book was titled Retire and Die, and she started explaining her philosophy of no retirement, ever, for anyone.

Bill said, "Uh, Ms. Noggins…"

"Okay, enough about me. Whatcha got, Ink—I mean, Bill?"

He gave her a carefully edited version of his decision to buy World of Reptiles, and explained that he didn't know what it was worth. She thumbed through the financial printouts he had brought and said, "There's a restaurant three blocks south that serves excellent gumbo. Go have lunch and come back in an hour or so. I'll tell what the business is worth for $500."

"You charge $500 an hour?" Jamie said, amazed. "Cool."

"I'm giving your man here a courtesy discount."

Wilma was right—the shrimp gumbo was excellent. And when they returned to Noggins Brokerage, she was beaming.

"Such a deal," she said. "Customs must really want to dump World of Reptiles.

I read all these numbers three times, and I know the accountants who prepared them. Top notch people. You're paying $500,000 for a company that's worth nearly $3,000,000."

"Wow," Bill said.

"Tell you what, Billy-Boy. Buy this place and turn it over to me. I'll find a buyer and flip it, take my commission, and you're home free to live the rest of your life the way you want—provided you promise not to retire."

"Oh, I won't retire, I do promise that."

Wilma looked at him intently. "What do you really, really want to do?"

Bill put his arm around Jamie's shoulders. "I really, really want to raise a family," he said and kissed her on the temple.

"Ah, ain't that cute. Look, Bill, I've got another meeting, so I'll get the paperwork together. Deal?"

"You bet, Wilma."

• • •

Back at the bungalow, shortly before midnight, Kevin adjusted the pentobarbital drip. "Once I stop the drip for our trip, they'll wake up in a few hours," he told Dalton.

"We'd better get some sleep," Phil suggested.

"Our last night together in our newly remodeled bungalow," Dalton said. "How romantic."

"Safe house, you mean," Kevin corrected.

"Just the three of us," Dalton said, suddenly serious. "No one else knows—ever. Zimmerman and Mozell, well they just got away." The three of them bumped fists simultaneously.

20

They are vicious, brainless, prehistoric, carnivorous monsters
that hunt in packs on land and in the water, and they are
running loose in south Florida. The truth is that the largest
Nile Monitors can be over nine feet long and weigh upwards
of 200 pounds (their lowballing '7 foot long' was just plain
wrong as that is the average length). Note that they are able
to out-run and out-swim humans. Imagine encountering a
hungry pack of these meat-eating monsters out in Florida's
back country. —Jeb, on LifesaCoast.com, 2013

Kevin's airboat was a black, 18-foot, 2014 Floral City Law
Enforcement model with an uncommon sunken deck that
was designed to hold captured offenders. Its custom-made tarp
covered the deck while it was in transit, fastened with a nylon
line snaked through grommets and attached to the small cleats
on the top of the deck. It wasn't perfect for concealing Zimmerman and Mozell, but it would have to do.

At 6:00 a.m., Dalton opened the gate to the alley, and Kevin backed the trailer past the storage shed and into the backyard. It was raining lightly. Zimmerman and Mozell, still in
the spare bedroom, were bound with silver duct tape on their
wrists behind their backs, around their ankles, and over their
mouths. Dalton and Phil had stripped and bound them right
after Kevin turned off the drip.

They moved Zimmerman to the airboat first, with Kevin on his torso, Phil on his waist, and Dalton, who was still bruised, on his feet. When they reached the boat trailer, they pushed him up onto the main deck then carefully maneuvered him into the sunken deck on the right side of the support frame for the three seats. Using bungee cords, they lashed his hands and feet to the frame so that he could not make a sound if he woke up too soon. With the same procedure, they loaded Mozell into the boat and fastened the tarp securely over both of them.

Dalton had already selected their destination: the far western part of the Everglades Wildlife Management Area near the border with Big Cypress National Preserve—an hour and 15 minute drive from Homestead. They would launch from the same boat ramp the Drone Squad had used at the Broward County Rest Area. With Dalton driving, they took US 27 north toward Alligator Alley.

Dalton's phone rang through his Bluetooth. It was George Tompkins, their former boss at the Conservation Commission. "Hello George," he said. "Phil's here with me, so you're on the speaker."

"Hello to both of you. Listen, I just had a call from Bob Mixon—remember him?"

"The former governor? Sure."

"Well, one of his do-gooder projects is the King's Bay Manatee Sanctuary over near Crystal River. It seems that somebody is killing their manatees—two of them, anyway. He asked me if any of our people could investigate. But I had to tell him that two of our best agents resigned yesterday."

"Aw, George, sorry about that."

"Don't worry, I told him what you two were up to and he wants to talk. Gave me his very private cell phone number. Call him if you're interested." He read off the number and Phil wrote it down. Dalton thanked him, disconnected, pulled his phone out of his pocket and handed it to Phil, who dialed.

"Bob Mixon," said a voice on the speaker after the second ring.

"Governor Mixon, this is Sam Dalton. George Tompkins asked me to call you."

"I'm not the governor anymore, so please call me Bob. Yes, two of our tagged manatees have been killed in the past week. Stab wounds that penetrated the skulls, according to the necropsy. George told me you'll be investigating environmental crimes, so I guess this qualifies. What do you charge for your service?"

"Well, sir, our resignations don't kick in for two weeks, so we're not even in business yet. Don't have a business license, and we don't have all the permits that private investigators need."

"I can grease the wheels for all of all that if you two can get up to Tallahassee right away."

Phil shrugged and nodded. Kevin, in the back seat of the extended cab, gave Dalton a thumbs-up. "What about first of next week? Monday afternoon? We could drive up there and come back via King's Bay."

"Sounds like a plan. I'll meet you at King's Bay first thing Tuesday."

"You gotta deal," Dalton said. "Say, could you email me the necropsy reports? We need to find out what kind of a knife can do that sort of damage. Manatee skulls are pretty damned thick."

"Text me your email. And thanks, Sam, I really appreciate you doing this."

"Our pleasure, sir. See you Tuesday."

Dalton disconnected and Phil and Kevin gave a little round of applause.

"Maybe the first job for ECIS," Phil said.

"Could be. I said Monday because Laura would kill me if I dropped everything and went up there. I haven't seen her for more than a week."

"Tell me about it," Kevin said. "Monday's perfect."

Traffic on US 27 slowed considerably as they neared I-75 for a Florida Highway Patrol check session in the middle of the divided highway right at the Recreation Road exit. Single vehicles were waved through, while enclosed trucks, vans, and trailers were checked.

When they reached a state trooper, he pointed to the right. "Please pull over there, sir. Won't take but a minute. License, registration, and proof of insurance, please."

Dalton added his Fish and Wildlife ID to the mix and passed everything to the trooper.

"Ah, fellow law enforcement personnel. I guess you guys are after the same boys we're looking for." He passed them a flyer with photos of Zimmerman and Mozell.

"We are, but not today. Just taking a day off."

"Sam Dalton," the trooper said. He was, a tall, blonde-haired man. "That sounds familiar. Weren't you with NCIS? In Key West?"

"I was."

"I remember the incident. I was Key West PD at the time. We thought it was a cluster-fuck and you got sandbagged."

Dalton laughed. "That's one way to put it. Meet Phil Everett—he was Coast Guard, on that patrol boat with me. We both had to resign."

The two of them shook hands, and Phil showed him his F and W ID. "And this is Kevin Cooper—he's a fishing guide out of Key Largo." A second round of hand shaking.

"What's under the tarp?" the trooper asked casually.

"Just two DBs," Dalton joked, and everyone laughed. "Keeping our gear out of the rain. We're going bass fishing."

"Good luck with that in this weather, guys. Nice meeting you."

"Was that close, or what?" Phil asked as they moved over the ramp to the interstate.

"Life in the fast lane," Kevin commented.

They reached the Broward County Rest Area and launched the airboat without further incident. All three pulled on their rain jackets and hoods. When the airboat floated, Dalton pulled up the ramp, parked the truck in the lot and hopped aboard at the dock. Phil set the Humminbird to N25.98, W80.83 and they pulled into the canal. Dalton loosened the tarp and checked on their passengers. Zimmerman and Mozell were still unconscious.

"No other parked trucks with trailers," Kevin said.

"I noticed that," Dalton agreed. "I guess people don't like the Everglades in the rain."

Phil, who had spent a lot of time in the general area with the Drone Squad, mostly remembered the route to one of the larger hammocks. About 40 minutes later, Phil cut the engine and the boat glided to the shore. All three of them pulled on galoshes and they carefully carried their captives, one at a time, to a flat area about 50 feet from the water. Kevin pulled out his flip knife and cut all the duct tape off the men's wrists and ankles, and pulled the short strips off their mouths.

When Kevin finished, they carefully picked up all the tape and took it with them. The only litter they would leave in the 'Glades would be that of the human kind.

• • •

Dalton hated lying to anyone, and particularly Laura, but what else could he do? If he told her the truth about Zimmerman and Mozell and what they had done to those two murderers, she might leave him. She had certainly done it before. So his major problem was, how the hell do you downplay being attacked by six guys and killing four of them?

"Booby traps," he told her, "that's what got them. Kevin's really good at that sort of thing."

"And one of them got you," she said, pointing the ugly purple bruise. "Does it hurt very much?"

"Only when you get on top and ride really hard," he teased.

He focused on the aftermath and how grateful he was to the FBI guy, Brad Richards, who had taken charge of the chaotic post-raid scene at the bungalow. Brad had stepped up and told the Homestead police, and even the Customs investigator, that the operation was a Fish and Wildlife and FBI joint operation (it wasn't), a sting on some reptile smugglers aligned with Bruno Zimmerman who were out for revenge against himself and Phil for the airport bust, which was pretty much true. And Brad had covered his ass in more ways than one.

Dalton had managed to lock the door to the spare bedroom, and opening it had come up only once, right when Brad had arrived with two other agents. He had taken the agent aside, pointed to the door, and said, "I locked it. No one goes in there, okay?"

Brad had given him the FBI stare for a couple of seconds, then said, "And I don't want to know what's in there, right?"

"Let's just say that would complicate this situation enormously. What you don't know won't hurt me," Dalton had replied. But he didn't repeat that part of the story to Laura.

One of Richards' agents came up. "Illegal Chechens, all the dead ones, anyway."

"Perfect. The best thing for all of us," Richards finally said, "is for the FBI to seal this crime scene. It's a national security issue."

And that's the way it was resolved. The bodies were carried away—the third Chechen, the one Dalton had shot in the legs, had died and the remaining one was on the loose. The official story was that no one knew if Zimmerman had been part of the attack. Like Mozell, his whereabouts were unknown.

So, in bed, Laura had calmed down considerably and Dalton changed the subject to the two murdered manatees in King's Bay, and that ECIS had its first case.

"Who would hurt a manatee?" Laura asked. It was rhetorical, but Dalton had been wondering the same thing.

"Apparently they were stabbed numerous times in their skulls," he said.

"Which means that the killer had to be in the water with them."

"Yes, swimming around with some 1,000-pound sea cows. You could be crushed to death between two of them, or even drowned. Most people don't know it, but manatees can swim 15 miles an hour in short bursts. If you were head-butted at that speed, you'd be in serious trouble."

"So why would anyone do that?"

"The only thing I can think of is for sport."

"Sport?"

"People up in Georgia hunt feral hogs with dogs and finish them off using just a knife. That's a very dangerous sport. Some people swim with sharks. Rodeo clowns get gored by bulls. People drown when noodling catfish—catching 80-pounders with their bare hands. All for sport."

Laura was finally done with it all. Her man was back in her life, which would now return to normal. She had other things to think about, domestic things.

"We have an important decision to make," she told him.

"And that would be…"

"Do we eat dinner now, or after we make love again?"

• • •

The first thing that jumped into Bone Mozell's mind when he woke up was that Scottie had beamed him up from the tunnel exit of the bomb shelter to the Enterprise and then beamed him back down to a hammock in the middle of the fucking Everglades. And he was buck naked. And thirsty. And so hungry he wasn't even horny. And weak. And mosquito-bitten, with poison ivy pustules on his face, neck, and the backs of his hands. And sitting next to a very naked Bruno Zimmerman, who was passed out on his back on a pile of twigs and leaves, snoring, a Florida bark scorpion walking over his genitalia. Serves him right, thought Mozell.

The eight tiny feet of the scorpion tickling his dick and balls caused an automatic reaction from Zimmerman, who clumsily tried to swat it away, but not before it stung him in his urethra. He grabbed himself, looked around, and saw Mozell. So, he thought, this is what Hell's like.

"Dalton," Mozell said bitterly.

"Gotta be," Zimmerman squeaked. He was beginning to feel the real pain of the sting kick in. "We're fucked, and it's your fault."

"My fault? You're the one who fucked it all up! You were infiltrated by two spies at the same time!"

"You burned down your own fucking warehouse, you moron."

"Look at us. Does any of that matter now?

"No, Bone," Zimmerman said, a trace of remorse in his voice, "it doesn't."

"Truce?"

"For now."

"We gotta think survival, Bruno, and when you're lost in the wilderness, you don't try to find your way back home. You stay in one place and wait for rescue."

"Oh, I've got that worked out," said Zimmerman. "I had a GPS locator implanted in my shoulder."

"You mean the shoulder with the stitches in it?"

"What?"

"Feel it, dumb ass. Somebody cut it out of you."

"Then we'll just walk out."

"Walk out? Are you crazy? Float out would be more like it. A canal over there, so we can swim with the 'gators. Saw grass in that direction, which would rip us to shreds. No, we stay here. What are our basic requirements? Water, food, shelter, clothing."

"We can weave skirts out of the saw grass," Zimmerman said sarcastically.

"Water. It's right there, and this far north it's not salty, but loaded with giardia. So we get the shits but survive until someone finds us."

"So what do we eat, Mr. Survival Expert?"

"See that bush right there? That's a red-tipped coco plum. Native to south Florida. My mother grew them and made jam with the fruits." Mozell walked to the bush and starting picking the purple fruits. He sat down beside Zimmerman, gave him some, and they started eating.

"Better than nothing," Zimmerman admitted.

"Finish your lunch. We're going to weave some palmetto blankets to keep the mosquitoes off of us tonight."

"You're a swamp homemaker," Zimmerman said.

And that's how they survived their first night on the hammock.

• • •

Dalton decided to bring Laura with him to the brunch with Diana and Jeff, and surprisingly, she was looking forward to it. "It won't be boring," she told him. "With Diana as the hostess, anything could happen. And I want to meet this Jeff character.

313

Diana hooked up with a snake guy? Who woulda thought?"

"He's not a snake guy, Laura, he's a poisonous tree frog expert."

"How do you know that?"

"I'm an investigator. I find out things."

"Well, show me your gun."

"Later, honey. Let's get going."

The first thing out of Diana's mouth when she opened the door to her condo was, "No, it's not catered. We made it all ourselves. Or rather, Jeff cooked it for us."

Jeff came out of the kitchen dressed in white shorts and a shirt with red hibiscus flowers on it. Dalton's first impression was that he seemed like a real nice guy.

Jeff served them café con leche, a tostada—simple buttered Cuban bread with sea grape jam, a Spanish omelet with chorizo, onions, and potatoes, and a bowl of mango and papaya chunks with lime juice and red chile powder. Dalton's second impression was that Jeff was an excellent cook. Maybe that's why Diana fell for him, he thought.

"Jeff and I know that you killed all the snakes in south Florida," Diana said, sipping on her Cuban coffee. Laura's eyes went wide.

"Really?" Dalton asked. "You haven't written about it."

"Because we can't prove it," she replied, not bitter, just matter-of-fact. "So now we don't care. We have bigger plans that may, on occasion, tie in with some of yours."

"I'm listening," Dalton said.

"Jeff took a six month sabbatical from the University of Florida. He's working on syndicating my new environmental column in major national newspapers and blogs."

Dalton chuckled. "Excuse me, but what does a tree frog expert know about the specialized business of syndication?"

Jeff smiled and said, "It's not about what I know or don't

know—I'm a quick study on just about any subject—it's Diana's credibility that will drive this boat when she wins a Pulitzer Prize."

"And this has what to do with me?"

"We heard that you resigned from Fish and Wildlife."

"True."

"And that you and Phil Everett are going to be environmental crimes investigators—private, of course."

"Also true."

"Well, you're going to need clients and Diana's going to need subjects for her columns. Maybe we could share some information down the road."

"That's not a bad idea, Jeff. There's bound to be some overlap. I'd have to get the clients' permission to share that information."

"Of course."

Diana changed the subject. "Are you two getting married?" she asked Laura.

"We've been talking about it," Laura admitted, "but no firm plans yet. What about you two?"

Diana laughed. "You never know, but this is the longest relationship I've ever had—more than a month now. And we're living together! That's never happened before."

"What was your longest relationship before this one?" Laura asked.

"Four days," Diana replied, and everyone laughed.

"And the ten-minute crush on this nearly 50-year-old?" Laura asked, and Dalton wondered where the hell this was going. So did Jeff, so Diana explained.

"It's gone now because of Dr. Jeff, but I did have a ten-minute crush on Dalton when he was helping me with that Zimmerman creep. Then he told me the Playtex story and my crush went away."

315

"What Playtex story?" Jeff and Laura asked nearly simultaneously.

"Tell you later," Diana said to Jeff.

"Tell you later," Dalton said to Laura. And then to Diana and Jeff, "If you win the Pulitzer, we'll talk."

"Fair enough," Jeff said, smiling. "And when you get your first case, we'll talk."

"Oh, I've got my first case," he told them. "Somebody's murdering manatees over at King's Bay." Diana and Jeff looked a little stunned.

Kevin called him while they were driving back to Laura's place. "What's up, Kevin?"

"I got the first safe house rental," he said. "Fort Lauderdale PD—they've got to keep a DA safe until a trial. She's had threats."

"How much?"

"Exactly $300 a day for at least two weeks."

"The first ECIS income. Congrats." They disconnected.

"A safe house?" Laura asked. "You never told me—"

"Your favorite bungalow is now rented," he told her.

• • •

Their second day on the hammock was as uneventful as the first—until night fell, that is. They spent the day attempting to make some sort of shelter, but that was extremely difficult without any tools to work with, not even a decent rock. That was because the only rocks in the Everglades were limestone—calcium carbonate, which rates a lousy three on the hardness scale. They were reduced to bending, twisting, and trying to snap branches and small trees in an attempt to build the framework for a small hut.

They dined on coco plums washed down with swamp water. As the sun was setting, they retreated to their half-built leaf hut and pulled the palmetto leaf "blankets" over their naked bodies. A half moon soon appeared in the night sky, casting an eerie light over the 'Glades. They heard yapping sounds, like small dogs, interspersed with hisses and soft splashes.

As the yapping grew more intense and Mozell asked, "What's that damn yapping from, the chihuahuas of the Everglades?"

"I think I know," Zimmerman replied. "Do you see what I see?"

"You mean the eyes? It's the moon reflecting off of alligator eyes in the water."

Zimmerman snorted. "You may know some things about plants, but you don't know shit about reptiles."

"What do you mean?"

"Alligators don't hunt in packs. I count 26 eyes, 13 pair."

"What are they?" Mozell asked, a tremor in his voice.

"Varanus niloticus. A pack of Nile monitors has tracked us down."

Mozell was frozen with fear. "Well, it was nice knowing you, Bruno."

"Fuck you very much. Now they're starting to come out of the water."

Bone Mozell's last coherent thought was of his mother's favorite cartoon that she had clipped from an old New Yorker magazine in her dentist's office. She had it laminated, then framed for display in her kitchen. It was a bullfrog sitting on a lily pad. In the thought bubble above his head were the words, "Life's a swamp, and then you croak."

AFTER

At daybreak the next day the vultures showed up on the hammock, but found that the pickings were slim. The scent was there, but where was the meat?

$$\bullet \ \bullet \ \bullet$$

Two and a half weeks after the disappointed vultures left the hammock, Bill Draper emceed the grand reopening of World of Reptiles in a reptile-free tent in the parking lot, with music by the Amazing Lizard Aces. During intermission, Bill introduced the new owner, one Emerson Stevens, president of RCA, the Reptile Corporation of America. Stevens told the crowd that RCA was committed to repopulating the native snakes in South Florida, and had acquired the assets of Save Our Snakes to assist in achieving that goal. He also announced that First Sunshine Bank of South Florida was sponsoring the Florida Native Herpetological Collection that would breed venomous rattlesnakes, coral snakes, copperheads, and cottonmouths for the restocking.

$$\bullet \ \bullet \ \bullet$$

A week later, the Manatee Fish Meal plant was sold to a company with alligator farms supplying frozen alligator sashimi to Tokyo. It was advertised in Japan as a new food to "radically increase the size and durability of the Asian penis by eating this powerful reptile's male parts." The lab reports from

Florida Department of Environmental Protection on Big Ink's fish meal finally were available, but were published so late they were useless. The meal was eight percent fish, 12 percent alligator, and eight percent python—and the mercury count could kill every chicken in Florida. But since that brand was no longer produced or sold, nobody paid any attention to the report, and the file was soon deleted from the Florida state database.

• • •

Two months later, Bill and Jamie were married at the Safari Base Camp at Monkey Jungle in a faux Indian wedding ceremony with sitar music. A langur monkey smoking a cigarette delivered their rings on a red pillow. Dalton and Laura were in attendance, and there were crackers at the ceremony too, but each one of them had a little blob of caviar in the middle of it. At the reception, Jamie announced that she was pregnant with their first child.

• • •

A week after that, Diana Ventura won the Pulitzer Prize for her python series in the category "Local Investigative Specialized Reporting." Diana and Dr. Jeff, who were still living together at her place, celebrated with dinner at the Miami Institute of Molecular Gastronomy. Diana had the gnocchi green dumplings with broccoli rabe, garlic powder, and anchovies, while Jeff tried the oyster with sea gel and aromas. They were starving when they left the restaurant and stopped at Apocalypse Pizza on the way back to Diana's.

• • •

At about the same time, Dalton, Laura, Phil, and Kevin officially opened ECIS, Environmental Crimes Investigative Service. And ECIS had its first contract: find out who murdered the manatees in King's Bay. Laura and Dalton were married on his birthday at Fairchild Tropical Botanic Gardens, and with the some of the proceeds from the stock sales, they bought a house together in Key Largo with a huge rec room that became their offices. Laura badgered him into writing a letter of apology to the Reverend Hixon Stemmons of the Deep South Baptist Church in Cape Coral. "Sorry I called you a sick puppy," he texted the reverend. "Looks like you had it right with the bounty idea after all."

• • •

A year after the vultures landed on Zimmerman-Mozell Memorial Hammock, a gravid female Burmese python, apparently IBD-immune, parthenogenetically produced 92 eggs in a now virus-free hammock, not too far from where her immigrant ancestors first landed in the 'Glades in 1992.

Read on for a
sample of the next
ECIS Eco-Thriller

THE MANATEE
HUNTERS

BEFORE

Within ten seconds after he finished reading the banner ad on the Global Hunting Group's website, Hamilton Jones was on his cell phone speaking with his in-house corporate counsel, Cyril McNaughton.

"The GHG is up to its usual dirty tricks, Cyril."

"What's it this time?" he asked with a weary voice.

"I'll read it to you. 'The most exciting hunting adventure we've ever produced! Bid for your chance to hunt a 500-pound fierce grizzly bear—in Texas! We're auctioning off our first Texas bear hunt ever, live on Facebook one week from today.' We've got to stop this atrocity, Cyril."

"Uh, pretty nasty stuff, Ham. Let me look into this and get some kind of strategy together. When's the hunt?"

"Three weeks from today."

"I'll get right on it. Call you tomorrow."

Hamilton Jones, the CEO and president of the fourth-largest animal support group in the U.S., the Animal Freedom League, was fuming as he poured himself a shot of Macallan's 20-year to calm down a bit. No wonder he was upset. The mission statement of his Animal Freedom League was terse and oddly negative: "We believe that animals are sentient beings. Therefore, we are anti-hunting, anti-fishing, anti-zoo, anti-rodeo, anti-circus, and anti-anything else that harms or exploits animals." A "canned" bear hunt, as they called the hunts on game ranches, certainly fit well into that statement.

Personally, Jones wasn't opposed to ranching or commercial fishing, figuring that those animal abuses were a bit morally superior to mass human starvation. But some of the devotees of the AFL disagreed with him. Sometimes violently. He struggled to answer questions from the media, like, "Some of your supporters are described as environmental terrorists. What is your response to that?"

"I do not monitor the political beliefs or actions of all my 43,000 members," was his weak stock answer. Well, it was true, anyway.

The second scotch relaxed him enough to stop thinking negatively. Somewhere out there, he knew, were probably hundreds of wealthy bear-loving ladies who grew up with little bears everywhere: on charm bracelets, in photo books, in beds littered with dozens of teddy bears, and all that other bear crap, who wouldn't want this grizzly shot to death. If they couldn't stop the hunt, they'd use it as a fund raiser. Perfect.

He noted that it was nearly six and he was hungry. Jones was a devout vegetarian in public, but in private loved lobster and prime rib Tonight he had no one to join him for dinner. Divorced at fifty-two with thinning hair and a bit overweight. Alienated daughter. No girlfriend. Two close buddies, both married. He ended up calling the Lazy Lobster and ordering a grouper sandwich and slaw with a side of fries, which would no doubt be delivered by a teenager driving a Smart Car.

• • •

Three days later, Jones welcomed Cyril into his office, which was in his house in Anglers Park, Key Largo. Cyril, one of Ham's only two buddies, was about 45—ten years younger than Ham—tall and slender, with thinning light brown air and a friendly face without facial hair of any sort. He contrasted with Ham, who was shorter with a thicker waist, and his face sported a moustache and a goatee. More a friend than an employee, Cyril had been AFL's corporate counsel for eight years after cutting his teeth at the National Animal Defense Fund, specializing, obviously, in animal law.

"Sorry this took so long," Cyril began, sitting across from Ham at his desk. "It was rather complicated and I had to call in a bunch of favors to piece it all together. Bottom line, there is a grizzly at the North Fork Ranch in the Hill Country and it came all the way from Alaska."

"Alaska!"

"Yep, specifically, around Anchorage. I tracked down the director of the Division of Wildlife Conservation Services for the Alaska Department of Fish and Game, a guy named Jeff Clarkson, and he didn't try to hide anything at all. He said he had been contacted by a hunter from Dallas who was duly licensed in Alaska and had a guide and all the permits necessary to kill a brown or a grizzly. The grizzly is a subspecies of a brown, as it turns out. He asked if he could trap a bear rather than kill it and said he worked for the Fort Worth Zoo, and had all the paperwork to prove it."

"Who is this guy?"

"We don't know—yet. But since the bear is now at North Fork Ranch, he obviously works for the opposition. Clarkson, of course is a statie, so the bear had to come from a state park, and it turns out that all the state parks and monuments have trouble with what they call subadult bears, the ones about four years old that just left their mothers and are fending for themselves for the first time. One of their biggest problems was bears coming into Anchorage from the nearby Chugach State Park. Anyway, to make a long story short, Clarkson took his plan to the Commissioner, some palms were greased, and this guy from Dallas got a trapping permit if he provided his own trap, which he did—a child/bear-friendly trap they call it, using 14-guage plate steel and steel mesh. That's as far as I got with how the Dallas hunter got the bear. When I mentioned to Clarkson that there was an Alaskan grizzly in Texas, but not at the Fort Worth zoo, he clammed up and told me to call the commissioner with the rest of my questions. I did, but his highness wouldn't take my call."

Ham shook his head. "How did the bear get to Texas?"

"Animal Airlines, on a nonstop flight from Anchorage to DFW. They transport both pets and zoo animals. The bear was transported in a cage. All it takes is a large fork lift."

"Isn't that against the law?"

"No. It's a domestic flight, and the Dallas guy got a permit from the U.S. Fish and Wildlife Service by filling out Form 3-177."

"But aren't grizzlies an endangered species?"

Cyril shook his head. "The grizzlies in Yellowstone used to be, but that ended in 2017 because their population had rebounded from 150 to more than 700. There's thousands of grizzlies—or brown bears—in Alaska and they are not endangered."

"Can we complain to the Texas authorities?" Ham asked.

"No. The game ranch industry in Texas is unregulated. The North Fork Ranch needs no local, state, or federal permit for their exotic animals. State hunting regulations do not apply to exotics, which can be hunted year-round. Game ranches are part of a billion-dollar industry in Texas, and they have a combined population of about one point three million exotics that are used for hunting and breeding."

"Well, shit. Why don't we file a civil suit against them for animal cruelty to a bear?"

"That falls under the Texas Health and Safety Code." Cyril opened up a manila folder.

"Let me read you the law about that in Texas. The Animal Protection Laws state, and I quote, 'This section does not create a civil cause of action for damages or enforcement of this section.' In other words, only the state can enforce those cruelty laws, and the authorities can prosecute the laws as either civil or criminal offenses."

Ham felt that familiar depression and negativity creeping back into his brain. "So what do we do now?"

"I'm tired of trying to solve this thing with just Google and my cellphone. I'm flying into Austin and driving to Fredericksburg, and then I'll start letting people know that there's a grizzly bear running around loose on a twelve-thousand-acre game ranch."

"*Fenced* game ranch."

"Fences not designed for a 500-pound predator."

"Good point, Ham. They're usually chain link, twelve-foot livestock fences. Some of the ranches have red kangaroos for your shooting pleasure but they can't jump that high."

"Cyril, I've heard enough. Would you like to clear your mind and go flats fishing with me before you leave? I've got a new guide now, since Phyllis got my Mako 18 in the settlement."

"Oh? Who is he?"

"Guy named Kevin Cooper. Claims to be the only African-American guide in the Keys. What a hook, huh?"

"Next time, Ham. I've got a date with a bear."

• • •

Kevin Cooper was 47 but still looked like a Marine Corps master sergeant because he worked out in his own gym every day, and every other day he jogged or walked five miles. He wore a bonefish cap on top of his shaved black skull, had a salt-and-pepper moustache, a strong jaw, and a winning smile.

He picked up Ham at the Key Mangrove Marina promptly at six a.m. As he pulled his Dragonfly 17 flats boat into a slip, he tossed a line to Ham, who wrapped it loosely around a piling.

"Permission to come aboard, sir," Ham said, grinning.

"Granted," Kevin replied, playing along. Ham complied and they shook hands. "Not your first trip to Florida Bay, I gather."

"Maybe my eightieth," Ham said as Kevin pulled away from the dock at idle speed. "I lost my own boat in the divorce."

"Got it. Your ex a fisherperson?"

Ham laughed. "Hardly, but I think her new boyfriend might be."

Kevin increased their speed until they were on plane and headed west. "What's your pleasure, Mr. Jones?"

"Call me Ham, short for Hamilton. My mom was a history teacher. It's been months since I've been out here, so whatever we run into is fine. I'm mostly a catch-and-release guy, but I'd like at least one eating-size red."

"You got it. Maybe some boners, too," Kevin said, using the common men's term for bonefish.

Florida Bay is an unusual body of water, some 850 square miles of it averaging four feet deep, with small mangrove islands scattered everywhere. What Ham liked most about it was stalking redfish in two feet of water and using light spinning tackle to drop a lure right in front of a small school of them. He was definitely not a fly fishing snob, although he knew how to do it. Already, Ham was relaxed and happy, his thoughts on the sea rather than game ranches.

By the time they quit at 9:30—Kevin's half-day limit, Ham had his three-pound red in the live well, had tied into five bonefish, landing and releasing one of them, and had also caught and released a small snook that was under the legal limit. Back at the marina dock, Ham went into the small store and bought a styrofoam cooler and some ice while Kevin gutted and filleted the red.

"I'd like to go out again," Ham said after he paid Kevin in cash. "When are you available?"

"Not for a while, I'm afraid. I'm starting a new job next week that will take most of my time."

"Too bad. What's the new work?"

"This." He took a card out of his shirt pocket and handed it to Ham.

"ECIS," Ham said aloud. "Environmental Crimes Investigative Service, interesting. So the only African American fishing guide in the Keys is going to be a private eye."

"Well, Ham, considering what you do, you might need us sometime."

"Then you know about the Animal Freedom League?"

"Of course. Google is a wonderful tool, and I always check out my clients. But I have a question for you."

"Shoot."

"The organization you head up is anti-hunting and anti-fishing, yet there's your dead fish in that cooler."

"Please don't tell anyone, Captain Cooper," Ham said, and his left eye winked.

1

"Although Florida manatees have gigantic, ponderous bodies,
their grace and speed underwater can hardly be exaggerated.
They typically swim at speeds of 1.2-4.4 miles per hour, but
they are capable of moving at 11.2-15.5 miles per hour in
short bursts, thanks to the incredible power of their fluke.
In comparison, the fastest recorded swimming speed for a
human is just above 5 miles per hour."
—John E. Reynolds III, *Florida Manatees: Biology, Behavior,
and Conservation*, 2017

The debate about the best hand weapon to use to kill an
adult manatee was held at The Crankcase, a mixed-race,
blue collar bar in south Miami decorated with custom car
parts. On one side of the debate was Stonewall Pickett Wilson,
a professional feral hog hunting guide from Tuscaloosa, who
favored multiple stabs through the eyes with a 9-inch commercial auto pick. On the other side was "Always Randy" Ran-
dolph York, the publisher, editor, and staff writer—all under
different names—for *Extreme and Deadly Hunting* magazine,
supposedly published in Cape Fear, North Carolina but with
a Miami P.O. box return address. For killing Mama Manatee,
Always Randy preferred a Battle Cleaver, a supermachete designed by the South Florida Survival School that could sever a
whitetail deer's ribcage with a single blow.

The centerpiece for their bar table debate was a full-sized replica manatee skull that had cost A-Rand $347 from the online Skull and Bones Supersite. These were the same people running the promotion to have a replica made of your own skull if you sent them x-rays and measurements. "A perfect gift for the wife," the copy for the cable TV spot ran. "You gave her your heart. You gave her your mind. Now give her your skull."

They were drinking shots of Blowtorch, a new rye whiskey spiced up with cinnamon and cayenne. "Look, A-Rand," Stoney said, picking up the skull in one hand and the small tape measure in the other. "The skull's sixteen inches long." He stuck the end of the tape into the eye socket and pushed it into the skull. "Just four inches in and you hit the brain. Piece of cake."

"Sure, if you can hit the eye socket perfectly while you're floundering in a canal," A-Rand commented. "Measure it."

"One and a half inches."

"A pretty small target when you're in the water with a buncha 'tees all around you," Stoney said. "I've done some research, and Florida manatees can get to twelve feet long and weigh up to thirty-six hundred pounds. Considering their size, I'd rather have the Battle Cleaver. Nine and a quarter inches of carbon steel with 30-degree flat grind edge. One blow anywhere on the 'tee's head and he's going to that big warm canal in the sky. Much more dramatic, too."

"It's hard to get leverage when you're in the water," said Stoney. "We gotta do some stabbing and cutting tests with both weapons."

"With manatees?"

"No, dumbass, *cabezas de vacas*, cow heads. I know a guy."

It was a very instructive testing session. In fact, they discovered that both weapons worked rather well on cow skulls lying on the ground, if that could somehow translate to 'tees in the water. They decided to let their backer make the final decision after putting all the data they collected into their final report on phase one of the killings.

But at the next meeting, their backer just laughed at them. "You idiots have no idea how to murder a manatee. Let me tell you the best way to do it." He did, and A-Rand and Stoney just stared at each other.

"That's the best method for sure," agreed Stoney.

"But you guys did okay," their backer said. "Now we have *three* options and each finalist will get one of them. Makes it a lot more interesting with multiple *modi operandi*."

"But how do they choose..." began A-Rand, but he got cut off.

"That's my problem, not yours," their backer said. "Start the implementation of phase one and the planning for phase two." He handed A-Rand a bulging gym bag. "This should get you started."

• • •

Double Dr. Janice Fields, D.V.M. and Ph.D., chief veterinary pathologist for the Florida Fish and Wildlife Conservation Commission, aimed the laser pointer at the image of an adult manatee projected on the huge monitor in the necropsy suite at the Marine Mammal Pathobiology Laboratory in St. Petersburg.

"Some background first, though you two probably know a lot of this," she said to Sam Dalton and Phil Everett.

"The manatee is a large marine mammal also known as a sea cow. However, despite the name, they are more closely related to elephants. Although they may seem like cumbersome creatures, manatees can swim quickly and gracefully when they want to. The average adult manatee is about 10 feet long and weighs between 800 and 1,200 pounds. It eats sea grasses and other aquatic vegetation, but can survive on heads of lettuce or cabbage."

The image on the monitor switched to three manatees with their snouts about the surface. "Because they are mammals, they must surface to breathe air. They may rest submerged at the bottom or just below the surface of the water, coming up to breathe on an average of every three to five minutes. When manatees are using a great deal of energy, they may surface to breathe as often as every 30 seconds. When resting, manatees have been known to stay submerged for up to 20 minutes. Ultimately, loss of habitat is the most serious threat facing manatees in the United States today. There is a minimum population count of 6,610 manatees in Florida as of February, 2018, according to the most recent synoptic survey. One thing we definitely do not need is humans killing them."

The image changed to a manatee skull and she pointed the laser at the right eye socket of the skull. "We have a complete photographic library of signatures of steel markings on bone," she told Sam Dalton and Phil Everett. The camera zoomed in on the eye socket and she moved the pointer to two grooves on the edge of the socket. "These troughs were not caused by a knife because they are too shallow. Instead of the "V" formations that you would expect from a blade, these "U" tracks indicate a thin, cylindrical weapon, like an ice pick. Went directly into the 'tee's brain."

"Some asshole killed a manatee by stabbing it in the eye?" asked Phil, incredulously.

"Looks like it," she said grimly. "This was no boat accident."

"The media got it right for once," Dalton added. "It's murder."

"Technically," Dr. Fields lectured, "murder is defined as the unlawful premeditated killing of one human being by another."

"Tell that to Animal Planet," Dalton countered. "It's their favorite term for animal killings."

The vet pushed a button on the console and another mutilated manatee skull appeared on the screen. "This skull of the other victim is cracked along the sutures between the frontal and parietal lobes. We don't know what weapon caused it."

"A boat motor propeller blade?" asked Phil. "A lot of manatees are injured that way."

"More like an axe blade," she replied. "Here at the pathobiology lab, we conduct between three and four hundred manatee necropsies a year and in about half of them the cause of death was propeller blade damage, mostly lacerations that became infected. The manatee skull is quite hard and usually the blades cause more damage to the skin, eyes, nose, and mouth of the manatee. I can't recall a single case of a skull fracture from a propeller blade, although they have caused rib fractures."

"So somebody cruised by in a boat and hit this manatee with an axe?" Dalton asked, shaking his head.

"Or a machete or an adze. We're not sure. Let's grab some coffee and discuss it."

They adjourned to the break room and sat at a small table after pouring coffee into mugs furnished by the Save the Manatees Club. "I hear you guys were Effin' Doubleyou special agents," Dr. Fields smiled.

"That's right," Phil told her. "We're private investigators now." He handed her a business card.

"E.C. I. S.," she read. "That's pretty clever."

"Dalton's idea. He was N.C.I.S. before he was a special agent for the Conservation Commission."

"First naval crimes then environmental crimes," she commented. "Who's your client?"

But before either one of them could answer, her cell phone's ringtone of "Yellow Submarine" interrupted them.

"Excuse me for a minute," she said and left the room, her phone to her ear.

"What's the motive?" asked Dalton. "Two of them deliberately killed."

"It happens with other animals," Phil said. "Remember the Miami serial cat killer?"

"Can't say that I do."

"The Oregon Bunny Lady? She had 250 rabbits hopping around her house—and a hundred dead ones in the freezer."

"Those are wackos. This feels different to me."

"Sam Dalton, psychic animal crimes investigator at work."

Dr. Fields came back to the break room in a real rush. "I have to drive over to Fort Pierce," she said with a curious combination of sadness and excitement in her voice. We've got a third manatee dead. This one's at the Manatee Observation Center."

"What happened?" asked Dalton.

"They're telling me it was disemboweled."

• • •

The first board meeting of E.C.I.S. was called to order by company president Laura Dalton at 10 a.m. on September 15, and all members were present—her husband Sam Dalton, Phil Everett, and Kevin Cooper. Since she had married Sam, she had let her blonde hair grow out from the pageboy style of her bachelorette days, and now wore it in what she called medium-bouncy waves. She was 43, slender, and had the body of a swimmer or skier. Laura was wearing her office clothes—namely shorts, a tee shirt adorned with a whole pineapple wearing sunglasses, and pink flip-flops.

The meeting was being recorded and would be transcribed later, as per Laura's order. She told them from the beginning that the only way she would leave her cushy job as media director and public face of the Fairchild Tropical Botanic Garden and work for a start-up environmental crimes investigation business was if she could run the show.

"You guys don't know how to operate a business and won't have time anyway," she had told them. "Who's going to handle the finances, the taxes? You, Kevin?"

"No ma'am," he had replied, military to the bone, "And I have my own guide business to run—if I have the time." Everyone had laughed.

"Laura," Dalton, had told her, "we agree to all your terms. You run the business and we investigate. Deal?"

Now, a mere three weeks after Laura had resigned from Fairchild, they were meeting not only to fulfill the requirements to establish a Florida corporation, but also to develop a plan to catch the person or persons responsible for killing—murdering, as the media was calling the crime—three beloved manatees. A contract was in hand, and the $10,000 deposit had been paid by the newly-formed organization called Manatees Forever, LLC. Wiseacres were already calling the group the seaweed huggers because seaweed, or more properly, aquatic plants, were the primary diet of the peaceful vegetarian manatees, also known as sea cows.

The four of them had founded Environmental Crimes Investigative Services after Dalton and Phil had resigned from their positions as special agents for the Florida Fish and Wildlife Conservation Commission. Kevin Cooper, a retired marine sergeant recovering from PTSD, had assisted Dalton when he was capturing feral pythons for the state to euthanize.

After the business formalities were completed, Kevin said, "You'll never guess who I took fishing last week. Hamilton Jones, the guy who runs the Animal Freedom League. Turns out he he's not really anti-fishing after all." That garnered laughs from Dalton and Phil and a rueful look from Laura.

"A hypocrite," she said, "but maybe a useful one. Kevin, why don't you call him and see if he might be interested in helping to fund the manatee investigation?"

"I'll do that," he promised.

"This company cannot survive on a single client," Laura said. "We need to drum up more business. I want you guys to go through all your contacts and collect email addresses. I'm going to put together a biweekly email newsletter about environmental crime and how we would go about investigating those crimes."

Then Dalton suggested a brainstorming session about the killings. "Let's just speculate. Ask a lot of questions. Does someone kill manatees for fun?"

"It's a lot of trouble and risk for some dubious fun," Phil said.

"Is someone killing them for money?" asked Laura.

"A manatee assassin?" After he said it, Kevin shook his head. "Doesn't make much sense."

"Why are there three different methods of killing?" That question came from Dalton.

"All of them were successful, but with varying degrees of difficulty," Kevin said.

"Disembowelment was the easiest and the eyeball stab the most difficult," Phil said.

Laura then shook her head. "It's more than just the difficulty of the killing—you have to figure in the skill set of the killer. Only a serious snorkeler or a scuba diver could attempt the disembowelment. Even the axe hit would be difficult say, for a woman without masculine arm strength."

"A killing contest of some kind?" asked Kevin, and they all went silent for a few seconds, thinking about the possibility.

Finally, Dalton made a suggest. "Let's substitute 'hunting' for 'killing.' A hunting contest of some kind, probably with money to the winner."

"Who runs hunting contests?" Phil asked.

"Let's find out," said Laura, who had her laptop on the table in front of them.

• • •

Aquatic animal rescue vet Metallica "Tallie" Jones was feeding baby Leslie for the second time that morning while trying to control her increasing anger. The 65-pound manatee calf now lived in her de-chlorinated swimming pool, and it was the daughter of the manatee that the media reported had been killed with an axe. The thought of that horrendous act infuriated Tallie, and she had made a vow to herself to track down the asshole responsible and stab him in the head with a Bowie knife.

But since she had no earthly idea how to accomplish that, she set that thought aside and focused on feeding Leslie, so named because it was nearly impossible to determine a manatee's gender when they were that young—hence a gender-neutral name. Tallie had developed the feeding formula herself using a soy-based commercial product designed for colicky infants, plus liquid protein and some oils to simulate the fatty acid composition of manatee milk. Leslie certainly loved it, especially when Tallie got into the pool and embraced the calf while feeding it. There was a bond forming here—she could feel it.

The problem was the fact that little Leslie had to be fed every three hours, or eight times a day, and that meant doing shifts with Susan, her neighbor's twelve-going-on-thirty daughter, who, fortunately, was in summer recess from middle school. But then it would take three years of life in a swimming pool before Leslie could be released into the wild. Tallie certainly couldn't do that and track down the murderer who made Leslie an orphan in the first place.

She left Leslie batting around his or her inflatable dolphins in the pool, and called her friend Brenda Gonzales at the Orlando Seaquarium. They had gone to vet school together at the University of Florida and Brenda—in Tallie's view anyway—had sold out to the corporate giants that made a fortune keeping marine mammals in captivity and forcing them to do tricks for audiences of suckers. Animal slavery, she called it. But they had remained friends, and did not usually discuss the subject of Seaquarium.

"Tallie! Good to hear from you! What's up?"

"I've got the cutest little 'tee calf who needs a home. About two weeks old, called Leslie. It's wearing me out and I'm not getting enough donations to hire anyone. You guys have a lot more clout than I do."

"Text me a pic."

"Just a second." Tallie fiddled with her iPhone and attached the pic Susan had shot the day before and sent it.

"Ahh," said Brenda, "So cute and cuddly. Your new brown baby looks like a slightly sad hound dog with a big snout."

"All sixty-five cuddly pounds of it. Can you help me, Brenda? I'm begging."

"I gotta speak to the boss. How was it orphaned?"

Tallie told her the story and minced no words, including her vow to track down the killer of Leslie's mother.

"With an axe? That's the most horrible thing I've ever heard. It's heartbreaking. Call you right back."

Tallie went online and soon learned of the death of the third manatee, this time by evisceration. Her first thought was, *It's a fucking hunting contest.* Then she started surfing hunting sites, magazines, and forums. She needed to know everything about high-end hunting—and in particular, hunting awards and contests.

Her phone rang—it was Brenda calling her back. "The boss

went for it. The story will get us enormous publicity. We're sending the truck tomorrow for the transport. Thanks so much for thinking of the Orlando Seaquarium."

Tallie almost laughed, but grinned and said, "You have saved my family life, so thank *you*."

"One thing."

"Sure."

"We want you up here for the press conference when you present Little Leslie, as we're calling him, to the Seaquarium."

"Count on it," Tallie promised.

"One more thing."

"Go."

"Track down that scumbag manatee murderer and..."

Tallie cut her off. "I promise to give it my best try."

They chatted for a while about personal stuff and mutual friends. After they said goodbye, the first thing Tallie did was go online and subscribe to the magazine, forum, blog, and newsletter of a media company called Extreme and Deadly Hunting, Inc.

• • •

Diana Ventura was on the computer in her office at the *Miami Herald* attempting to figure out a lead for her follow-up article detailing the third manatee "murder" when two articles were handed to her by Emma Martinez, the intern from Miami-Dade Junior College who distributed all the press releases, regardless of if they came via snail mail or email.

"Diana, I think I have what you're looking for. You asked me to grab anything related to manatees for you, and two just came in. I printed them out for you."

Diana looked them over, and said, "Thanks, Em." The headline on the first one read, "Seaquarium to Accept Orphaned Manatee," and the second was "Manatee Investigation

Contract Awarded to ECIS." She had a contact at the Seaquarium, but what the hell was Manatees Forever—or ECIS, for that matter? It took her less than a minute to find out, and she grinned as she pressed the call button in her contacts list.

"Hey there, Diana, what's up?"

"Sam, you never write, you never call, you never text me sweet nothings. Are you mad at me?"

"Of course not. You haven't accused me of anything in weeks."

"Well, I didn't accuse you in print."

"You knew I would sue you and the paper."

"Let's talk about something positive, Sam. Congrats on ECIS and the manatee contract."

"You're fishin', aren't you?"

"Of course. That's what I do. I'd like an interview. Give you some free publicity."

"Can I have my attorney present?"

"*Sam!*"

"Just kidding. Sure. You buying lunch?"

"The *Herald* is buying."

"Then what cafeteria do you suggest?"

"Ha! Let's go to the Manatee Bay Café."

"Clever as always," said Sam. "At the Seaquarium?"

"Yes, tomorrow noon. Give my love to Laura. Bye, Sam."

Not surprisingly, seafood was absent from the menu of the Manatee Bay Café, but at least they had beer. He ordered a Twisted Trunk Rasta Stout and took a seat in front of a giant tank of arowanas winding their way through the fake foliage as he waited for Diana. He liked and admired the woman, but didn't trust her. For Diana, the story was everything. During the invasion of the Burmese pythons and their subsequent demise due to a snake virus, she had accused Sam of masterminding the spread of the virus, which he vehemently denied. Of course, she was right, and he was fortunate that she had no evidence whatsoever.

When Diana arrived, only a few minutes late, he stood to greet her and she gave him a big hug and a kiss on the cheek. She had made moves on him at least three times and he was slightly wary, but she was being sisterly rather than sexy.

"How's my favorite wildlife warrior?" she asked, waving to a server. She ordered a glass of white zin and winked at Sam.

"Busy," he answered with a smile. She looked great, as usual, in lime capri pants, heels, and an off-white short-sleeved cotton shirt with the blue initials DYWYCFM on it. Her long black hair was tied at the nape of her neck, and she wore very light makeup, except for her bright red lips. He ignored the initials, knowing that she wanted him to guess their meaning. She ordered a fruit salad and he went for a bacon cheeseburger with hot sauce.

"Why are we meeting here?" Dalton asked.

"I have an appointment with the director at one. Seaquarium is adopting an orphaned baby manatee that was rescued. Cute little 'tee named Leslie. Sidebar to the main story I'm working on. Can you give me a status report on the manatee murders and maybe a theory I can run with?"

"Well, the definition of murder is one human deliberately killing another human, so killing is a better term."

"Phooey. All the media in south Florida are using the phrase. It's alliterative."

He grinned at her, then got serious. "Okay, the necropsies were done by Dr. Fields at the Marine Mammal Pathobiology Lab in St. Pete. First one, penetration of the brain through the eye socket; second one, fractured skull; and the third, disembowelment. The doc thinks some kind of long ice pick for the first one, axe or adze for the second, and a long knife or bayonet for the third."

"You think it's over?"

"Could be. Last killing was five days ago. We had three in four days when they started."

"Theories?"

"I think it's some sort of sick hunting contest, and you can quote me on that. Please ask your adoring readers if they've heard any rumors about such a contest. Set up an 800 number and an email response. Help me and I'll send you email updates as things develop."

"I'll do that." Their lunches arrived and Dalton asked, "So what's new with you?"

"Not a damn thing. Work, work, work. I need a big story. And a new man in my life." Diana sighed dramatically. Dalton did not bite on that line, concentrating instead on his burger.

"You know, Diana, I would like to in…another time-space continuum."

"What on earth are you talking about, Sam?"

"The initials on your, uh, chest. 'Don't You Wish You Could Fuck Me?' That is my answer."

Diana laughed so hard she spit out a piece of cantaloupe. "You know me too well. Laura is such a lucky woman."

"Thank you, and I agree. Friends?"

"Always, Sam."

• • •

Lawrence "Lash" Lambrick, the founder and CEO of Global Hunting Group, Inc. watched the grizzly pace back and forth in its enclosure, hungry and anxious for dinner. The bear didn't have a name—as Lambrick told his inner circle, "It's not a fucking pet, it's a game animal. Giving him a cute name personalizes the bear and then people will feel sorry for him instead of fearing him."

It was difficult for Lambrick to play the role of a cowboy, mostly because he was born and raised in Ohio, not exactly a hotbed of riders and ropers. But that didn't stop him from wearing jeans and lizard boots, rodeo shirts, and a black Stetson. He was also tall and skinny and looked like an idiot on a horse. His face was nondescript—slightly rounded, a little bug-eyed, with no facial hair. His accent was like a guy from Cleveland trying to talk Texan. But nobody said anything. He paid their excellent salaries and the ranch had three chefs who all graduated from the C.I.A. in Hyde Park, New York. Life was good. Lash's style was a little weird and he liked to shoot defenseless animals. So what?

It was feeding time and Steve Emerson drove up in a golf cart pulling an enclosed cart on wheels. He was the 40-some ranch zoologist and the person responsible for the feeding and care of all twenty-seven species of game animals on the ranch—now twenty-eight, including the grizzly.

"Afternoon, Lash. Ready for a feeding?"

"Lookin' forward to it."

"These bears are the ultimate omnivores so I had to work out a plan for a varied and rotating diet both daily and seasonally. He gets a different meat or fish, vegetable, fruit, grain, and nut combo every meal, and I feed him like a dog, twice a day, but he gets thirty pounds each time. Today it's feral hog meat, spinach, very ripe bananas, some dog chow, and hard-boiled eggs. He's been here a week and has not been aggressive. Look, he's just sitting over there now, waiting. He's learned the routine. I'll get him started with this."

Steve reached into the cart and his hand came out holding a rabbit struggling to free itself. A ranch hand opened the feeding door and Steve tossed the rabbit into the enclosure. The bear, moving faster than you would ever imagine, trapped the rabbit in a corner of the fencing, pinned it down with one swipe of his huge claws, pulled it up to his jaws and swallowed after one loud crunch. As Steve opened up the cart and began to unload the metal food trays, the bear retreated to his sitting spot and waited.

"That is one smart animal," Lambrick said.

"And in short spurts he can run as fast as a horse," Steve added, pushing the food trays through the slot but leaving the retrieval ropes outside the enclosure. The bear ambled over and began methodically eating his dinner.

"Happy hour, Steve. Care to join me at The Watering Hole?"

"Sure. Thank you, sir."

"Some people are joining us. Not customers."

"Okay with me."

Steve was a new employee of Northfork Ranch. He had specifically been hired to deal with the care of bears and other animals to be on display at the new Northfork Menagerie—the bear enclosure being the first of the animal display units. Steve had realized that it was state-of-the-art zoo keeping. He didn't particularly like the idea of working at a game ranch, but his entry-level job at the Naples Zoo at Caribbean Gardens had been eliminated in a budget crunch, so he applied to an ad on the American Association of Zoo Keepers website and was shocked when Lash called him. Despite the new job, he still wondered if it had been worth the expense and trouble to get a doctorate in zoology.

At The Watering Hole, with bar customers waving at him, Lambrick led Steve to a reserved table and introduced him to Jonathan Harris, his vice president and chief operating officer, and Anne Traynor, who was director of marketing and public relations. Harris was a graying, button-down executive type with a very serious demeanor, while Traynor was an energetic fortyish brunette go-getter. He shook hands with them and then joined the others in ordering drinks. Lash asked for a Texas vodka—Tito's, of course—rocks, olive. Harris was a water, no ice guy, Traynor wanted a lemonade, and Steve requested a Shiner Bock.

Lambrick opened the meeting with three negatives: "We have a bear image problem, a marketing problem, and a public relations problem. First, our bear doesn't seem to be particularly fierce. Any ideas, Steve?"

"This bear is acclimated to humans," he answered. "He was labeled as a 'problem bear,' which usually means that he was a garbage hound, and garbage means humans. He has learned that humans provide food—like me. I would imagine that all the animals on the ranch are similarly acclimated."

"But when we release him into the ranch land for the hunt, what's he gonna do, hang around the enclosure waiting for lunch?"

"Mr. Lambrick, releasing him into the ranch would be extremely dangerous for all of us, Steve replied."

"Most of our employees will have the day off, and the rest will be inside. Now please answer my question."

Steve was flustered. "I don't know what will happen. I never said I was a bear expert."

"Well, then, call a fucking bear expert. Jon, what's best bid so far?"

Harris pulled out his phone and checked their account on SilentAuctionware.com. "Twenty-two thousand. Break-even for this hunt is thirty-five."

"Well, shit. Anne, it's your turn."

"It's early in the game, Lash. We've only been accepting bids for a week. I can buy stock footage of enraged grizzlies, if that's what you're looking for. We can get a voiceover done and run some TV spots in Dallas and Houston on the hunting shows."

Lambrick perked up. "That's a great idea. Get a budget together. Now, we're getting attacked by all the animal do-gooders—Humane Association, National Animal Defense Fund, Animal Freedom League, all those assholes. Very bad publicity. What should we do?"

"Nothing," Anne said, and that one word seemed to hang in the air for hours.

"Explain," Lambrick directed.

"Any way we attempt to explain the hunt or defend ourselves will just backfire, drawing even more attention to it. I say we clam up. Say nothing, do nothing. The controversy will just fade away."

Lambrick frowned but did not reply. There was silence at the table and a lot of drink-sipping. Finally, Harris said, "I agree."

"Whose bright idea was this bear hunt, anyway?" Lambrick asked with a smile, and the tension evaporated. "It'll all work out. We have a plan. Steve will figure out how to prepare the bear, Anne will get the advertising together, and Jon and I will keep our mouths shut when the media calls. We'll be nice about it, though, take their calls, and say, 'Sorry, Jim, I just can't discuss company business. Orders from the boss.' Okay, gang, this meeting's over. Jon, I need to see you."

Lambrick and Harris stood up and left the bar. Anne and Steve remained at the table, both a little shell-shocked. Their server came by and Anne said, "Dewars scotch, straight-up."

"Is he always like that?" Steve asked.

"Pretty much," she replied, and sang the refrain of the Queen song, "Under Pressure."

Steve laughed. "Well, Lash never told me that I was feeding a doomed bear. He said it would be in the menagerie."

"The plan is to have a bear hunt every month. The auction is to determine the highest price they can charge."

"That's obscene."

"This is a game ranch, Steve, everything's part of the hunt."

"Even humans?"

"Ask our highly effective ranch security goons."

"This place creeps me out. I'm turning in my resignation."

When Anne's scotch arrived, she downed it in one gulp and looked him in the eye. "That would not be a healthy thing to do at this stage of the game."

• • •

"It looks like your lunch with Diana worked out fine," Laura said, handing Dalton the *Miami Herald*. It was a page three story with the headline reading "Local NGO to Investigate Manatee Killings." Diana had interviewed the co-founder of Manatees Forever, former governor Bob Mixon, and had asked him why they had hired ECIS rather than leaving the investigation to the Florida Fish and Wildlife Conservation Commission. He had replied diplomatically that he realized the Conservation Commission was understaffed and didn't have enough experienced wildlife investigators. "ECIS has three investigators," he said, "and two of them, Sam Dalton and Phil Everett, are former CC agents. They know what they're doing."

Diana then explained the status of manatees in Florida. "Manatees are protected by the Marine Mammal Protection Act of 1972, the Endangered Species Act of 1973 and the Florida Manatee Sanctuary Act of 1978. It is illegal to feed, harass, harm, pursue, hunt, shoot, wound, kill, annoy, or molest manatees. However, the manatee population has grown from about 800 individuals in 1979 to more than 6,000 today, and last year the U.S. Fish and Wildlife Service changed their status from endangered to threatened."

She had asked former governor Mixon about the penalties for killing manatees. "The state law is essentially a slap on the wrist," he said. "Anyone convicted of killing a manatee faces a maximum fine of $500 and/or imprisonment of up to 60 days for each incident. But the perpetrators would also be charged with violating federal protection laws, which are stricter, and the punishment is fines up to $100,000 and/or one year in prison."

Diana had concluded her story with a quote from Dalton: "ECIS, of course, lacks the authority to arrest anyone, so if our investigation uncovers the perpetrators, we will turn over our findings to the Conservation Commission and the U.S. Fish and Wildlife Service. We appreciate any leads from the public, particularly those that might indicate some kind of killing contest."

"Diana did us a big favor. This is instant credibility for ECIS."

"And what did you have to do for her?" Laura was teasing and Dalton knew it.

"I had to figure out what the initials DYWYCFM on her shirt meant."

"And they mean what?"

"Think about it for a while," he teased back.

• • •

Cyril McNaughton planned his trip from Florida to Fredericksburg, Texas with great care, as he knew he was headed into enemy territory. It was precisely for this kind of situation that he had become a Monroe County Auxiliary Deputy Sheriff. He was officially allowed to carry his Glock 21 Gen 4 .45 automatic to any state in the country, so he packed it unloaded in a Pelican 1170 hard case with foam, along with two boxes of ammunition, and used a TSA-approved lock to fasten it. He filled out a Firearm Unloaded Declaration Form, which he would leave at the American Airlines check-in counter—the only carrier with nonstop flights from Miami to Austin.

His wife Eileen had sewn a pocket into his black adjustable Taclite Uniform Cap that would hold his tiny GoPro Hero 6 video camera with just the lens visible from the front; it was a black lens on a black cap and hardly noticeable. He gave it a test and found it took only four seconds to start the camera and put the cap on his head. If he ran into any trouble, he wanted to make sure that the encounter was recorded. The rest of his gear included a Canon with a telephoto lens and light tubular tripod, Zeiss binoculars, his MacBook Pro laptop with two six-packs of flash drives, and his iPhone X. He was ready.

Cyril rented a black Toyota RAV4 at the Austin-Bergstrom International Airport and took Highway 290 to Fredericks-burg, keeping his speed under the limit. He had two stops to make before he checked into the hotel—the Fredericksburg Police Station and the Gillespie County Sheriff's Office. In both places, he didn't make a big deal about it, just one visiting law enforcement officer informing the authorities that he was in town but just on vacation, not on official business. He left his Monroe County business card at both places, asked a few questions about local things to do and see, and only spent about ten minutes at each office. He punched the address of the Hangar Hotel into the RAV4's GPS and soon found himself just off Airport Road in front of a hotel near an active runway of the Gillespie County Airport. It looked like an actual airplane hangar from the 1940s. He checked in and then checked out the bar, which was called the Officers' Club. It had a neon martini sign and was a classy room with lots of wood and brass. A sign read "Rules of the Bar," and one of the rules was "No Reading of the Rules." He sipped on a martini, called his wife to give her an update, and then asked his server to bring him a menu.

"We don't serve food here except for bar snacks in a lit-tle bowl," he was told by the server, who looked like a college freshman. She went on, "They have burgers and meatloaf at the Airport Diner next door, or you can go some place fancier, like the Cabernet Grill or Vaudeville."

Cyril didn't want to go to a fancy restaurant alone, so he opted for the diner and had a Bomber Burger with jalapeños, then went back to the Officers' Club and watched the Dallas Mavericks bounce the ball around. He went to bed before ten to get plenty of sleep for the next day, which he suspected would be busy.

By eight a.m. he had taken a shower, shaved, and eaten a breakfast of huevos rancheros with a side of cheese grits and was driving toward the Northfork Ranch. Cyril had a simple mission that morning. He was going to videotape himself and the Northfork fence line, and, assuming that the fence was not strong enough to prevent a grizzly bear from leaving anytime he wanted, he was going to record himself measuring the gauge of the chain link with his handy circular wire gauge measuring tool that he had bought online for thirty-five bucks.

Chain link fencing appeared on his right, about ten feet high with poles about twelve feet apart. Every other pole had a small sign attached to it that he couldn't read from the road. Cyril pulled over to the shoulder, stopped the SUV, turned it off, and walked over to the fence. The sign read, "Northfork Ranch. Game Animals. No Trespassing." It took him ten minutes to set up for the first scene in his video, removing the GoPro from his cap and screwing it onto the top of the tripod, which he placed so the sun was behind it. He turned on the camera and stepped up to the fence.

"Hello, my name is Cyril McNaughton. I'm the corporate attorney for the Animal Freedom League and also a Monroe County Florida Auxiliary Deputy Sheriff. I'm here on the fence line of Northfork Ranch, a game ranch in Gillespie County in the Texas Hill Country. Inside this fence, the ranch has a large male grizzly bear that was captured in Alaska. It is now in a secure enclosure, but the ranch management is auctioning off a hunt for the bear, which means—"

He lost his train of thought. "Start again. "Which means that the bear will be released from the secure enclosure and this fence will be the only thing keeping him away from neighboring farms and houses. My question is, "Can this fence stop a grizzly bear? Let's find out."

Cyril turned off the camera, took down the tripod, put the GoPro back in his cap. He turned it on, and placed the cap on his head. He stepped up to fence and looked at the sign, then took the wire gauge measuring tool out of his pocket.

"I'm now going to measure the wire used in this chain link fencing. Remember, the lower the gauge, the stronger the wire. The gauge recommended for bear enclosures is nine. Let's see what this measures."

He ran the tool along the wire until it fit neatly into one of the semi-circular holes in the round disk. The he moved his head closer to the tool. "As you can see, the gauge of this fencing wire is 12 point five, which is fine for fencing deer and antelope, but far too light to hold a grizzly bear. Scientists from Montana State University have proven that grizzlies are two and a half to five times stronger than humans."

He did four takes until he felt that he had done the best job he could. Then he set up the tripod again and finished his pitch. "A determined grizzly could take out this ten-foot pole in about a minute because it's so far away from the poles on either side. He would push it right over and walk on it to freedom. In a proper bear enclosure, not only is the wire gauge much stronger, but the poles are only four feet apart. So it makes sense for the safety of the general public for Northfork Ranch to keep the bear in his secure enclosure and cancel the hunt."

He had packed everything up, put the GoPro back in the cap and placed it on the passenger seat when two white Ford Fusions with flashing police lights arrived, one blocking him from behind and the other diagonally in front of him. He was trapped. Smiling, he turned on the camera, put the cap on his head, and thought, now the fun begins. He turned his head so the camera would pick up the oryx head logo and the lettering on the side of the Fusion in front of him: Northfork Ranch Security. He quickly memorized the coordinates on his GPS unit. Two beefy guards emerged from their cars, wearing badges and state police hats. They both had filled weapons in holsters on their right hips and collapsible black batons in sheaths on their left hips. Flick and Flack, he thought until he had their real names. Flick was blonde and built like a fat linebacker while Flack had black hair and a build like a six-foot-two basketball guard.

Flack came up to the driver's window. "License, registration, and proof of insurance," he said.

To which Cyril replied, "Fuck you. You have no authority over me."

"You're trespassing, parked on private property."

"Bullshit," Cyril said. "The shoulder of a county farm road is not public property, Billy." The name "Ofc. William D. Brandt" was embroidered on Flack's uniform shirt just above his bogus badge. Flick pulled his baton from its sheath and expanded it.

"Get out of your vehicle," ordered Brandt, "or we'll drag you out."

"That would be assault and I will sue your ass off," Cyril threatened. "Go away and leave me alone."

It was evident to Cyril that these two bozos had never had anything like this happen to them. Flick gestured to Brandt and they moved about ten feet away from the RAV4 for a little conference, and then Flick smashed his baton into the left side rear window, breaking it into little diamonds of glass. As Flick stepped back, Cyril quickly and violently opened the car door, catching Flick on his right side and knocking him to the ground. Cyril scrambled out of the SUV and before either of them could react, pulled his Glock out of his right hand pocket.

"Okay, you fucking rent-a-cops, unbuckle your belts and drop them. You, drop the baton.

"You asshole," screamed Billy, coming at him, and Cyril fired the Glock, the bullet landing between Billy's two boots. That changed the situation dramatically, and both of them unbuckled their heavy belts, holsters and all, which slid to the ground. They were now officially scared to death and Billy was visibly trembling. Cyril calmly pulled out his iPhone from his left pocket, dialed 911 and put the phone on speaker.

"Gillespie County Emergency Services," said a female voice. "What is your emergency?"

"This is Cyril McNaughton. I'm an attorney and a deputy sheriff from Monroe County, Florida. I'm afraid we've got a Mexican standoff here with two security bozos from Northfork Ranch.

"Any injuries?"

"Just my car window, which they smashed."

"What is the exact status there?"

"I'm holding them at gunpoint. Their weapons are on the ground."

"I'm sending two cars. Don't do anything rash, deputy."

"No, I'm cool."

"Are you the one who came by yesterday?"

"Yes."

"Good thing you did. I'll tell the deputies. They're on the way."

Cyril disconnected and looked at the two guards. "You jerks are totally fucked."

• • •

"Are you going to press charges against these two, Mr. Mc-Naughton?" asked Deputy Luther Hodges, who had confiscated their weapons and wallets. He looked like he might laugh at any second.

"I'm not sure what good that would do," Cyril replied. "Tell you what, if they pay me two hundred for the window and both apologize, I won't."

That's precisely what happened, and Cyril had it all digitally recorded.

Back in the Officers' Club at the Hangar Hotel, Cyril ordered a Chupahopra IPA from the Twisted X Brewing Company in Dripping Springs, transferred the raw footage from the GoPro to his MacBook, and began editing. It took him two and a half glasses of Chupahopra to finish the edit, and he wished he had some music for the audio track, but he didn't. His favorite scene had been a subdued Billy Brandt apologizing for the "misunderstanding" and calling him "sir" three times in twenty seconds. Cyril then transferred the finished MP4 video files to the twelve flash drives. Using Google, he found the addresses of the major TV stations and newspapers in Austin, Houston, and Dallas/Ft. Worth. He used the business center at the hotel to print out the cover letters he had composed on Animal Freedom League letterhead and then took a drive to the Fredericksburg FedEx Office and sent off eleven Overnight Letters. He dropped the final letter and flash drive off at the offices of the *Fredericksburg Standard*. It had been a highly productive day, so he rewarded himself that night with a Lobster-Topped Chicken Fried Certified Angus Beef Ribeye at the Cabernet Grill—Texas Wine Country Restaurant on State Highway 16.